G.J. KEMP

THE ACRE SERIES

Miles and the Soldier Book 2

This edition published in 2022 by TB5 Publishing

gjkemp.co.uk

ISBN 978-1-915379-06-1 (paperback)
ISBN 978-1-915379-07-8 (ebook)

For Davie

ACKNOWLEDGMENTS

To my incredible team, who have yet again helped me produce a lovely piece of work.

Jess and Isabelle, for your guidance. My beta readers, Nanna and Lara. My editors, Claire from Cherry Edits and Andy from The Narrative Craft. Andrei, for your wonderful cover. And Latifa (@latifahdesign) for all your design work.

To the countless professionals who dedicate their valuable time to helping disabled people. I wouldn't be where I am today without you.

Davie, my brother, this one is for you.

Thank you.

THE ACRE SERIES

From their windows, balconies, and gardens, the residents of the land of Acre stare north at the ominous black clouds that crawl across their beloved skies, overshadowing their homes. Under the clouds, a darkness has befallen the majestic City of Lynn. Within the city, a cornered Queen, once true and just, now plays a game of cat and mouse with the races of Acre. Each season, as the Queen fights for control, the 'Unknowns' from the North approach. With them comes the stench of evil, fear, and death.

But… there is hope. A lost legend now awakened.

A set of dormant orbs lay in the gnarled hands of an old man. One by one, the dull orbs spark and swirl to life. Somewhere within the City of Lynn, the scroll of equals remains hidden. It's text, supplied by the gods, awaits the chosen who may one day save the land of Acre.

Or so the legend says.

Thank you for your interest in The Acre Series. I

recommend you read the principal novels in order as the characters and the story grow with the series. The novellas are prequels and sequels to the principal novels. You can read them in any order you wish.

The Acre Series

Juno and the Lady (An Acre Story Book 1)
Valen and the Beasts: A Juno and the Lady Novella (An Acre Story Book 1.1)

Miles and the Soldier (An Acre Story Book 2)

CHAPTER 1
A CUP OF TEA

Tiny beads of sweat formed above the thick black hairs of Miles's eyebrows. He dragged the back of his hand across his brow and blinked at the salty liquid that dripped into his eyes. The blanket fluttered as he ripped it from his legs. With his hands placed on either side of his hips, he pushed himself into a sitting position.

The pain rippled through his lower back, down his legs, and into his toes. He filled his cheeks and placed his palms on his thighs, before exhaling while he massaged the muscles with the heels of his hands. Looking down at his toes, he willed each one to show some sign of life. Just before the waves of anger rose inside him, the little toe on his right foot spasmed, then twitched. Miles froze and, trying not to blink, he glared at his toes, waiting for one or more of them to move again.

'Come on,' he whispered. 'Move.'

Minutes passed until the forgotten pain in his lower back and in his legs brought him back to the present. The mattress puffed out dust as Miles slammed his fists on either side of his legs.

Miles glanced at the door as the familiar clump of Dr Viktor's cane sounded from the top floor of the house. The banister of the horseshoe staircase creaked as Miles's surrogate father leant his weight against it.

The blanket fluttered as Miles dragged it back over his legs and tucked the corners under his thighs.

'Are you awake, son?'

Miles cleared his throat just loud enough for Dr Viktor to hear.

The door opened an inch. 'May I come in?'

'Yes,' Miles said, with a slight quiver in his voice.

Dr Viktor entered the room and sat on the chair next to the bed. 'Pain in your back again?'

Miles bit his bottom lip. 'Pins and needles across the small of my back, which turn into jolts down my legs and into my feet.'

'Are you sure you don't want a draught? It will only take a moment for me to make it.'

Miles shook his head. 'I don't want to numb the pain.'

'I don't understand,' Dr Viktor said, tilting his head to one side.

'I want to feel it.'

'What on earth for?'

Miles gave Dr Viktor a quick glance. 'If I can feel pain, it means there is still some life left. And where there is some life, there is some hope.'

Dr Viktor tapped his cane on the floor.

'You don't think I should hope?' Miles said.

'It's been all summer and autumn,' Dr Viktor said. 'The winter snow will be here shortly, and the cold will not be good for your injuries.'

Miles rubbed his eyes. 'Distract me. Tell me about the others. How is the town of Fairacre?'

Dr Viktor struggled to his feet and hobbled over to the door. 'I will bring us tea,' he said over his shoulder. 'When I get back, we can talk about your friends and Fairacre.'

Miles waited for the door to click closed. With a flick of his hand, he removed the blanket and peered at his toes. A minute later, with a grunt of frustration, he grabbed the tops of his thighs and gave them a hard squeeze. A wave of pins and needles spread across the small of his back. An electric shock zapped down his calves and through his toes. The small toe on his left foot twitched.

Miles froze. A second later, his toe moved again.

The door of his room swung open and Dr Viktor, concentrating on the tray in his hands, shuffled over to the desk at the wall, where he dumped the tray with a clatter.

Miles pulled the blanket back over his legs and tucked it under his thighs and calves.

'Here you go, son,' Dr Viktor said, holding out a mug of tea with a trembling hand.

'Silly man,' Miles said, grabbing the mug's handle. 'No reason to burn those fingers of yours.'

Dr Viktor shuffled to the table and, picking up his own mug, he grabbed his cane, and walked back to the chair where he sat with a groan.

Miles took a sip of sweet tea, then lifted an expectant eyebrow at Dr Viktor. 'Well?'

'Why the sudden interest in Fairacre?' Dr Viktor said.

'I am not that interested. It's just something to talk about.'

Dr Viktor eyed him through the steam rising from the mug of tea. 'What about your friends? Every time I see them, they ask about you, and I am running out of excuses as to why you are not seeing them.'

Miles dipped his head. 'I miss them, but I cannot train them because I cannot face it right now.'

'I understand, but that's not the only thing you are good at.'

'Let's talk about other things,' Miles said. 'What did you see when you visited the town last month?'

'A town I do not recognise,' Dr Viktor said, snorting into his tea. 'Women running their own stalls in the market. Men sweeping the streets. Women owning shops. Men working for women. That is just not proper.'

Miles's shoulders shook as he laughed. 'I will tell Chloe you said that.'

Dr Viktor's head snapped up. 'You wouldn't!'

'For a cup of tea this good, you can convince me to keep my mouth shut,' Miles said, taking another sip.

'I will admit she is doing a fine job leading the Fairacre council. Although it took her some time to get the northern district in line.'

'She is learning as she goes,' Miles said. 'What about Juno and Chax?'

'Chloe has received messages from the schools in the south, asking to validate Juno's claims. She sends a sewer rat once every two weeks with a reply.'

'Not a good idea to call the ladies sewer rats anymore,' Miles said, smiling.

Dr Viktor raised his eyes to the ceiling. 'I don't know if I can live in this new, alternative world of yours.'

'Things progress, old man,' Miles said. 'What of Valen? I haven't seen him since he finished this house for you.'

'He still operates his arts and crafts shop,' Dr Viktor said. 'There are rumours of a planned wedding.'

'A black woman from the east marrying a white man from the south,' Miles said. 'Are you sure your brain isn't about to explode?'

Dr Viktor filled his cheeks and blew out a long breath. 'I don't think I will be attending.'

Miles smiled. 'They will be happy and it will send a wonderful message through our land. Will you not go if they invite you?'

The end of Dr Viktor's cane tapped the floor with each bounce of his leg. 'If it is Billy who asks me, I don't think I can say no.'

'What of Billy and Tilly? Are they not to be wed?'

'Chloe agreed to turn half of the town hall into a hospital. Billy is creating his draughts and Tilly is training people who are interested in the art of healing. As for a wedding, I am not sure that is something they are thinking about.'

'Are they together?'

'Chloe says they are taking it slow. Tilly is still trying to make sense of what happened to her. She did take someone's life.'

Miles averted his eyes and looked down at his legs. The haunting sound of the jagged dark sword whistling through the air filled his senses. He flinched as he remembered it slicing across the small of his back.

'Sorry, son,' Dr Viktor said. 'I sometimes forget who did this to you.'

'It is OK,' Miles said, raising a hand. 'The visions are a lot less often now. I am just glad we got rid of her.'

'You haven't mentioned these visions before,' Dr Viktor said.

Miles's eyes glazed over as he gazed off into the distance. 'I keep wondering what I could have done differently. It is unlike me to lose control like I did.'

'I am glad you are speaking of the events,' Dr Viktor said.

Miles flashed a look at Dr Viktor. 'I have needed time to process what has happened.'

'Acceptance maybe?' Dr Viktor said with a small glint of hope in his eye.

'I wouldn't go that far,' Miles said. 'I am still angry at everything.'

Dr Viktor laid his head on the back of the chair and peered up at the ceiling.

'You think I am taking too long to process all of this?' Miles said.

'I think it will be wise to get out of this house and get to Fairacre for the winter,' Dr Viktor said up to the ceiling.

'It's colder there than it is here,' Miles said.

'There is no escape if you stay here with me, my boy,' Dr Viktor said. 'You know the black snow blocks everyone from coming and going during the winter.'

'I will think about it,' Miles said.

Dr Viktor brought his head level and rubbed his chin. 'Will you see your friends the next time they visit? They have respected your wishes and stayed away, but they will soon tire of this.'

'Chloe will nag me to join the council. I don't know if I can handle that.'

'Your mind is just as valuable as your sword, my son.'

'I am a warrior,' Miles said, then checked himself. 'I was a warrior. How can I expect warriors to take orders from a man who cannot lead from the front?'

'You don't have to be on the battlefield to lead, son. Kings and queens have done so for centuries.'

Miles plunged his head back into his pillow and sighed.

'You will need to decide what you want to do before the snow falls,' Dr Viktor said.

Miles's eyes widened before he let out a sharp hiss.

'What is it?' Dr Viktor said, sitting up straight.

Miles lifted his index finger and wagged it at Dr Viktor. After a few more intakes of air, he exhaled slowly.

Dr Viktor stood, wrung out a cloth, and dabbed Miles's forehead. 'I don't like seeing you like this.'

Miles waved Dr Viktor's hand away. 'I will be OK. Pain equals hope, remember.'

Dr Viktor sat back down. 'Are you sure the pain is only in your back and legs?'

Miles nodded.

'OK,' Dr Viktor said. 'Billy brought some bread from Fairacre yesterday. Compliments of Gem and Jen. Would you like some for dinner?'

'With vegetables, if that isn't a bother?'

Dr Viktor pulled himself to his feet. 'I will be back shortly.'

Miles waited for the door to click closed. He removed the blanket from his legs and grabbed the tops of his thighs, giving them another squeeze. After a minute of staring at his toes, he released his thighs and leant back into his pillow. Turning his head, he looked out of the big bay window at the yellow and brown leaves stubbornly holding onto their branches. They wouldn't last long with the first fall of black snow.

Miles jerked awake as Dr Viktor pulled open the door and walked in with two plates of food precariously balanced on one arm. Miles reached up and removed a plate, then waited for Dr Viktor to sit.

'The bread is some of the best I have ever tasted,' Dr Viktor said, breaking off a crust and placing it into his mouth.

'Gem and Jen kept two camps fed during the time on the cliffs,' Miles said. 'I miss their cooking.'

Dr Viktor snorted.

Miles gave him a withering smile. 'Your cooking has got better.'

'Since you have been in this room and Billy has abandoned me, I have had no choice but to learn.'

'You knew he would go as soon as he met someone.'

'I know, but I would like to have finished his training.'

'I imagine he is getting plenty of training in the new hospital. And he now has a new pupil. You learn just as much from training someone as you do from being trained.'

They sat in silence and finished their meal.

Dr Viktor put his plate on the side table. 'It is time for me to turn in, my son. Will you need anything tonight?'

Miles shook his head. 'I am fine.'

'Ring the bell if the pain gets too much.'

Miles passed his plate over to Dr Viktor. 'I can handle the pain. Don't worry about me.'

Dr Viktor got to his feet, stacked Miles's plate onto his, and left the room.

Miles leant back into his pillows and watched the last of the sun fall over the horizon. The gnarled tree's branches, with their brown and yellow leaves, no longer swayed with the gusts of wind. In the distance, thick, dark clouds hid the moonlight. Miles turned his nose up at the acrid stink from the advancing vapours. With a sigh, he closed his eyes and began his nightly meditations, which helped to block out the pain.

Miles opened his eyes and shook his head at the throbbing that ran down his legs. His chin rested on his chest as he spoke his meditation words to help himself focus. At the end of the bed, the blanket's right side twitched. Miles pulled it off his legs and let it drop to the floor. He looked at his toes and, ignoring the waves of pain, willed them to move again. The muscles in the top of his feet shuddered, and then his toe moved up and down. He grabbed his right thigh, swung his leg off the side of the bed, then followed with his left leg. The end of his toe touched the ground, sending electrical shocks up through his calf and up into his lower back.

'Come on,' Miles said. 'Please work.'

He placed the rest of his foot on the floor, then covered his mouth with his hand to stifle a yell. The carpet underneath felt coarse and unwelcome. His toes, feeling the roughness, twitched and shuddered.

Miles's fingers wrapped around the bedpost, and with a heave, he pulled himself to his feet. He raised his head to the ceiling and growled, sending spittle down his chin. Thighs and calves shook with each wave of electrical shocks that shot out of his back. Using his left hand, he grabbed the back of his left thigh and moved his leg forward. His foot hit the ground, sending another stab of electricity streaking from his heel. He released his thigh and applied weight onto his left leg. Red dots exploded through his head, and with a gasp, he collapsed onto the floor.

'Son,' Dr Viktor said, his voice distant. 'What the hell are you doing?'

Miles blinked up at Dr Viktor.

'What happened?'

'I must have rolled out of bed,' Miles said, with a croak.

Dr Viktor gave him a confused look. He propped his cane against the side table and offered a hand.

Miles waved him away. 'You will hurt yourself if you try to lift me, old man.'

Dr Viktor slapped his hand away. 'I am old, but there is still life in me.'

Miles grabbed the bottom of the bedpost and dragged himself closer to the bed.

'How do you want me to help, son?' Dr Viktor said.

'Pass me your cane, if you will,' Miles said.

Dr Viktor planted his cane next to Miles's hand.

His left hand on the bedpost, and his right on Dr Viktor's cane, Miles got himself up onto his knees.

'Can you feel something?' Dr Viktor said.

Miles shook his head. 'No. Hold the cane steady, will you?'

Dr Viktor placed more weight onto the cane.

Miles pulled himself up and slid onto the end of the bed. His lips rattled together as he sighed from the effort. With both hands, he shifted his weight until he sat in the middle of the mattress. He grabbed the underside of each thigh and pulled his legs back onto the bed.

Dr Viktor picked up the blanket and spread it across Miles's legs.

His head back in the pillows, Miles closed his eyes and brought his breathing back under control.

Dr Viktor sat down in the chair next to him and eyed Miles through his knitted brow. 'What were you dreaming of? Something must have made you move in your sleep.'

Miles scanned the window. 'Black snow,' he said. 'I can smell it coming.'

Dr Viktor grabbed his cane and hauled himself out of the chair. With a clump of the cane on the carpet, he walked to the bay and pulled the top window closed. He grabbed his handkerchief from his pocket, coughed loudly, then returned to the chair.

'This black snow does not agree with you,' Miles said, giving Dr Viktor a concerned look.

Dr Viktor waved his hand dismissively. 'It will soon be time to lock this house down to keep the stink out.'

'You should have asked Valen to build this house closer to Fairacre.'

'This house has been here for centuries,' Dr Viktor said, his gaze growing distant. 'I could never move away.'

'Maybe you are feeling some guilt for building those machines that are causing all of this destruction?'

Dr Viktor snorted. 'The destruction would be worse if they were not there.'

Miles opened his mouth, then closed it again.

'What is it?' Dr Viktor said.

'You speak little of the machines and the City of Lynn.'

Dr Viktor spun the cane in his hand. 'Your brother is due here the day after tomorrow. Would you like to see him?'

Miles closed his eyes and shook his head. 'Subtle change of subject, and no, I don't like to see the pity in his eyes.'

'You cannot ignore your brother forever.'

Miles opened his eyes and trained them on Dr Viktor. 'I will think of it and tell you tomorrow. Right now, I am getting tired and I need to rest.'

Dr Viktor hauled himself up and shuffled to the bedroom door. 'I will say goodnight. Please don't fall out of your bed again. It will further the complications in your back.'

Miles dropped his head onto the pillow and ignored his adoptive father.

The door closed with a gentle click and the familiar thud of Dr Viktor's cane grew softer as he made his way up the stairs.

Miles removed the blanket and sat staring stony-faced at his toes. Ignoring the pain, he willed each toe to move over and over again until exhaustion hit. With trembling hands, he pulled the blanket over his legs, placed his head on his pillow, and stared at the ceiling.

The light in his room faded and the dark, now moonless night dragged by. The once-clear windows were slowly coated with streaks of wet as the black snow began to fall. Miles dozed in and out of sleep, only awakening when the pins and needles in his lower back prickled intensely.

The next morning, Miles sat bleary-eyed, watching the rays of the new day's sunlight crawl over his bedroom. The clumping of Dr Viktor's cane through the house signalled the precise time of six o'clock in the morning. Thirty minutes later, Miles said, 'Come in.'

Dr Viktor, chuckling, walked in with a bowl of steaming porridge. He stopped and frowned at Miles. 'Have you not slept?'

'A bit,' Miles said, taking the bowl. 'The pain awakens me

sometimes.'

Dr Viktor frowned and opened his mouth, but then thought better of saying anything.

'What are your plans for today?' Miles said.

'I will spend some time in my study, then prepare for the visit tomorrow. The entire group is visiting from Fairacre before they get cut off by the black snow.'

Miles stirred his porridge and waited for the question.

'I have something for you. Valen built it.'

Miles stopped stirring and glanced at Dr Viktor with a surprised look. 'Valen made something for me?'

'You may not like the gift, but understand it's with the best of intentions.'

'What is it then?'

Dr Viktor placed his bowl on the side table and, using his cane, he propped open the bedroom door and shuffled out of the room. A minute later he returned wheeling a wheelchair.

Miles closed his eyes and took a breath to still his rising anger.

'It will do you good to get out of this room, son,' Dr Viktor said. 'It does not mean this is permanent.'

'I do not want you to wheel me around in some chair like a useless cripple.'

'You won't need anyone to wheel you around,' Dr Viktor said, rolling the chair over to Miles's bed. 'You are more than capable of operating it.'

Miles stared at the wheelchair with a look of disgust. With a shake of his head, he dumped the empty bowl of porridge on the side table, sending the spoon clattering to the floor.

Dr Viktor, remaining silent, bent over, picked up the spoon, and placed it back in the bowl.

'I will use it when only you are at home. I will not use it when the others are here,' Miles said.

The corners of Dr Viktor's mouth rose. 'I can live with that. Would you like to try it now?'

Miles stared at the chair, then raising his head, he gave Dr Viktor a single nod.

'Here, let me help you,' Dr Viktor said, struggling to his feet.

Miles held up a hand. 'Sit down. I will do this myself.'

Dr Viktor fell back into the chair. 'Suit yourself.'

Miles pulled the blanket away, and using his hands to move his legs, he worked his way to the edge of the bed. With the bedpost in one hand and the mattress underneath the other, he lifted himself off the bed, then lowered himself into the wheelchair.

'I see your upper body strength hasn't disappeared,' Dr Viktor said.

Miles shuffled himself deeper into the wheelchair, then clipped the straps over his legs. 'My upper body strength is nothing like it used to be.'

'Is it comfortable?' Dr Viktor said.

Miles nodded. 'You said Valen created this?'

'Yes. He is a master technician. I noticed it in the changes he made in this house when he rebuilt it.'

'It is comfortable.'

'You cannot get upstairs just yet, but Valen has an idea to fix that,' Dr Viktor said.

Miles ran his hands over the rubber wheels. 'What is the layout of the house?'

Dr Viktor pulled himself to his feet. 'The house is exactly the same. Your room upstairs is waiting for you when you are ready. This room, your old training room, we can change to whatever you want it to be.'

Miles gripped the tops of the wheels, spun the chair, and manoeuvred himself out of the room. The wheels turned smoothly as he made his way to the large entrance hall. The chandelier at the top twinkled small spots of sparkling light over the floor and up the horseshoe stairs. With a turn, he made his way past the lounge and through the double doors into the kitchen. The wheels squeaked on the floor as Miles moved past the breakfast table and up to the pantry door, which he opened.

'I can rearrange that for you to get items more easily,' Dr Viktor said, standing behind him.

'Thanks. Valen has done an amazing job with this chair. It is easy to use.'

'He has done a lot for us,' Dr Viktor said.

'How are you taking to the new house?' Miles said, scanning the pantry shelves.

Dr Viktor sighed. 'I still feel a bit out of place. New things, although the same, don't have the history tied to them.'

'Too many ghosts in your past.'

Dr Viktor chuckled. 'You and me both, my boy.'

'Time to get back,' Miles said, wheeling himself away from the pantry.

The wheelchair whirred over the stone floor of the kitchen and entrance hall. Miles banged open his bedroom door and, moving through it, he parked the wheelchair on the opposite side of the bed, where he pulled himself up onto the soft mattress. The blanket rustled as he pulled it over his legs, and the pillows sagged as he dropped his head against them.

'Tired, son?' Dr Viktor said from the doorway.

'Yes, I would like to rest now if I may.'

'Call me if you need me,' Dr Viktor said, closing the door behind him.

Miles opened his eyes and, after removing his blanket, he moved his toes. A smile crept across his face as, after a long spring and summer, a glimmer of hope shone with the first falling of the black snow.

CHAPTER 2
I HAVE NOTHING TO OFFER

Dr Viktor tapped the cane on the door.

Miles pulled himself into a sitting position and tucked the blankets under his legs. 'Come.'

The door banged open, and Dr Viktor cursed as the trolley holding the plates of food jammed against the door frame.

'Don't drop the food,' Miles said, straining to see the plates' contents. 'I see you have been busy.'

Dr Viktor grunted as he shoved the trolley closer to the bed. 'Your comment about my cooking left a wound deep in my soul.'

'I said it was getting better,' Miles said, scanning the different plates of food.

Dr Viktor filled two bowls with steaming vegetables and an assortment of meats. He handed Miles a bowl, then lowered himself into the chair.

'Not bad,' Miles said through a mouthful of food.

Without looking up from his bowl, Dr Viktor hummed his agreement.

'I heard you locking down the house this morning,' Miles said.

'The black snow fell lightly through the night,' Dr Viktor said, waving his spoon at the window. 'A few days from now and it will smother the entire house.'

Miles glanced at the window and scrunched up his nose at the long streaks left by the snow.

'Billy will be here tomorrow,' Dr Viktor said. 'Have you decided what you are going to do?'

'I would like to see him, but I do not want to hear anything about coming back to Fairacre.'

'I am sure he will understand,' Dr Viktor said.

'Is it just Billy that is coming through?'

'This will be the last time anybody can get to us, so I am sure there will be more than just Billy.'

Miles shook his head.

'Son,' Dr Viktor said, resting a gnarled hand on Miles's forearm. 'Even if they wanted you back in Fairacre, there is no way we could get there now.'

'A man with a cane and a man with a wheelchair,' Miles said. 'You might have to call this house the school for the disabled, old man.'

Dr Viktor chuckled. 'For both boys and girls?'

'Ha,' Miles said, then grimaced as the pins and needles turned into stabs of pain that shot down the backs of his legs.

Dr Viktor grabbed his cane and struggled to his feet.

Miles waved a hand. 'It will pass.'

'I am not used to feeling helpless, boy,' Dr Viktor said.

Miles looked over at Dr Viktor. 'If it was not for you, I wouldn't be here, old man. Not easing the pain is my choice.'

Dr Viktor grabbed the trolley's handle and, with a push, he bashed open the door. 'I will return with tea. Don't go anywhere,' he said without looking back.

Miles placed his head back onto the pillow.

A few minutes later the door swung open and Dr Viktor shuffled in with two cups of half-filled tea. The tea sloshed onto the bedside table as he dumped a cup next to Miles. 'The snow is falling a bit harder.'

'Have we enough in our stores for the winter?'

'Billy is bringing the remaining supplies in the morning,' Dr Viktor said. 'We have enough to last two winters.'

Miles adjusted his seating position to hide another stab of pain that shot down the backs of his legs.

With a tut under his breath, Dr Viktor stood. 'I am going to begin my work in my room. You have the bell if you need anything.'

'I have the wheelchair, old man, which makes you somewhat redundant,' Miles said with a half smile.

Dr Viktor slammed the end of his cane into the ground and chuckled until another fit of coughing took over. 'I will be in my room, son,' he said, replacing his handkerchief and banging the door open with his cane.

Miles waited for the door to close before he collapsed back into his pillows. He turned his head and looked out of the window at the black snow covering the trees and shrubs. The forest, once alive, now lay silent. Animals that stayed within the warmth of the trees had all but migrated south. Leaning over, he reached under his bed and lifted the sheathed greatsword, placing it across his lap. Next came the covered sharpening stone, which he placed on the table next to the bowl of water. With one fluid movement, the sword sang as Miles pulled it free from its protective cover. He picked up the sharpening stone, splashed it with some water and began the hypnotic work on the shiny steel sword. The scraping filled his ears and his eyes narrowed as he fell into the zone of sharpening his prized possession.

After what felt like minutes, he shook his head to bring himself out of the hypnotic flow. The angle of the rays on his bedroom floor told Miles he had been going for hours, as it was just after noon. With a jerk, Miles pulled a hair from his head and, with the softest of touches against the sword, he watched the blade slice the hair in two. The sword sang back into its sheath, then rattled as he dropped it under his bed. Reaching for his sharpening stone, Miles's jaw slammed shut, and his fingers curled into claws. His body shook as the pins and needles in his back turned into pulsing electric shocks. The muscles in his legs shuddered as the nerves connected back to Miles's brain. Miles focused on controlling his breathing. In the distance, a long, mournful howl broke through the rasping of his breaths. Sweat poured down from Miles's brow and into his eyes. The jolts turned into waves of low, dull pain as each muscle came back to life.

Another long howl, this time closer, sounded through the trees in the forest.

Miles tilted his head to one side and listened.

A scratching sound whispered through the house.

Miles pulled the blankets away, swung his legs over the side of the bed, and held both feet an inch off the carpet. Tentatively, he let the bottom of his left foot touch the carpet. A shock pulsed up through his leg and into his back as his toes curled, claw-like, into the fibres. A few seconds later, he watched as his toes uncurled, letting the rest of his foot settle onto the ground.

Miles lowered his right foot onto the carpet and felt nothing.

'Come on,' he said, squeezing the top of his right thigh.

The nerves in his lower back shifted, sending stabs of pain down his right leg. With a crack, the toes on his right foot curled into the carpet and then, a few seconds later, they slowly uncurled.

Miles pushed himself off the bed and stood with both knees wobbling. The wheelchair was two steps away. The bed shuddered as he let go of the bedpost and, leaning on his left leg, he took a step forward. He planted his left foot into the floor and tried to take another step. The sound of muscle and bone hitting carpeted floor echoed through the house.

Miles cursed colourfully as he lay sprawled over the carpet.

With a shake of his head, he got onto his hands and knees, crawled up to the wheelchair, and hauled himself into it.

The bedroom door banged open, and Miles wheeled himself into the entrance hall, where he stopped and listened.

A small yap and insistent scratching came from the big wooden door.

Miles wheeled himself to the door and pulled one of Dr Viktor's canes from the holder. He turned the lock and, opening the door an inch, he immediately gagged at the acrid air that hit him square in the face. With his eyes scrunched up, he scanned the gnarled trees sitting beneath the growing layers of black snow.

A deep-throated growl sounded beyond the trees. A set of green eyes peered around a tree trunk and glared without blinking at Miles. Slowly, more eyes of varying colours appeared from behind the tree trunks.

Miles pulled open the door the rest of the way and wheeled himself out into the cold, gusting air.

An enormous black timber wolf, with his head lowered, stalked into the clearing and stopped just below the steps.

With his breath catching in his throat, Miles froze and stared back at the wolf.

Time slowed as the two glared back at one another, unmoving and unblinking.

A streak of light brown dashed from the forest and underneath the legs of the alpha wolf. With a yap, a wolf pup bounded up the steps and stopped in front of Miles.

The alpha wolf let out a long, soft growl.

'I don't think your dad is happy with you being up here,' Miles said, leaning forward.

The wolf pup yapped again, then spun in a circle.

Miles lifted the cane and poked it at the wolf pup. The pup stopped spinning, grabbed the end of the cane with sharp needle-like teeth, and growled playfully.

Miles shook the cane, trying to break it free from the wolf pup's mouth.

The alpha wolf took a step forward and growled menacingly.

The pup turned and growled at the alpha wolf.

'You better get out of here, little one,' Miles said.

The small pup stalked down the steps, and with a final snap at the alpha wolf, she darted off into the trees.

The alpha wolf raised his head, and with his lips dragging over his fangs, he snarled at Miles.

'What is going on, son?' Dr Viktor said from inside the house.

Miles lowered his gaze and reversed the wheelchair back through the open door.

The wolf snorted and backed away into the forest, his yellow eyes disappearing into the darkness.

Miles closed the door.

'Son?' Dr Viktor said from the top of the staircase. 'Are you OK? Why was the front door open?'

'It's nothing,' Miles said, spinning his wheelchair round.

'I heard wolf howls,' Dr Viktor said.

'Yes. Unusual for them to be here after the black snow has fallen.'

Dr Viktor made his way down the stairs. 'They used to stay in these forests before the snow came. The forests were a rich food source for them.'

'They probably got caught on their way south,' Miles said, turning his wheelchair for the kitchen.

'I see you are using the chair.'

Miles wheeled into the kitchen. 'It is good to move about,' he said over his shoulder.

Dr Viktor walked down the stairs and, following Miles, he entered the kitchen and lit the cooker to heat water.

Miles wheeled his chair up to the counter. 'You say little about these machines that pollute the snow. The ones you created in the City of Lynn.'

Dr Viktor grunted. 'I don't want to talk about it.'

'If I can bring myself to use this blasted wheelchair, you can talk about what is happening in the City,' Miles said.

Dr Viktor pulled two mugs from a cupboard. 'There is not much to tell,' he said. 'We created large machines to melt ore and craft large metal objects. We found a black rock that burns for a long time and creates an enormous amount of heat. We used the heat from those rocks to power them.'

'Which fills the clouds with black, acrid smoke?' Miles said.

Dr Viktor poured hot water into the mugs. 'It creates a fog that gets sucked up into the clouds, yes.'

'So why are you so reluctant to speak about these machines?' Miles said.

'They used them to create machines for war,' Dr Viktor said.

'Which war? It is peaceful down south.'

'Not in the north,' Dr Viktor said, picking up the mugs and walking over to the counter. 'War has raged there for some time.'

'Is that why you never wanted me to go to the east to train for the Queen's Guard? Because of this war?'

Dr Viktor rested his hands on the counter top. 'It is part of it, my son. Few soldiers survive the battles in the north.'

Miles kept his gaze trained on Dr Viktor.

'Do you remember what Valen does with his essence?' Dr Viktor said.

Miles nodded. 'He shares it with his metal creations to give them life.'

'Yes, and that is what the machines in the City need to work. These machines are on the front line, fighting the forces in the north. The Queen's Guard are the protectors of these machines.'

'Who are these invaders?' Miles said.

Dr Viktor handed Miles a mug of tea, then he sat on a stool and peered off into the distance.

Miles took a sip of his tea. 'Father?'

Dr Viktor grabbed his cane and thumped it on the ground. 'I have never seen them. And this is the last I shall speak of it.'

Miles dragged his hands through his hair. 'Why are the women taken to the City?'

Dr Viktor shook his head. 'That is a mystery to me. They kicked me out of the City before they started stealing the women.'

Miles sighed.

'It is late, and I am tired. I think I will go back to bed,' Dr Viktor said.

'We need to tell the others this information, old man. Chloe needs to understand how important it is that we supply food to the City.'

Dr Viktor leant over until his face was inches from Miles. 'You will do nothing of the sort. I have only told you because I know you can keep this to yourself. And, if you had taken your seat at the council, you could have ensured the City its supply of food.'

Miles reversed his wheelchair. 'This will reach them, eventually. Don't you think they deserve the chance to prepare?'

'If it reaches them, son, no preparation will save them. Let them live in happy ignorance.'

Miles spun the wheelchair and made for the kitchen exit.

'I trust you to behave like an adult,' Dr Viktor said. 'Leave this be, son.'

Miles wheeled himself back to his bedroom and stopped short of the bed. He removed the blanket, stretched both his legs out, and wiggled his toes. In one fluid movement he stood, wobbled, then caught himself on the bedpost. The bed creaked as Miles lowered himself into it. Through the rest of the afternoon the scraping of sharpening stone onto blade filled Miles's room and the entrance hall. The sun's rays crept across his bedroom floor until sunset.

Dinner with Dr Viktor was a silent affair, as the two of them lived with their own thoughts.

'Have you decided what you are going to do tomorrow?' Dr Viktor said from the bedroom door.

Miles shook his head. 'I will tell you in the morning.'

Dr Viktor turned and pushed the trolley out into the entrance hall. Miles lay back in his pillow and, hearing the door click shut, he closed his eyes for the night.

'Son, they are here,' Dr Viktor said, knocking on the bedroom door.

Miles rubbed his eyes with the heels of his hands. 'They?'

Dr Viktor cracked open the door. 'Billy, Tilly, Chloe and Valen.'

Miles turned his head and looked out at the black snow-covered trees.

'Would you like me to ask them to come in?' Dr Viktor said, opening the door further.

Miles looked at the wheelchair. 'Can you come in, remove the wheelchair, and then send Billy in?'

Dr Viktor pulled the door open, walked around the bed and, resting his cane across the wheelchair, he moved it to the door.

'Billy will be here in a moment,' he said, closing the door behind him.

Miles double-checked the blankets, making sure they covered every part of his legs. He closed his eyes and listened to the laughter coming from the kitchen.

A soft knock sounded on the door.

'Billy?' Miles said.

The door opened and Billy walked in. 'Hello, brother,' he said, a lopsided grin spreading across his face.

Miles smiled thinly. 'I see the sun has been good to you.'

'When I can get out of the hospital,' Billy said, removing his dark-black cloak and sitting down on the chair. 'How have you been?'

Miles shrugged. 'Nothing much has changed.'

Billy scanned the length of the bed, then cocked his head to one side.

Miles reached down and rubbed the tops of his thighs.

'Can you feel them?' Billy said with a frown.

Miles remained silent.

'You can feel them, can't you?' Billy said.

'Pins and needles in my back and some pain down the backs of my legs.'

Billy sat up and, with his eyes shining, he laid a hand on Miles's shoulder. 'You know what this means, don't you?'

Miles couldn't help the smile that crept across his face.

'I need to tell the others,' Billy said, standing up.

'No, don't,' Miles said, reaching out and grabbing Billy by the hand.

Billy sat down and gave Miles a long, hard glare. 'What are you up to?'

Miles ignored the question and said, 'What news have you for me? How is Tilly?'

Billy turned a slight pink. 'She is in the kitchen with Chloe, Valen and Janie.'

'Janie is here?'

A light knock brought their attention to the door.

'Hi,' Janie said.

'I will leave the two of you alone,' Billy said, leaving the room.

Janie walked into the room, sat on the chair, and with a smile, she shyly cupped her hands in her lap.

'Please leave,' Miles said, looking down at his legs.

Janie's smile fell. 'Have I done something wrong?'

Miles continued to look at his legs. 'I don't like you seeing me like this. Please can you go now?'

'I don't care about that,' Janie said.

Miles looked at Janie with narrowed eyes and a clenched jaw. 'You might not care, but I certainly do. Please leave, now.'

Janie stood, sending her red hair cascading over her shoulders. 'I am not giving up on you, Miles. I am not giving up on us.'

Miles's face softened. He opened his mouth to say something, then closed it with a snap.

Janie waited for a response and, not getting one, she nodded once and left the room.

Miles let out a long breath. He bunched his hands into fists and pounded the mattress on either side of his legs. The door to his room swung open.

Chloe marched in and stood above Miles with her hands on her hips. 'You silly little man,' she said. 'You have upset Janie.'

'Why did you bring her here?' Miles said, snarling.

Chloe bent over and placed her face inches from Miles's. 'Maybe we brought her here because you need something good in your life. But no, you sit here and wallow in your own misery.'

'Get out,' Miles said, his voice lowering.

'I am not going anywhere until you apologise to Janie.'

'I am not apologising. You should have asked me if I wanted to see her.'

'Love, leave him be,' Valen said from the doorway.

Chloe swung around and glared at Valen. 'I will not have him treating Janie like that.'

Valen walked into the room and, wrapping an arm around Chloe's waist, he gently directed her to the door. 'Go, my love.'

With a shake of her head, Chloe shoved Valen's arm off her waist and, stalking out of the room, she slammed the door.

'I don't need a lecture, Valen,' Miles said, bowing his head.

Valen sat down. 'Everyone misses you in Fairacre. Chloe has saved you a seat at the council. Janie talks about you often.'

Miles shook his head. 'I cannot sit on the council like this, and I have nothing to offer Janie. She needs to find a man who doesn't need looking after all day.'

'Men with greater disabilities have served on councils before, Miles, and don't you think that is Janie's choice?'

Miles turned his head away from Valen and looked down at his legs.

Valen stood and made his way to the door. 'You are going to have to decide soon, Miles. You cannot sit in this room forever. The council is waiting for you, and you are going to lose a woman who loves you.'

Miles continued staring at his legs.

Valen opened the door and, peering over his shoulder, he said, 'As Chloe mentioned, you owe Janie an apology.'

The door closed behind Valen.

Miles wiped the back of his hand across his face to hide the tears that sprang from his eyes. Angry voices trickled from the kitchen, and Miles flinched at the mention of his name. He heard the front door of Dr Viktor's house open and close.

The house fell into silence.

A few minutes later, Dr Viktor's cane thumped along the wooden floor and stopped in front of Miles's door. Miles braced himself for the door to slam open. He waited and heard Dr Viktor's cane thump again as he moved away. Miles leant back into his pillow and bit his bottom lip. The shock and hurt in Janie's face brought another tear to his eyes.

Later, he lifted himself out of bed and hobbled to the door, which he cracked open to listen for movement. Hearing nothing, he walked into the entrance hall and over to the front door where Dr Viktor's canes sat in a bucket. The canes rattled as Miles searched for one with a rubber stop on the end. With the cane in his right hand, he went into the kitchen and over to the pantry, where he opened the door and searched for food that would not perish.

With the food items he found packed onto one shelf, he closed the pantry door, and then made his way back to his room. Sweat beaded his forehead as he walked to his wardrobe and pulled out a dark-green rucksack. He packed two sets of clothing, a rain sheet and a sleep mat. The sound of scraping metal drew his eye to a small box sitting at the back of the shelf. Miles dropped the rucksack and, picking up the box, he flipped open the lid. His breath caught in his throat at the sight of the round, crested patch of the Queen's Guard.

Retrieving the patch, Miles turned it around in his fingers. With his brow furrowing and his jaw clenching, he kissed the patch and said, 'I will not keep myself from my dreams any longer. I will be a member of the Queen's Guard.'

With a nod, he slipped the patch neatly into his breast pocket and placed the box on the shelf. He closed the rucksack and threw it under the bed.

A knock sounded on the door.

Miles climbed into bed and pulled the blankets over his legs. 'Come,' he said.

Dr Viktor walked in with a tray of cheeses and bread, which he placed on the bedside table. 'Sorry I am late. Got carried away with work.'

Miles reached over and helped himself to the food.

'This morning went well,' Dr Viktor said with a snort.

Miles ignored him and carried on eating his food.

'They only mean well,' Dr Viktor said. 'You know that, don't you, son?'

'They pity me,' Miles said. 'Sending Janie here like I need someone to cheer me up.'

'Would she have cheered you up if you had given her a chance?'

'She deserves better than what I can offer.'

Dr Viktor lowered his eyebrows at Miles. 'Is that for you to decide?'

The muscles in Miles's jaw clenched. 'You sound like Valen.'

Dr Viktor sighed. 'You cannot stay like this forever, son. You are going to need to decide what you want at some point.'

'Now you sound like Billy.'

Dr Viktor spread his hands. 'Well, they are both my former pupils.'

'I know they mean well, but I need to do this in my own time.'

Dr Viktor finished his cheese and bread and struggled to his feet. 'I will leave the rest of the cheese and bread here for dinner. I am going to Fairacre this late afternoon.'

Miles turned and frowned. 'Are you sure that is wise? How are you getting there and what if the snow cuts you off?'

Dr Viktor smiled. 'Chloe is sending a team here to escort me and I will be back by morning.'

'Make sure you wrap up, old man. You know what this black snow does to your cough.'

Dr Viktor grunted and hobbled to the door. 'I will see you tomorrow, son.'

After Dr Viktor left the room, Miles removed the blankets and sat on the edge of the bed. He leant over and pulled his greatsword and rucksack out from under the bed. Double-checking the bag's contents, he closed the straps and swung it onto his back. With a roll of his shoulders, he checked that the bag sat comfortably. Satisfied, he removed the rucksack and placed it underneath the bed. The pillows sagged as Miles climbed back into bed and rested his head against them.

A few hours later, the thump of Dr Viktor's cane stopped at the bedroom door. 'I will see you tomorrow, son.'

'Keep warm, old man.'

The front door opened, then closed with a bang.

Miles climbed out of bed, pulled on some thick socks, then slipped his feet into a pair of thick-soled boots, which he laced up. He reached under his bed and picked up his greatsword, cane and rucksack.

The cane thumped on the floor as he hobbled towards his cupboard. He stopped short and, with a tilt of his head, he looked at the long black cloak sitting in the corner of his room.

'You knew,' Miles whispered. 'You knew I was going, didn't you, Billy?'

The thick cloak smelt of his brother as he picked it up and wrapped it around himself. He swung his greatsword onto his back and tied the leather straps to secure it. The rucksack sat over his cloak and greatsword.

Miles walked out of his bedroom, through the entrance hall, and into the kitchen. He opened the pantry door and, throwing the rucksack off his back, he stuffed the food into it. The cane thumped against the floor as he hobbled back into the hall and stood at the front door. Miles turned and, for the last time, scanned the place he grew up in.

The door opened and a blast of acrid, cold air hit him in the face. With his head lowered, Miles pulled the cloak's hood over his head and braced himself against the wind. The door behind him slammed closed, and with a last glance over his shoulder, he walked to the path and turned south.

CHAPTER 3
A PUP

The overlapping branches of the trees that lined the southern path created a wind tunnel. Miles pulled the drawstring of Billy's cloak tighter around his neck to protect himself from the gusting wind.

'Not sure this is such a good idea,' Miles said to himself, squinting to keep the path in focus.

The sun, which had lost its war against the thick black clouds, disappeared over the western horizon, leaving the forest in darkness.

Through the icy wind, Miles felt the pins and needles crawl across his lower back. With each step, they turned into jolts of painful electricity down his legs. His right foot facing inwards grew more tired as it dragged a long groove through the snow. The knuckles on his right hand turned white as he leant more heavily on his cane.

A howl broke through the gusting wind.

Miles froze.

From behind a tree, a wolf's snout appeared.

The end of Miles's cane dug deep into the snow as he threw his full weight against it.

With a snort, the snout disappeared behind the tree.

Miles scanned the darkness, squinting at each tree, searching for any movement.

With the cold starting to work through his clothes, Miles tightened his cloak around his body and continued walking down the southern path. After another hour, he reached the fork in the road and, without stopping, he turned left and walked towards the eastern land.

A flash of fur caught his eye. Miles stopped and crouched. He scanned the forest, and stopping at the base of each tree, he searched for movement.

A long, menacing growl spun his head back along the eastern path. The black-haired alpha wolf, standing in the path, lowered his head and snarled at Miles.

'Whoa there, big boy,' Miles said, holding out his hand while getting back to his feet.

The wolf lowered his head and took a step towards Miles.

Miles reached behind his back and, with one practised fluid movement, he drew his greatsword.

Growls from both his left and right broke through the gusting wind.

Miles kept his focus on the alpha wolf in front of him.

The black wolf raised his snout, sniffed the air, then lowering his head, he let out a deep, gurgling growl. With his lips sliding across his thick white teeth, he advanced on Miles.

A sudden jolt sent a new powerful set of pins and needles across Miles's back. His hands trembled as the nerve endings in his lower back knit together. He watched his right foot turn outwards until it faced the way it always had. The cane dropped out of his hand and fell softly into the snow. Miles adjusted his stance, shifting some of his weight onto his right leg. His foot held steady and strong.

The alpha wolf, his muscles rippling across his shoulders, broke into a trot.

Black snow puffed up into the air as a barking wolf pup bounded through the trees and jumped onto the path in front of the alpha wolf. The alpha skidded to a halt and snapped his jaws at the pup. The pup dodged the sharp white teeth and, lowering her front legs until her chin touched the snow, she let out small ear-piercing barks.

'Get out of here,' Miles said under his breath.

With her eyes trained on the alpha wolf, the pup shuffled back towards Miles.

'We don't want any trouble,' Miles said, pointing the greatsword at the wolf. 'Leave us alone.'

The alpha wolf's muscles rippled across his shoulders as he continued stalking forward.

Miles spread his legs as the pup backed in between his feet.

The pup spun in between Miles's legs, growling and yapping.

Miles reached behind his back and rubbed the muscles running along his spine. The nerve endings felt like fire coursing through his back and down his legs.

The pup stopped her ear-splitting yapping and looked up at Miles.

'Have you got something to do with this, little one?' Miles said.

Big brown eyes gazed up at Miles.

Paws padded on the black snow as the alpha wolf again picked up speed.

Miles placed the greatsword across his chest to protect himself.

Bits of snow sprung up from between Miles's legs as the pup, her small limbs scrambling, darted towards the alpha wolf.

A sickening yelp reverberated through the trees as the alpha wolf clamped his jaws around the pup's tiny neck and threw her into the black snow.

Billy's cloak slipped from Miles and fluttered to the path. The muscles rippled across his shoulders as he looked at the pup's lifeless body. His head jerked back to the alpha wolf, and with a yell, he charged.

The wolf, in one fluid movement, squatted, then sprang, sending his enormous body to the height of Miles's head. Miles sidestepped and slammed the flat side of his greatsword into the wolf's side. The wolf slashed out its front claw and narrowly missed the tip of Miles's nose before he crashed into the snow on the side of the path. Miles moved his feet through the snow, searching for a solid footing. The wolf, his teeth bared, scrambled to his feet, and sprang again. Miles turned his greatsword and rammed the hilt into the side of the wolf's head. The wolf yelped and crashed to the ground.

'I didn't want to hurt you,' Miles said. 'I told you to leave us alone.'

The wolf got to his feet and shook his coat, sending black snow spraying into the air. With a low growl, he cautiously backed up into the trees.

Miles shuffled backwards with his eyes focused on the alpha wolf. Out of the corner of his eye, he saw the fur of the lifeless pup. The snow crunched under him as he knelt next to the pup. After placing his sword across his knee, Miles ran a hand along the pup's body and sighed with relief as he felt the rapid thudding of her heart.

'Come on, little one,' Miles said, massaging the pup's neck and shoulders.

With a jolt, the pup scrambled to her feet and shook the black snow out of her brown coat.

Miles ran his hand from the top of her head and over her back.

The little pup's coat was free of wounds.

'I knew it,' Miles said. 'You are like Juno's Chax, aren't you?'

The wolf pup licked Miles's hand.

Miles stood and, turning in a full circle, he tried to count the number of wolves that stood silently staring at him.

The alpha wolf, standing on the other side of the path, pricked his ears and growled.

Miles held out a hand in resignation. He slid his greatsword back into its sheath and said, 'I mean you no harm.'

The alpha wolf turned his gaze to the wolf pup.

Her head held high, the pup bounded over to the alpha wolf and snarled.

After sniffing the pup, the alpha wolf turned and walked into the trees. The surrounding wolves, one by one, turned and disappeared after the alpha wolf.

The wolf pup turned and tilted her head at Miles.

'Go,' Miles said. 'I will be OK.'

The wolf pup looked at the disappearing pack. Then, with one final glance back at Miles, she bounded after them.

Miles walked back onto the path and picked up his cane. He slid the cane onto his back and continued walking eastwards. The muscles in his back and legs moved freely with the newly knitted nerves, sending instructions down his legs.

In the distance, a solid iron gate appeared out of the darkness. On each side, a smooth wall disappeared north and south into the mist. The closer to the gate Miles got, the bigger and higher it became, until, standing in front of it, he had to lift his head to see the top.

Miles grabbed the handle of the gate and tried to move it. Locked and frozen solid, it stayed stubbornly in place.

'No way I am going to get through this,' Miles said, peering north then south. 'Time to choose a direction.'

The yap of the wolf pup came from the north.

Miles immediately walked north with his right hand dragging along the high, smooth wall. The black snow crunched under his boots as he stepped over fallen branches and sharp stones. The wolf pup let out a long, high-pitched howl.

Miles stopped. Up ahead, wolf eyes vanished one by one. With the last set of wolf eyes disappearing, he walked up to where the snow was littered with paw prints. Miles dragged his hand along the wall until it disappeared into a black hole. Going down to his knees, Miles placed his forearms in the snow and peered into the blackness. Resting back on his haunches, he shrugged while tightening the straps of his rucksack and greatsword.

'If that alpha wolf can fit through this hole, so can I,' Miles said, pulling his face mask over his mouth.

Miles edged into the hole and banged to a halt as the hilt of his greatsword caught on the edge. With a curse, he dipped lower and crawled into the darkness. Hand over hand, he inched forward through the hole. After a few minutes of crawling, a gasp escaped his lips. The nerves in his back began to separate. His right thigh trembled, and his right foot turned inwards. With a shake of his head, he continued to place one hand over the other until suddenly, his head popped out of the other side of the wall. Bugs scampered off his arms and shoulders, trying to escape the cold black snow. Miles stood and placed his back against the border wall. He scanned the surrounding area, taking in the tall, dead, gnarled, snow-covered trees. Mist swirled around the tree trunks, hugging the bases like piled-up blankets.

With no stars and moon to guide him, Miles pushed off the wall and shuffled up to the first tree. He pulled his rucksack off, unfastened the buckles, and pulled out one of his shirts. With one hand on the tree trunk, Miles knelt and ripped the shirt into long strips. He stuffed all but one of the strips into his pocket. He stood and tied one piece of cloth to the tree's lowest hanging branch. Miles pushed away from the tree and, shuffling east, he stopped at each tenth tree and tied another piece of cloth to its lowest branch.

An hour later he froze as a groan murmured through the thick mists. Miles sank to a knee and, placing one hand on the tree trunk, he reached behind his back and drew his greatsword.

A man shuffled through the trees. His clothes lay tattered over his body. One arm bounced lifelessly off his side. He moaned as he bumped into a tree, sending the mist swirling in all directions. Another man, groaning, appeared behind the first man. After the second man, a woman appeared also wearing tattered clothes.

Miles slid his greatsword back into its sheath. The end of the cane pushed into the snow as he hauled himself to his feet. One of the shuffling men stopped walking, turned his head and peered in Miles's direction.

Miles walked around the tree trunk then froze as all around him, men and women appeared out of the mist.

A flutter of a dark cloak whisked past a tree.

Miles remembered his training and steadied his breathing.

'What are you doing here, boy?' a voice said from inside the mists.

Miles removed his rucksack and placed it with his cane next to the tree. His greatsword sang out of its sheath.

A hiss whispered from his left side.

'Who are you?' Miles said.

A chuckle from inside the mist filtered to his ears.

'I don't want any trouble,' Miles said.

'You are no trouble, boy.'

Miles narrowed his eyes as he scanned the areas between the trees.

Another flick of a black cloak. 'You shouldn't be out at night, boy.'

'What do you want?' Miles said.

'Shall we play with him?' another voice from inside the mist said.

Miles took a step away from the tree to create some space for his sword.

A blur of black darted out from behind a tree and stopped dead in the black snow. His hooded cloak covered everything from his face to his feet.

'Who are you?' Miles said.

The figure extended his hands and lifted his hood partially off his face. Dark-black eyes gazed back. A smile slowly crept across his face.

A breath touched the nape of Miles's neck. With a sharp intake of air, Miles dropped to one knee and slashed his greatsword behind him.

'You will need to be a lot quicker than that, my boy,' the man said.

'He is slow,' a woman's voice said. 'And we do not have time to play these games.'

The man in front of Miles sighed. 'You take all the fun out of the hunt, my dear.'

'We are not hunting,' the woman said. 'Take him or kill him, just make it quick. We need to get moving.'

Miles straightened and pointed his greatsword at the man. 'You won't take me without a fight.'

The man chuckled. 'I think I will keep this one, my dear.'

'Hurry it up, Gerald,' the woman said.

Gerald pulled his hood back over his head.

Miles spread his feet and winced as his right club foot caught in the snow.

Gerald extended a hand and flicked out sharp, claw-like nails. 'He looks injured.'

A howl echoed through the mist.

Gerald hissed in the howl's direction.

'We move now,' the woman said from behind Miles.

Gerald looked at Miles. 'I will be quick, dear.'

'No. We move now,' the woman said, fear etched in her voice.

Another howl, this time closer.

The nerves in Miles's back began to knit together. The familiar electric shocks pulsed over his back and down his thighs.

'I will come back for you, boy,' Gerald said.

Several black cloaks blurred into the mist. The woman flashed past Miles and, grabbing Gerald, she dragged him into the darkness.

A flash of wolf tail followed the hooded figures.

With a groan, the dishevelled men and women turned and shuffled south into the mists.

Miles straightened his back and watched as more wolves sprinted after the dark-robed figures. His club foot turned outwards.

A yap sounded and Miles turned and smiled at the wolf pup who bounded up to him. She sat and lifted a paw, then dropped it and ran after her wolf pack.

The dark woods turned silent.

Miles walked back to the tree where his rucksack rested and sat down in the snow with his back to the tree. He unbuckled the flap of his rucksack, took out the dried foods and stuffed them into his mouth. Then, without warning, the nerves in his back split apart. A grimace spread across his face as he pulled himself to his feet. His foot turned inwards. In disgust, he swung his greatsword into the trunk of the tree. Black snow rained down on him. Having forgotten to keep track of where he was going, Miles stumbled forward through the snow. The food in his belly gave him some energy but did nothing for the pains running down his legs.

The cane suddenly dipped forward. A yell escaped Miles's lips as the world disappeared below him. He rolled head over heels down a slick, black snow-covered bank until he hit a road. Miles looked up into the dark night sky. Once the pain had subsided, he worked his way onto his hands and knees and crawled over to where his cane lay. The cane shook as he pushed himself up onto his feet.

A light glow appeared in the east as the sun broke over the horizon.

Miles stood on a road's corner. He peered east, then south. The cobblestones disappeared into the mist.

Across the road, Miles caught sight of a small cluster of green plants growing under a rocky overhang. After walking across the road, he crouch-walked underneath the overhang and instantly felt the wind's chill disappear. Dragging his rucksack off, he opened the buckles and pulled out the bed sheet, which he lay underneath the overhang. He pulled out the rest of the clothes and, after pulling off his cloak, he undressed and re-dressed into dry clothes. The warm clothes brought on a deep exhaustion and Miles, slipping back into his cloak, rolled up onto his bed sheet and rested his head on his rucksack.

The shivering woke Miles up. Stiffness in his back and legs only added to the throbbing ache of pain. He opened his eyes and took in the darkness outside the rocky outcrop. The mist had cleared slightly, and he could see the black snow-covered trees across the road. Miles sat up and, grabbing the last of the food out of his rucksack, he wolfed it down hungrily. With the aid of his cane, he struggled to his feet, secured the rucksack onto his back, and peered out of the rocky outcrop.

The sun had passed overhead and set in the west. He had slept through the entire day. After a few deep breaths, he left the overhanging rock and shuffled out onto the road. With his head lowered, he walked along the eastern road with his cane in his right hand to help support his club foot. Nothing around him moved. The wind was no more, and the mist hung eerily still. All around, the black snow covered the dead trees, the steep banks and the cobblestone road.

As the hours passed by, Miles fell into a rhythm where he concentrated on putting one foot in front of the other. The pain and aches increased over time, making him lean heavily on his cane. His right foot occasionally caught on a cobblestone as it left drag marks through the snow.

A twig snapped.

Miles stopped dead and automatically reached for his greatsword.

Up ahead, a lone figure, with their head down, walked out of the mist.

The snow crunched underfoot as Miles moved off the road. He pulled his cloak tightly around himself and leant against the trunk of a tree.

The person walked with a hunch as they carried something big on their back.

Miles crouched and strained his eyes to get a view of the stranger's face.

The stranger stopped walking and looked left and right.

A flutter of black cloak flashed out from the trees, and in a second, the stranger on the road disappeared.

Miles stared at where the person had once stood. After waiting a few minutes, he used the cane to pull himself up. He left the trunk of the tree and, staying off the road, he used what cover he could find among the trees and mist. At the place where the person had been, Miles walked into the road, bent down, and checked the snow for tracks. Footprints walking along the road ended and another set of footprints from the side disappeared into the trees. Long grooves from dragged feet followed the footprints into the forest.

Miles searched the forest for a few moments, and finding nothing, he pulled his cloak tighter and made his way back into the trees.

He continued east, keeping the road to his left. As the hours ticked by, Miles felt his strength start to fade. Thirst wracked his body.

'Don't give up, boy,' a woman's voice said.

Miles stopped and tilted his head as a hazy light broke through the stagnant mist.

'Can you see the light, boy? Not far to go,' the woman said.

Miles's jaw chattered as the cold worked its way through his clothes. The knuckles of his right hand stayed white as he gripped the end of his cane.

The light disappeared.

Miles searched the area where the light had been. Seeing nothing, he continued forward with the road on the left.

The light blinked into view.

With his eyes not leaving the growing light, Miles moved into the road and quickened his shuffling step.

The road widened, large enough to take two carts and horses.

Miles stopped as the outline of a three-storey wooden building broke through the mist. A light hung over a wooden door.

Engraved on the door was a crest of a rearing horse. Below the horse's crest, the name of the inn shone in white letters.

The Dancing Horse Inn.

Miles walked closer. A dim light shone through the windows on the bottom floor.

A soft tinkling of glass on glass came from inside the inn.

Miles placed his hand on the door and pushed. The door opened, and Miles covered his eyes at the bright light from inside the inn. He took a step inside and gasped at the rush of heat slamming into his face.

The door thudded closed behind him. He reached up and pulled the hood off his head. To his right, through a doorway, a long wooden bar spanned the length of the wall. High empty stools sat pushed underneath the bar. Tables and chairs filled the rest of the room.

A man behind the bar stopped cleaning the glass in his hand and stared at Miles. At the bar, a figure in a long dark hooded cloak sat with his back to Miles.

The bartender's eyes darted towards the person sitting at the bar, then back at Miles.

Miles frowned at the fear etched across the bartender's face.

'Serve the boy, will you?' the familiar voice said.

The bartender cleared his throat and plastered a smile across his face. 'Come in, young man. Sit where you please.'

Miles removed the rucksack from his back and hobbled to the table in the corner closest to the door.

The bartender walked around the bar and waited for Miles to remove his cloak.

Miles pulled out his coin purse and undid the knot in the string. 'May I have some hot tea? And what do you have to eat?'

'Tea I cannot make. Coffee, dried meats and bread is all I have.'

Miles nodded. 'Coffee, dried meats and bread then, please. How much coin?'

'Three bronze,' the bartender said over his shoulder.

Miles pulled out four coins and placed them on the table. He glanced at the back of the man sitting at the bar.

The bartender hurried off and returned with a tray that he slid onto the table. He picked up the coins, and while turning them in his hands, he frowned at Miles.

'Everything OK?' Miles said.

The bartender pocketed the coins. 'Perfectly good, young sir. Enjoy your meal.'

Miles didn't wait for the man to leave. He buttered the bread and wolfed it down. He chased the bread with the salty dried meats. The coffee burnt the back of his throat as he washed the food down.

The bartender returned with a steaming kettle and refilled the coffee mug.

'What is a young man doing wandering these roads at this time of night?' Gerald said.

Miles remained silent.

'You would do well to answer me, boy.'

Miles moved in his chair to free up access to his greatsword. 'I got lost in the mist and my horse became lame.'

'That is unfortunate to hear,' Gerald said. 'Which road were you travelling?'

'What is it to you, sir?' Miles said, his voice lowering.

Gerald chuckled. 'Idle conversation is all.'

The bartender pursed his lips at Miles and shook his head.

Gerald cocked his head to one side. 'Is there a problem, bartender?'

The bartender lowered his head. 'No, sir.'

Gerald turned around and trained his unblinking eyes on Miles. 'You cannot be from these parts.'

'What makes you say that?' Miles said.

A smirk crept across the man's face. 'Because you are not one of us.'

Miles stared wide-eyed as Gerald's canines grew out of his mouth and down his chin.

CHAPTER 4
STONE-COLD SERIOUS

Miles's chair fell over with a clatter.

Gerald, with unnatural grace, slid off the bar stool, faced Miles, and hissed.

'What are you?' Miles said, his greatsword sliding from its sheath.

Gerald chuckled. 'This boy still has time to ask questions, bartender.'

Glasses toppled from shelves as, behind the bar, the bartender plastered himself against the wall. 'He is not from here, Gerald. Please, I have nothing to do with this.'

Gerald snarled at the bartender. 'I will deal with you later.'

The bartender's mouth fell open. He grabbed a cloth and patted his brow.

Miles inched away from the corner of the room until he had enough space to swing his greatsword.

'What are you doing in these parts?' Gerald said. 'And no lies about lame horses.'

'I don't have to tell you anything,' Miles said, pointing the tip of his greatsword at Gerald.

Gerald peered over at the bartender. 'Will you be able to stop me from getting to Jon?'

Miles looked over at the bartender.

'Please tell Gerald what he wants to know,' Jon answered, fear etched across his face.

Miles took a step back, bent over and picked up the chair he had sent clattering to the floor. The muscles in his jaw tensed as he tried not to show the pain from his foot. He sat and lay his greatsword across his knees. 'I am here to prove myself fit to join the Queen's Guard.'

'You?' Gerald said, frowning. 'You are trying for the Queen's Guard?'

Miles lifted his chin. 'Yes, me, why the surprise?'

Gerald looked at Jon, then back at Miles. 'Is this a joke?'

Miles, keeping a stony face, glared at Gerald.

'He is serious, Jon,' Gerald said. 'Stone-cold serious.'

'I don't think he knows, Gerald,' Jon said.

Miles glanced at Jon, then resumed his unblinking stare at Gerald.

'My boy. It is nigh on impossible for even the strongest man to join the Queen's Guard. How you, a cripple, think you're going to get in, is beyond me.'

The knuckles of Miles's hands turned white as he tightened his grip on his greatsword. He couldn't stop a quick glance at his right foot and how it turned inwards.

Gerald chuckled. 'It looks like he has left everything behind for nothing, Jon. Shall I show mercy and put him out of his misery?'

Miles stood and flicked the greatsword at Gerald.

The vampire took a step back and watched the blade harmlessly swish by.

Miles, with his greatsword still pointing at Gerald, backed up towards the inn entrance.

'There are more of us out there, boy,' Gerald said. 'I would suggest you take your chances in here with me.'

'I didn't come here looking for trouble. All I wanted was a meal and a place to stay before I move on.'

Gerald tapped a sharp fingernail on his chin. 'Maybe I should turn him, Jon?'

'Turn me?' Miles said, looking at Jon.

The bartender cleared his throat. 'Into a vampire, son.'

'I don't know what a vampire is.'

Gerald threw his head back and laughed heartily, giving Miles a view of his sharp, pointy teeth. 'Definitely not from around here, is he Jon?' Gerald said after his laughter.

Jon flicked his head at the inn entrance. 'Get out of here, son.'

Gerald tutted. 'Why chase my food away, Jon?'

Miles drew back until his foot hit the inn door. With a shove of his elbow, it opened a crack, letting in a blast of cold air.

Gerald, walking towards Miles, licked his teeth and lips.

Miles backed out of the entrance, then turned and hobbled up the path and onto the road.

Gerald stood in the doorway and chuckled. 'Look how broken his body is, Jon. Yet here he is, trying to run.'

Miles stood on the road that ran east to west. With a resigned sigh, he turned, set his greatsword across his body, and tried to move his feet into a defensive stance. His right foot, catching against a crack in the cobblestones, made Miles stumble.

'And you want to be part of the Queen's Guard,' Gerald said, stalking out of the inn and launching himself at Miles.

Miles slashed out his greatsword and hit nothing. Claws lashed out and opened up a thin red gash in his chest. The black snow soaked Miles's trousers as he fell backwards onto the road.

Gerald stood above him with his hands on his hips and his

head cocked to one side. 'I know you are a cripple but I thought you would have more fight in you, boy.'

Miles leant over to grab his greatsword.

Gerald rested his foot on the greatsword and pulled it inches away from Miles.

The snow puffed as Miles fell back onto his elbow. He touched the wound in his chest and, looking up, he growled at the vampire.

Gerald sank to his haunches, extended a clawed finger, and lifted Miles's chin.

Miles slapped the finger away.

'You once had some fight in you, didn't you, boy?' Gerald said, looking deep into Miles's eyes. 'But now, all I see is an angry, weak little boy.'

Miles's breathing came fast and shallow as the pain in his chest increased. The blood seeping from the wound turned his shirt dark red.

'I see no fear in you, though,' Gerald said. 'Nothing to live for, have we?'

An image of Janie popped into Miles's head. He curled a lip and said, 'You know nothing about me.'

Gerald struck Miles across the face. 'Humans. If you didn't taste so good, we would have got rid of you centuries ago.'

Miles kicked out with his left foot and struck Gerald in the chest.

'Enough with the games,' Gerald said. 'I take little pleasure in hunting someone so pathetic.'

A blur of brown fur sprang out from the trees across the road. Gerald looked up, bared his teeth and hissed at the wolf pup. The wolf pup bounded across the black snow and onto the path, where she skidded to a halt behind Miles.

Miles slammed his mouth shut and closed his hands, digging his nails into his palms. The nerves joined across his back.

The pup let out a low growl and launched herself over Miles at the vampire.

Miles's head jerked back as he gaped at the size of the wolf. Her legs were long and gangly; she had turned into a teenage wolf.

Gerald, in one swift elegant move, sprang to his foot and kicked the wolf as hard as he could in the face.

The wolf launched back over Miles and, with a yelp, landed on the road and lay still.

Gerald looked at the lifeless body and growled.

'I am getting very tired of people hurting my wolf,' Miles said, grabbing his greatsword as he rolled onto his knees.

'Your wolf?' Gerald said.

Miles sprang to his feet and, raising his greatsword above his head, he moved into his attacking stance.

Gerald looked down at Miles's newly straightened right foot and, frowning, he said, 'How is that possible?'

Declining to explain, Miles moved through a rapid series of attacks with his greatsword hacking and slashing through the air.

The vampire, with unmeasurable speed, danced away from each sword attack.

Miles spun, slashed his sword, then gasped aloud as he felt the vampire's claws rake down his back.

'I sense an apology is in order,' Gerald said with a chuckle. 'You are an extremely gifted fighter.'

With a drop of his right shoulder, Miles sent the greatsword singing through the air and over the top of Gerald's head.

Gerald rolled and, with a flick of his wrist, he flipped up into the air and landed on his feet above the unmoving wolf pup.

'Get away from her,' Miles said, pointing his sword at Gerald.

The black snow crunched underneath Gerald's boots as he went down to his haunches. He snapped open his hand and extended his razor-sharp claws.

'No,' Miles screamed.

The ground underneath Gerald shuddered. With a look of surprise, he retracted his claws and placed a hand in the snow to steady himself.

Miles raked his hand through the air and roared as small stones shot out of the black snow and flew into Gerald's body.

Gerald blinked. A second later, he collapsed to one knee. His eyes turned a dark red as small stones, one at a time, fell from his body back into the black snow. The holes where the stones once were, closed up and healed.

'Get away from her,' Miles said, taking a step towards Gerald.

'What are you?' Gerald said, his fangs fully extended.

Miles took another step. 'I said, get away from her.'

With a grimace, Gerald got to his feet and, lifting a boot, he aimed it at the wolf's head. A snarl from the other side of the road made him freeze. The black alpha wolf sprang out from the trees with his jaws snapping. Gerald's boots sprayed up black snow as, in a flash of cloak, he disappeared into the dark forest. The alpha wolf bounded off into the forest in chase.

'Jon,' Miles shouted over his shoulder. 'Come and help me.'

The inn door remained closed and quiet.

'Coward,' Miles spat, walking over to the wolf. A few steps short, he felt his right foot turn in. 'No, please, no,' he said, kneeling and running his hand across the wolf's side. No heartbeat, no rise or fall of her chest.

'Jon, come here,' Miles said over his shoulder. 'Now!'

The inn door banged open, and Jon, with nervous eyes, looked into the darkness.

'Come and help me get her into the inn,' Miles said.

Jon remained planted to the ground just inside the inn door.

'I promise you, Jon, if you don't come and help me, the vampires will be the least of your worries.'

With a last glance left and right, Jon hurried up the path and onto the road.

'You will need to carry her,' Miles said. 'I will hold her head.'

'What if she wakes and bites me?' Jon said.

'I will hold her head. She will bite me before she bites you,' Miles said. 'Let's move.'

In one fluid movement, Jon bent over and picked up the wolf. 'She isn't breathing.'

'I know that,' Miles snapped. 'Get her into the inn.'

Jon turned and moved swiftly towards the inn. Not able to keep up, Miles stumbled after until he walked through the front door. From behind him, he heard the snap of a branch and a hiss through teeth.

Miles slammed the door. 'Can you lock this, Jon?'

Jon stood frozen at the end of his bar.

'Jon,' Miles said, his voice rising. 'Can you lock this door?'

'Yes, yes,' Jon said, shaking himself, then hurrying around the bar. 'There is a plank that goes across.'

Miles held the door closed and waited for Jon to get the plank. He moved to one side and watched Jon slot the plank in place.

Jon turned and eyed the wolf that lay on the bar. 'Is it dead?'

A lump caught in Miles's throat. 'She is not dead,' he said, hobbling to the bar. 'I need to check where her wounds are.'

'She isn't breathing,' Jon said again.

A crash hit the inn door. 'Come out, little boy,' Gerald said.

Jon looked wild-eyed at the door. 'What have you done? He will come for me now.'

Miles ignored Jon and gently ran his hands along the wolf's body, searching for the wounds. Finding the claw marks along her belly, Miles spun the wolf around.

'She is dead. Nothing can survive that,' Jon said.

'Shut up,' Miles said. 'Get me a cloth that I can tie around her.'

Jon walked to the end of the bar and pulled out a tablecloth, which he flung over to Miles.

Miles wrapped the cloth around the wolf and tied a knot to secure it in place.

Another crash hit the inn door.

Jon placed his head in his hands. 'Gerald has friends. They will get in and that will be the end of me and my inn.'

Miles reached over and shook Jon's shoulder. 'If that is the case, then why don't we try to go out with a fight? Do you know what hurts these vampires?'

Jon's brow furrowed. 'The only thing I know is fire.'

Miles snorted.

'What?' Jon said.

'I know just the person, but she is a long way away from here.'

Jon shook his head in confusion.

'Nothing,' Miles said. 'Have you got more cloth?'

Jon's knees cracked as he crouched. He rummaged inside the cupboard and pulled out an armful of tablecloths.

'Get behind the bar and keep an eye on her,' Miles said, flicking his head at the wolf.

With a hesitant look, Jon shuffled behind the bar and placed the tablecloths on the counter.

Miles hobbled over to a table, scraped the chairs out of the way, and flipped it upside down. He drew his greatsword and, with four swipes, he removed the table legs. 'Wrap the cloth onto one end of each of these poles, then soak the cloth in alcohol,' he said, slamming the wooden stakes onto the counter.

Jon stared at Miles, then jumped as another crash hit the inn door. The wooden plank rattled and shook against its metal hooks.

'Jon, you need to move,' Miles said.

'They are playing with us,' Jon said. 'They could have got in here long ago.'

'Come on, Jon. Snap out of it,' Miles said, slapping his hand on the bar. 'Help me out here.'

'OK,' Jon said, shaking his head. 'Wrap the cloth around the poles, then wet the cloth with alcohol.'

'You got it,' Miles said, walking along the bar to the wolf.

'Is she breathing?' Jon said.

Miles laid his ear on her side and listened. 'No,' he said. 'That bastard killed her.'

The inn door shuddered as Gerald slammed his weight against it. The wooden plank split, sending splinters flying across the floor.

'Have we got another?' Miles said.

Jon flicked his chin at the room on the other side of the front door. 'It's lying on the ground next to the wall.'

With a grimace, Miles hobbled into the room and dragged out the wooden plank. Back at the door, he grunted with the effort of lifting the heavy piece of wood.

'One is ready,' Jon called from the bar.

Miles walked over, grabbed the table leg, and held it for Jon to set the cloth alight.

A loud rap rattled off one of the inn's windows.

'What are these windows made of, Jon? Why are they not breaking them?'

'It's just glass, which they can break easily,' Jon said. 'I told you, they are playing with us. It is all part of the hunt.'

Miles grabbed a table leg from Jon and, placing it against the first, he waited for the flame to take hold. 'What is the best way to use these?'

'Stab it in their faces or the chest,' Jon said. 'It won't kill them but it might drive them off.'

'If we had the time, we could make stakes out of these,' Miles said.

Another slam against the front door sent wood splinters from the second plank spraying across the floor.

'I have just about had enough of this monster,' Miles said, walking over to the front door.

'Are you scared yet, boy?' the vampire said from outside. 'There are more of us here now to have some fun with you and Jon.'

Miles stood in front of the door and, placing both torches in one hand, he drew his greatsword. Counting to three, he heaved up the sword and rested the blade's tip on the plank that lay across the door.

'I can smell your blood and your fear from here,' Gerald said.

'Come and get me,' Miles said. 'You killed my wolf and I am going to make you pay for it.'

Gerald slammed himself against the front door. With a snap, the plank fell in two pieces onto the floor, leaving only the lock to hold the door in place. The door shuddered then split as Gerald's fist slammed through.

Miles drove his greatsword through the split and felt the blade sink deep into Gerald. Taking a step forward, he followed the blade with both burning torches.

Gerald screamed.

The two burning torches disappeared through the split in the door. Miles yanked on his greatsword until it came free from Gerald.

The world outside the inn suddenly turned silent.

'We need another beam for this door, Jon,' Miles said.

Jon scuttled to the end of the bar, where he opened a door to the back storage room. 'I have only two left in here.'

Miles hobbled to the bar and laid a hand on the wolf. He froze as a tiny heartbeat kissed the palm of his hand.

Jon appeared from the door with a plank over his shoulder.

'She is alive,' Miles said.

'That is a miracle,' Jon said. 'Nothing should survive that wound.'

Miles took the plank from Jon and placed it onto the hooks. Cold air gusted through the hole in the door.

'Let's pile up some tables behind this door,' Miles said, hobbling over to a table and dragging it towards the front door.

Jon fetched a second table and, between the two of them, they piled it onto the first table.

A whine sounded from the counter top.

Miles walked over to the wolf. 'Easy, little one,' he said, stroking the top of her head.

'What is she?' Jon said, his eyes darting to the wolf.

'Don't worry about her,' Miles said. 'Is there anybody else living in the inn?'

Jon shook his head. 'The vampires usually take them away. The men they either kill or turn, and the women just disappear.'

Miles frowned. 'Are they taken to the City of Lynn?'

Jon shrugged. 'I don't know. They don't tell me anything.'

'Why haven't they turned you?'

Jon lowered his head. 'They ordered me to keep the inn open.'

Miles curled his lip. 'So you are assisting them?'

Jon looked up with wide eyes. 'No! I would never help them. I try to warn people when I can.'

Miles walked over to a table, turned it upside down and, using his greatsword, he chopped off the legs. He picked them up and placed them in front of Jon.

Jon walked to the end of the bar, grabbed some more cloths, returned and started wrapping them around the table legs.

'They will come in from everywhere now,' Jon said. 'They won't bother with the door.'

Miles counted five windows along the room's wall. 'We cannot defend all of those windows.'

'I suppose this is the end,' Jon said. 'Gerald will kill me after what we did to him.'

'He will kill me, Jon. You have done nothing.'

With the last torch wrapped and ready, Jon pulled out two glasses from underneath the bar and placed them on the counter. He grabbed a bottle of white liquid from the top shelf, flicked off the cork, and poured a shot into each glass. He held up his glass and said, 'I am glad I heard that monster, Gerald, scream.'

Miles picked up the glass, clinked it against Jon's drink, threw his head back, and downed the shot.

Jon chuckled at Miles's watering eyes and puffed-out cheeks. 'Never tasted anything like that before?' he said.

Miles leant both hands on the bar and shook his head. 'How is that even enjoyable?'

'It's what it does to you afterwards that is enjoyable,' Jon said.

Miles cleared his throat. 'One more then.'

After Jon had refilled the shot glasses, they held them aloft and, giving each other a nod, they threw the burning alcohol down their throats.

Miles shook his head and wiped the water from his eyes. 'That is awful.'

A window shuddered, cracked, then shattered. Splinters of glass showered across the bar's floor.

Gerald stuck his head through the broken window and said, 'Any more burning sticks you feel like shoving into me?'

'Come in here and I will show you,' Miles said, grabbing two of the table legs.

The glass crunched underneath Gerald's boots as he hopped through the window and strode towards the bar.

Miles took a step forward with the table legs raised.

'I wouldn't,' a woman said from outside the broken window. 'Your wolf will not like what I do to her.'

Miles lowered the table legs.

Gerald sat on a stool at the bar and signalled to Jon for a drink.

Jon nervously rubbed his hands together while looking over at Miles.

Miles nodded.

Jon grabbed a glass from behind the bar and filled it up with the white liquid. He reached over and placed it in front of Gerald.

Gerald grabbed the glass, threw his head back, and downed the drink. The glass slammed back onto the counter. 'Give me another,' he said, using a clawed finger to tap the bar next to the shot glass.

'I see my greatsword and burning table legs had little effect on you,' Miles said, leaning against the bar.

'We are not that different are we, boy?' Gerald said, spinning in his stool and staring at Miles with red-ringed irises. 'You seem to have some healing capabilities yourself.'

Miles's hand instinctively shot to the wound across his chest.

'Did you not notice it has healed?' Gerald said.

The thick, pink welt began to itch. Miles pulled his shirt over the wound, hiding it from Gerald.

'So what are you?' Gerald said, looking at Miles through his eyebrows. 'Tell me or I will end you, Jon, and this wolf.'

Miles grabbed a table leg off the bar and took a step towards Gerald.

'Didn't I warn you not to do that?' the woman said from outside the window.

Miles curled a lip at Gerald. 'I see you have brought backup.'

Gerald chuckled. 'The type of backup you pray you never have to meet.'

Miles glanced at the broken window. A pair of red-rimmed irises stared back. Thick incisors, longer than Gerald's, glinted in the light that shone out of the inn.

'Your greatsword has guaranteed you a slow and painful death, boy,' Gerald said. 'I don't take too kindly to being stabbed.'

The familiar singing of Miles drawing his greatsword filled the inn.

The glass around the broken window crunched as three more vampires entered the inn.

Miles lowered his greatsword. 'Coward,' he spat at Gerald. 'Fight me like a real man.'

'I have lived for many years, boy,' Gerald said, striding over to the broken window and leaning against the wall. 'I have stayed alive by picking my fights carefully.'

'Are you going to stay hidden behind that bar?' a vampire said, pulling a knife from his belt and pointing it at Jon.

Jon took a step back and bumped into the wall behind the bar. 'I have nothing to do with this. Please tell them, Gerald.'

Miles faced the three vampires. 'If we do this, you will leave Jon and his inn alone.'

Gerald chuckled. 'You have no bargaining power here, boy.'

Miles moved his feet into an attacking stance and pointed his sword at the nearest vampire.

The vampire smirked, then he whipped past Miles.

Miles dropped his greatsword and looked down at his side. A wound, long and deep, dripped blood from above his hip. The inn's floorboards creaked as Miles collapsed to his knees.

'Well, that was pathetically easy,' the vampire said, walking back around to face Miles.

Gerald walked up behind Miles and, grabbing his hair, he pulled his head back and exposed his neck to the vampires.

A vampire walked up to Miles, opened his mouth and extended his fangs.

A low-throated growl came from the end of the bar. All three vampires' heads shot up and turned to look at the wolf that stood on the counter. The hairs across her body bristled, standing on end.

Gerald hissed. 'That wolf should be dead. Take care of it,' he said, eyeing one vampire.

The vampire drew a blade, and with fear etched across his face, he took a step towards the wolf.

The wolf raised her head and let out a long howl.

A long, mournful howl answered from the forests outside the inn.

The vampires froze.

Miles smiled up at the vampire. 'I think we have just evened the odds.'

Gerald let go of Miles and walked over to the window. 'Genevie, where are you?' he said, sticking his head through the window.

Miles fell on his hands and winced at the pain shooting down his legs.

Another long howl sounded from outside the inn.

'That howl was closer,' a vampire said. 'We need to get out of here.'

'Finish that boy quickly,' Gerald said. 'The wolves will have this inn surrounded in minutes.'

The vampire grabbed Miles's hair and pulled his head back. He opened his fanged mouth and aimed for his throat.

Miles closed his eyes and waited for the bite to break the skin on his neck. A moment later, he snapped his eyes open as a sickening thud sounded through the inn. The vampire raised his hand

and touched the side of his head. Blood dripped down his clawed fingers.

'Sorry,' Jon said, backing away. 'I don't know what I was thinking. I didn't mean to hurt you.'

The vampire let go of Miles's hair and took a step towards Jon.

Miles grabbed a table leg and, with as much force as he could find, he hurled it at the vampire's head. Another sickening thud sent more blood onto the floor.

Another howl, this time much closer, sounded through the broken window.

'We need to go,' Gerald said. 'Now.'

The vampire spun round, and with a flash of claws, he raked a deep slash across Miles's throat.

A deep growl reverberated through the inn. Through the window, a snout, then a mouth full of sharp, white teeth, slowly appeared.

Gerald scrambled backwards, knocking over a table and chair.

The alpha wolf stalked into the inn and, with his head lowered, snarled at the vampires.

The three vampires, holding up their clawed hands, backed away towards the inn door.

Gerald's eyes never left the alpha wolf as he retreated and joined the other three vampires.

Miles blinked to clear the dark haze of unconsciousness that crept over him. Warm blood soaked his shirt. He opened his mouth to take in a breath, but only felt thick blood enter his lungs.

'We need to get out of here,' a vampire said.

Gerald hissed at the alpha wolf.

Another wolf crashed through the broken windows and stood next to the alpha wolf.

Gerald lifted the bar from the front door and swung it open.

Growls and snarls from the darkness echoed through the open doorway.

'I will be back for you, Jon,' Gerald said. 'Say your goodbyes to the boy. He will be dead in seconds.'

Miles jerked his head around and stared at the space where the vampires once stood. He swung his head back around and blinked at the advancing, snarling alpha wolf. He opened his mouth again to take in another breath. Panic flooded through him as the black world of unconsciousness crept over his eyes.

The wolf from the counter dropped to the bar floor and, limping badly, she placed herself between Miles and the alpha wolf.

The alpha wolf stopped and bared his teeth at the wolf.

'Get out of here.' Miles heard Jon shout from the bar. 'Go on, get out of here.'

The alpha wolf looked over at Jon, then back at Miles. The young wolf backed up, blocking Miles from the alpha wolf. She threw back her head and let out a long, mournful howl before collapsing onto her side.

The alpha wolf sniffed the air. Then he backed up and jumped out of the broken window.

Miles fell onto his side. His last breath had come before the vampire's claws had opened his throat.

Jon's faced appeared above him. 'Can you hear me, son?' he said. 'Stay with me.'

Miles felt a cloth wrap around his throat. Darkness flooded over him. A moment later, the soft touch of a mattress spread under his body. The whine of a wolf filled his ears.

'Who is this?' a deep voice said. 'And why the hell is there a wolf here?'

Miles's eyes fluttered open, then slowly closed. An image of a man tied to a chair faded into the blackness.

CHAPTER 5
COWARD

'Who is he, Jon?'

'I don't know, sir,' Jon said. 'He arrived during the night.'

'Untie me.'

'What about your cover, sir?' Jon said.

'That's entirely blown now.'

'I don't understand. Why is your cover blown?'

Thick rope thudded onto the floor. 'You, this boy and his wolf have chased Gerald away. Gerald wouldn't expect you to keep me prisoner, now, would he?'

The floorboards creaked as Jon moved around the room. 'I guess you are right.'

Miles opened an eye to get a look at the man that was once tied up. As he approached the bed, he snapped his eye shut.

'Will he wake up, Jon? His wounds looked bad when you brought him in.'

Jon hesitated, then cleared his throat. 'His wounds are all healed.'

'His wounds have healed? How?'

'I don't know, sir,' Jon said.

'Have you checked if he is one of them?' the man said.

Miles opened his eyes. 'Don't touch me,' he said, pointing a finger at the man.

The man walked over and placed his face inches from Miles. 'Who are you?'

With his elbow planted into the mattress, Miles pushed himself until he sat with his back against the wall.

'Well?' the man said, moving even closer. 'Who are you and where have you come from?'

'Get away from me,' Miles said, turning his head. 'You smell like you belong in a sewer.'

The man threw his hands up in the air, then turned to Jon. 'Can you get this boy some food please, Jon? I am going to have a little chat with our friend here.'

Jon took his cap off and placed it on his chest. 'Yes, sir,' he said, giving a curt nod.

The man waited for Jon to leave, then dragged his chair up to the bed. With a lunge, he grabbed Miles by the hair and pulled his head back. 'What are you?'

Miles grabbed the man by the wrists. 'Let me go.'

'Why are your wounds healed? The only things I have seen heal wounds that quickly are vampires.'

Miles tried to pull the man's hands away and gasped as the man tightened his grip on his hair.

'Let me see your teeth,' the man said, letting go of Miles's hair, grabbing his chin and lifting his lip.

'I said, let me go.' Miles sprayed spittle onto the man's face.

He let go and sat back in his chair. 'Your teeth are fine.'

Miles ran the back of his hand across his mouth. After checking for blood, he looked at the man and said, 'Do that again and I will kill you.'

The man leant back with his arms folded. 'You haven't

answered my question. If you are not a vampire, then what are you?'

Miles remained silent as, for the first time, he looked at the man properly. His broad, stubbly chin sat under a wide mouth. Blood-caked teeth peeked out from under the man's cracked lips. Bruises spread across both cheeks, which left thick, purple stains under the skin. A scar ran from his forehead down over his eye and finished mid-cheek. One eye, fully opened, stared a crystal-blue, while the other eye hid behind an angry purple bruise. The man, seeing Miles staring, instinctively touched his face.

'What are you staring at?' the man said. 'I don't look that bad.'

'You remind me of someone who lives in Fairacre. A man with the same facial features as yourself,' Miles said.

A flicker of pain shot across the man's face.

Miles ignored the man's discomfort. 'What happened to you?'

The man's face hardened. 'I don't think you are in a position to ask me questions, boy,' the man said. 'Who are you, what are you, and where have you come from?'

'I don't have to answer to you,' Miles said, cupping the bottom of each thigh and pulling his knees up to his chest.

The man's good eye glanced at Miles's foot.

Miles grabbed the blanket and threw it over his legs.

'Are you a cripple?'

'I am no cripple,' Miles said, lifting his chin.

'You should go home, cripple,' the man said, sitting back in his chair. 'You won't survive a week in these lands.'

'I survived last night, didn't I?' Miles said.

The man placed his hands behind his head and, pushing back, he balanced the chair on its back legs. 'And tell me, boy, how did you manage that?'

Miles opened his mouth, then shut it as a knock came from the door.

'Come,' the man said, his eyes still trained on Miles.

Jon bumped the door open with his hip and walked in with a tray full of food.

'Jon, my good man. I am absolutely starving,' the man said.

'Can you pull the table up?' Jon said, flicking his head at the back of the room.

The chair's front legs thumped onto the ground as the man stood.

'That one over there,' Jon said.

'There is only one table in the room, Jon,' the man said, walking over to the table and dragging it up alongside Miles's bed.

'Ah yes, so there is,' Jon said, placing the tray onto the table.

The man took in a breath and let it out gradually. 'I am sorry, Jon. I didn't mean to snap. Thank you for the food. It is much appreciated.'

A wide smile broke across Jon's face. 'It is my pleasure, sir. I will leave you to it.'

Miles waited for the door to close behind Jon. 'Sir?' he said, looking at the man. 'Are you some big important person?'

'What were your very words?' the man said, tilting his head to one side. 'I don't have to answer to you. Yes, I think those were the words.'

'Whatever,' Miles said, wrapping his arms around his legs.

The man picked up a plate and filled it with the cold meats and hot bread.

Miles let go of his legs and reached for a plate.

The man grabbed the table leg and pulled the table away from Miles. 'You will get food when you tell me who and what you are and why you are here.'

'Keep your food,' Miles said. 'I am not hungry.'

With a shake of his head, the man pulled the table back to

Miles's bed. 'Eat,' he said. 'I do not take pleasure in seeing a cripple go hungry.'

Ignoring the comment, Miles piled a plate with food and, after dropping his legs, he balanced the plate on his thighs. The first piece of food that touched Miles's mouth set his stomach growling.

After a couple of minutes and with his plate empty, the man sat forward and said, 'I will tell you why I am here, but then you need to meet me halfway.'

Miles thought for a second, then gave the man a single nod.

'I am here trying to find out information about those things that come during the night,' the man said.

'You mean, the vampires,' Miles said.

The man curled a lip, showing his red-stained teeth. 'Yes, the vampires. I am here from the barracks trying to find out information.'

Miles leant forward. 'The barracks? Where they train the Queen's Guard?'

'What do you know about the Queen's Guard?' the man said.

'I travelled to these lands to become one,' Miles said.

The man glanced at the blankets covering Miles's legs. He opened his mouth, then closed it quickly.

'What were you going to say?' Miles said, his eyes narrowing.

The man held up a hand and shook his head.

'You don't think I can become one?'

'Most men cannot become a guard for the Queen. No crippled men have ever been on the Queen's Guard.'

Miles leant further forward. 'I am not a cripple,' he said through thin lips. 'I am a better warrior than most I have met.'

The man held up his hand. 'It is not for me to judge.'

'You already have,' Miles said, shaking his head. 'You don't know anything about me.'

The floorboards creaked as the man sat back into his chair. He laced his fingers behind his head and sat staring at Miles.

Miles finished his food and placed his plate on the table. 'What are these vampires?' he said, pulling his knees back up to his chin.

A look of disgust stretched across the man's face. 'Creatures that need our blood to survive. Predators that hunt humans with glee like a cat playing with its food.'

'And why are you gathering information about them?' Miles said.

'They have been increasingly bold over the last few seasons,' the man said. 'The vampire royal family are hunting for something. I hear whispers about some animal with a gift of some kind.'

Miles squeezed his legs closer to his chest. 'Gerald? He is part of the vampire family?' he said, moving the conversation away from the gifted animal.

The man chuckled and pushed back the chair so it balanced on its back legs. 'No, Gerald is not a royal.'

'He said he was deciding whether to turn me. What did he mean by that?' Miles said.

The man rubbed his stubble. 'They can turn us humans into one of them.'

Miles eyed the man. 'So if we are food to them, why didn't he kill you? Or why didn't he turn you?'

The man laced his fingers behind his head and gazed out of the window.

'What have you promised them?' Miles said. 'You must be offering them something?'

'That is no concern of yours,' the man said, looking back at Miles.

Miles folded his arms. 'You expect me to tell you everything, but here you are, playing games with me.'

The chair's front legs hit the ground. 'I have told you plenty. It is you that has not told me anything.'

Miles curled a lip, then turned his head to stare out of the window.

'Do they hurt?' the man said.

Miles looked down at his legs, then up at the man. 'My legs ache most of the time. My right foot is what hurts.'

The man nodded. 'And how did you do that?' he said, pointing at the red welt that spanned Miles's side. 'That was an open wound last night.'

Miles pulled his shirt tighter around himself. 'I don't know.'

'Don't lie to me, boy,' the man said. 'Has it got something to do with that wolf? Her wounds healed up last night, too. I saw it with my own eyes. Is she perhaps this gifted animal?'

'I don't know what you are talking about,' Miles said, looking back out of the window.

The man snorted and laced his hands behind his head again. 'What's your name, boy?'

Miles looked back at the man. 'My name is Miles. What's your name?'

'People call me the Soldier,' the man said.

'What?' Miles said. 'People call you the Soldier?'

'You can call me whatever you want to call me,' the Soldier said. 'My name is not important.'

'You mean you are some big-shot person from the barracks and you don't want anybody to know your name?' Miles said.

The Soldier slammed the chair's front legs onto the ground and, slapping the top of his thigh, he roared with laughter.

The bedroom door slammed open. 'Is everything OK?' Jon said. 'I heard noises.'

'You heard everything, Jon. Next time, give it a few seconds before you charge in,' the Soldier said.

Jon sheepishly ripped off his hat. 'How was the food, sir?'

'Excellent, Jon, thank you very much,' the Soldier said. 'Your cooking has always been a treat.'

Jon gave the Soldier another wide smile.

'It is time for me to leave,' the Soldier said. 'Since this young pup here has blown my cover, there is nothing left for me to do here.'

'You can't leave, sir,' Jon said, his eyes pleading. 'They have only spared me and my inn because you are here.'

'I am sorry, Jon,' the Soldier said, standing up. 'This problem is bigger than you and this inn.'

'But, sir,' Jon said.

The Soldier held up a hand. 'Thank you, Jon, for your help. I will get my things and leave shortly.'

'Coward,' Miles said.

Stopping in the doorway, the Soldier stood with his back facing Miles. Jon stared at Miles, wide-eyed. The Soldier grunted and continued out of the room. The door closed gently behind him.

'That is us done for,' Jon said, staring at the door. 'We have no protection now.'

Miles slid sideways down the wall until his head hit the pillow. Shallow breaths came as the exhaustion hit him full force.

'What am I going to do now?' Jon said, leaving the room.

With his eyes closing, Miles cupped his hands and put them under his cheek. An image of a smiling Janie sat above him just before the darkness took hold.

'Get up, boy,' the Soldier said from the doorway. 'It will be nightfall in a couple of hours.'

Miles sat up. 'I thought you were leaving?'

'And what, leave a bartender and a cripple to fight for themselves?' the Soldier said.

'I am not a cripple,' Miles said under his breath.

'Get downstairs,' the Soldier said. 'We need to survive the night so we can travel to the barracks in the morning.'

Miles's eyebrows raised. 'You are taking us to the barracks?'

The Soldier smirked. 'Get any idea of the Queen's Guard out of your head, boy. The best thing you can hope for is work in the blacksmiths district. Now get out of bed before I get you out.'

Miles pulled the blankets off and moved to the end of the bed. His lip curled in anger at the sight of his right inwards-turning foot. He placed his left foot on the floor and pushed himself up. His right foot touched the ground and bent slightly out as he put weight on it. He grabbed his cane and, moving to the back of the room, he got dressed. Billy's cloak flapped around him, covering everything but his boots. Miles left the room and hobbled down the stairs, leading with his left foot and holding onto the banister with his right hand. He entered the bar and sat on a stool.

Behind the bar, the Soldier banged open a door and walked in carrying thick boards. 'Good of you to join us,' he said, flicking his head towards the inn's front wall. 'We need to nail these boards across those windows.'

Miles spun in his chair and looked at the windows, which were just big enough for a man to crawl through. 'Are those going to hold off Gerald?' he said, turning back to the Soldier.

The Soldier looked at Miles, then at Jon, then back to Miles before he burst out laughing. 'Of course they won't. I don't want to keep them out, I want to keep them in.'

Miles jerked his head back. 'You want to keep them in?'

The Soldier walked over to the first window and dumped the thick wooden boards onto the floor. 'My boy,' he said, turning back to Miles. 'We have more chance of seeing pretty rainbows in this black snow-covered hellhole than we have of surviving. If I am going down, I am going down after I have lopped a few vampire heads off.'

Miles looked over at Jon, who was nodding his head vigorously.

'OK then,' Miles said. 'What do you need me to do?'

'Give the man a hammer, Jon,' the Soldier said. 'Take the two far windows and hammer in as many nails into those boards as you can.'

Miles and the Soldier spent the rest of the daylight hours hammering the boards into place. Once done, the Soldier came back from the storeroom with thick, heavy planks, which they suspended across the inn door.

'What about upstairs?' Miles said. 'Can they not just come down the staircase?'

'Aye, son, they sure can, but that is where I will have fun piling them up,' the Soldier said, showing his blood-stained teeth. 'Jon, how is the food looking?'

'It will be ready in a few minutes, sir,' Jon said.

'I am going to get myself cleaned up,' the Soldier said. 'Save some food for me.'

Miles watched the Soldier climb the stairs and disappear down the corridor. He walked back to the bar, unclipped his greatsword, and propped it up against a stool before hauling himself onto the weathered padded cushion.

'Would you like a drink, sir?' Jon said.

Miles gave him a nod. 'Who is this man, Jon? Do you know where he comes from?'

Jon looked left and right and leant in. 'He is the General. The ruler of Battleacre.'

Miles frowned. 'Battleacre? The General?'

Jon's eyebrows jumped up in surprise. 'You don't know of Battleacre?'

Miles shook his head before resting his elbows on the bar counter and leaning closer. 'I have only heard of the barracks.'

'Battleacre is the major city to the east. It is the place where they train the soldiers for the City of Lynn. The barracks is part of the city.'

'And the Queen's Guard? They train the soldiers in the barracks inside the city?' Miles said.

Jon nodded. 'Yes, they are the elite soldiers from the land. The only way we know who is selected is by their sudden disappearance.'

'What about their families?' Miles said, sitting back.

Jon shrugged. 'They are not told anything, but they figure it out.'

Miles folded his arms and thought of his friends in the south. His head looked to the ceiling as a thump came from one of the rooms on the second floor. 'Why would the leader of these lands be here?' Miles said. 'Isn't that a job for someone else?'

'I think he is trying to get the royal vampires to show themselves. And what better bait than to use himself?'

A clink sounded from the staircase.

Miles swung around and gawked at the mountain of a man standing before him. A gold and silver breastplate sat snuggly to his chest. A matching helm with metal cheek plates rested on his head. The hilt of a greatsword sat above his left shoulder. On both the breastplate and helm, the image of a wolf's head sat gazing at Miles.

'Close your mouth, cripple,' the Soldier said.

Miles slammed his mouth closed and growled under his breath. 'I am not a cripple.'

The Soldier waved a dismissive hand. 'What have you been telling our young guest, Jon?'

Jon picked up a glass and rubbed it furiously with a white cloth. He held it up to the light, checking for blemishes, then continued rubbing.

The Soldier looked back at Miles. 'I suggest you find a place to protect yourself. I will be concentrating on taking as many of these monsters with me. If you get in the way, well, then that is your own problem.'

Miles pushed himself off the stool and, in one fluid movement, he drew his greatsword, which he pointed at the Soldier.

The Soldier took a step back with surprise etched on his face.

'I do not need to hide in a corner or find a place to protect myself,' Miles said. 'I am capable.'

In a flash, the Soldier drew his greatsword and slashed it at Miles's sword.

Miles parried and moved further away from the bar. He gripped the hilt with both hands and moved into an offset defensive stance. The big toe of his right foot danced in front of him as he used his left foot to balance the bulk of his weight.

The Soldier, with abnormal speed for a man so large, darted right, then left, slashing his sword at Miles.

Miles slowed his breathing and concentrated on his training. Parrying, dodging and only moving when he needed to, he kept the Soldier's attacks at bay.

'Not bad for a disabled boy,' the Soldier said, taking a step back. 'You may survive a round in the games.'

A red mist descended over Miles. He looked down at his inwards-turning foot and looked back up at the Soldier. With a growl from deep within his chest, Miles attacked. He feigned right, then darted left and attacked the Soldier with overhead swipes and slashes. Tables and chairs scattered across the inn's floor as Miles, hopping on his left foot, advanced on the Soldier.

His eyes wide, the Soldier backed up more and more until he found himself stuck in a corner.

With all senses gone, Miles drove his sword forward, aiming it at the Soldier's heart.

The Soldier sidestepped and crashed his sword hilt into Miles's nose.

Miles slumped as blood ran down over his chin and onto his shirt. His greatsword clattered to the floor as he covered his face with both hands. The tears streamed through his fingers and mixed with his blood. Wracking sobs coursed through his body as his dreams of being a Queen's Guard faded. Images of Janie flashed across his mind. His father and brother, Dr Viktor and Billy, the only two men he had ever loved, were now an entire land away.

A gentle hand touched his shoulder. 'It's OK, son.'

Miles wiped the back of his hand across his nose.

'Come on,' the Soldier said. 'Up you get. Let's get something to drink.'

Miles placed a hand on a chair and pushed himself to his feet. He took the white cloth the Soldier held out for him and wiped his nose.

The Soldier bent over and picked up Miles's greatsword. Rubbing the blade with his hand, he turned the sword and held it, hilt facing forward for Miles to take. 'You are a formidable fighter for someone who has such a disability. I am suitably impressed.'

'Not good enough to be a Queen's Guard though,' Miles said, taking the greatsword. 'It is all I have ever dreamed of.'

'Maybe one day you will find someone who is truly worthy of your protection,' the Soldier said.

'I cannot even protect myself,' Miles said. 'Besides, I have thrown all of that away.'

'Well, then join me in bringing some destruction to these monsters that have brought horror to my land,' the Soldier said.

Miles gave the Soldier a single nod. He sheathed his greatsword and walked over to the bar.

'You fight well,' Jon said, handing Miles a drink.

Miles threw back the shot of alcohol. He placed the glass back onto the bar, spun on the stool and faced the windows.

'It will be dark in a few minutes,' the Soldier said.

'Why don't the royals attack during the day?' Miles said.

'They would never risk themselves coming into here,' the Soldier said. 'They will send the turned. The royals have the power to influence the turned. They are like their little pets.'

'How many do you think they will send?' Miles said.

'I do not know, but try to stay alive until we get hold of Gerald,' the Soldier said. 'That monster needs to pay for what he has done to me.'

The last of the sun's rays disappeared. The wind picked up and buffeted the boards that lay across the windows. Miles and the Soldier sat at a table facing them. Both sat back, their fingers interlaced behind their heads and their greatswords resting across their thighs.

Behind the bar, Jon hummed quietly to himself as he methodically cleaned one glass at a time.

A board on one of the windows shuddered.

The Soldier sat forward and looked at Miles. 'And so it begins, my crippled friend. And so it begins.'

CHAPTER 6
MOANS AND GROANS

'I said, don't call me crippled,' Miles said, shaking his head.

'Are you out there Gerald?' the Soldier shouted while dodging Miles's foot. 'Or are you being a coward and sending in your little minions?'

The boards on the windows shuddered. With each hit, the nails slowly worked free.

Miles looked over at Jon and shook his head as he picked up a fresh glass and began polishing furiously, ignoring the commotion.

The Soldier unsheathed his greatsword and walked up to a shuddering, boarded window. 'Shall we wait for them to break the boards or shall we give them a surprise?'

Miles unsheathed his greatsword and shuffled over to where the Soldier stood. 'They are going to get in regardless, so let's give them a surprise.'

'That's the spirit, boy,' the Soldier said, a wide smile spreading across his face. 'We jab through the gaps in the boards and let's see what we hit.'

Miles wedged the tip of his greatsword against the board and, using his full weight, he thrust the blade through the wood. A scream shattered the new night sky. Miles heard a pop and then the sound of dust spraying against the boards.

'You got one,' the Soldier said, moving to another window. 'My turn.'

A deep-throated chuckle sounded outside the inn as another vampire became dust.

'Is that you, Gerald?' the Soldier said. 'Come here and let me play with your head.'

'I should have turned you when I had the chance,' Gerald said. 'Our elders would love a trophy like you.'

A board broke off a window and fell to the ground. The head of a vampire peered through the window, which was immediately lopped off by the Soldier's greatsword. The head tumbled to the ground, then turned into a cloud of dust.

'It looks like Gerald has brought himself a small army, my boy,' the Soldier said. 'Let's see how many of these we take out before they take us.'

Nails pinged out of the boards and shot across the bar. The rest of the boards clattered to the ground.

'Back to back,' the Soldier said, moving into the centre of the room.

Vampires jumped through all five windows with teeth bared and claws out.

Miles and the Soldier brandished their greatswords in wide arcs to keep the hissing and snarling vampires at bay.

The inn's front door shuddered.

'You don't need to use the door, Gerald,' the Soldier said. 'Come through the windows like your pets.'

'It won't be long now, General,' Gerald said. 'Genevie, my princess, will be so proud of me when I bring you to her. She has been looking for a pet for quite a while.'

The bars across the front door rattled.

'I shall tell her you were too much of a coward to come and get me yourself,' the Soldier said. 'Or does your princess prefer her men to be cowards?'

The vampires in the inn stopped hissing and one by one, they jumped through the windows, leaving the inn eerily silent.

Miles gave the Soldier a confused look. 'What are they doing?'

'I have no idea,' the Soldier said with a shrug. 'Are you OK?'

Miles's right leg buckled slightly. 'I don't think I can go on for much longer,' he said, reaching for a stool.

The Soldier caught Miles by the elbow and pulled him onto the stool. 'You have fought well.'

Miles grabbed the Soldier by the wrist and lifted a finger to his lips. 'Can you hear that?'

'Hear what?' the Soldier said, taking a step away from Miles and moving into a defensive stance.

'Jon, put that glass down and keep quiet,' Miles said.

Jon looked at Miles, opened his mouth, then slammed it shut as a woman's scream sounded through the windows.

'It's coming from outside,' Jon said, waving his glass in the direction of the noise.

The Soldier crept to the closest window and, taking a deep breath, he glanced out of it.

Another scream shattered the night's silence.

'That was a different woman,' Miles said to the Soldier. 'We need to help them.'

'I don't think we would stand a chance out there, lad,' the Soldier said.

'We will not survive in here either,' Miles said. 'So why not try to save them?'

The Soldier gave Miles a quizzical look. 'I thought you wanted nothing more than to go to the barracks tomorrow?'

Miles slid off the stool, picked up his greatsword, and pointed it at the Soldier. 'Are you telling me you are going to leave those women to these things?'

'How do you know it's not just the vampires screaming?' the Soldier said. 'Sounds like a nice little trap to me.'

'That scream doesn't sound fake,' Miles said. 'I will not stand idly by.'

'Why the sudden nobility? Making amends for another girl, perhaps?'

'Yes,' Miles said, matter-of-factly. 'I cannot be a guard for the Queen and I have hurt the only girl that has ever liked me, so I am going to make amends.'

'Well, son, that is extremely stupid, and it is exactly something I would do,' the Soldier said with a grin. 'So let's go and have some fun shall we?'

Miles sheathed his greatsword and, grabbing his cane from the bar, he made his way to the front door.

'Slow down,' the Soldier said, laying a hand on Miles's shoulder. 'Let's at least try to find out what we are walking into.'

'What do you suggest?' Miles said.

'Fire,' Jon said, his polished glass glinting in the flickering flames of the fireplace.

Miles and the Soldier jerked their heads and stared at Jon.

'What?' Jon said, spreading his hands. 'It's dark and the vampires burn. Fire solves both problems.'

The Soldier shook his head and, with a chuckle, he walked up to a table and struck it in the middle with his greatsword.

'Oh, come on,' Jon said. 'Do you have to keep breaking my inn?'

The Soldier sheathed his greatsword, picked up two chair legs and approached the bar. Jon wrapped two cloths around the wooden stakes, then soaked the cloth with alcohol. The Soldier walked back to Miles, gave him a torch, and unsheathed his greatsword.

'Doubt these little things are going to do anything,' Miles said, waving the feeble torch around in a circle, then slipping it into his belt.

'Might come in handy later,' the Soldier said, sending the two boards to the ground with a clatter. The inn door slammed open, and a blast of cold air hit Miles in the face. Black specks of snow whipped in through the door and fluttered to the floor. Miles shuffled out of the inn and into the gusting wind. He looked west as the screams of another woman pricked his ears.

'Can you see anything?' the Soldier said.

'No,' Miles said. 'The screams are coming from the west.'

'Strategically placed upwind so we can hear them,' the Soldier said. 'Let's walk straight into this trap, shall we?'

Miles pulled Billy's cloak closer around him as he trudged up the small path onto the road. His cane crunched into the black snow and hit the cobblestones beneath.

'So much for you being the all-conquering smart General,' Gerald said.

Miles and the Soldier stopped and, with squinting eyes, scanned the treeline until they spotted Gerald.

The vampire stood leaning against a tree while picking his fingernails. 'A few screaming dames and you come running. Such chivalry.'

The Soldier, moving towards Gerald, reached his hand over his shoulder and gripped the hilt of his greatsword.

Miles placed a hand on the Soldier's shoulder.

'Your protégé is more aware than you are, General,' Gerald said. 'I would suggest you look around you.'

Countless red eyes shone through the forest trees. The Soldier withdrew his hand from the hilt of his greatsword.

'What do you want from me, Gerald?' the Soldier said, stepping back towards Miles.

'With all due respect, General. I am not here for you,' Gerald said, moving his gaze to Miles. 'This cripple has something Genevie wants.'

The Soldier spread his hands. 'Then why doesn't she come out and ask him for it?'

Gerald placed his hand on his mouth and snickered. 'That's why I am here, General. Genevie doesn't have time for games.'

The cries of another woman came from the west. Miles flicked his cloak aside and drew his greatsword. A moment later, the Soldier's greatsword left its sheath.

'What are you not telling me, boy?' the Soldier whispered. 'What is it you have that a royal vampire wants?'

'The wolf,' Miles said. 'She is here for the wolf.'

'Yes, she is here for the wolf,' Gerald said. 'And how did you know that?'

'A previous tale,' Miles said, thinking of Juno, Chax and the Lady.

'Where is this Genevie?' the Soldier said. 'Is she as much of a coward as you? Why is she hiding in the shadows and letting her pathetic minion do her dirty work?'

Gerald sighed. 'A warrior's jibe. Calling me a coward has no effect on me. Surely you should know this by now?'

The Soldier spat into the black snow. 'Your murderous, disgusting kind has no honour.'

Gerald yawned, then waved a hand at Miles and the Soldier. Flashes of cloth blazed out of the forest. With shining red eyes and long, white extended incisors, the vampires descended onto the two men. Cracks filled the night as heads flew into the air and bodies exploded into clouds of smoke.

'There are too many of them,' Miles said, gasping quickly. 'They are everywhere.'

The Soldier swung his greatsword in a great arc. 'I don't wish to be one of them, my boy.'

Miles hesitated a second, then with a flick of his sword, he took another head.

'Do it now, boy,' the Soldier shouted. 'Take my head.'

'I cannot,' Miles said, hearing the crack of bone as his elbow found the nose of a vampire.

'You must,' the Soldier said. 'There is too much at stake.'

Suddenly, the wind escaped Miles's lungs as vampires from all sides tackled him to the ground. The Soldier, with a loud curse, hit the ground next to him.

'It is not your time, General,' Gerald said, walking out of the trees.

The Soldier hissed through his teeth.

'Now who is the coward?' Gerald said, moving his face close to the Soldier's. 'Asking this young boy to end your life.'

The Soldier snapped his teeth at Gerald.

'Stand them up,' Gerald said. 'Bind them and let's take them to Genevie.'

Miles felt the rope's coarseness as they bound his wrists. His fingers ached as less blood flowed into his hands.

The Soldier, still kicking and spitting, exhaled a long breath as Gerald punched him in the gut. 'Behave or I will take limbs off the boy.'

'Gerald,' a vampire said.

'Not now,' Gerald said, waving a dismissive hand.

'Gerald, sir,' the vampire said, his voice rising.

'What?' Gerald said, spinning and looking at the vampire with annoyance.

The vampire pointed towards the inn just as a twirling bottle, filled with alcohol, slammed into his face. The burning cloth poking out of the bottle's neck ignited the liquid and set the vampire ablaze. With a scream, the vampire dropped into the black snow and thrashed about.

Gerald chuckled at the burning vampire who, writhing on the ground, sent hissing steam into the air. Eventually the flames disappeared and the vampire, coughing a cloud of smoke, stood and patted himself down. The burnt skin flaked off and new skin grew back, healing all the burn wounds.

'Lucky vampire,' Gerald said, facing the Soldier. 'It seems your yellow-bellied innkeeper has a spine after all.' He turned to a vampire and said, 'Bring him to me.'

Vampires dodged the thrown flaming bottles and, tackling Jon to the ground, they bound him, picked him up and brought him over to Gerald.

Gerald moved his face close to Jon's and sniffed. 'You are of no value to me. I think I will have you for my dinner.'

'Leave him alone,' the Soldier said. 'He has done nothing but serve you, Gerald.'

Gerald placed a long fingernail under Jon's chin and, his fangs extending, said, 'And he will serve me one more time.'

'Gerald,' Miles said.

Gerald looked over at Miles with a raised eyebrow. 'What do you want, cripple?'

'Do you hear that?' Miles said.

'Hear what?' Gerald said, his head tilting to one side.

Miles spat a wad of blood out onto the black snow. A ghost of a smile spread across his face. The knitting of his nerves, which once made him grimace with pain, now brought a welcome sensation of freedom across his body.

A long, beautiful howl broke through the gusting wind.

A vampire took a step back and bumped into Miles. 'Waya,' he said, before flashing off into the trees.

The vampires let go of Miles and the Soldier and began creeping towards the trees.

'Hold your ground,' Gerald said. 'Or I will see that all of you will meet the sun today.'

With fear etched over their faces, the vampires stood frozen while they anxiously searched the surrounding trees.

Along the east–west road, a pair of yellow eyes appeared out of the darkness. A long stream of steam followed a rumbling growl that broke the eerie night's silence. The alpha wolf stalked out of the mist and, lowering his head, he sniffed the black snow. A moment later, he lifted his head and looked behind him. Dark, narrow amber eyes appeared glowing through the mist. The enormous head of a brown-haired wolf followed the amber eyes. The enormous wolf stopped next to the alpha wolf and, lowering her head, she let loose a deep thumping growl at the vampires.

'Impossible,' Gerald said, taking a step back. 'I have never seen a wolf so big.'

'She seems very annoyed with you, Gerald,' the Soldier said.

'If you untie us and give us the women, I will call her off,' Miles said.

Gerald snorted. 'And how would you control her?'

The massive brown wolf took a step forward, her eyes never leaving Gerald.

'I don't control her,' Miles said. 'But I can always ask.'

A woman's voice, so clear and beautiful, sang out from the darkness. 'Take the wolf.'

'Genevie,' Gerald said, his eyes widening.

A look of serenity flooded the faces of the surrounding

vampires. Their cowering crouches disappeared as, one by one, they stood tall and determined. As one, they swivelled to face the wolves. A flutter of snow from the soles of boots sprang into the air. The night's silence shattered with the snarls and snapping of both vampires and wolves alike. Miles marvelled at the alpha wolf's speed as he sprang at the nearest vampire and, with one bite, transformed the vampire into a cloud of dust.

The enormous wolf that once stood next to the alpha wolf ignored the fighting and trotted over to Miles, where she, with one bite, cut the ropes that bound him.

Miles placed his hand on the side of the wolf's head. 'So it is true. You are like Chax.'

The wolf shook her head and snorted.

'Waya,' Miles said. 'A fitting name. Remind me to thank the vampire personally for that idea.'

'Um, son,' the Soldier said. 'We need some help here.'

Miles picked up his greatsword and cut the ropes binding the Soldier's and Jon's hands.

The Soldier wrung his hands to get the blood flowing. With a glance at Miles's feet, he said, 'Your foot, it's healed.'

'It's the wolf,' Jon said.

'An explanation for another time,' Miles said. 'Now I think Waya's pack needs some help.'

A wide smile spread across the Soldier's face. 'I can certainly help you with that.'

'Get back to the inn, Jon,' Miles said. 'You have done what you can.'

Jon nodded and dodged a growling, snarling wolf before scuttling off to the inn.

Miles, his sword swinging through the air, sprang into the fray of wolves and vampires. Waya, her jaws snapping, protected his back.

'The Queen's Guard would accept you now,' the Soldier said.

With a stab of pain running through his heart, Miles channelled his anger and fought harder still.

'Where are you, Gerald?' the Soldier said. 'Have you run off again?'

A yelp spun Miles around. Waya held a paw close to her chest. Her blood dripped into the snow, sending out a cloud of steam. Four vampires, their nails drawn, slashed at her body.

Miles stumbled as a rush of blood roared through his ears. The ground beneath him shuddered. He gripped the side of his head and, with a scream, he dropped to his knees.

'What is it, boy?' the Soldier said, appearing by his side.

Miles pushed the Soldier away and, holding onto consciousness, he directed the pain in his head at the four vampires. The earth below them shuddered. The black snow shimmered. Suddenly, pebbles ripped up through the black snow and through the vampires. The four vampires collapsed to the ground. Waya pounced and, with her massive jaws, she turned the vampires into dust.

'Disengage,' the woman's voice said.

The vampires, in an instant, disappeared into the forest.

Miles blinked to clear the fog in his head.

'What was that?' the Soldier said.

Waya trotted over to Miles and butted her head against his.

'I said, what was that?' the Soldier said, taking a step back from Miles and Waya.

Miles struggled to his feet. 'I will explain later.'

'Your foot healed. Stones are exploding out of the ground. And you have a monster wolf as a pet,' the Soldier said. 'I need you to tell me what is going on, son.'

The screams of women shattered the quiet darkness.

Miles began walking east up the road. 'I said I will explain later.'

The Soldier reluctantly replaced his greatsword and followed Miles up the road.

Waya sniffed the air then bounded down the road. Miles sheathed his sword and, with his body healed, he sprang after her.

The Soldier appeared alongside him. 'Truly incredible,' he said. 'I assume your whole body is in good working order?'

Miles nodded. 'When Waya is close, my body heals.'

The Soldier remained quiet as they moved along the path.

Miles glanced at the Soldier. 'While my body is able, I will hunt until we find these women.'

Waya skidded to a halt and, after sniffing the air, she turned north into the dark forest.

Miles pulled the torch from his belt and held it for the Soldier to set alight. With the torch held high, Miles followed Waya through the dead trees looming out of the darkness. The swirling mist created moving shadows along the ground. Waya's paws crunched in the snow as she moved past the blackened trees. After a minute, she came to a halt and whined.

Miles touched Waya's shoulder. 'What is it?'

A moan sounded from up ahead.

'Undead,' the Soldier said. 'We shouldn't be here, boy. One bite from these can turn you into a shuffling corpse.'

'Waya is leading us to the women,' Miles said.

The Soldier spat onto the ground. 'These undead are worse than vampires. At least vampires kill you quickly.'

Waya trotted past a few more trees and then slowed as a larger tree appeared out of the mist. Around the tree trunk, women sat tied together. Their heads lolled forward onto their chests. Another moan came from the darkness.

Miles sheathed his greatsword and walked up to the closest woman.

'Be careful, son,' the Soldier said. 'She could be undead or a vampire.'

Miles grabbed the woman's shoulder and shook her. With a start, she opened her eyes, looked wildly about her, and began struggling against her bonds.

'What do I look for?' Miles said over his shoulder.

'Lift her lips. You will see holes where the incisors extend from,' the Soldier said.

Miles lifted the woman's lips and checked her gums.

The woman shook her head, and finding her voice, she said, 'Please help. They are everywhere.'

'Who is everywhere?' Miles said.

'Disgusting creatures with limbs and faces missing,' the woman said.

The Soldier circled the tree. 'Where are you from?'

'Horse farms,' the woman said.

'In the south?' the Soldier said.

The woman nodded.

'Let's get them untied and back to the inn,' the Soldier said.

Miles and the Soldier walked around the large trees and cut the women's bonds.

'Help her up, and stay together as a group,' Miles said, pointing the woman to a young girl who had collapsed in the snow.

A moan, much closer, came from the darkness.

'Hurry, boy,' the Soldier said. 'Get those last four over there.'

Miles walked over to the tree, then froze. Waya trotted up to him and bared her teeth. 'Steady girl,' Miles said, laying a hand on the top of her head.

'What is it?' the Soldier said.

Miles raised a hand to silence the Soldier.

'Please help us,' a woman said.

'Who are you?' Miles said, looking past the woman.

A young boy with black, misty eyes and shocking white hair stood staring back at Miles.

Miles sank to one knee. 'Where are your parents?'

The boy stared back, unblinking.

Waya growled, which made the boy flinch.

'Steady,' Miles said, rubbing Waya's shoulder. 'He is just a young boy.'

'Please untie us,' the woman said.

Miles stood and tentatively walked over to the tree. The bonds that tied the four women to the tree fell to the ground. Three of the women shuffled off towards the Soldier. The last woman turned and looked at the young boy.

'Do you know who he is?' Miles said.

The woman looked back at Miles and shook her head.

'Go back to the group,' Miles said. 'I will see if I can speak to him.'

The woman turned and walked off to the group.

Miles waited until the woman was back with the Soldier before he took a step towards the boy.

The young boy lowered his eyebrows and curled his lip.

Waya sniffed the air, then nudged Miles before she took a step backwards.

The striking blue eyes of the young boy shimmered and glowed. The boy's mouth began moving, but no sound came out. All around Miles, moans and groans sounded from the darkness.

'We need to go,' the Soldier said.

'I am not leaving a kid in this dark forest,' Miles said.

'He is the one controlling the undead,' the Soldier said.

'What do you mean?' Miles said, his breath catching in the

back of his throat.

The young boy, his mouth still moving, pointed at Miles and Waya. Out of the darkness, a wall of bodies shuffled towards them. Waya, walking backwards, snapped her jaws at the grotesque undead.

'Now, boy,' the Soldier shouted. 'Before they surround us.'

Miles turned and ran over to where the Soldier stood.

'I have sent the women to the road,' the Soldier said. 'Let's move.'

Miles dodged the trees' low-hanging branches as he ran to the road. He slid down the bank and came to a halt on the roadside. Waya followed him and turned to sniff the direction they had come from. The women chattered nervously among themselves.

'Keep it down,' the Soldier said. 'The wolf is with the boy. There is nothing to worry about.'

Miles knelt and placed his hands on either side of Waya's head. 'Best you get back to your pack,' he said. 'But don't go too far.'

Waya whined, then backed away from Miles.

Miles strode over to the Soldier and placed a hand on his shoulder. Pins and needles shot across the small of his back. His foot turned inwards, with shots of pain pulsing through the backs of his thighs.

The Soldier gripped Miles by the elbow. 'Hold on, son.'

Spittle ran down Miles's chin as he sucked in sharp breaths through his teeth. He fought the desire to pass out by slowing his breathing and familiarising himself with the throbbing pain.

'OK, lad?' the Soldier said.

'Let's move,' Miles said, hoarsely.

'Take the lead,' the Soldier said. 'We will move at your pace.'

Miles pulled out his cane and jammed the end through the snow until it hit the cobblestones. With a grimace, he took the first painful step back to the inn.

CHAPTER 7

He Has a Right!

'We need to move quicker,' a woman said. 'They are catching us.'

The Soldier offered Miles an arm. 'Hold on to me,' he said.

Miles swatted the Soldier's arm away, and gripping the cane harder, he pushed the end deep into the black snow as he tried to pick up the pace.

A grunt came from behind the trees.

'They are on both sides of us,' a woman said.

Trees shuddered, dropping snow onto the ground, creating a cloud of black mist.

'Faster,' another woman at the back said.

'Miles, take my arm,' the Soldier said. 'You are putting us in danger.'

Miles ignored the Soldier and shuffled quicker.

'Enough of this,' a woman said, walking up behind Miles. 'You are coming with us.'

Before Miles could say anything, he felt his feet leave the ground. Hands on his arms and legs forced him into a horizontal position. 'Let me go,' he said, struggling against the horsewomen's many firm hands.

The Soldier chuckled.

'Put me down,' Miles shouted.

The undead broke the treeline. Their shuffling gait turned into a limping jog as they descended on the group.

Miles felt his greatsword leave its protective sheath.

'Give me back my sword,' Miles said, still struggling. 'Put me down and let me fight.' The firm hands that held him high in the air tightened their grip. Miles stopped struggling as the shouts of the fighting women rang out into the night.

'Go,' the Soldier said. 'We will hold them back.'

The women holding Miles broke into a well-coordinated jog. Sweat formed across their brows and their breathing laboured with the effort.

'What is happening?' Miles said, turning his head to get a look.

'Lights ahead,' one of the women said. 'Is that where we go?'

Miles looked forward. 'That's the inn. We will be safe in there.' A minute later, they slid down the path to the inn's front door. The women lowered Miles to his feet and ushered him in. 'I need to help them,' Miles said, looking out into the blackness.

'There is nothing you can do that isn't already being done,' Jon said, appearing next to him and placing a hand on his shoulder. 'These are horsewomen, son.'

Miles peered out into the darkness, then jumped as the Soldier and the horsewomen came charging down the path.

'Get inside,' the Soldier said, waving a hand. 'We need to board the inn up.'

Miles hobbled back through the front door, around the wall and to the first window. He picked up a board and slammed it against the gap.

'I will get nails and hammers,' Jon said, scuttling to the door at the back of the bar. The horsewomen picked up the other boards and held them in place over the windows.

After the last of the horsewomen ran through the door, the Soldier slammed it shut. 'They are everywhere,' he said, throwing his shoulder against the door. 'Hurry with those hammers and nails, Jon.'

'I have them,' Jon said, running out of the storeroom holding boxes of nails and hammers.

The horsewomen began hammering the nails into the boards.

'Jon, help me with these beams,' the Soldier said, flicking his head towards the planks on the floor.

Jon picked up a plank and, turning red in the face with the effort, he slid it through the hooks on either side of the door.

Miles took a step back and examined the nailed-up board.

'Your sword,' the horsewoman said from behind him.

Miles inclined his head and took the sword by the offered hilt. 'What is your name?'

'Heather,' the woman said, extending a hand. 'Pleased to meet you.'

Miles, shaking Heather's hand, felt a pang of regret streak through him as an image of Chloe appeared in his head. The tall, fierce-eyed woman reminded him of the passionate leader of Fairacre.

A ghost of a smile crept across Heather's face. 'You are thinking of someone,' she said, pulling her hand away.

Miles cleared his throat. 'Yes, a leader in the south. You remind me of her.'

Heather picked up a hammer and knocked a nail into the board that Miles held. 'She must mean a lot to you.'

'She, funnily enough, carried me once too,' Miles said. 'Or, more accurately, her friends did.'

'Good to see you got here safe, son,' the Soldier said.

Miles closed his eyes and sighed. 'I was just explaining to Heather that being carried by women is becoming a habit.'

'And I am not used to dying,' Heather said, hammering in another nail. 'And we would have all died if we had waited for you.'

Miles moved his hand away from the board to let Heather hammer in the last nail. As it went in, the board shuddered as an undead slammed his face into it. The moan that followed made Miles's skin crawl. 'I am grateful for your help,' Miles said.

Heather gave Miles a nod, then pulled a face at the boarded-up window. 'Foul creatures.'

The doors and windows creaked, shuddered and moaned as the bodies of the charging undead slammed into them. Then, as quickly as it had begun, it stopped, leaving an eerie silence behind.

The Soldier walked over to the front door and pressed his ear against it. 'They are moving away,' he said.

'Can you get our guests some food, please, Jon?' Miles said.

Jon threw a cloth over his shoulder and disappeared into the storeroom.

Miles righted a few chairs and tables then, sitting, he frowned at Heather, who stood staring at the Soldier.

'I didn't know it was you, sir,' Heather said, giving a small curtsey.

The Soldier walked around the room, picking up the remaining chairs, and asked the ladies to sit. Once they had all sat around a few tables, he picked up a chair and sat next to Miles.

With a wave of his hand, he said, 'Meet the horsewomen from the south, lad. They breed and supply the City of Lynn and Battleacre with all the horses. A strong fierce lot who will give most men a good thrashing if they get out of line.'

Miles inclined his head. 'Again, thank you for saving me out there.'

'I think it was the two of you that saved us,' Heather said. 'I didn't think we would make it through the night being tied up on those trees.'

'What happened?' the Soldier said, leaning back and interlacing his fingers behind his head.

'Sorry, sir, but before I continue, why are you out here?' Heather said, raising an eyebrow.

Miles snorted. 'Seems like the big, bad soldier has quite a following.'

The Soldier rolled his eyes at Miles then, looking back at Heather, he said, 'Our women in Battleacre have been going missing. I have been tracking down those responsible.'

'It's them vampires,' a woman from another table said. 'Bloodsucking vampires. Them's the ones that took us.'

'Aye, that they are,' the Soldier said. 'So what happened down south on the horse farms?'

'Excuse me,' Jon said, sliding trays of food onto the table.

'Thank you, Jon,' the Soldier said. 'That looks wonderful as usual.'

'Unfortunately, this is the last of our fresh food, sir,' Jon said, grabbing his hat off his head and clutching it to his chest. 'I am sorry. All I have is a bit of dried food. I cannot cater to anyone anymore.'

The Soldier stood and placed a hand on Jon's shoulder. 'You have done well, Jon. You have nothing to worry about. We will get things worked out.'

Jon scratched the stubble on his chin, then walked back to the bar.

The Soldier sat. 'You were about to say,' he said, looking at Heather.

'Vampires flooded the horse farms and captured all the women,' Heather said, glancing back at the women, who sat quietly eating. 'They threatened to destroy our children, husbands and horses if we did not go with them.'

Miles slammed his hand down on the table. 'This happened in the south. At Fairacre. We should have found out why this was happening.'

'Steady, son,' the Soldier said.

Miles sat back and folded his arms. 'I am tiring of this,' he muttered.

'Was there a woman with these vampires?' the Soldier said. 'A woman named Genevie?'

Heather shook her head. 'The only vampire who told us his name was Gerald.'

A glass slammed on the bar, making everyone jump, then spin around. 'I dislike that man more and more,' Jon said. 'He was unkind to you, sir.'

The Soldier burst out laughing. 'Jon, my good man. Glad you have reached the decision that Gerald is not the model citizen.'

Jon, grumbling, picked up another glass and polished furiously.

'Did they harm any of you or any of your family members?' Miles said.

Heather lowered her head. 'We do not know. We left with Gerald and his band of vampires. Some of his vampires stayed behind though.'

'Go back in the morning, we will,' a woman said.

'Its two days' trek at least to get back,' the Soldier said. 'Which means you will be out there for a night.'

Heather glared at the Soldier. 'If I may be so bold. None of this would have happened if you had supplied protection like you promised.'

The Soldier looked back at Heather with a confused expression. 'They did not present a request to me asking for Battleacre to protect you?'

Heather stood abruptly. 'You are lying, sir. We had multiple people say you would send protection.'

The Soldier stood and held up his hands. 'Please, Heather. I can guarantee you – they did not consult me.'

Heather calmly sat, but the fierceness in her eyes remained.

'Battleacre promised me protection too,' Jon said from the bar.

Anger creased the Soldier's face. 'And you tell me of this now, Jon.'

Jon shrugged. 'When you got here, sir, the vampires had already taken over and you were a captive. It was not something I thought you would want to discuss.'

The Soldier closed his eyes, tilted his head back and aimed a long growl at the ceiling. A deep breath later, he looked back at Heather and Jon and said, 'I can promise you both they sent no such request to me. I would have sent guards immediately.'

'Undead, vampires and wolves have terrorised us through autumn and into the winter,' Heather said, clasping her hands in her lap. 'Usually, the three of them war between themselves, but they have turned their focus on us. Wolves, undead and the vampires.'

Miles rubbed his chin. 'I can understand the vampires showing interest. But why the undead and the wolves?'

'Why would the vampires show interest in us?' a woman said.

Miles looked at the Soldier who gave him a nod. Looking back at the woman, he said, 'The City of Lynn is stealing women. We found a book with thousands of women's names ordered by each region. We do not know why this is happening. All we know is they have marked thousands to be taken to the City.'

'Horse hay fever,' a woman cursed. 'Why were we not warned of this?'

'I sent warnings,' the Soldier said. 'But it seems my people did not reach you.'

'I am not surprised with vampires, undead and wolves running about,' Miles said.

'Why the undead and the wolves?' Heather said, nodding at Miles. 'I never even knew the undead existed.'

'I think the wolves want the horses,' Miles said. 'Food is scarce with the spread of the black snow.'

Heather's eyes narrowed. 'It's been falling for several years. If it is our horses they want, why now?'

'We are used to the wolves coming to the south in the winter,' Miles said. 'But the black snow has chased their food to the west.'

'The wolves didn't get any of our horses though, did they, ladies?' a woman said.

The women in the room straightened their backs and held their heads high.

'The undead is a mystery,' the Soldier said. 'I have only heard of them through mythical tales told by court jesters. Yet here I sit, having seen them with my own eyes.'

The group sat in thought while chewing on the food Jon had provided.

The Soldier sat up. 'Who told you I would provide you with protection?'

'The Hammer, sir,' Heather said. 'We asked your son.'

The Soldier rubbed his eyes with the heels of his hands.

'What is it?' Miles said, reaching over and placing a hand on the Soldier's forearm.

The Soldier stood and walked over to the fireplace where, leaning on the mantel, he dropped his head into his hands.

'Did I say something wrong?' Heather said, worry creasing her face.

Miles shook his head, stood, and made his way to stand by the Soldier. 'I take it that wasn't the news you wanted to hear?'

The Soldier looked at Miles with wet eyes. 'My son went missing weeks ago. I had hoped he had made his way to the City of Lynn. But it seems he came south with false promises.'

'Well, at least you know he is alive,' Miles said.

The Soldier cleared his throat. 'He is not alive, lad. They have turned him. Why else would he be feeding everyone false information?'

'You cannot be sure of that,' Miles said. 'Let us not jump to conclusions.'

The Soldier lowered his head back into his hands. After a few moments, he took in a deep breath, stood tall, squared his shoulders and looked down at Miles. 'There is a place for you on the Queen's Guard,' he said.

Miles took a step back, stumbled, then threw out a hand to grab the mantelpiece.

'Careful, son,' the Soldier said.

Miles composed himself. 'What do you mean, there is a place for me? Just moments ago, women carried me back to the inn. How am I suddenly capable?'

'I select, train, structure and oversee the Queen's Guard,' the Soldier said. 'It is an honour that has run through my family for generations. I am the General of Battleacre, and therefore, the General of the Queen's Guard.'

'But you said they would never select me,' Miles said. 'Why the change of mind?'

'I would not select you as a warrior, but as a strategist and a leader.'

Chloe's voice echoed through Miles's head. She, too, wanted him to lead and strategise. 'I always wanted to be the one protecting with my greatsword,' Miles said, his hand reaching for the hilt of his sword.

The Soldier huffed. 'Any clown can wield a sword, lad. Not every person can lead a group into battle.'

'Who would follow a cripple?' Miles said, lifting his hand from the sword's hilt to rub his right thigh.

'Nobody will follow you if you act like a victim,' the Soldier said. 'I think it is time to take some responsibility for your life.'

Miles glared at the Soldier.

'Well?' the Soldier said, raising his hands. 'Are you ready?'

'It would be an honour,' Miles said, inclining his head.

'We need to get back to Battleacre,' the Soldier said. 'But first, let's get these fierce horsewomen back to their farms.'

Miles surveyed the women who sat at the table talking among themselves. Turning back to the Soldier, he said, 'The Queen's Guard or not, I will not abandon these people.'

'And that, lad, is the voice of a man taking responsibility,' the Soldier said, before leaning in and continuing. 'But remember to offer your help, rather than impose it. I feel our wondrous horsewomen will take unkindly to being told they need our help.'

Miles looked back at the women and smiled. 'You would love Juno, Chloe, Alexa and the sewer rats,' he said, looking back at the Soldier.

'Sewer rats?' the Soldier said, scrunching up his nose.

Miles snorted, then placed his hand over his mouth as laughter shook his body.

Miles left the fireplace and sat back down. He turned to Heather and said, 'We are going to escort you to the horse farms. We will leave at first light.'

A grin broke across Heather's face. 'Thank you,' she said before lowering her voice. 'Is the General OK?'

'His son is worrying him,' Miles said. 'He thinks the vampires have him.'

Heather pulled her lips into a tight line. 'His son filled us with hope. And we did not put plans in place to protect ourselves. We thought the soldiers from Battleacre were coming.'

'I am sorry,' the Soldier said, sitting down next to Heather. 'Please know I would never abandon you.'

Heather's eyes softened. 'You will make this right by getting us home?'

'You have my word,' the Soldier said. 'As the lad has said, we leave at first light.'

Jon cleared his throat. 'What of my inn, sir?'

The Soldier stood and walked over to the bar. 'I would like you to come back to Battleacre with me, Jon. I have several inns that need managing.'

For the first time all night, Jon stopped his constant polishing. With care, he placed the glass down on the bar, then looked slowly around his inn.

'I can always get you back to your inn when this is over,' the Soldier said. 'I know this inn means a lot to you.'

Jon gave the Soldier a confused look. 'You can burn this place to the ground for all I care. It's a piece of rubbish.'

The Soldier dropped onto a stool and spread his hands. 'I thought you loved this place. It is part of your family, is it not?'

'My family left for the City of Lynn,' Jon said. 'That's how much they loved this place. Have the inn as a present, they said. Look after it for everyone, they said. Well, I am done with that, sir.'

'It's decided then,' the Soldier said. 'Jon will travel with us.'

Heather sat up and tilted her head to one side.

'What is it?' Miles said.

'I hear the whine of horses,' Heather said, standing up and facing Jon. 'Do you have horses in the back?'

Jon jabbed a thumb at the storeroom. 'A mare and her foal. The foal has a deformity, though. I cannot bring myself to end its life.'

A high-pitched scream brought all the horsewomen to their feet.

'They are distressed,' Heather said. 'The undead must have found them.'

'We wait for sunrise,' the Soldier said. 'It is dangerous out there and they are just two horses.'

Heather rounded on the Soldier and jabbed a finger into his chest. 'Horses that make soldiers out of your mediocre men,' she said.

The Soldier's eyes widened as he realised who he was talking to. With his hands raised, he said, 'I do not wish offence. I am just saying it is dangerous to go out there for a pair of horses.'

Heather stalked over to the bar. 'Take me to them,' she said, pointing a finger at Jon.

Jon shook his head. 'I am not going out there with those things.'

'Coward,' Heather said through her teeth.

Jon spun on his heel. 'I am no coward. I will take you to them.'

'You will?' the Soldier said, his eyebrows raised.

'Yes, I shall,' Jon said, walking to the storeroom door.

The Soldier looked up at the ceiling and sighed before slamming the front chair legs back down on the ground. 'Wait,' he said, walking over to the bar. 'Where are they, Jon?'

'Across the courtyard, through the double doors of the stable, turn right, and they are in the last loose box.'

'We need to clear a path, so wait at the back door until I say we can go,' the Soldier said to Heather.

Heather folded her arms. 'Whatever you say, sir.'

The Soldier, shaking his head, walked through the storeroom and stopped. He looked back and placed his finger on his lips. Moans and groans sounded from the other side of the door. The mare's screams grew louder.

Heather barged past Jon and walked up to the door, which she ripped open before the Soldier could stop her. An undead woman with one eye and no lips spun around and stared back at Heather.

With a yell, the Soldier jumped through the door, took the undead's head and disappeared.

Heather stepped out of the door into the darkness.

Miles hobbled over to the back door and stepped out into the cold, dark night. Ahead of him, the Soldier took the head of another moaning undead. Heather, standing behind the Soldier, kicked any undead that approached his back. Miles moved across the courtyard and entered the stables. Heather came next, then the Soldier, who rolled the stable door shut.

The thump of the undead walking into the closed door made the Soldier spit at the ground in disgust.

'They are at the end,' Miles said, squinting to see through the darkness. 'I can hear them.'

'There is someone over there,' Heather said, her voice a whisper.

Miles took a step forward, then froze as, at the rear of the stable, the little boy from the barren forest turned, showing his glowing eyes.

'Who are you?' Miles said, walking forward.

The boy looked down at Miles's club foot.

Miles stopped walking and instinctively grabbed his right thigh.

The boy turned and walked out of a side door.

Heather strode forward, past the open door and along the corridor, until she reached the last loose box. The Soldier, close behind, closed the door the little boy had disappeared through.

The moans and groans of the undead faded into the night.

Miles peered into the loose box. A mare stood shivering in the far corner. Behind her, the foal stood with his side pressed against the wall of the box.

Heather opened up the loose box and clicked her tongue. 'It's OK there,' she said, taking a step in. The mare's ears, once flat, pricked up at the soothing sound of Heather's voice. With a shake of her head, she took a careful step towards Heather's outstretched hand.

'The horsewomen have a gift,' the Soldier said. 'See how quickly the mare responds?'

Miles watched in fascination as the mare took another step forward. The foal, now released from being trapped between his mother and the box wall, stumbled out on unsteady legs.

'Poor thing,' the Soldier said. 'He won't live for long.'

Miles frowned at the deformed shoulder bones protruding from the small horse's back.

'How has this happened?' the Soldier said. 'His front legs are too long. Is he in pain?'

Heather used her other hand to feel the back of the foal. 'We should put him down.'

The small foal turned his head and stared with enormous eyes at Miles. Both eyes, the colour brown, had a small blue ring surrounding the iris.

'Will he not survive?' Miles said.

'He will survive,' Heather said. 'But he will be of no use and a costly burden.'

'Is that what I am?' Miles said.

Heather turned her eyes on Miles. 'What do you mean?'

'Am I a costly burden? Did carrying me from the undead cost you dearly?' Miles said.

Heather cleared her throat. 'That is not what I meant.'

'He has a right to live, just like every other horse,' Miles said.

'Horses are not pets. They serve a purpose. Nobody will look after this crippled horse. I promise, I will put him down humanely.'

'No, you will not,' Miles said. 'I will look after him.'

Heather stared at Miles, then looked back at the Soldier.

'Don't look at me,' the Soldier said, with raised hands. 'The lad can make his own decisions.'

'Do you have stables in Battleacre where I can keep him?' Miles said.

'There are,' the Soldier said. 'I have personal stables where we can keep them.'

'Then he comes with us,' Miles said, looking back at Heather. 'I trust you will look after him if I or the General ask you too.'

Heather looked the foal over. 'He will slow us down.'

'I will stay behind with them,' Miles said. 'Can we get them ready to travel?'

Heather grabbed stirrups from the wall and placed them over the mare's head. Waving her hand to move the two men out of the way, she led the horse out of the loose box and up the aisle to the sliding doors. The foal, still slightly unsure on his hooves, trotted behind his mother. His bones at the top of each shoulder jabbed up and down with every step he took.

The Soldier opened the sliding door a crack and peeked out. 'It's all clear,' he said. 'Let's get these two into the storeroom.'

Miles followed the two horses across the courtyard.

'What are you doing?' Jon said from inside the bar. 'They cannot bring those horses into my storeroom.'

'What do you care?' Miles said from the back door. 'You said you couldn't give a damn about this place if I remember correctly.'

Jon, remembering he was going to leave the inn behind, shrugged.

'It is about an hour from daylight,' the Soldier said, walking back into the bar. 'We move as soon as the first sliver of light appears.'

An hour and a half later, Miles opened the door and stepped out into the early morning light. The mist, which had felt cold during the night, now had a slight warmth to it. The clop of horse hooves turned his attention to the side of the inn. Heather appeared around the corner, leading the mare and the foal. The foal bounced up and down on his front legs, then shook his head at Miles.

'Are you sure about taking those horses, lad?' the Soldier said. 'I will not put our women in danger over them.'

'There is something about them,' Miles said. 'I cannot leave them behind.'

The Soldier glanced down at Miles's inwards-turning foot.

'It's not what you think,' Miles said, using the cane to shift his weight.

'You don't have to explain yourself to me,' the Soldier said. 'Let's be clear, though. We will not wait for them if we need to move quickly.'

Miles inclined his head.

The Soldier adjusted his breastplate, took a step back, and cast his eye along the horsewomen's determined faces. At the end of the row, Jon stood looking back at his inn.

'I thought he hated this place?' Miles said, his voice low.

'He spent most of his life here, lad,' the Soldier said. 'Must still hurt to leave her behind.'

‘Can we get going?’ Heather said from the road. ‘If we are to go east, then south, I would rather this be two days than three.’

Miles leant on his cane as he climbed the small hill to the road. He moved to the front of the line and stood next to the foal, who looked up at him with blue-tinted brown eyes. ‘Will they be able to go long distances?’ he said, looking over the foal at Heather.

Heather rubbed the mare’s neck. ‘They will outwalk the both of us. Even the little one with his deformity will be OK. It’s when we need to move at speed we may have a problem.’

Miles rubbed the foal’s chin, who nickered and shook his head.

‘Let’s go,’ the Soldier said from the back of the group. ‘Lad, keep that sword handy.’

Miles looked over his shoulder and gave the Soldier a nod.

With a click of her tongue, Heather got the train moving along the east road towards the eastern wall. They walked in alert silence. The women strode purposefully forward, their eyes constantly scanning the dead trees on either side of the road.

Miles just about kept pace, his cane thudding against the cobblestones beneath the black snow.

An hour passed, then two, three and four, with no sound other than the squelching of feet and hooves cutting through the black snow and hitting the cobblestone road.

On the eighth hour, Miles squinted into the light mist. ‘The curve in the road is up ahead.’

‘We should rest,’ Heather said. ‘Even the horsewomen will have aching muscles after this amount of time.’

Miles tried to smile, but he grimaced as the pain of his foot shot up through his thigh. At the curve in the road, he led them to the rocky outcrop he had slept under when he had come from the east. With no more sound than a sigh of comfort, the horsewomen sat in circles on the dry rocks underneath the rocky overhang.

'We camp here for the night,' the Soldier said. 'It is an excellent defensive position.'

'What do we need to do?' Heather said.

'Take the horses as far under this outcrop as possible. Lash them down so they cannot bolt,' the Soldier said. 'The rest of us, we form an outwards-facing half circle.'

'Thus watching every angle,' Jon said.

'Yes,' the Soldier said. 'Every second person sleeps for two hours while the others watch. Jon, can you prepare the leftover food?'

Jon turned and hurried deeper under the outcrop. The women, wrapping their clothes tighter around themselves, organised themselves into the correct positions. Silence descended onto the camp as the last light faded. The mist descended like a thick blanket, bringing icy-cold air. Jon walked from person to person, handing each a few small pieces of dried food. The two horses, deep under the outcrop, occasionally tittered.

Hours later, in the dead of night, a low moan floated into the camp. The women's heads shot up as one by one they woke each other up.

'Undead,' the Soldier said into Miles's ear. 'If we stay quiet, they may miss us.'

Miles leant over and gave the message to the woman sitting next to him. Another moan broke through the heavy, swirling mist. The mare snorted and slammed her hoof on the hard dirt. The sound of Heather's soothing voice tickled Miles's ear.

A moan and grunt, this time closer, made Miles tense. The Soldier, once sitting cross-legged, now spun and knelt, his hand over the head of his sword hilt. There was a moan to their right, another to their left, and a long sigh up in front of them.

'They are everywhere,' the horsewoman next to Miles said.

Miles turned and crouched, his hand on the hilt of his greatsword, just like the Soldier.

'What do you think, lad?' the Soldier whispered.

'I think this is the end,' Miles said. 'I can hear shuffling and moaning in all directions.'

There was a movement up ahead in the swirling mist. Miles narrowed his eyes to get a better look.

'As soon as we can make out their faces, we attack,' the Soldier said.

The horsewomen, now on their knees, pulled out old daggers and swords from their belts. A long, high-pitched howl shattered the night. The moaning and groaning of the undead stopped.

'Waya,' Miles said.

The shadows of the undead melted away into the mist. An eerie silence descended on the camp with only an occasional sniff breaking the silence.

'Is she close?' the Soldier eventually said, glancing down at Miles's legs.

Miles shook his head. 'Howls travel great distances, it seems.'

The Soldier crouch-walked along the row of horsewomen and whispered in their ears. Returning to Miles, he sat cross-legged and lay his greatsword across his legs. Every second horsewoman curled up into a ball and fell asleep, while the rest kept a steady eye on the swirling mist.

'Time for you to get some rest,' the Soldier said.

Miles shook his head. 'Not going to happen. Why did the undead not attack?'

'They couldn't find us, lad,' the Soldier said.

Miles grunted. 'Not sure that's true. When the boy saw us in the stables, he disappeared out of the door and then the undead followed. I don't think he wants to hurt us.'

'Well, I am not taking any chances,' the Soldier said. 'If they come near us, I am taking heads.'

'I agree,' Miles said. 'Let's get through the night and get everyone home.'

The Soldier nodded, then jerked his head to the side as Jon appeared with a plate of food. 'You're going to get yourself killed one day, Jon.'

Jon smiled then gave the Soldier a quick bow before sitting next to him. They sat in silence as they worked their way through the plate of food. The mist in front of them swirled, making dark shadows dance out of the nothingness. Every minute, one of them squinted into the mist to try to figure out what the changing shapes were.

Finally, through the mist, the first sliver of light appeared in the east.

The Soldier stood and stretched. 'Let's get moving.'

They packed the camp up and made their way to the road. The mist, refusing to lift, gave them limited visibility. Miles and Heather, with the two horses, took to the front and began the walk south.

Miles wrapped Billy's cloak tighter around himself. 'I thought it'd get warmer the more south we go.'

Heather gave him a half smile. 'We are still in the rolling valleys. The farms are on the plains where the weather is more agreeable.'

'And what about this horrendous snow?' Miles said, slashing at the black snow with his cane.

'We get the snow but lightly,' Heather said. 'Sometimes it is white, and sometimes it is black. There has been more black than white snow over the last couple of years.'

The mare suddenly bounced her head and let out a scared nicker.

Heather stood tall and squinted to survey the road in front of her.

'What is it?' Miles said, using his cane to make himself taller.

'Something out there has spooked the horses,' Heather said.

'Why have we slowed?' the Soldier said, walking alongside Miles.

Heather held up her hand asking for silence. The mare shook her head. The foal, sensing his mother's fear, tucked himself up closer to her.

Down the southern road, the shadow of a person appeared.

'Do you see the figure in the mists?' Heather said, her voice dropping to a whisper.

The slow scraping sound of two greatswords leaving their sheaths made the mare stamp her foot harder.

The shadow grew clearer as it walked towards the group. Around the shadow, the mist stirred then cleared. Miles's breath caught in his throat. A tall woman stood in the centre of the road. Her wide catlike eyes moved from the Soldier, to Miles, to Heather then back to Miles. She opened her mouth, showing long thick, curved fangs. In a voice that sounded like ocean waves crashing against rocks, she said, 'Where is the wolf, boy?'

'Genevie,' the Soldier said, his voice cracking.

CHAPTER 8

RATTLING LIPS

Miles frowned as a captivated look spread across the Soldier's face. 'What's wrong with you?' he said, jabbing the Soldier with his elbow.

The Soldier jumped, then shook his head while clearing his throat.

'I remind him of his dead wife,' Genevie said, placing a hand on her hip. 'Do you still pine for her, General? Or is it me you see in your dreams?'

Sadness etched onto the Soldier's face. 'You are nothing like her. Absolutely nothing like her.'

'Let us pass, Genevie,' Miles said. 'We don't want to hurt you.'

Genevie touched her mouth and tittered. 'Even if you wished me harm, my dear boy, I am certain you wouldn't get close enough to try. How is your troublesome crippled foot?'

Miles pressed harder on the cane to lift himself to his full height. He bit the inside of his cheek to stop himself from showing any pain.

'You poor boy,' Genevie said. 'I can see you hiding your pain. Hand me your wolf and I will take all that pain away for you.'

'You are an abomination,' Heather said, stepping alongside Miles. 'Your disgusting kind have killed many of our children.'

Miles sneered at Genevie. 'Children? Really?'

'You are a murderer,' Heather said, spitting into the snow.

Genevie tutted. 'I do not condone vampires killing children. And if any of my brethren kill children, we deal with them in the most severe way.'

'You use our children to threaten us,' Heather said. 'To control us.'

'Now that is a different story,' Genevie said. 'Yes, we use your offspring to control you. How are your children, my dear Heather?'

Heather's mouth hung open. 'How do you know my name?'

'I know the names of everyone in our shared land,' Genevie said. 'We have been part of you for thousands of years. Haven't we, General?'

Miles gripped the Soldier's elbow. 'What is going on? What are you not telling us?'

A few moments later, the Soldier finally found his voice. 'Humans and vampires have had a pact for centuries. They take what they need to feed but mostly leave us alone.'

'You let them take humans?' Miles said, his eyes widening at the Soldier.

'The worst of the criminals,' the Soldier said. 'Once convicted, we hand them over.'

'Until recently,' Heather spat. 'Now vampires run riot across our lands, killing children and stealing women.'

Genevie took a step forward to move out of the thickening swirling mists.

Miles involuntarily took a step backwards. The mare, sensing the predator, nickered and shook her head. With his coat trembling, the disabled foal stepped closer to his mother.

'That is close enough,' the Soldier said, his eyes narrowing. 'Why are you stealing our women? What does the City of Lynn want with them? And if your brethren are killing children, Genevie, I will declare the pact broken.'

Genevie laughed. 'Your wits have returned, General. I suppose my beauty is effective for only a short time.'

'Humble as ever,' the Soldier said. 'I asked you some questions.'

Genevie placed her hand back on her hip then turned her grey, red-ringed eyes onto Miles. 'Where is your wolf?'

'What's your preoccupation with this wolf?' the Soldier said, throwing his hands up into the air. 'Vampires and wolves are deadly enemies. Answer my questions, Genevie.'

'The City of Lynn has instructed the vampires to bring the wolf to them, haven't they?' Miles said.

Genevie looked at Miles down her nose. 'How do you know this?'

'The wolf is the earth element,' Miles said. 'The City of Lynn has decided it needs to capture these elements. They did this with the fire element in the south.'

The Soldier looked at Miles, then Genevie, and then back at Miles. 'Elements?' he said.

Miles spread his hands. 'I don't control the wolf, Genevie. You know this.'

Genevie's sweet smile broadened. 'But the earth element seems to want to protect you, doesn't she, my dear boy?'

Miles's face hardened but he kept his mouth shut.

'And she also seems to want to protect the ones you love or wish to protect,' Genevie said. 'Truly two beings joined at the hip.'

The Soldier reached for the hilt of his greatsword. 'I asked you questions, Genevie. Are you killing children?'

'We have not been killing children. Heather is lying, General,' Genevie said, the tip of her tongue dancing onto one of her fangs. 'All I want is the wolf and I will let you be on your way.'

Heather spat at the snow. 'I am not lying, sir.'

'You still haven't answered my other question,' the Soldier said, holding up his hand. 'Why are you taking our women?'

Genevie adjusted a sleeve on her blouse. 'A request from the City,' she said. 'For a sizeable reward.'

'What could the City offer that you don't already have?' the Soldier said.

A sound in the forest turned Genevie's face from serene beauty to predatory anger. With a flick of her hand, she summoned vampires who listened for a second, then flew into the forest.

'I would never have guessed you would be afraid of the undead, Genevie,' the Soldier said.

'Afraid?' Genevie said. 'I am not afraid, General. I am annoyed. Their bites will ruin my precious children.'

'An undead vampire?' the Soldier said. 'Positively disgusting.'

Genevie scratched her neck with a perfectly formed nail. 'Diabolical and dangerous,' she said.

Another groan from among the trees made the mare fight against Heather's grip on the reins.

'You need to give me your wolf,' Genevie said. 'If we stay here too long, the undead will surround us and leave us no escape. I will survive, but none of you shall.'

'I told you, I don't control her.'

Genevie closed her eyes and let out a long sigh. As she opened her eyes, she waved a hand. 'I didn't want to do this, but I have no choice.'

Miles jumped as a scream came from one of the horsewomen.

'They took Amy,' another horsewoman said, her eyes darting.

'Yes, and we will turn her,' Genevie said. 'No doubt she will become one of Gerald's playthings.'

Miles faced Genevie. 'What am I supposed to do? I cannot call the wolf. I don't know how many times I need to tell you this.'

'The boy is telling the truth, Genevie,' the Soldier said.

'Maybe something else will convince the boy,' Genevie said, waving her hand behind her. 'A guest perhaps.'

Two silhouettes, one large and one small, took form in the mist.

Miles reached for the hilt of his greatsword. To the south, the howls of wolves sounded.

Genevie's face turned from predator to angel. 'Is that her? Is that your wolf?'

Miles drew his greatsword. 'What do you mean, a guest?'

The two silhouettes grew larger as they walked closer to Genevie.

'Call her,' Genevie said, lifting her head and pointing her chin at Miles. 'Call your wolf.'

'I told you, she doesn't heel on my command,' Miles said.

'This is your last chance, boy,' Genevie said.

Miles looked at the Soldier. 'What is she up to?'

'I don't know,' the Soldier said.

Out of the mist, Gerald walked towards them. Next to him, with her neck firmly in the grasp of his hand, stood a girl with wavy red hair.

'Janie,' Miles said, stumbling forward. He fell as his right leg collapsed underneath him.

. . .

The Soldier caught Miles by his elbow and hauled him up. The knuckles on Miles's right hand turned white as he gripped the handle of his cane.

'Miles,' Janie said. 'Help me, please, he is hurting me.'

'Let her go, Gerald,' Miles said, pointing his greatsword at him.

'What are you doing, lad?' the Soldier said, still holding his elbow. 'They have turned her.'

Miles frowned at the Soldier. 'What do you mean, turned? It's Janie. The girl I told you about.'

'They have turned her,' the Soldier said.

With his entire body shaking, Miles looked back at Janie.

'Pesky General,' Genevie said. 'Why destroy the fun? You should have kept quiet.'

'Janie?' Miles whispered.

Janie waved Gerald's hand away, then squared her shoulders, before smiling at Miles.

'This cannot be happening,' Miles said. 'What have they done to you?'

'Where is the wolf?' Janie said.

Miles stood frozen to the ground. The top of the cane wobbled as he fought to keep his balance. His greatsword, now too heavy, shook in front of him.

Genevie reached out a hand, grabbed Janie by the throat, and lifted her off the ground. 'Tell me where she is, or I will snap your little girlfriend's neck.'

'Janie,' Miles whispered again.

Janie looked back at Miles with fear in her red-ringed eyes. Her red hair flew about her shoulders as Genevie shook her.

'She is no longer human, boy,' the Soldier said. 'There is nothing you can do for her.'

Miles opened his mouth to say something, but his breath

caught in his throat. The muscles in his jawline tensed. His right foot turned outwards until it pointed straight. The nerve endings in his back knitted together. In one swift movement, Miles sprang forward and slashed at Genevie. His sword swishing through the air, Miles landed on his feet and stared at the place where Genevie and Janie had stood.

Gerald chuckled. 'You are going to need to be quicker to catch these ladies.'

'I will have your head,' Miles said, springing towards Gerald with his sword swishing through the air. Miles hissed as his sword hit nothing. The mare neighed in terror. Miles spun to see vampires descending on the group. The Soldier's sword flourished in wide arcs, lopping off heads. The horsewomen with their short swords hacked and slashed. A vampire slashed his long claws at Heather, missed, but cut the reins that held the mare. Sensing freedom, the mare bolted down the south road. The foal, losing sight of his mother, slipped and slid into the forest towards the eastern wall.

Miles turned in a full circle to scan the mists in search of Janie.

'Run,' the Soldier shouted, barrelling past Miles.

Miles watched them run down the southern road and disappear into the mist. The footsteps of his friends crunching in the snow grew softer until he stood on his own in silence. Miles sheathed his greatsword, picked up his cane and slipped it next to the greatsword. Rotating his shoulders, he felt the power of Waya course through his veins. He crouched, undid his laces, removed his boots and, tying the laces together, he hung them around his neck. The earth under his bare feet thumped with the same tempo of his heart. Through the black snow, Mother Earth felt solid, warm and reassuring.

Deep in the forest, near the eastern wall, Miles heard the foal scream. With earth's energy resonating through his legs, Miles sprang into the forest. The mist swirled around him as he dodged the blackened, dead trees. To his right, an undead person shuffled along, searching. To his right, he glimpsed the flap of leather as a vampire sprang among the dead trees. The eastern wall loomed above him as Miles skidded to a halt. The foal stood with his right side against the eastern wall. With their fangs extended, the vampires jumped in and out, toying with the disabled horse. With the power of Waya running through him, Miles jumped forward, whipped out his greatsword, and separated the vampires' heads from their bodies. Two swipes and their remains disappeared into dust.

Miles replaced his greatsword. 'It's OK,' he said, walking up to the foal with an outstretched hand.

With eyes bulging, the foal pushed against the eastern wall and kicked a back leg at Miles.

Miles dodged the kick before reaching over and stroking the foal's neck.

The foal jerked his small head around and snapped his teeth at Miles.

'Steady little one,' Miles said. 'I am not going to hurt you.'

At Miles's touch, the foal's coat rippled along the length of his back. With a snort, he turned his head and buried his snout into Miles's armpit. Miles ran his hand over the horse's ears and down over his deformed shoulders. 'Let's get out of here,' he said. 'We need to get you back to your mother.'

Miles walked south, keeping the eastern wall to his right. The foal, now more certain on his feet, kept close to Miles. The mist swirled around the trees, making shadows dance along the grey wall. In the distance, the sound of fighting rang through the forest. With his hand on the horse's neck and the foal walking next to the eastern wall, Miles continued south.

Suddenly, the foal jabbed his snout against Miles's ribs. He froze.

The small boy with glowing eyes and shocking white hair stepped out from behind a mangled tree trunk.

Miles held out a hand, his palm facing the boy. 'I don't want trouble,' he said. 'Who are you?'

The ground behind the boy rumbled, shuddered, then split open. The remains of a human crawled out of the hole, stood, and shambled off into the mists. With a sniff of the air, the foal took a step back and placed his nose into Miles's armpit.

'It's OK,' Miles said, rubbing the foal's ears.

The boy turned and, walking south, he looked over his shoulder and beckoned for Miles to follow.

'Looks like we are following him, little one,' Miles said, giving the foal's ears another rub. 'Good idea, do you think?'

The foal removed his nose from Miles's armpit and shook his head.

'I don't think it's a good idea either,' Miles said. 'But we are going to anyway because it's the direction we need to go.'

The foal sighed and trotted forward. Miles kept his eye on the shock of white hair as they continued south through the black snow. The boy occasionally looked over his shoulder with his glowing eyes to make sure he was being followed. After a few hours, the mist lightened, but the black snow still covered the trees and ground.

The boy suddenly froze. Miles stopped and wrapped his arm around the foal's neck. The boy turned around and, walking back past Miles and the foal, he melted quietly into the mist.

Miles bent a knee and, while rubbing the foal's snout, he tilted his head and listened carefully. 'Why did the boy leave, little one?' he said. 'Vampires about I bet.'

The foal swished his tail and nodded his head.

'All alone with nobody to help you,' Genevie said from somewhere in the mist.

'I was right,' Miles said, standing.

'Your foot is healed,' Genevie said, raising an eyebrow. 'How did that happen?'

'You hurt Janie,' Miles said.

'She isn't hurting, my dear boy,' Genevie said. 'She is one of us now.'

The foal nickered and pressed himself against the eastern wall. Miles turned his head to the soft crunching of snow. Out of the mist, Waya stalked with her teeth bared toward Genevie's voice. The foal, seeing the massive wolf, shuffled his legs, trying to escape to the north. Miles wrapped his arms around the foal's neck and tutted in his ear. Waya stopped in front of Miles, sat, and sniffed the air. A few moments later, the foal accepted he would not escape and hung his small head.

'There she is,' Genevie said. 'I am going to come and fetch her.'

A smirk crossed Miles's lips. 'You can try.'

'You know wolf bites are deadly to the turned,' Genevie said. 'If your wolf bites your little girlfriend, she will die slowly and painfully. Not the quick and painless pop of a removed head.'

'Waya, don't hurt Janie,' Miles said, laying a hand on the wolf's back. Waya looked over her shoulder and snarled back at Miles.

'Looks like you were telling the truth,' Genevie said. 'You don't control her at all.'

Waya flung her head to the west and sniffed the air. Out of the mist, from the same direction that Waya had come, the black alpha wolf stalked. Waya snorted, making him stop a small distance away. The foal, sweating heavily, turned his head and placed it against the wall.

'Where is Janie?' Miles said. 'Let her go, Genevie.'

'She is free to go where she pleases,' Genevie said. 'Why don't you call for her?'

'You know that isn't true,' Miles said. 'You have influence over her.'

Genevie's laugh tinkled through the mists. Waya rumbled deep in her chest at the sound of the royal vampire's laugh. The alpha wolf stalked up to Waya and, standing next to her, he sniffed the air in Genevie's direction. Slowly, the fading mists showed the advancing Genevie. With her fangs and claws fully extended, she looked predatory and beautiful. Another shadow appeared as Gerald stepped out of the mists and stood next to Genevie. The vampires eyed the wolves; the wolves, their heads lowered, growled at the vampires. The foal turned his head and rammed his snout into Miles's armpit.

'Waya,' Miles said. 'You need to go.'

Waya turned her head and whined.

'You need to go,' Miles said again. 'You need to stay away from me.'

Waya swung her enormous head and stared at Genevie.

'Yes,' Miles said. 'She wants to take you away. You need to stay away from me.'

Waya looked back at Miles, then turned her head and growled at the alpha wolf. Sensing what she needed, the alpha wolf raised his head and howled into the mist. Long howls from around the area answered. Waya backtracked north, with the alpha wolf staying between Miles and the vampires.

'So you can control her,' Genevie said.

Miles smiled. 'I can ask, but that doesn't mean I can control her.'

'No matter,' Genevie said, pointing at Waya. 'I will catch her without you.'

Dark shadows sprang out of the mists as Waya's pack of wolves sprang at Genevie and Gerald. Both vampires disappeared into the mists, with the alpha and his wolves giving chase.

Miles let go of the foal and, stepping backwards, he knelt and slid an arm over Waya's neck. 'You cannot get captured by those vampires,' he said. 'We need to stay apart.'

Waya whined and butted her head against Miles's chin.

Miles looked down at his foot and, with the thought of losing his ability to walk properly, he sighed. 'You need to go,' he said, shoving Waya away from him. 'Don't let them catch you, and don't come near me even if I am in danger.'

Waya growled.

'You need to trust me,' Miles said, remembering that if he got hurt, Waya would also get hurt. 'I will stay out of danger.'

With a swish of her tail, Waya bounded north into the mists.

Miles stood, walked back to the foal, and rubbed his neck. 'It's just you and me again, little one.'

'Miles,' Janie said.

The breath caught in Miles's throat. 'Janie?' he said, spinning around.

'Yes,' Janie said, appearing out of the mists. 'It's me.'

The foal whined and shoved his head back in Miles's armpit.

'Shh,' Miles said, running a hand over the foal's ears.

'I don't mean to scare your little horse,' Janie said. 'What is wrong with his shoulders? Did someone damage him?'

'He was born that way,' Miles said, his eyes narrowing. 'It seems they have damaged you too.'

Janie dropped her head. 'I came to look for you. I came through the eastern wall.'

Miles bit his bottom lip. 'I wish you hadn't,' he said. 'Look what they have done to you.'

Janie looked up with anger in her red-ringed eyes. 'I wouldn't have needed to come if you hadn't left.'

'We won't be talking about this now,' Miles said, looking down at his hands. 'I need to get this foal back to safety and find my friends.'

'You never wanted to talk,' Janie said, taking a slow breath. 'What new friends? Have you already given up on your old friends?'

Miles let out a grunt before grabbing his cane and leaning on it. His foot turned inwards as the nerves in his lower back separated.

Janie took a step forward.

Miles reached over his head and grabbed the hilt of his sword. 'Don't come any closer,' he said, his eyes narrowing.

'Don't you trust me?' Janie said, spreading her hands.

'Genevie controls you,' Miles said. 'Why should I trust you?'

'I always like how smart you are. Please join me,' Janie said, holding out a hand. 'I will heal you and we can be together.'

Miles let go of his sword's hilt. 'How do you know you will heal me?'

'When I turn you, everything that is broken will heal,' Janie said.

A distant look crossed Miles's face.

A wolf howl sounded in the distance.

With a shake of his head, Miles snapped out of his thoughts. 'I can't,' he said. 'Genevie wants Waya, and I promised I wouldn't leave my friends.'

'You left me,' Janie said, her voice softening to a whisper.

Miles's voice cracked. 'I know. And I wish I never had.'

'Give Waya to Genevie,' Janie said. 'We can be together forever.'

The foal nickered and butted Miles in the arm. Miles shook his head. 'You know I can't do that, Janie. I need to get this foal to safety. My friends need my help. I cannot abandon them.'

Janie opened her mouth, exposing two small fangs. 'Don't make me hurt you, Miles,' she said, taking another step forward.

Miles reached for his sword. 'I knew it. You are playing games with me, aren't you? Is she controlling you?'

A shuffling undead appeared from behind a tree. With an outstretched hand, the undead rapidly closed in on Janie.

'Watch out,' Miles shouted, hobbling forward, reaching for his greatsword.

Janie jerked her head around, let out a hiss, and kicked the undead in the chest, sending him sprawling onto the ground. More undead shuffled into view, all walking towards Janie with their arms extended.

'You need to get out of here,' Miles said. 'Please, Janie, don't let them hurt you.'

Janie, in a blur, knocked three more undead to the ground. 'What do you care?' she said. 'You left me, remember.'

Miles pointed his greatsword at Janie. 'I care,' he said. 'But I will take your head before one of these things gets to you. I will not let you turn into some undead beast.'

Janie hissed at Miles before disappearing into the mist. The undead spun in circles in confusion then, choosing a direction, they disappeared into the mist.

Miles sheathed his greatsword, then frowned as, out of the mist, the little boy appeared. With his index finger, the boy beckoned Miles to follow them southwards.

'Why are you helping me?' Miles said.

The boy, looking over his shoulder with his piercing, glowing eyes, beckoned Miles to follow.

With his arm wrapped around the foal's neck, Miles led the horse after the young boy. The mist continued to lift, exposing more undead surrounding them. The stench of decaying flesh overpowered the acidic smell of the black snow. The sun disappeared below the western horizon, bringing darkness to the forest. Suddenly, the ground disappeared down a steep bank. The young boy stopped at the top of the bank and, looking back at Miles, he pointed to the cobblestone road that led to the west.

'Why are you helping us?' Miles said again.

The little boy jabbed his finger to the west then, with a small nod, he walked north, past Miles and into the dark forest.

'This will not go well,' Miles said, looking down the steep bank. The foal rocked his head and snorted.

'Ready?' Miles said.

The horse peered down the bank, then shook his head. They slipped and slid for the first part of the hill until both of them lost their balance and, with a puff of black snow, landed in a jumbled-up pile at the bottom. Miles sat up and brushed the black snow off his clothes. The foal struggled to his feet, his shoulders looking like they would break through the skin.

'I told you,' Miles said, rubbing the foal's nose. 'That didn't go well, did it?'

The foal stumbled onto the road, then looked back at Miles.

'We need to camp,' Miles said, seeing the foal's trembling legs and feeling his own right leg collapsing. 'The pair of us will never make it through the night.'

The foal's body trembled harder as the cold set in. Miles walked off the road and searched for a dry place. Eventually, he stumbled down a small incline and found a place covered by a small cluster of bushes. Rocks packed along the incline formed a protective wall they could place their backs against. Miles led the foal down the incline, then gently buckling his legs, he laid him next to the rocks. After spreading branches over the foal, Miles sat with his back to the rocks and drew his legs up to his body.

'If they find us here, we will have no escape,' he said. 'Stay quiet under those branches.'

The foal sighed, then rested his head on Miles's feet. With one last look around, Miles sank his head on his knees and fell asleep.

Miles jerked awake. The foal was nowhere to be seen. With the aid of his cane, Miles scrambled to his feet and walked out of the small hole. He brought his hand up to cover his eyes as the morning sun glowed from the east. With a slow turn, he surveyed the area until, with a sigh of relief, he saw the foal's tail poking out from behind a tree. 'What are you doing? You shouldn't walk off like that,' Miles said, smacking his cane onto a rock.

The foal lifted his head and stared back at Miles.

Miles shuffled over to the foal. 'We need to move,' he said, running his hand over the foal's coat.

The foal lowered his head and crunched down on some yellow roots.

'The snow,' Miles said. 'It's white.'

The foal lifted his head and rattled his lips together.

'We must be near the gate to the south,' Miles said, looking to the west. 'Come on, we need to get to the horse farms.'

They both moved onto the middle of the cobblestone and began the walk east. With the sleep under the bushes having refreshed them both, the two disabled friends walked with renewed purpose and little pain. As the sun rose, its glow gave some warmth to their backs. The path undulated with the terrain moving from flat to rolling hills. The foal, his legs steadier, hopped from front-to-back legs while swishing his tail. Miles chuckled at the foal's playfulness. Hours passed and the snow on the ground thinned into small patches of black and white as they walked up and over the hills.

As they came close to the crest of a hill, the foal's ears pricked up.

'What is it?' Miles said, slowing and scanning either side of the cobblestone road.

The foal nickered and, picking up speed, he trotted to the top of the hill.

'Slow down,' Miles said, leaning on his cane harder as he tried to keep up.

The foal disappeared over the crest of the hill.

Miles, breathing hard, grimaced at the pain in his thigh and foot. At the top of the hill, he slowed to a walk and peered down the winding path. The land at the bottom spread out into a long, flat valley. At the valley's bottom lay differently sized horse farms. The foal, having made it down the hill to the farms, trotted along a fence, calling to the horses in the fields. A man with a long pole appeared out of a farmhouse and strode to where the foal danced along the fence.

'Excuse me,' Miles shouted as he walked down the path.

The man, getting closer to the foal, raised the long pole. A flash of light reflected off the top of the pole and hit Miles in the face. Miles dropped the cane and, ignoring the pain in his thigh and foot, ran down the hill.

The man raised the bladed pole high over his head.

'Stop,' Miles shouted. 'Leave him alone.'

The foal, hearing Miles's voice, darted away from the fence and ran up the winding cobblestone path.

'Get back here!' the man said.

'I said, leave him alone.' Miles reached over his shoulder for his greatsword.

The foal came charging up the path and, spinning around next to Miles, he jammed his nose into his armpit.

'That foal has deformed shoulders,' the man said, walking up the hill. 'He has no place on the horse farms.'

'You get away from him,' Miles said, his greatsword singing out of its sheath. 'Do not come any closer.'

A neigh, followed by the pounding of hooves, spun the man around. The foal's mother galloped up the path with her tail swishing side to side. The foal pulled his snout out of Miles's armpit and squealed at the sight of his mother.

'Leave them be,' Miles said, his greatsword trained on the man. 'We don't need any trouble here.'

The man spat at the ground. 'I will have your head for bringing that abomination into our farms. Keep him away from my horses.'

With his greatsword trained on the man, Miles backed off down the hill until he reached the fence. Miles found a gate, opened it, and let the two horses run into the enclosure. Miles crossed the horse enclosure, climbed the fence, and walked over to the inn. At the door, he placed his head against the wood and listened. Men having conversations filtered back to him. He shoved the door and walked in. The inn went silent, and all eyes turned to him.

'It can't be,' a woman's voice said.

'It certainly is,' Jon said, walking around the bar. 'How on earth did you make it here, son?'

'Get the Soldier,' Heather said. 'He has been worrying himself silly and was just about to go searching for you.'

Miles smiled. 'No need for the old man to go searching.'

'Lad,' the Soldier thundered from the top of the stairs. 'I knew you were OK.'

'Just about OK,' Miles said, walking into the inn and embracing Heather. 'It got scary out there.'

'And the foal?' Heather said.

'He is with me,' Miles said. 'He is in the horse enclosure. Some man tried to take the foal's head with a long blade.'

'That would be Adam from the horse farm next door. We will need to hide the foal,' Heather said, hurrying to the inn door. 'I will store the horses in my stable for tonight, but tomorrow morning you will have to find another place.'

Miles gave Heather a small smile. 'That is kind of you, Heather.'

'Let me look at you,' the Soldier said. 'Tell me everything.'

'May I trouble someone for some food, please?' Miles said. 'I haven't eaten in two days.'

'Yes, yes, of course,' Jon said. 'We only made it here early this morning. Sit and I will sort you something, then you can tell us everything.'

'He will do nothing of the sort,' a woman said. 'Once he has eaten, he is up to his room to rest.'

The Soldier sat back and laced his fingers behind his head. 'It is good to see you safe, lad. I think the woman is right. Eat and off to rest you go.'

Miles looked at the platter of food that had been slid onto the table. After devouring as much as he could, he walked up the stairs to a room and collapsed on the bed.

CHAPTER 9
CHARMING

'Just men,' the Soldier said, walking out of the inn and scanning the fields. 'Not a woman in sight.'

'Heather mentioned she was the last woman to be taken,' Miles said. 'Do you know where the children are?'

'They are being hid in the houses,' the Soldier said, walking around the side of the inn. 'I asked Heather if she wants us to take them to Battleacre. She refused and said their homes are here.'

'We need to protect them,' Miles said, leaning more heavily on his cane to keep up.

'That is why we must get to Battleacre as soon as possible,' the Soldier said.

'I don't know if I want to go.'

The Soldier stopped walking. 'Why? I need you there. Does my offer not excite you?'

'I need to help Janie,' Miles said, walking past the Soldier. 'I can't leave her out there.'

'They have turned her, son,' the Soldier said, double-stepping to catch Miles. 'I don't know of any way we can help her.'

'My father, in the south, Dr Viktor, he will know.'

'You want to go back to the south?'

'I've got to speak to him,' Miles said.

'And if he knows how to save her, he will want to come to the east, won't he? Why not send a messenger? It is a waste for you to go all that way to just return.'

Miles rubbed his chin. 'That is a better plan. Plus, if I go to the south, I am sure Genevie will follow me.'

The Soldier continued walking to the back of the inn. 'There is a stable down the road where we can board the horses. Heather has given me directions.'

They walked into the small barn where the mare and foal stood. The foal's ears pricked up at the sound of Miles's cane hitting the ground.

'Throw that blanket over the foal,' the Soldier said.

Miles untied the mare and handed the reins to the Soldier. Once they moved the mare out of the way, Miles dragged the blanket over the foal. 'It's OK,' Miles said, holding a bit of sliced apple in his hand. The foal's ears lay flat as his lips grabbed the apple.

'You ready in there?' the Soldier said.

Miles walked out of the inn and grinned as the foal followed close behind.

'He has taken a shine to you,' the Soldier said.

'In the short time we have known each other, we have been through a lot,' Miles said, rubbing the foal's ear.

They walked through the farms where horses pranced around the gated enclosures. Miles and the Soldier's raised-hand greetings to the farmers went mostly ignored.

'This is it,' the Soldier said, walking down a small dirt path and stopping at the entrance of a farmhouse.

Miles knocked.

'Who's there?' A gruff voice came from behind the door.

'A soldier from the barracks,' the Soldier said. 'We wish to house our horses in your stable.'

A panel in the door slid open.

The Soldier gave the two small eyes his best grin.

The thump of bolts ended with the door being opened a small crack. A short man with a pudgy face peered through the gap. He eyed the Soldier, then pulled the door open. 'Cannot be too careful during these times,' he said, looking right and left. 'Name is Norman.'

The Soldier extended his hand. 'We have a need for a stable for our horses, and the purchase of two fresh horses please, Norman.'

Norman frowned at the mare and the foal. 'Why is that foal still alive? We do not allow deformed horses at the horse farms.'

Miles touched the foal's neck.

'You have a good eye, Norman,' the Soldier said, reaching into a small purse and retrieving two silver coins. 'The foal is special to the young lad. I trust it won't be a problem?' he said, pushing the coins into Norman's hand.

Norman looked down at the coins with wide, greedy eyes.

'And there will be two more of those on our return,' the Soldier said.

Norman cleared his throat. 'Certainly, sir. I will have to hide him. I must uphold my reputation, you see.'

'Any harm comes to this foal,' Miles said, pointing his cane at Norman, 'you will feel the sharp end of my sword.'

Norman glimpsed the hilt of the greatsword that appeared over Miles's head. 'I will look after her as if she is my own. I promise you that, sir,' he said.

The Soldier reached into his purse, pulled out two gold coins and held them up to the light.

Norman's mouth fell open and his eyes grew wider and greedier still.

'This is for the purchase of two of the finest horses,' the Soldier said, spinning the coins around.

'I have never seen the like,' Norman said, reaching for the coins.

The Soldier closed his hand. 'Two horses, and the best care for the mare and her foal.'

Norman pulled his hat off his head and placed it against his chest. 'It will be my honour, sir.'

The Soldier opened his hand and watched Norman retrieve the coins with a trembling hand. 'Send word to Heather's inn when you have the horses ready, Norman,' the Soldier said.

Norman took the reins from the Soldier and led the mare and her foal to a door at the end of the stable.

'You sure he will be OK?' Miles said, looking at the Soldier.

'He has never seen that type of coin before,' the Soldier said. 'I think they will be safe with him.'

Miles and the Soldier walked back through the fields and entered Heather's inn.

'Did you secure boarding for your horses?' Heather said, walking out of the storeroom.

'Yes, thank you, Heather,' the Soldier said. 'We persuaded Norman easily.'

'And he is organising us two horses,' Miles said, sitting on a stool.

Jon placed two tankards of ale on the bar.

'Bit early, isn't it?' Miles said.

'It's midday,' Heather said. 'Lunch will be ready in half an hour. There is a table ready for you.'

Miles and the Soldier, with drinks in hand, left the bar and sat at the table in the corner. The sunlight streamed through the window, but the warmth came from the crackling fire on the other side of the room.

The Soldier took a long draw from his tankard, then banged it back down on the table. 'That was much needed,' he said, leaning back and lacing his fingers behind his head.

Miles took a few gulps of the ale then wiped his mouth with his sleeve. With a sigh, he leant back in his chair and rubbed the top of his right thigh.

'We need to do something about that foot,' the Soldier said, looking down at Miles's feet. 'The people of the barracks frown upon people with disabilities.'

'Horse farmers wanting to kill helpless disabled foals, and people in Battleacre frowning on people with disabilities,' Miles said. 'You realise that we just want to be treated like everyone else and that we are useful?'

The Soldier eyed Miles but kept quiet.

'You don't think we are useful?' Miles said.

'You have changed my mind.'

Miles took another drink from his tankard. 'So what do we do with my foot?'

'We use a brace,' Heather said, sliding a tray of food onto the table. 'The brace will help pull your foot straight and keep it straight.'

'Very painful,' Jon said, sliding a smaller tray onto the table.

'It will be ready in the morning,' Heather said. 'Eat up.'

'Charming,' Miles muttered. 'What's a bit more pain, right?'

The chair's legs slammed onto the floor as the Soldier leant forward to fill his plate with food.

'What are the games like?' Miles said, with a mouthful of food.

The Soldier smirked. 'Still thinking of participating, are you?'

Miles shrugged. 'I don't know.'

The Soldier signalled to Jon, who brought two fresh tankards to the table. 'In the past, they would fight to the death and the surviving combatants would have the honour of joining the Queen's Guard.'

'They don't fight to the death anymore?' Miles said, looking up from his plate.

The Soldier leant back on the chair legs. 'No, they need soldiers for the war in the north. The weapons they use now are not actual weapons but well-crafted practice weapons. The winners still get sent to the Queen's Guard. As for the rest, we transport them north to take part in the wars.'

Miles took another draw of his ale. 'All I ever wanted was to be a member of the Queen's Guard.'

'For a warrior, it is one of the highest honours of our land,' the Soldier said. 'Being a strategist, though, we regard even higher. It is the strategist that keeps the Queen safe.'

Miles sat eating, lost in thought. 'How do the games work?' he said, filling his mouth with more food.

The Soldier interlaced his fingers behind his head. 'You don't know?'

Miles shook his head. 'Fairacre is a farming region. Nobody travels to the east. Even for trade, we send to the City of Lynn.'

The Soldier's chair dropped on its front legs with a bang. 'A magnificent amphitheatre stands in the middle of Battleacre. In the amphitheatre, rows and rows of spectators look down into the sandpit. The sound they make is wondrous, thunderous, magnificent.'

A grin crept across Miles's face as he imagined the baying and screaming crowds.

'The walls surrounding the fighting arena are high – three to four men high. We broke the arena up into quadrants. In each quadrant, there are five panels on the wall. Within the four bottom panels sits a random practice weapon.'

'And the fifth?' Miles said, his eyes never leaving the Soldier.

'In the fifth panel sits the fighter's practice weapon of choice.'

Miles scraped his chair closer to the table. 'So in the beginning, you don't get to choose which weapons you can use?'

'No. You may be lucky enough to receive a weapon you have trained with before, but you rarely get the weapon you want.'

Miles cast his mind back to his training room and all the weapons lined up on the racks.

'The battle starts with four fighters and the aim is to disarm your opponents. When an opponent disarms another opponent, the disarmed fighter must retrieve another weapon from their quadrant. The fight continues until two opponents have no more weapons in their four panels.'

'So four become two?' Miles said.

'Yes, the first two to use all their four random weapons get eliminated,' the Soldier said. 'Once four become two. The remaining two open the fifth panel, which houses their preferred weapon.'

'And the final two fight until one disarms the other?'

'No,' the Soldier said, a grin spreading across his face. 'They fight until one submits.'

Miles took another drink of his tankard. 'You can continue to fight if they disarm you?'

The Soldier smirked. 'When your opponent has their preferred weapon, and you don't have your own weapon, do you think that continuing is advisable?'

'It would seem like a silly thing to do,' Miles grunted. 'What if one doesn't submit?'

'They continue until one cannot continue,' the Soldier said.

'To the death if need be?'

'If that needs to happen,' the Soldier said, spreading his arms.

Miles slumped back into his chair and pictured the warriors fighting in the arena.

'Imagining taking part?' the Soldier said.

Miles shook his head. 'No.'

'Janie?' the Soldier said, raising an eyebrow.

Miles gave the Soldier a half smile. 'Before meeting her, all I could think of was being part of the Queen's Guard. Now she is all I think of.'

'It's called love, my boy,' the Soldier said, slapping his hand on his knee. 'It is cruel and wonderful at exactly the same time.'

Miles lowered his head into his hands. 'But they have changed her into one of those things.'

'Yes, it seems you were late to this game of love, weren't you, lad?' the Soldier said.

'I need to save her,' Miles said through his fingers. 'I owe her that much.'

'The best thing you can do is stay away for now,' the Soldier said. 'Genevie will take great pleasure in hurting her to get to you.'

Miles massaged his temples. 'And Waya needs to stay away from me too.'

'Come on, son. It's mid-afternoon. Let's get you into your room.'

Two copper pieces tinkled onto the table. Jon looked across and signalled a thank you. Miles followed the Soldier through the bar and up the narrow staircase to the rooms.

'Lie in tomorrow,' the Soldier said, standing at his door. 'Tomorrow, we try this new brace from Heather.'

Miles entered the small room, kicked off his boots, and climbed onto the single bed. With his hands folded behind his head, he closed his eyes and imagined the sights and sounds of the grand amphitheatre.

. . .

The next morning, Miles glared at the black leather boot that sat on the floor in front of him. His bed creaked as he placed an elbow on each knee and his chin on the knuckles of his hands. The three belt buckles across the top of the boot sat firmly as a symbol of pain. With a guttural growl, he clutched the back of his right calf, turned his foot, and slid it into his boot. Once inside the boot, his foot turned inwards, pulling the boot with it. Miles grabbed the first strap, which lay across the foot at the base of the shin, and he pulled hard until the buckle reached the last hole. His foot slowly turned outwards. With sweat beading across his forehead, Miles grabbed the second strap and pulled hard. A sharp blast of air escaped his lips. His foot turned outwards even further. He closed his eyes, balled his hands into fists, and bit his bottom lip. After a few deep breaths to control the throbbing pain, he opened his eyes and sneered at the last buckle, which lay close to his toes. Holding his breath, he pulled on the last strap and placed the buckle's pin into the hole. His foot turned the last piece until it pointed straight ahead. He swallowed hard to stop himself from throwing up all over his bed. Miles climbed off the bed and put pressure on his right foot. Sharp stabs of pain shot up through his leg. He leant on his cane and walked over to the small window where he stood gazing out at the horses galloping across the fields. Slowly, the pain disappeared. Miles spun at a rap on the door. 'Come in,' he said, walking back over to his bed.

The Soldier swung open the door. 'Our horses are ready. How is your foot?'

'It is manageable,' Miles said with a quick glance at the ugly boot.

'They will turn you away from the barracks if they spot any sign of your disability. Are you sure that boot will hold?'

'Yes, it will hold,' Miles said, holding up a hand. 'Don't worry about it.'

The Soldier bowed his head then disappeared down the narrow corridor.

Miles gathered his things, gave the room a last check, then walked through the corridor and down the staircase into the inn. He sat next to the Soldier and filled his plate with porridge. 'How long will it take to get there?' he said, dripping honey onto his breakfast.

'Two days if all goes well,' the Soldier said. 'We need to get to Battleacre before sunset tomorrow, otherwise we wait for another day.'

After finishing their breakfast, they walked over to the bar where Heather and Jon stood.

'Are you ready for your journey?' Jon said.

The Soldier placed a hand on Jon's shoulder. 'We are ready. Are you sure you don't want to come with us?'

'I am going to stay here and give Heather a hand,' Jon said with a quick glance across at her.

A wide smile stretched across the Soldier's face. 'Sounds like a plan to me.'

Heather, her face a slight pink, rolled her eyes, then said, 'Will you be sending help when you get to the barracks?'

The Soldier placed his fist on his chest. 'You have my word.'

Heather smiled. 'Thank you.'

Miles embraced Heather, then shook Jon's hand. 'Please, can you check in on the mare and the foal?'

Jon nodded. 'They are still my horses, you know.'

'Ha, that they are, sir,' Miles said with a chuckle. 'I may negotiate for their release in due course, Jon.'

'As you wish, sir,' Jon said with a small bow.

'Let's get moving, son,' the Soldier said, striding to the inn entrance.

Miles walked to the front door, then stopped and looked over his shoulder. 'Thanks for the boot, Heather. It fills me with joy and dread all at the same time.'

Heather put a hand up to her mouth, chuckled, then with the other, shooed Miles away. 'Get out of here.'

Miles caught up to the Soldier and raised his hand above his brow to block out the sun so he could see the path up to Norman's. 'Looks like spring is going to come early,' he said.

The Soldier glanced at Miles. 'Unfortunately, son, we will still have a couple of months of winter left. And the worst is yet to come.'

'We don't get that cold snap down south in the last of the winter months,' Miles said.

'We will have more snow before the season is out,' the Soldier said, raising a hand at Norman. 'Morning, Norman. What have you for us?'

'Morning, sir,' Norman said, running his hand down the nose of a horse. 'Two of the finest horses.'

The Soldier walked around the horses with a critical eye. 'Very fine horses, Norman. They have names?'

'Raven and Nina,' Norman said. 'Nina, the smaller, is the easier to ride.'

'How are the mare and the foal doing?' Miles said. 'I would like to see them.'

'Certainly,' Norman said, removing his cap. 'Follow me.'

Miles followed Norman through the doors and down the corridor to the centre of the stable, where he opened the top half of the stable door.

Miles scanned the box. 'The mare is here. Where is the foal?'

Norman opened the bottom half of the door and moved the mare to one side. On the back wall sat a latch, which Norman undid before swinging open a secret door. The foal, with his large, brown eyes, peered out of the hidden stable. 'He is safe in here, sir,' Norman said. 'I take him for a walk along the stables twice a day.'

'You built this just for him?' Miles said.

Norman chuckled. 'Ask no questions, sir. Just know he is safe.'

'And two gold coins for you when we return, Norman,' the Soldier said, slapping Miles on the back.

The smile on Norman's face stretched from ear to ear.

'Let's move, son,' the Soldier said. 'We shall see you soon, Norman.'

Norman placed his cap back on his head and put his hand on his breast. 'Safe travels, sir.'

The Soldier led Miles out of the stable to the two black horses. 'Come on, son,' the Soldier said, lifting himself up onto Raven's back.

Miles placed the wrong hand on the saddle and the wrong foot in the stirrup.

'You haven't ridden before?' the Soldier said, his eyebrow shooting up.

Miles shook his head.

The Soldier filled his cheeks with air and blew out a long breath. 'Let's make it three days to get to Battleacre,' he said, climbing off Raven and walking around Nina. 'Stand on the left side of the horse. Place your left hand on the saddle and your left foot in the stirrup.'

Miles bounced on his right foot, then sprang onto the horse's back.

'I see the boot is helping your foot,' the Soldier said. 'Now don't pull the reins, it will hurt her mouth. Just let her follow Raven.'

Miles sat on top of Nina with white knuckles gripping the reins. The Soldier clicked at Raven and moved into a slow walk away from the farm. Nina trotted forward until she walked alongside Raven.

'Feel the way the horse moves and move with her,' the Soldier said. 'We will walk for most of today so you get used to it.'

Miles looked straight ahead with a face set in concentration. After a few hours, he lifted his head and relaxed. The horse farms disappeared behind them and in front lay long rolling hills. Every mile, the path changed from a light blanket of black snow to white snow, then to dry cobbles.

'There is no cover out here,' Miles said, placing a hand on his brow.

'There are small rivers that run south from the great river under the City of Lynn,' the Soldier said. 'We will turn north to the barracks tomorrow morning.'

Miles settled into Nina's rolling movements. He lifted his head higher and sucked in deep breaths of clear, fresh air. The black snow's toxic smells faded as they moved south but hit their noses hard as they moved back into the north.

'There is the first river,' the Soldier said, pointing down the hill. 'We cross that and continue to the second river where we will camp.'

'I can see campfire smoke,' Miles said.

The Soldier slowed their walk to a crawl as they reached the bottom of the hill. In front of them, a low stone bridge spanned across the river. At the entrance to the stone bridge, a small group of travellers camped off the side of the path.

'Trouble?' Miles said.

The Soldier raised his hand and waved his finger to call for quiet.

As they walked past the camp, Miles frowned at a group of black people who, dressed in rags, sat around a fireplace. A man dressed in fine colourful clothes stepped out of the largest tent and barked an order at the people. The black people scrambled away from the fire and began packing the camp. The man looked down his nose at Miles and the Soldier with a sneer.

The Soldier looked at the man through his eyebrows then turned his head forward as Raven and Nina's hooves clacked across the stone bridge.

'Who were those people?' Miles said, as they exited the bridge.

'Slaves from the west.'

Miles stared at the Soldier. 'I thought they had abolished slavery. A friend of mine in the south told me her parents have returned to the west.'

'They abolished it, but they need slaves because of the wars in the north.'

Miles thought of Chloe and bit his bottom lip. 'I need to get a message to my friend.'

'Only way to do that is through the City of Lynn,' the Soldier said. 'Sending people from the east to the south will just attract vampires and the undead to the south.'

Miles lowered his head and closed his eyes. 'As soon as we get to Battleacre, we need to send a message.'

'I will see to it,' the Soldier said.

They continued east until the light faded and the wind from the north picked up. The wind brought a chill from the snow-covered hills. 'We need to pick up the pace,' the Soldier said. 'We have no chance out here in the open.'

Miles bounced in the saddle as the Soldier picked up the pace. Just like the Soldier, he moved his head from left to right, searching for any movement on the horizon.

A few minutes later, Miles pointed. 'Wolves, on the ridge.'

'Keep close. We don't want these horses to bolt,' the Soldier said.

Miles kept Nina's head close to the Soldier's knee to keep her alongside Raven. A long howl broke through the northern wind. Miles scanned the undulating hills until he found a second line of wolves standing on the hills to the south.

'Do you think your wolf is with them?' the Soldier said.

'No, she isn't close,' Miles said, running his hand down his thigh.

'Hold on, son,' the Soldier said, standing up in his saddle. 'The second river is up ahead.'

The horses picking up the wolves' scent from the north flicked their heads and their tails. Raven let out a nervous whicker, which made Nina roll her eyes. The Soldier spurred the horses into a canter and Miles, bouncing in his saddle, held on with all his might. Ahead, the bridge's white stone pillars rose into the sky.

'Where do we camp?' Miles said, trying to catch breath as Nina knocked it out of him.

'Other side of the bridge,' the Soldier said, slowing Raven before the bridge. The sound of the horse's hooves changed as they entered the bridge. Up ahead, the flickering of fires lit up a well-organised campsite that contained three circles. A high-fenced inner circle housed the traveller's horses. The travellers filled the middle circle with fires. In the outside circle, the campers stored their carts, protecting the travellers from the darkness.

The Soldier brought Raven to a stop and hopped off. Miles lifted his leg, slid off his horse, and collapsed onto the ground.

'Hold on, son,' the Soldier said, moving around Nina and offering a hand.

Miles struggled to his feet. 'Right foot gave way. The boot works but stops the blood sometimes.'

'Settle over there at that empty fire,' the Soldier said, before ushering Raven and Nina into the fenced circle. Once he had stowed the horses in the inner circle, the Soldier walked up to a pile of firewood where he picked up an armful and brought it to the fire.

Miles lowered himself onto a broad log.

With a flint, the Soldier started the fire then nursed it until the flames darted up into the sky.

Miles scanned the fire pits surrounding the fenced-off horses. At each fire, at least one person kept watch.

'We always have one person awake,' the Soldier said, seeing where Miles was looking. 'If there is any trouble, we band together. It is the traveller's rule.'

Miles removed his greatsword and laid it on the log next to him. He opened up his pack and pulled out dried meats and a metal canister of water. They both sat in silence, eating and listening.

'Are you going to take that boot off?' the Soldier said, ripping up a piece of dried meat before placing some into his mouth.

Miles shook his head. 'The blood has returned and, if something happens, I won't have time to put the boot back on.'

The Soldier slipped off his log, crossed his arms, closed his eyes, and said, 'Wake me after two hours, son.'

Two hours passed, and Miles nudged the Soldier signalling a change of shift. Miles slipped down the side of the log and closed his eyes. In what felt like a moment later, the Soldier's boot nudged his side. Miles rubbed his eyes with the heels of his hands, then sat up as the Soldier slid down from the log and immediately fell back to sleep.

An hour passed with Miles staring at the crackling fire.

'Miles,' a voice whispered from the darkness.

'Who is there?' Miles said, rubbing his eyes.

'Miles,' the voice said again.

Miles got to his feet and took a step away from the fire. To his right and left, the lookouts at each fire pit saw Miles scan the darkness, and so they stood and drew their weapons.

'What is it?' a man said from the fire next to them.

Miles held up his hand, calling for quiet.

'What is it, son?' the Soldier said into his ear.

'Someone calling my name,' Miles said.

The Soldier dropped onto his haunches and scanned the darkness.

'Miles,' the voice whispered.

The Soldier stood up sharply and placed a hand on Miles's shoulder. 'Vampires. They are playing with you.'

'It sounds like Janie,' Miles said.

The Soldier squeezed his shoulder. 'It is her, and she is playing tricks on you. Don't respond.' Miles tried to take a step forward, but the Soldier dragged him back. 'You are not going out there. We stay here and stick together.'

Miles shrugged the hand off his shoulder and peered into the darkness.

'They are reminding you they want you to give them your wolf,' the Soldier said.

'She is out there. I can feel it,' Miles said, stepping back to the fire pit.

'Sit and get some rest. I will take the watch for the rest of the night.'

'Why don't they attack?' Miles said.

'Fire is their biggest enemy,' the Soldier said. 'It's why we have set out the camp like this. It gives us everything we need to defend ourselves.'

Miles slid off the rock and curled up next to the fire, but his eyes stayed open. With every sound, Miles turned his head to figure out what it was.

The hours dragged by until the Soldier tapped Miles with the toe of his boot. 'I will get the horses. We saddle up and get going immediately.'

Miles sat up and dragged a hand through his hair.

'How did you sleep?' the Soldier said.

Miles shook his head. 'Not very well.'

The Soldier walked over to the horse pen and returned with Raven and Nina. Once they strapped the saddles on, the Soldier stood next to Nina and cupped his hands to give Miles a leg-up. Miles gripped the saddle and hauled himself onto the horse. The Soldier led them to the crossroads and turned north up the cobblestone path. After some time, Miles slouched in his saddle and closed his eyes.

'Hand me the reins,' the Soldier said from in front of him.

'I am fine,' Miles said, his head snapping up.

'Hand me the reins and try to get some rest,' the Soldier said, extending his hand behind him.

Miles threw the reins into the Soldier's outstretched hand. Then Miles crossed his arms and let his chin drop onto his chest. The steady clank of Nina's hooves on the cobbles sent Miles into a fitful sleep.

'Food time,' the Soldier said, bringing them to a halt alongside the river.

'How far have we come?'

'Not far enough to reach the barracks today,' the Soldier said. 'We are going to need to find a place to camp tonight.'

Miles straightened his back to ease the stiffness. He reached over and took the food the Soldier offered. They sat side by side, eating, while Raven and Nina continued forward. The cobbled road disappeared under a blanket of black snow. Miles pulled up his face mask to reduce the toxic smell. The chilly northern air worked its way between his clothes and made him shiver. With their meal finished, the Soldier spurred the horses on. Each hill came and went, with each looking like the last. The light faded as the sun set in the west.

The Soldier sat up in his saddle and scanned the area. 'There is not much cover. I suggest we make our way to the river and try to find something there.'

Miles turned in his saddle to scan the tops of the hills.

The Soldier, seeing Miles freeze, turned and looked in the same direction. 'Genevie,' he said.

Genevie sat on top of her own horse. A horse with two glaring red eyes. Sensing the danger, Raven and Nina stomped their feet and shook their heads.

Vampires appeared over the hill and stared unblinking, with shining red eyes.

'They know we have given up on Janie and that we are going to the barracks,' the Soldier said.

'You have given up on Janie,' Miles said.

'I didn't mean it like that, son,' the Soldier said. 'I will do everything I can to help you get her back.'

Miles gave him a single nod. 'What do we do now?'

The Soldier turned his gaze onto the top of the hill. 'There is only one thing we can do. Run and, if we have to, fight. Wrap your legs into the stirrups and hold on tight. Nina will follow Raven.'

Miles reached down and wrapped each of the stirrups around his legs.

'Ready?' the Soldier said, looking over his shoulder. 'As soon as we take off, they will come.'

'I cannot promise I can stay on this horse,' Miles said.

'Trust in Nina. Keep your head down until they get close, then use both hands for your weapon.'

Miles shook his head. 'This will not work.'

'It's time to stretch the legs of these horses,' the Soldier said, running his hand over Raven's neck then digging his heels into her side. The two horses flew forward, black snow kicking up from their hooves.

Miles lowered his head onto Nina's mane as his eyes watered with the wind whipping through his face. He looked under his armpit. 'They all have horses,' he shouted at the Soldier. Nina's big brown eyes bulged at the strain of galloping and the sound of the vampiric horses chasing her.

'You won't get far, boy,' Gerald yelled with a cackle.

Miles sat up and drew his greatsword. To his left, a vampiric horse snapped its fanged jaws at Nina's hindquarters. Miles swung his sword behind him, and the horse backed away.

A vampire horse melted into a sandy pile as the Soldier's greatsword took off its head. The vampire on the horse rolled once, sprang to his feet and continued running.

Miles looked forward and got his first glimpse of the lights of Battleacre.

'Enough playing,' Genevie said. 'Take them down and bring them both to me.'

A vampire spurred his horse forward, then jumped through the air onto Nina's back. Miles swung his greatsword over the top of the vampire's head, missing completely. The vampire sank his long fangs into Miles's forearm. With a yell, Miles let go of his greatsword and watched it clang off the cobblestone road and disappear into the night.

The vampire hissed, grabbed his throat, then fell off the back of Nina.

'Gerald, take his horse down,' Genevie said. 'Don't bite the boy if you want to live.'

The Soldier spun round in his saddle and flicked his greatsword at another vampiric horse. The horse exploded into a cloud of powder, and he watched the vampire plough into the cobblestone before turning into dust.

A vampire drew his sword and thrashed wildly, catching the Soldier on the forearm and opening a long gash.

'Can you not do any of that earth stuff?' the Soldier said, swiping his sword at the vampire.

Miles drew his dagger and jabbed it into the face of a fanged horse, who snapped his jaws back at him. 'I have no control over it.'

A vampiric horse at the back of the pulsing wave let out a terrifying scream. Behind the galloping group from over the rolling hills, streaks of fur with snapping jaws bounded towards them.

'Wolves,' Gerald said, backing his horse away.

'Stay with them,' Genevie said.

Ignoring the royal vampire, the group broke away, leaving Genevie and Gerald.

'I see you are leading a bunch of cowards,' the Soldier said, swinging his sword at Genevie.

'I thought she influenced all of them,' Miles said under his breath.

Genevie released the reins of her horse and pulled out two throwing axes. One axe whistled past the Soldier's head, but the other lodged itself in his shoulder. He grabbed the handle, pulled out the axe and threw it back at Genevie. The axe whizzed past her head and disappeared into the darkness.

'Waya,' Miles said, feeling the nerves in his back knit together. The wolf, now fully a shoulder higher than the rest of the wolves, showed her teeth as she came alongside Gerald's horse. With a snarl, she jumped onto the back of his horse and snapped her jaws inches away from Gerald's back. The horse bucked, sending Waya tumbling to the ground.

Genevie slowed her horse and looked back at the tumbling wolf. 'There she is.'

'Run, Waya,' Miles shouted over his shoulder.

Waya sprang to her feet and stood snarling and snapping at the advancing Genevie and Gerald.

'Keep moving, boy,' the Soldier said.

'We can't leave her,' Miles said.

The Soldier reached over and grabbed Nina's reins. 'She will be fine. She has her entire pack with her.'

Miles watched the vampires surround Waya. 'I can't leave her there. I can fight.'

'Open the gates,' the Soldier said, standing on his stirrups. 'Open the gates!'

'I said I can fight,' Miles said, struggling to get his legs out of the stirrups.

'Who goes there?' a man shouted from the top of the wall.

The Soldier ripped open his cloak, exposing his breastplate. 'I said, open the gates!'

With an almighty crash, the drawbridge slammed on the ground. The Soldier led the horses over the drawbridge and through the gate.

Miles slumped against Nina as the nerves in his back ripped apart. 'I said I can fight.'

CHAPTER 10
A CRACKLING FIRE

'Don't touch him,' the Soldier said, jumping off Raven and grabbing Nina's reins. 'Those vampires have injured his right leg.'

'Yes, sir,' a guard said.

The Soldier walked over to Nina and grabbed Miles by the elbow as he slid out of the saddle. 'Steady, son.'

Miles opened his mouth but closed it quickly to stop the cry of pain that stuck in his throat.

'Take these horses to my stable, please,' the Soldier said, signalling to the guard.

The guard saluted and, gathering the reins of both horses, he led them down a path along the city wall.

'How are you feeling?' the Soldier said, pulling Miles's arm over his shoulder. 'We have quite a way to go.'

'The blood is flowing again. I will be able to walk in a second.'

'Does he need a doctor, sir?' a guard said, walking up along-side them.

'A blunt object has given him a dead leg,' the Soldier said.

'Can you make haste to my villa and make sure Rafa knows we are coming?'

'Yes, sir,' the guard said, sprinting up the wide road leading into the city.

The Soldier took it slowly as they walked up the wide cobblestone road. Residents stopped and stared, then turned and whispered to each other.

'Seems like you are as famous as you say you are,' Miles said.

The Soldier chuckled. 'I am known, yes, but I feel they are looking at you more than me.'

'I think I can walk now,' Miles said, straightening up and pushing his shoulders back. 'There is no more pain in my back and I can feel the blood in my foot.'

'I am letting you go,' the Soldier said, removing Miles's arm from his shoulder. 'I will stay close so you can grab me.'

Miles lifted his head to take in the surrounding sights. His mouth hung open at the sheer size of the small city. 'I haven't seen anything this big before,' he said. 'Is that the amphitheatre at the top of this road?'

'Yes,' the Soldier said. 'Although it is a long walk from here. We are turning right in a moment to make our way into the officers district.'

Miles cast his mind back to the districts in Fairacre. He shook his head in amazement at the enormity of the district ahead of him.

The Soldier pulled Miles out of the way of an old woman. 'Careful, lad. I know there is a lot to take in but keep looking where you are going.'

Miles raised both hands. 'Sorry.'

She cackled something unintelligible as she carried on down the road.

At the crossroads, the Soldier turned right and began the long walk up the winding road into the officers district. Miles cast his eyes over the long driveways leading to large houses deep within each property. Large iron gates sat in front of each driveway and on the gate was the resident family's crest. The road turned up a steep incline, then flattened out as an extensive park came into view. In the middle of the park sat a children's play area of slides, swings and climbing frames.

'We cross over the park to the road and continue up,' the Soldier said. 'How is your leg holding up?'

Miles wiped the sweat beading over his forehead. 'It doesn't hurt that much. I just get tired quickly.'

'We are not far,' the Soldier said, walking into the park.

'It's quiet,' Miles said.

'Yes,' the Soldier said with a touch of sadness in his voice. 'They have taken most of our women and most of the officers are in the war. This park used to be filled with the laughter of children.'

Miles said nothing as they crossed over the park. The Soldier's sombreness reminded Miles of the Fairacre men's loss when their own children went missing. They stepped back onto the road and continued walking up a smaller meandering path. At the top, the Soldier stopped at an iron gate. The latch came away easily, and the gate, on well-oiled hinges, swung open without a sound. The path turned dark as the trees' branches overhung it, forming a tunnel. At the end of the path, a wide set of steps led up to the front door of a double-storey house. At the top of the steps, a man dressed in formal trousers and a blazer waited patiently at the front door.

'Welcome back, sir,' he said with a small bow.

'Good evening, Rafa,' the Soldier said, placing a hand on the man's shoulder. 'Please, can you make up a suite for young Miles here?'

Rafa opened the right door of the double doors and waited for the Soldier and Miles to walk into the entrance hall. He gently closed the front door. 'It is good to have you back, sir, and it is a pleasure to meet you, Miles. What suit shall I make up for the young man, sir?'

'As we have no visitors, I will leave it up to you.'

Rafa gave a quick bow before walking up the staircase and entering the furthest door on the landing.

'Follow me,' the Soldier said, walking to a large wooden door. 'We can relax here while Rafa gets your room sorted out.'

Miles followed the Soldier through the door and into a room where two single deep-set chairs sat facing a crackling fireplace.

'Sit, and get that boot off, son. Let the blood flow freely.'

Miles sat and pulled open the boot's three buckles. As he slipped the boot off, he winced as his right foot turned inwards.

'Are you in pain?' the Soldier said, lowering himself into the opposite chair.

Miles shook his head. 'It throbs but the well-made boot helps with the pain.'

The Soldier laced his fingers behind his head. 'I think we made it here without too much of a commotion.'

'Am I that much of a burden?' Miles said.

'I apologise,' the Soldier said. 'To me, you are not a burden and I didn't wish it to come across that way. To the city of Battleacre, though, you are a burden.'

Miles peered into the fireplace for a few moments then, turning to the Soldier, he said, 'What is happening in the north? I have heard of this war, but nobody has told me what it's about.'

The Soldier untangled his fingers and leant forward. 'You do not know?'

Miles shook his head. 'The south is pretty isolated.'

With a long sigh, the Soldier sat back and said, 'They swarm, son. They devour everything that gets in their way.'

'What are they?' Miles said.

'We don't know. And I haven't seen one close by. They form a dark cloud with the amount of them.'

The chair Miles sat on creaked as he leant back. He looked into the fireplace and watched the flames dance over the logs.

'Our machines keep them at bay for now, but I don't think that will be forever.'

'Why are the women being taken?' Miles said.

The Soldier spat into the fire. 'I thought it was the vampires taking them for themselves. But you have told me it's the City of Lynn. I will send a messenger tomorrow to find out if this is true.'

'You haven't any idea then?'

'I don't. Sorry, lad,' the Soldier said.

The door of the room swung open. 'Your room is ready, sir,' Rafa said.

'Thank you, Rafa. I assume not much food is ready because of my unexpected return?'

Rafa bowed. 'The chef is on his way, sir.'

The Soldier slapped his hand on the armrest. 'Always one step ahead of me, Rafa. Tell me, who else is home?'

'Your daughter is visiting a friend, sir. Your son, I have not seen for several days.'

The Soldier slumped into his chair. 'Are you sure he hasn't been home?'

'His bed has also been untouched, sir.'

'Thank you, Rafa.'

'Yes, sir. I shall return when your meals are ready.'

'Oh, and Rafa, I do not want any gossip about my guest. He is a gentleman in my household from now on.'

Rafa smiled at Miles. 'Yes, sir,' he said, then closed the double doors.

'Very formal,' Miles said.

Sadness stretched across the Soldier's face. 'My wife helped raise Rafa after his parents left for the west. She was the one for formalities.'

'I am sorry about your wife,' Miles said.

The Soldier waved his hand. 'She passed many seasons ago.'

Miles brought his right foot up onto the couch and turned it outwards while massaging the arch.

The Soldier leant forward and placed his elbows on his knees. 'So do you think you can fight wearing that boot?'

Miles closed his eyes but continued to massage his foot.

The chair creaked as the Soldier sat back and interlaced his fingers behind his head.

'I can fight,' Miles whispered. 'I need to practise though.'

'You are in Battleacre, son. Where else in the world would you want to practise?'

Miles opened his eyes and grinned.

'I feel that something is distracting you though,' the Soldier said. 'What is on your mind?'

'Waya and Janie,' Miles said.

The Soldier chuckled. 'A wolf and a vampire. Mortal enemies. You will have to pick one, you know.'

Miles dropped his club foot, stood, and walked over to the fireplace. 'I cannot choose either.'

'You need to tell me more about this wolf,' the Soldier said.

'I am worried about her,' Miles said.

'She had her pack with her, and a wolf bite is certain death for a vampire. She will be OK.'

'I think I would have felt it if something had happened to her,' Miles said. 'I am more worried about her being hunted.'

The Soldier rocked in his chair. 'How would you know? Is it to do with that mark on your back?'

'It is, but it is different to what happened to Juno and her elemental animal.'

With a wave of his hand, the Soldier said. 'I have welcomed you into my home. Care to fill me in on this story?'

After a few minutes of silence, Miles cleared his throat. 'I am linked to the wolf. She is the earth element and I have the earth element mark on me. It is different to Juno and Chax though.'

'Juno and Chax?' the Soldier said.

'Juno is the vessel for the fire elemental. Chax is the fire elemental. The elements are too powerful for one vessel, so it needs two to survive. A person and an animal.'

'And why are you and Waya different?'

Miles scratched the side of his face. 'Juno and Chax wanted to be near each other. Chax would heal Juno if she got injured.'

The Soldier waited for Miles to continue.

'Waya fixes me when she is nearby, but when she leaves, the healing disappears. With Waya and me, the connection isn't there like Juno and Chax.'

'You have had little time to bond with her. And she seems to pop up when you need her.'

Miles bit his bottom lip. 'That is true.'

'Did you not speak to Juno about how it worked with her and Chax?'

'I helped in building the connection between the two of them. It involved getting Juno to dig deep to find her inner lioness to release it,' Miles said.

'And you cannot find your inner wolf?' the Soldier said, with a smirk of amusement.

'I do not know where to look,' Miles said with a shrug.

A knock sounded at the door.

'Yes,' the Soldier said.

Rafa pulled open the door and walked in with two bowls of

pasta on a silver tray. He cleared the side tables of the glasses and placed the bowls on them.

A hint of chilli tickled Miles's nose as he twirled the pasta onto a fork and fed it into his mouth. 'This is great,' he said, slurping on the long pasta strands.

'I suggest we finish our dinner and then get some rest,' the Soldier said. 'There is a lot we have to do tomorrow.'

Miles raised an eyebrow.

'Heather and Jon,' the Soldier said. 'We need to send help, remember?'

'Ah, yes,' Miles said, with another mouthful of food.

'Father,' a woman shouted from further inside the house.

'My daughter,' the Soldier said, his face lighting up.

'Where are you, Father?' the woman shouted.

'In the study,' the Soldier bellowed.

The door slammed open and a tall regal woman stepped into the study.

The fork in Miles's hand fell to the bowl with a loud clatter.

'What is it, boy?' the Soldier said, leaning forward and grabbing the bowl of pasta. 'It looks like you have seen a ghost.'

Miles looked wide-eyed at Raquel.

'Well?' Raquel said, tilting her head to one side and crinkling her forehead. 'Are you going to answer my father?'

Miles regarded the Soldier then Raquel. 'It cannot be.'

'What cannot be?' the Soldier said, with irritation in his voice. 'Talk, boy!'

'I am not feeling well,' Miles said.

'Catch him, Father,' Raquel said. 'He is going to fall on his face.'

. . .

Miles jerked awake. With the back of his hand, he wiped the sweat from his forehead. A quick scan of the room revealed luxury he had never seen before. Dressers and wardrobes made from a dark wood stood against the walls. Gold-framed pictures showing battle scenes covered all four walls. Miles scooted to the end of the bed and placed his club foot on the floor. With his elbows on his knees, he dropped his face into his hands where he used the heels to wipe sleep out of his eyes. With a shove, he left the bed and hobbled over to the bay window where rain drops pattered the glass. The sky flashed a blinding white as lightning streaked across the dark-black clouds.

A knock on the door spun Miles around. 'Who is it?' he said.

'It is Rafa, sir. Here is a change of clothes.'

Miles walked over to the bed and pulled the wool blanket around himself. 'You can come in.'

Rafa entered the room with clothes draped over his arm. He walked to the end of the bed and placed them on the chest.

'What happened last night?' Miles said.

Rafa brushed the creases out of the crisp white shirt. 'You passed out, sir. It was a long day.'

Miles studied Rafa's black face and thought of Chloe. His thoughts then wandered to the slaves on the side of the road.

'The General and his daughter are downstairs at breakfast, sir. Will you be joining them?'

'His daughter,' Miles said under his breath. 'Raquel.'

'Yes, sir,' Rafa said, tilting his head. 'You fainted when she walked into the room.'

'The Lady,' Miles whispered.

'I beg your pardon, sir?'

Miles rubbed his face. 'It is nothing, Rafa. She just reminds me of someone I once knew.'

Rafa smiled. 'The woman you knew must be an exceptional woman then, sir.'

'Did the Soldier's wife look the same as Raquel?'

'The Soldier?' Rafa said.

'I am sorry. The General. Did his wife look the same as his daughter?'

'There are pictures in the study, sir,' Rafa said. 'You can look for yourself on the way to breakfast.'

'Thank you, Rafa.'

The door closed behind Rafa with a soft click.

After a hot shower, Miles dressed in the soft cotton trousers and the crisp white button-up shirt. He laced up the newly oiled left boot, then struggled into the right boot. His right foot turned slowly outwards as the buckle of each strap took hold. Miles left the room and walked down the stairs to the study door. He held his breath as he turned the handle.

'We are in the kitchen, son,' the Soldier said.

Miles let go of the door handle and, closing his eyes, he let out his breath.

'Come and join us,' Raquel said.

Miles walked through the kitchen door and stopped at the sight of her.

'Are you feeling better?' Raquel said.

'Um, yes,' Miles said, scratching his chin. 'It was a long day.'

'It looked like you saw a ghost,' Raquel said, sitting back and folding her arms.

'I am sorry,' Miles said. 'I was telling Rafa you remind me of someone back in the south.'

'My father has been filling me in on the journey you two have been following,' Raquel said. 'And here I thought my father was in the City of Lynn.'

'I couldn't tell you, love,' the Soldier said. 'Word would have got out to the vampires.'

'Your breakfast, sir,' Rafa said, sliding a plate in front of Miles.

Miles looked up at Rafa and grinned. 'Thank you. This looks amazing.'

'My father tells me it is the City of Lynn stealing the women,' Raquel said, tapping an index finger on her forearm.

'Yes,' Miles said, with a mouthful of food. 'We don't know why they are taking them though.'

'I have sent messengers to the City,' the Soldier said.

'I am surprised you didn't know about this, Papa,' Raquel said, frowning at her father.

'If I had known, I wouldn't have gone to some inn out east, now would I?' the Soldier said, throwing his hands up in the air. 'I have not heard of the City kidnapping women.'

'Dr Viktor, my father, said it has something to do with the war.'

'Why would they need women for the war?' Raquel said, spreading her hands.

Miles shrugged. 'What other reason would there be?'

Raquel filled her cheeks and sighed.

'Let's wait for the messengers to return,' the Soldier said.

Everyone remained silent as they watched Rafa remove the cutlery from the breakfast table.

'I am not finished talking about your journey, Father,' Raquel said. 'And we haven't even started on you,' she said, leaning forward and narrowing her eyes at Miles. 'A wolf? Earth elements? Is this some kind of joke?'

'Raquel,' the Soldier said. 'I've seen the elemental wolf myself. You saw the brown marks all over his back. Stop pressing the poor man.'

As Raquel sat back, Miles released the white-knuckled grip he had on the chair's armrests. Each time Raquel moved in close, all he could see were the eyes of the Lady turning black and the swing of her sword before it sank into his back.

'You are scaring the boy,' the Soldier said with a smirk.

Raquel folded her arms and continued tapping a bicep with an index finger.

'Marks?' Miles said, clearing his throat. 'There is more than one?'

All three nodded. 'Multiple marks, sir,' Rafa said. 'Brown and in the shape of tree roots. They spread out from the base of your back.'

Miles instinctively looked over his shoulder.

Raquel huffed and shook her head. 'Silly boy.'

'I think we should continue this later,' the Soldier said, rising. 'It is morning and I am going to show this young man the city.'

'Do not forget your gift, sir,' Rafa said.

'Oh yes,' the Soldier said, slapping his thigh.

'What gift?' Raquel said, rising and placing her hands on her hips.

'Miles lost his weapon in our escape. I wish to replace it for him if that's OK with you?' the Soldier said, raising an eyebrow.

Raquel turned to Miles. 'We haven't finished our conversation. I want to know everything before I go and sit at the council table.'

Miles bowed his head but kept quiet for fear the quaver in his voice would give him away.

'Can you stop hounding the boy and lead the way, daughter?' the Soldier said.

A gentle smile stretched across Raquel's face. She leant over and grabbed Miles's hand, then marched him out of the kitchen, past the study and down a long corridor to a set of double doors. With a swift kick, Raquel banged the door open and pulled Miles into a large padded room with a high ceiling. Along three walls lay weapons of all shapes and sizes. Miles stood very still with wide eyes and his mouth hanging open. Raquel walked up to the wall at the back of the room and stood next to the rack where the Soldier's greatsword stood. She reached behind the Soldier's greatsword and pulled out an identical sword, which she presented to Miles.

Miles gaped at her, then over at the Soldier.

'Take it, son,' the Soldier said with a wide grin.

'But this is your sword,' Miles said, tentatively placing his hand on the hilt.

'A sword fit for a man who has protected my father,' Raquel said. 'It is the twin of my father's greatsword. Only a family member can present this sword to another.'

'Why do you not take it then?' Miles said to Raquel. 'Or your son?' he said, looking at the Soldier.

Raquel chuckled. 'I prefer wielding the pen rather than the sword, and my brother has never been one for fighting.'

Miles ran his finger along the shining blade. He took a step back and tested the weight and balance. 'It is much lighter than what I am used to.'

'Forged in the same place we make the machines in the City of Lynn,' the Soldier said.

Miles placed both hands on the hilt and twirled the sword in a figure of eight. The wind whistled as the blade cut through it.

Raquel reached behind the Soldier's greatsword and retrieved a scabbard. 'I have an idea,' she said, walking over to Miles. 'Give me the sword and I will return it to you by day's end.'

Miles slipped the sword into the scabbard and stared after Raquel as she disappeared out of the training room.

The Soldier chuckled. 'Heed my warning, young man. My advice is to stay away from her. She has her mother's temperament.'

Miles closed his eyes and shook his head.

'I am sorry,' the Soldier said. 'That was insensitive of me. I know you care for this vampire girl.'

Miles gave the Soldier a thin-lipped smile. 'Can we get that message to my father?'

'I will send messengers today. They will need to go through the City of Lynn to get to the south. It could take some time as they will have to go as traders.'

'Thank you,' Miles said.

'Sir, you have a visitor,' Rafa said from the training-room door.

'Not one day's rest,' the Soldier said to Rafa. 'Let me deal with this, then we can take a walk to the games.'

A smile broke across Miles's face. 'The games are on today?'

The Soldier slapped his thigh and belly laughed. 'They are on every day, son.'

'I have repaired and cleaned your cloak, sir,' Rafa said, looking at Miles. 'It is in your room.'

'Thank you, Rafa,' Miles said, walking out of the training room. 'That cloak is my brother's. I miss him dearly.'

'I hope the job is to your satisfaction,' Rafa said.

Miles walked up the stairs and into his room. The cloak lay neatly over the chest at the end of his bed. He picked up the cloak and wrapped it around himself. The familiar hood and mask surrounded his face. He left his bedroom, walked down the stairs, and waited in the large foyer.

'Are you sure it was him?' the Soldier said from inside the study.

'Yes, sir,' a man said.

'Keep me informed,' the Soldier said. 'Rafa, please see these gentlemen out.'

Two men wearing dark, clean-cut uniforms walked out of the study, nodded at Miles, and walked out of the front door Rafa held open.

The Soldier, with a beetroot-red face, followed them out of the study. 'My son has been enjoying the company of top officials' daughters.'

'I thought you said he was a vampire?' Miles said.

'I don't know if he is or isn't,' the Soldier said. 'He needs to answer for not sending help to the horse farms.'

Miles clasped his hands behind his back and waited for the Soldier to calm down.

'Any reason for the face mask?' the Soldier said, his voice now measured and calm.

'I cannot promise that people will not see my disability. I cannot completely hide it, but I can hide my face,' Miles said. 'If there is no face, then nobody knows who I am.'

'I see your logic, but I do not think you should hide. You are my guest.'

Miles waited a moment then unclipped the mask.

'Let's go,' the Soldier said, walking out of the enormous doors and down to the front gate. The two of them retraced the steps they had taken the day before. After walking through the park and down the winding road, they reached the crossroads and turned north. The huge amphitheatre stood up ahead. Unlike Fairacre's narrow streets, Battleacre's roads were double lanes and filled with carts, horses, children and gossiping groups of people. Small dogs roamed around looking for scraps of food, and cats hissed and darted into rubbish bins in the alleys.

As they continued up the long road towards the amphitheatre, Miles heard the clashes of steel followed by cheers and hollers from the crowds.

'It is huge,' Miles said as the road widened into a large square. 'Is that the entrance?'

'We have eight entrances,' the Soldier said. 'This is the southern one.'

Miles followed the Soldier through the entrance and onto a circular walkway.

'We have a lot of floors to cover,' the Soldier said. 'Are you going to manage?'

'Yes,' Miles said, his eyes filling with amazement.

Round and round they went until the circle flattened out. Walking through the archway, Miles gasped at the sights laid out in front of him.

CHAPTER 11
THE HAMMER

'Are you OK, son?' the Soldier said with a smirk on his face.

Miles gripped the Soldier's forearm to steady himself before casting his sight to the amphitheatre. The circle at the bottom of the arena, covered in light soil, was being raked by four people. The colours they wore, red, yellow, brown and blue, matched the flags running along the top of each wall that split the arena into quadrants.

With effort, Miles tore his eyes away from the arena and gazed at the rows of seated spectators who sat talking, eating and placing the occasional bet. Traders walked up and down the aisles, hollering the prices of the food and drinks they carried on their trays.

'Over here, son,' the Soldier said, sitting on a high-backed chair and pointing to the chair on his left. 'This is Raquel's chair, but she isn't here.'

Miles walked along a platform and slid onto the chair that the Soldier had pointed to.

On the right of the Soldier sat two empty chairs. Four chairs for a family of four. A hint of sadness flickered across the Soldier's face as he rested his hand on the arm of the chair next to him.

'Who usually sits there?' Miles said, flicking his head at the larger high-backed chairs that sat behind them.

'Battleacre's mayor and family,' the Soldier said with a hint of annoyance.

Miles opened his mouth then closed it again, thinking better of it.

'Lean in, son, so I can walk you through what happens in the games.'

Miles pulled himself to the side of the chair and bent his head so he could hear everything the Soldier said.

'Who's your friend, General?' a man shouted two rows below them.

The Soldier lifted an eyebrow at the gentleman sitting below him.

The man showed a palm. 'Not looking for trouble, sir.'

'He is a guest of my house. That is all you need to know,' the Soldier said, his brow lowering.

The people around the General fell into hushed whispers as the man who asked shrunk into his seat.

'Who was that?' Miles said.

'A councillor's son,' the Soldier said with a look of disdain. 'They always seem to have a lot to say.'

Miles jumped as horns blasted across the amphitheatre.

The crowd screamed, cheered and clapped with fists pumping into the air. Above their heads, strips of coloured material twirled.

The Soldier leant over to Miles. 'And so it begins.'

A grin spread across Miles's face as he leant forward and craned his neck to see every inch of the arena.

Wrought-iron gates clacked open and four men wearing brown shorts, sandals and a helmet walked into the arena. On top of their helmets, a plume of their quadrant's colour fluttered in the wind. They walked up to the wall in their quadrant and faced the centre of the arena.

'No armour?' Miles said to the Soldier.

'The trial gives each combatant equal opportunity. Armour will give the combatants an edge.'

'What of the colours?' Miles said.

'Colours of the elements, son,' the Soldier said. 'Red being fire, blue being water, yellow being wind.'

'And brown being earth,' Miles said, his hand squeezing his thigh.

The Soldier placed a hand on Miles's shoulder. 'Forget about all of that and let's enjoy the games.'

Miles's smile returned.

Below them, on the ring of the arena, the gamekeeper lifted his hands, calling for quiet. Within a few seconds, the crowd's roar reduced to a whisper. The gamekeeper read out the combatants' names before placing his lips against the oversized alphorn and, with one deep breath, blasted a booming note that bounced through the amphitheatre. The pent-up electricity in the crowd burst and Miles placed his hands on his ears at the reverberating roar.

'Heard nothing like it, son?' the Soldier said, chuckling.

Miles shook his head. 'My ears are ringing.'

The Soldier slapped his knee and roared with laughter.

'What happens now?' Miles said. 'They have no weapons.'

'Listen carefully, son,' the Soldier said. 'As I said before, can you see the five panels in the walls of each quadrant?'

'Four panels next to each other in a row, and a fifth panel above the four panels,' Miles said.

'Yes. Each panel contains a weapon. The four panels at the

bottom contain a random weapon. The fifth panel contains the participant's preferred weapon.'

'Why not give them their preferred weapons in the beginning?' Miles said.

'To be selected for the Queen's Guard, one must fight with every weapon you get.'

'Does the winner of each bout go to the Queen's Guard?' Miles said.

The first panel of each quadrant slammed open. Each combatant reached in and pulled out their first random weapon.

'The winner of today's games goes to the City of Lynn,' the Soldier said. 'There they take part in the trials to become a guard for the Queen.'

'So whoever wins this contest must fight the winners of the other contests?' Miles said.

The Soldier held up his hand and ticked off fingers. 'Process of elimination, my boy. The contest runs the whole day.'

With an almighty crash, the combatants met each other in the middle of the arena. The crowd roared while shaking their fists into the air.

'The object of this round is to remain in the game,' the Soldier said. 'If they disarm you, you must go to your quadrant and retrieve the next random weapon.'

'Can you not wait in your quadrant and let the others fight it out?' Miles said. 'Then they wouldn't have disarmed you.'

'That is dishonourable,' the Soldier said. 'And the other three combatants would round on you and take you out.'

Miles bit his bottom lip. 'I am assuming you're eliminated if they disarm you of all four random weapons?'

'Yes,' the Soldier said, slapping Miles on the back. 'Once two have left the arena, the remaining two get to open the fifth panel for their preferred weapon.'

'If they were smart, they would get rid of the big man,' Miles said, squinting at the four fighters.

'My thoughts exactly,' the Soldier said, his eyes narrowing as he scrutinised the combatants.

A moment later and the first random weapon went flying. A game watcher ran in and retrieved the weapon from the arena floor. The disarmed man ran to his quadrant and slammed his fist against the panel. He reached into the hole, retrieved the weapon, cursed at it, then ran into the fray.

'With that colourful language, I don't think he liked that weapon,' Miles said.

The Soldier's forehead crinkled in surprise. 'You heard him?'

'Yes,' Miles said. 'You didn't?'

'I didn't,' the Soldier said, leaning in closer and lowering his voice. 'Keep that little trick to yourself. You don't know who could be listening in.'

Miles inclined his head, then locked his eyes back into the games.

The big man thrashed his club in a wide arc, which the first man ducked. The club crunched into the second man's head, sending him flying to the dirt.

'What happens now?' Miles said, pointing at the lifeless body.

'He still has his weapon,' the Soldier said. 'If he gets up with it, he can continue. But he must get up before they disarm the next man.'

'So the other fighters just leave him there?' Miles said.

The Soldier shrugged. 'Nobody said it would be safe, lad.'

A minute later, a disarmed weapon slammed into the ground. The gamekeepers ran in and retrieved the discarded weapon and the lifeless man.

'Now there are three,' the Soldier said.

A shorter, stockier man ran to his quadrant, punched open the last panel, and retrieved his weapon. He looked down in disgust at a wooden ball on a chain.

'He is not best pleased either,' Miles said.

'Hardly anyone likes what they get out of the random panels,' the Soldier said, resting his elbows on his knees. 'He will do well to let the other two fight it out.'

As if the other two heard the Soldier, they ignored each other and advanced on the man with the ball and chain. With a look to the heavens, the combatant threw the ball and chain to the ground and stalked out of the arena.

The Soldier roared with laughter. 'Queen's Guard material, he is not.'

'Saving his own skin,' Miles said, shaking his head. 'Such little honour.'

'Aye, lad,' the Soldier said, slapping Miles on the back.

The two remaining combatants ran to their quadrants and slammed open the fifth panel.

With a smirk, the large man threw a two-sided battleaxe into the air and caught it expertly by the handle. The smaller man slipped on a shield and slammed his short sword against it.

'Fancy a wager, my boy?' the Soldier said.

Miles pulled a copper from his coin purse and signalled to a bookie. 'One copper on the man with the short sword and shield.'

The bookie grabbed the coin and handed Miles a coupon.

The Soldier slapped his knee. 'You have been paying attention.'

Miles grinned. He leant forward and watched the men circle each other. 'The big man is quick for his size.'

'But relying on brute strength,' the Soldier said. 'And they have been fighting for a time. I feel he will tire.'

With a smash, they engaged. Back and forth they went, trading blows until the man's sword flew through the air. The crowd roared and cheered.

'Looks like we got this one wrong,' Miles said, shaking his head.

The Soldier chuckled. 'His shield, not his sword, is his preferred weapon, lad. Not one swing of that axe has got anywhere near that man.'

The smaller man ducked and dodged the axe's wide swings until the larger man slowed with tiredness. With his shield blocking a swing of the axe, the smaller man sent a punch into the larger man's jaw. The larger man took a step back, shook his head, and spat blood into the dirt. A bloodied sneer stretched across his face.

'Overconfident,' the Soldier said. 'This will be over soon.'

The larger man charged and swung his axe over his head and down at the smaller man. His opponent stepped into the larger man's inner circle and slammed the edge of his shield into his jaw. Dust puffed up from the arena floor as the man hit the dirt. The gamekeeper blasted a victory note into the alphorn.

'I knew it,' the Soldier said, sitting back in his chair and lacing his fingers behind his head. 'Well done on your wager, my boy.'

Miles handed the coupon to the bookie, who checked the ticket and handed over two copper coins.

The gamekeepers rushed into the arena and closed the panels. Behind the arena walls, new weapons were banged into the chambers, ready for the next fight. The alphorn sounded and four more men entered the arena.

'And here we go again,' the Soldier said.

'Hello, gentlemen,' Raquel said from behind Miles. 'I see you have taken my seat.'

Miles stood. 'I am sorry.'

Raquel placed a hand on Miles's shoulder. 'Sit, I will use my brother's chair. He is hardly here anyway.'

The Soldier growled under his breath and shifted in his chair.

'I am sure he is fine, Father,' Raquel said. 'Let's enjoy the games. I am sure Miles will leave with a lot more coin.'

Throughout the rest of the day, they sat and watched the rounds of combatants. As dusk took hold, torchlight illuminated the arena, giving it a theatrical look. The amphitheatre filled all its seats as the people of Battleacre finished their workday and joined the games. As the night drew on, the winning fighters fought each other until the last four fighters remained. Miles checked his coin purse and counted an extra twelve copper pieces he had won.

'Going to bet on the last match, lad?' the Soldier said.

Miles shook his head. 'This is going to be too close to call.'

'We may have to organise him a larger coin purse, Papa,' Raquel said, leaning over her father.

The Soldier chuckled. 'Leave the poor boy alone, sweetheart.'

Raquel gave Miles a half smile, then stood and walked behind them to the mayor's area.

The alphorn blasted through the amphitheatre, and the crowd jumped to their feet with an almighty roar. The four combatants entered the arena, saluted towards the Soldier and made their way to their quadrants. With a bang, the first panel on each quadrant slammed open, signalling the start of the match. Miles watched in awe at the skill the four fighters displayed with the weapons they did not prefer. A few moments and they were down to three.

'Your fighter with the shield is still in it,' the Soldier said. 'I think that tall, thin one is more skilful though.'

Miles took in a sharp breath of air.

'What is it, son?' the Soldier said.

'Knife slinger,' Miles whispered.

The Soldier placed a hand on Miles's shoulder. 'I can't hear you, lad.'

'It's a knife slinger from the City of Lynn,' Miles said. 'I have fought one before.'

With his elbows on his knees, the Soldier narrowed his eyes, creating a frown as he studied the knife slinger.

'He will win,' Miles said. 'He is lethal.'

A thud rang through the amphitheatre as the third combatant bounced off the wall and fell face-first into the dirt. Two game-keepers sprinted out and dragged the fallen combatant through the arena doors. The doors slammed shut and the fifth panels in two quadrants crashed open. The knife slinger retrieved his long, thin sword and the second combatant grabbed his shield and short sword. With his narrow-set eyes staring down his nose, the knife slinger stood still with his sword behind his back.

'He is goading him,' the Soldier said.

The second combatant darted in and jabbed his sword at the knife slinger. With a step to the right, and a whip of his sword, the knife slinger caught the combatant across the back of the neck. In slow motion, the man fell onto his knees before slowly falling head first into the dirt. The amphitheatre went deathly quiet for a few moments before it exploded into a thunderous roar.

'I think I would like to go back now,' Miles said, gripping his right thigh.

The Soldier rose immediately and offered Miles a hand. 'Let's get going. Best beat all the traffic, anyway.'

Miles followed the Soldier out of the seated area and down the gangway.

As they left the southern entrance, the Soldier turned right towards the east. 'Who was that person? The knife slinger?' he said, glancing at Miles.

'An elite set of fighters working for the Queen,' Miles said. 'They tried to kill all of my friends.'

The Soldier laced his hands behind his back as he strode away from the amphitheatre.

Miles tripped as he tried to keep up. 'Where are we going?'

'I wish to show you something,' the Soldier said.

'Can we slow it down a bit?' Miles said.

'I am sorry, lad,' the Soldier said, turning and waiting for Miles to catch up. 'Sometimes I forget.'

With a grimace, Miles caught up and said, 'So where are you taking me?'

'Listen,' the Soldier said, as he continued walking. 'Can you hear it?'

The clang of steel being pounded and the hiss of cooling metal danced around the night air.

'The famous blacksmiths,' Miles said, his eyes widening. 'I have heard tales.'

'More famous than the City of Lynn?' the Soldier said.

Miles chuckled. 'Not sure about that.'

The Soldier chuckled. 'The blacksmiths here specialise. Most of them work on one particular style of weapon. In the City of Lynn, each blacksmith does many things.'

'Do they just create weapons?'

'The city blacksmith at the bottom of this road is where the trainee blacksmiths create everything we need for Battleacre. Once they graduate from there, we send them to a specialised weapons blacksmith.'

Miles walked along the street and stopped to peer into the open doorways. Blacksmiths waved back with soot-covered faces. Black aprons with the insignia of their chosen weapon hung from their necks. The fires cooked cauldrons of red-hot liquid steel.

'When a warrior wins the games, he comes here to have a

weapon specially made,' the Soldier said. 'The only payment we ask for is their allegiance to Battleacre. They need to protect the city at all cost.'

'You are going to make the knife slinger a weapon?' Miles said, the muscles in his jaw twitching.

'It is tradition,' the Soldier said. 'But worry not, I will have people keep an eye on him.'

'I would like to know why he is here,' Miles said, following the Soldier back into the middle of the road.

'Let's get moving,' the Soldier said. 'Rafa will have dinner waiting.'

Miles and the Soldier walked back through the blacksmith's district, past the southern entrance of the amphitheatre, and back into the officers district.

Back at the estate's gated entrance, the Soldier halted. 'Let's keep this knife slinger between you and me for now, son. I don't want anyone to tip him off that we know about him.'

'I was hoping you would say that,' Miles said, walking through the gate.

Rafa stood at the front door with his hands behind his back. His white shirt, crisp and creaseless, contrasted with his black skin. He stood tall and proud, giving him the regal look of a man whose household ran like a well-oiled machine.

The Soldier walked up the steps and handed Rafa his coin purse. 'Sorry we are late, Rafa.'

Rafa gave a small bow. 'The chef and I thought you might be, sir. Dried meats and warm bread await you.'

'Fantastic,' the Soldier said, smiling.

'How were the games, sir?'

'Young Miles here won some money,' the Soldier said,

glancing back down the stairs. 'It looks like he has a knack for choosing winners.'

Rafa inclined his head. 'Your coin purse, sir.'

Miles tilted his head at the Soldier.

'Battleacre is not the safest of places, son. Rafa will keep your valuables under lock and key,' the Soldier said.

Miles lofted his coin purse into the air, which Rafa caught.

'Time for food,' the Soldier said, walking into the study.

Miles sat on the high-backed chair, picked up a plate from the side table, and filled it with meats and buttered bread. Rafa walked in, holding two mugs of steaming coffee. Miles and the Soldier sat staring into the crackling fire while they ate. With the last of the food finished, Miles washed it down with coffee. Closing his eyes, he sunk back into the chair, and sighed at the fire's warmth.

'I am going to need you to help me tomorrow,' the Soldier said.

Miles opened an eye and frowned at the serious look on the Soldier's face. 'What do you need?'

The Soldier looked over at Miles. 'There are vampires in our city and they have been stealing our women for the City of Lynn.'

'You want me to keep an eye out for them in the city?'

'No,' the Soldier said. 'I want you to hunt them. Hunt them and rid this city of them.'

'I don't think I can run around your city killing vampires,' Miles said.

The Soldier walked over to a cabinet at the far end of the study where he knelt and opened a glass door. He retrieved a small wooden box, which he handed to Miles.

Miles placed the box on his lap and waited for the Soldier to sit. 'What is it?'

'Open it.'

The box's latch snapped open. Miles frowned back at the Soldier. 'I don't understand.'

'It's my sigil,' the Soldier said. 'You are free to do what you need to do under my banner.'

Miles pulled out the large gold coin and turned it around in his hand. On one side sat the emblem of a crossed set of vambraces, and on the other the symbol of a greatsword.

'Rafa,' the Soldier shouted. 'Can you bring in the chest?'

The door of the study opened and Rafa walked in, holding a small chest. He walked around the chairs and placed it at Miles's feet. With a small bow, he exited the room and closed the door. The Soldier signalled at the chest with his head. Miles leant over, snapped open the two locks, and flipped the lid open. Inside sat two vambraces side by side. As per the coin, one held the symbol of crossed vambraces and the other the symbol of a greatsword. Miles pulled out one vambrace and slipped his hand through until it covered his entire forearm. With his palm facing up, he used his other hand to lace it up until it sat tight like another skin.

'Those vambraces are your signal to the people of Battleacre that you work for me,' the Soldier said. 'The coin and the vambraces both have my insignia.'

'One without the other does not count?' Miles said, turning the coin over in his hand.

'The coin allows you to investigate under my house banner. The vambraces give you licence to use a weapon.'

Miles unlaced the vambrace and placed it in the box. He sat back and closed his eyes.

'You don't wish to take this on?' the Soldier said.

'I want to help Janie,' Miles said, keeping his eyes closed. 'We need to send that messenger.'

'I have already sent the messenger,' the Soldier said. 'You can use these items to question the vampires you find. You may find some information.'

Miles opened his eyes. 'I should be out there looking for her.'

'You will fail unless you have an army with you,' the Soldier said, folding his arms. 'Even with your wolf pack, those vampires will take you and Waya down.'

Miles sighed, then shook his head. 'The one and only time I find someone I care about, and they take her away from me.'

'I think you mean the only time you find love,' the Soldier said with a gentle smile.

Miles bit his bottom lip.

The Soldier chuckled. 'Your first love?'

'Hopefully my only love,' Miles said.

'So, my boy, do you accept?'

Miles turned and stared into the fire. A few minutes later, he looked at the Soldier and bowed his head.

'Excellent,' the Soldier said, slapping the armrest.

'We have one problem, though,' Miles said. 'How do we tell who is and who isn't a vampire?'

'I may have something for that,' the Soldier said. 'Rafa,' he shouted over his shoulder.

The door swung open and Rafa walked in. 'Yes, sir.'

'Where is that socialite daughter of mine?'

'She returned from the games but ten minutes ago, sir. She is eating in the breakfast area.'

'Ask her to come and see us after her dinner, please.'

Rafa bowed his head. 'Most certainly, sir.'

The study doors clicked closed. The Soldier stood and poured yellow liquid into two thick glasses. He sat back down and handed Miles a glass. With an incline of his head, he said, 'To ridding our lands of these monsters.'

Miles raised his glass and inclined his head. 'And to saving Janie.'

The Soldier chuckled and took a sip of his drink. He scrunched his eyes and blew out a long blast of air. 'The first sip always takes me by surprise.'

Miles turned his gaze towards the study door as it banged open. Raquel strode in, holding a plate of food in one hand and an empty glass in the other. She offered the empty glass to her father. 'Will you please sort me a drink, Papa?'

The Soldier got to his feet and filled up a glass at the mantelpiece. He turned and harrumphed at his daughter, who had stolen his chair. Raquel looked up at him sweetly then took the glass. The Soldier opened his mouth then closed it again as the study door opened and Rafa walked in, pulling in a chair.

Miles shook his head. 'How does he know?' he said, whispering to Raquel.

Raquel looked over at Rafa. 'He knows because he is the most professional man I have ever met.'

Miles smiled at the way Raquel let her eyes rest on Rafa. She turned back to Miles and, noticing his look, she dropped her eyes and cleared her throat.

The Soldier pulled the chair over and settled in front of the fire. 'Miles has accepted.'

Raquel flicked her hair. 'Our own little mercenary.'

The Soldier kicked the edge of Raquel's chair. 'Behave, daughter. He is not a mercenary and you know full well we have a problem in Battleacre.'

Raquel smirked at Miles. 'Oh, how I love getting Papa riled up.'

'You would like my brother,' Miles said. 'He has the same painfully annoying side.'

'Is he available?' Raquel said, wagging an eyebrow.

The Soldier raised his eyes to the ceiling and groaned.

'Unfortunately not,' Miles said with a grin. 'He found love very early on.'

'Typical,' Raquel said, dropping her chin onto her hand.

'Can we get on with this, daughter?' the Soldier said, rolling his eyes.

'We certainly have a problem in Battleacre. Most of our younger women have gone missing,' Raquel said. 'The council is looking for answers. Our assumption is they are all being turned.'

'They are being stolen,' the Soldier said.

Raquel's mouth hung open. 'Stolen? By whom?'

'The City of Lynn,' the Soldier said.

'I think both are happening,' Miles said, looking over at the Soldier. 'Some are being turned and some are going missing. The missing women are being taken to the City of Lynn.'

Raquel sat back and tapped her chin with her finger. 'Why are they taking them to the City?'

'We never found out,' Miles said with a shake of his head. 'Chloe, who is head of the council in Fairacre, is trying to find out through her trade routes.'

'A woman is head of the council in Fairacre?' Raquel said, with a perfectly formed raised eyebrow.

'It is a long story, but yes, women have equal rights in the south and the men and women voted Chloe in to lead the council.'

'I would never have thought,' Raquel said, turning and staring into the fire.

'What do your contacts say about finding these vampires in our city, love?' the Soldier said.

'Not much,' Raquel said. 'Direct sunlight is something they cannot take. But they can come out during the day if there is heavy cloud cover.'

'Their skin is paler than most,' the Soldier said.

Raquel looked down at her white forearm. 'Most of us are not sun-kissed.'

The Soldier ran his hand through his hair. 'Their eyes are predatory.'

'How so?' Raquel said.

'There is a red ring around the irises, if you look closely. That red ring expands over their irises when they are hunting.'

Raquel tapped her finger on her chin. 'I will get this information to the council.'

'I want the two of you to partner up,' the Soldier said. 'My daughter with the pen, and Miles, I want you to be the Hammer.'

'So dramatic, Father,' Raquel said with fondness. 'What about brother? Is he not your Hammer?'

'Where is he?' the Soldier said, swishing his hand in an arc in front of him. 'He has done nothing but dishonour this house. I need someone I can trust.'

Raquel rose and sat on the armrest of her father's chair. She waited for her father to sit back in his chair, then she rested her arm across his shoulders. 'I am sorry, Father.'

The Soldier gave a single nod then looked at Miles. 'So, son, do you accept?'

'What does it involve?' Miles said.

'See it as the sheriff of our household,' Raquel said. 'You protect the interests of mine and Father's name. It is of great responsibility.'

Miles sat forward. 'This is a great honour. I will start tomorrow.'

Raquel stood and, walking out of the study, she peered over her shoulder and said, 'I will be back shortly. Wait here.'

The Soldier laced his fingers behind his head and gazed into the fire.

'I am going to need another set of weapons,' Miles said. 'The greatsword you have given me is too large to use effectively in the city.'

'Go to the blacksmiths tomorrow and get what you need,' the Soldier said. 'Just show your coin.'

Miles turned the gold coin in his hands, then slipped it into a pocket.

Raquel returned and sat in the empty chair next to the fire. She pulled out a purse and handed it to Miles. 'There are street couriers throughout the city. Young children who are looking to make a few coppers. Hand them one of the coloured tokens and wait at the correct entrance of the amphitheatre.'

Miles pulled out the different coloured tokens. 'They match the quadrants.'

'I will meet you at the amphitheatre entrance that matches the specific colour. If I cannot meet you, I will send someone I can trust.'

Miles closed the purse and slipped it into a pocket.

The Soldier clapped his hands. 'Excellent. I think it is time to turn in for the night.'

Miles stood. 'Are there times I can come and go from your residence?'

'My house is your house,' the Soldier said. 'Anything you need, speak to Rafa.'

'Go and get them, Hammer,' Raquel said, saluting Miles.

A groan escaped the Soldier's lips.

Miles smiled, gave them both a nod, and left the study.

CHAPTER 12

LIGHT AND DARK

The mist hung thick around the amphitheatre's southern entrance. Miles pulled his cloak around his neck to chase away the biting cold.

'Good morning, sir,' a street sweeper said. 'It seems we are entering the final cold snaps of winter.'

'It sure does,' Miles said. 'Keep warm, my friend.'

'Good day, sir,' the man said, bowing.

With the amphitheatre to his right, Miles followed the curved road to the north, then turned left into the blacksmiths district. Fires burnt bright within each smithy as each blacksmith melted their steel to create the correct shapes for their weapons. As Miles walked along, he checked the signs hanging above the black-smiths' doors. A greatsword, a shield, a hammer, but not the one he was looking for. At the end of the street, Miles turned and faced the way he had come.

'Can I help you, sir?' a blacksmith shouted.

'I am looking for the short-sword blacksmith.'

'That would be Almond,' the blacksmith said. 'Go back down

the street and walk down the alley between the shield and greatsword blacksmiths.'

Miles gave the blacksmith a thumbs-up, then walked back to the blacksmith with the shield above the door. He turned down the dark misty alley until he found the sign of a short sword. Unlike all the other smiths, this one sat in icy darkness.

'Anyone home?' Miles said through the doorway.

A thin man wearing a small cap on his bald head scampered out from a room in the back of the workshop. 'How can I help you, sir?' the man said, wiping his mouth.

'Have I disturbed your breakfast?'

'No, no,' the man said. 'Name is Almond. What can I do for you, sir?'

Miles pointed to the sign above his head. 'Do you make short swords?'

Almond frowned. 'You want short swords, sir?'

'Yes, is that a problem?' Miles said.

'No, sir, of course not. It is just that nobody ever orders them anymore. Please come in,' he said, waving his hand into the smithy.

Miles walked into the cold smithy and sat on a stool.

'Have you won in the games, sir?' Almond said.

Miles retrieved his purse and pulled out the Soldier's gold coin. 'I have the General's coin, and here are the vambraces of the Hammer,' he said, pulling up a sleeve and showing his arms.

Almond gasped and took a step backwards.

'Almond? Are you OK?'

Almond's entire body shook with his knees tapping against each other. He ripped off his all-too-small cap and held it close to his chest. 'Yes, sir. Right away, sir.'

Miles lifted an eyebrow and smiled.

'Of course, sir,' Almond said, his feet sticking to the spot. 'What an honour, sir. Right away, sir.'

Miles reached over and placed a hand on Almond's shoulder. 'Calm down, Almond. How long do you think it will take to make them?'

Almond continued to tremble.

'Almond?' Miles said, giving him a shake.

'Sorry, sir. This is such an honour.'

'I will make sure the city of Battleacre knows you are the best short-sword blacksmith. If, of course, the short swords are the best you have ever made,' Miles said.

A wide smile stretched across Almond's oval face. He scuttled to an empty wall at the back of his smithy. 'Where is it?' he said, running his hands against the smooth surface. 'Here it is,' he shouted at the top of his voice. With a click, the wall slid away, exposing three thick blocks of metal. He looked over at Miles, while pointing at them with both hands.

Miles walked over. 'There is something special about this steel?'

'Yes, sir,' Almond said, hopping from foot to foot. 'Very rare. My brother, may the gods rest his dark soul, brought these blocks back from the northern lands.'

'They look like glass,' Miles said, running a hand across a block.

'Just very smooth, sir,' Almond said.

'How long to create the swords?' Miles said. 'I don't want you to rush them.'

'Them?' Almond said.

'Yes, Almond, I need two.'

'Tomorrow morning, sir,' Almond said, scratching the side of his head. 'I will not rest until I have them done.'

Miles pulled out a gold coin from his purse and pushed it into Almond's hand.

Almond looked at the coin, then at Miles, then back at the coin. 'This is unnecessary, sir. The General will not be pleased if I take his gold coins.'

Miles chuckled. 'The General is paying for one, Almond. I am paying for the other.'

Almond nodded frantically. 'OK, sir!'

'Make sure it is your best work, Almond,' Miles said, walking to the exit of the smithy. 'I will be here first thing in the morning.'

'Of course, sir,' Almond said, still staring down at the coin. 'Right away, sir.'

Miles walked through the alley and onto the main road of the blacksmiths district. To the west, the mighty amphitheatre grew higher as he approached. At the east entrance of the arena, he turned north and followed the side of the amphitheatre until the entertainment district appeared on his left. Shops, bars, restaurants and inns all lined the district's roads. As Miles walked through the quiet entertainment district streets, people glanced down at his shuffling foot. Miles bit his bottom lip as he pulled his right foot straight to reduce the limping. After walking up and down several streets, Miles reached Battleacre's east wall. He turned north up the alleyway until he entered a square with a fountain in the middle.

'Can I help you?' a girl said.

'What district is this?' Miles said.

'The weavers district,' the girl said with a smile.

With a thump of his heart, an image of Janie crept into his head. The red-headed girl covered in needles, cotton, scissors and measuring tape turned into a monster in his mind. His breath caught in his throat as he bit his bottom lip.

'Are you OK, sir?' the woman said.

Miles drew in a long breath, held up his hand and turned back south into the alleyway. Back at the entertainment district, he walked towards the amphitheatre. Halfway to the arena, he jumped as, with an almighty blast, the horns of the amphitheatre broke the mid-morning silence of Battleacre. Suddenly, the entertainment district came alive. Doors of bars and restaurants banged open. People stepped out and shouted their good mornings and what wares they had for sale. A young girl ran out of an inn and dodged her father's lunging grasp. Her long blonde hair flew out behind her as she ran giggling away from her father and his pretend bear growls.

Miles reached the end of the entertainment district and turned south, then left into the officers district. At the park, he slowed as the pain in his right leg intensified. At the top of the hill, he pushed the gate open, and hobbled up to the steps.

'Can I help, sir?' Rafa said, reaching forward.

Miles held up a hand. 'I am fine thanks, Rafa.'

Rafa gave a small bow. 'Are you sure, sir?'

Miles struggled up the steps, through the entrance, and into the kitchen breakfast area, where he sank onto a stool.

'I suggest you come and have your lunch in the study, sir,' Rafa said. 'It is a lot more comfortable and warmer.'

Miles hobbled out of the kitchen and into the study. He sat in the soft high-backed chair, which sighed as he sighed.

Rafa walked in with a bowl of steaming soup and thick white bread. He placed it on the side table.

'Rafa,' Miles said.

'Yes, sir,' Rafa said, adjusting the white cloth that draped over his forearm.

'Excuse me for asking, but are you from the western lands?'

A smile broke across Rafa's face. 'It has been a while since someone has asked me that, sir.'

'So you are from the west?'

'I am, sir. They brought my great-grandparents here as slaves. The General's parents freed my mother and father from that slavery. They stayed here and had me.'

'Where are your parents now?'

'When I turned thirteen, they decided to return to the west,' Rafa said. 'They could not convince me to leave this home. It is where I grew up.'

'What would you think if I told you a black woman by the name of Chloe is the head of Fairacre council in the south?'

Rafa chuckled. 'I would say you need to see a doctor as you must have lost your mind, sir.'

Miles smiled up at Rafa. 'Looks like you might need to call me a doctor then, Rafa,' he said, keeping his gaze.

'You jest, sir?' Rafa said, his mouth dropping open.

Miles shook his head. 'I hope one day you meet her and the rest of my friends. She is one of the best leaders I have ever met.'

'Well, I never thought in all my life I would hear of such a thing,' Rafa said. 'She would not be able to lead in my land. Yet here she is, leading in another land. Do you miss them, sir?'

Unable to speak, Miles sighed and nodded.

Rafa straightened his back. 'You will see your friends again, sir. Friends are never more than a thought away.'

'Thank you, Rafa. Oh, and I have another request for you.'

Rafa inclined his head. 'Anything, sir.'

'Tomorrow, I will receive my weapons from the blacksmith. Two short swords I wish to wear on my back. I would like a fresh set of black clothes, and my cloak amended to fit the short swords.'

'Leave that with me, sir,' Rafa said. 'The General has people who will do this for us.'

'Thank you, Rafa.'

Rafa adjusted the white cloth on his forearm, then turned towards the study door.

'Is that the picture of his wife?' Miles said, pointing his chin to a small table in the room's corner.

'Yes, sir,' Rafa said, walking over to the table and retrieving the picture. 'She passed away many seasons ago.'

Miles placed the bowl on the side table. 'May I have a closer look?'

'Certainly, sir,' Rafa said, bringing the picture over.

Miles took the black-and-white picture and held it out in front of him. Instantly, his knuckles turned white and sweat beaded over his forehead. A twinge of pain shot across his lower back. From the frame stared a picture of the Lady.

'Are you OK, sir?' Rafa said.

Miles handed the picture back to Rafa. 'I am fine,' he whispered.

'As you wish, sir,' Rafa said, taking the picture and placing it back on the table.

'I think I will finish my meal and turn in for the rest of the day,' Miles said. 'I need to rest my legs and my back.'

Rafa bowed. 'Call me if you need anything.'

Miles waited for the study door to close. With a sob, he leant forward and covered his eyes with the heels of his hands. His whole body shook as the image of the Lady's sword cut across his lower back. After a few minutes, he drew in a ragged breath, rose and made his way up the stairs to his room. Closing the door and the curtains, he fell onto the bed and wrapped his arms around his knees. The darkness eventually arrived after no more tears came from his eyes.

'Sir?' Rafa said, softly knocking on the door.

Miles opened the door. 'Rafa, what can I do for you?'

'Here are your clothes, sir.'

Miles's forehead crinkled at the black clothes draped over Rafa's arm. 'That was quick.'

Rafa tilted his head to one side. 'It is early morning, sir. The sun will rise shortly.'

'I slept all the way through?' Miles said, opening the door further. 'I must have needed the sleep. Can you leave them on the chair for me?'

Rafa walked in and placed the clothes on the chair. 'We have especially crafted them with the sign of the Hammer. And we have adjusted your cloak.'

'Thank you, Rafa,' Miles said. 'I will call you if I need anything else.'

'If you wish to talk about yesterday, sir. Please don't hesitate.'

Miles turned his head away and bit his bottom lip. 'I am fine, Rafa.'

Rafa bowed and left the room.

Fifteen minutes later, Miles stood in front of the full-length mirror. The black clothes fitted perfectly. Across the breast sat the Hammer insignia – a pair of crossed vambraces with a gold coin sitting above them. His cloak, now altered, narrowed at the top so the two short swords would be easy to retrieve with a flick of his shoulders. With a last look at himself in the mirror, Miles left the room, walked down the steps, and exited the estate. As he walked through the park and down to the south entrance of the arena, the icy cold formed small crystals along his eyebrows. In the distance to the east, the smiths' fires burnt bright.

'Good day, sir,' the street sweeper said. 'Do you feel the cold snap?'

'I do, sir,' Miles said, rubbing the crystals off his eyebrows. 'How long will this last?'

'Hard to tell,' the sweeper said. 'The black snow is changing our climate. The weather is unpredictable. One week or four weeks. Nobody knows.'

Miles turned his head to the sky and squinted at the black-and-white snowflakes. With a sigh, he waved at the sweeper and continued to the blacksmiths district.

The lights in Almond's smithy flickered shadows across the alley walls. With his shoulder leaning against the entrance, Miles watched him run around the shop. He cleared his throat.

Almond skidded to a stop. 'Sir, yes, sir,' he said, bowing at Miles.

'How are you, Almond?'

An enormous grin spread across Almond's face as he whipped his cap from his head. 'I am well. Your swords are ready, sir.'

Miles walked into the shop and sat on a tall stool next to a workbench.

Almond's body trembled as he stood in front of Miles.

'I am ready,' Miles said, smiling down at Almond.

Almond dropped his cap on the floor and jogged over to a covered workbench. He tugged away a blanket, revealing a box with the two symbols of the Soldier's house. 'Sir,' he said, stepping back and waving his hand at the box.

Miles walked to the bench, snapped open the latch and carefully raised the lid. His breath caught in his throat as the two blades glinted back at him.

'Do you like them?' Almond said, his voice quavering.

Miles reached in and gently removed one sword. The blade curved slightly from the middle to the end. The steel glinted like fire dancing off smooth glass, and the handle, wrapped in gold, ended in a pommel of the same glasslike steel. With his finger in the middle, he measured the blade's balance. He flicked it up into the air and caught the sword by the handle.

'Such perfect balance,' Miles said, looking down the short sword's length.

'Try the other one, sir,' Almond said.

Miles replaced the first blade and picked up the second sword. Just like the first, the blade curved from the centre to the tip. However, this one shone a dark swirling black. The handle, wrapped in silver, ended in a pommel with the same black seal.

'These are fantastic,' Miles said, turning to Almond. 'I have never felt such balance. Why are they different?'

'Light and dark, sir,' Almond said. 'Made from two different blocks of steel. The closer they are together, the more powerful they are.'

Miles picked up the second blade and held both up to the light. 'How so, Almond?'

Almond shrugged. 'My brother, may the devil's earlobes let his soul rest, told me so.'

Miles ran a blade over his forearm and smiled as the hairs fluttered to the ground.

'The only thing to break one blade is the other blade,' Almond said. 'Nothing else can destroy them.'

'Such amazing work,' Miles said.

Almond reached down, picked up his cap and held it to his chest. 'I thank you, sir.'

'The General will praise your skills, Almond.'

Almond's eyes went wide. 'It is my honour.'

Miles moved to the centre of the smithy, where he slid into a defensive stance. The wind whistled as he performed his moves. Once finished, he walked back to the bench and placed the swords in the box. 'Where can I get some scabbards, Almond?'

'Lift the panel, sir.'

Miles pulled both swords out and lifted the panel. Criss-crossed scabbards sat nestled at the bottom.

'I should have guessed,' Miles said over his shoulder. 'You have thought of everything.'

'Thank you, sir.'

Miles placed his cloak on the stool and adjusted the scabbards. He slipped his arms through the straps and worked his shoulders until the scabbards lay comfortably across his back. He removed the light sword and slipped it into the sheath. Next, the dark sword slid perfectly into its new home. Miles picked up the cloak and wrapped it around himself, hiding the two swords from view. He replaced the panel and clicked the latches closed. Reaching into his purse, he pulled out two gold coins, and handed them to Almond. 'Yesterday's coin is for one sword. These two coins are for the second sword and the scabbards.'

'I cannot accept these, sir,' Almond said, holding the coins out. 'Please, take them. It is not proper.'

Miles sighed and took the two coins back. 'I will praise your name throughout the whole of the land, Almond. Nobody has skills like your own.'

Almond grinned from ear to ear. 'Such an honour. Will you name the swords, sir?'

'I shall think on the matter,' Miles said, walking to the smithy's entrance. 'Almond. If I may ask a favour of you?' he said, turning around.

'Yes, sir?'

'If you see anybody suspicious, anybody out of place, can you please call for me?'

'Suspicious, sir?' Almond said.

'Anything unusual, Almond,' Miles said. 'People you wouldn't expect in the blacksmiths district.'

'Certainly, sir. How do I contact you?'

Miles removed a token from his purse and flicked it over to

Almond. 'Give that to any messenger. I will meet you at the south entrance of the arena.'

Almond bowed. 'Thank you, sir. And have a good day.'

Miles bowed and walked out into the alley. He exited between the greatsword and shield blacksmiths, then walked into the wide street and towards the arena. At the entrance to the arena, he turned north and walked until he reached the entertainment district. The amphitheatre's horns trumpeted the day's beginning. Doors banged open and people of the entertainment district stepped out onto the road to greet one another. Miles walked up the street until he found the inn the young girl had run out of. A sign saying The Alphorn spread across the inn's entrance. Miles walked through the main doors and slid through the throng of people to the bar. He perched on a stool and signalled to the bartender.

'Yes, sir,' a man with a braided beard said. 'Can I help you?'

'A coffee please,' Miles said.

The man sidestepped to a coffee drip pot and poured hot water into the upper chamber. He waited patiently for the coffee to drip through.

Miles assessed the crowd, scanning for anyone who looked out of place.

'Here you go, sir,' the bartender said, placing a mug of steaming coffee on the bar.

Miles retrieved a silver coin from his purse and placed it on the bar.

The man frowned. 'It's a copper, sir.'

'A silver for the coffee and some information, my friend.'

The man took the silver coin. 'Name's Jarod,' he said, pocketing the coin and moving away to another customer.

Cheers and whistles came from the other side of the bar as a group of people played a board game. Trays of ale, held head-high by staff, moved through the bar until they reached their destination.

'What you looking for?' Jarod said, eyeing the vambraces.

'You serve ale this early?' Miles said.

'Ale is served regardless of the hour,' Jarod said.

Miles raised an eyebrow in the noisy group's direction.

'I thought the General's son was the Hammer,' Jarod said.

Miles darted a glimpse at his exposed vambraces. 'Have you seen the General's son?'

Jarod picked up a glass and rubbed it with a cloth. 'He is in the city.'

Miles placed his coffee on the bar. 'You are sure about that?'

'I am,' Jarod said, replacing the glass. 'He is a vampire and you can often find him in the entertainment district.'

Miles scanned the room again before turning to Jarod. 'The General and I have noticed several women have disappeared.'

Jarod rested his elbows on the bar. 'A few of our servers have not showed up for work throughout winter.'

'Any communication from their families?' Miles said.

'Their families have come here enquiring about them.'

Miles watched Jarod walk away to serve another customer. Another cheer erupted from the revellers as they were delivered more ale.

'Any idea where these women have gone?' Jarod said, holding up another glass and drying it with a cloth.

Miles shook his head. 'Any suspicious patrons lately?'

Jarod replaced the glass and dropped his elbows back onto the bar. 'It's a big place, and it is never empty.'

Miles stood, finished his mug of coffee, and slipped Jarod another silver coin. 'The General will hand out a substantial amount of coin for any information about these women.'

Jarod slipped the coin under the bar. 'How do I get hold of you?'

'Send a messenger with this token to the south entrance of the amphitheatre,' Miles said, handing Jarod a token.

Jarod flicked the token over in his hand, then gave Miles a nod.

Miles continued. 'If you see the General's son. Don't tell him anything but send for me.'

'Anything for the General's Hammer,' Jarod said.

Miles left the inn and spent the rest of the morning walking the streets of the entertainment district. At noon, he made his way south and west until he reached the Soldier's estate.

'We are in the study, lad,' the Soldier shouted.

Miles walked into the warm room and sat on the chair next to the fireplace.

'A certain man named Almond claimed his weapon badge this morning,' the Soldier said. 'What a trembling little man.'

'You spark the fear in most men,' Raquel said, smiling at her father.

The Soldier chuckled. 'I am surprised you chose short swords, lad.'

'Almond needs to be praised. I have never seen work this good,' Miles said, reaching behind his back and pulling out the light short sword.

'Oh my,' Raquel said, placing a hand over her mouth. 'That is beautiful.'

The Soldier leant forward and delicately ran a finger along the length of the blade. 'May I?' he said, looking up at Miles.

Miles spun the sword, pointing the golden handle at the Soldier.

'Such balance,' the Soldier said, resting the middle of the blade on a finger.

'It is but part of two,' Miles said, reaching over his shoulder and pulling out the dark sword.

A gasp escaped Raquel's lips.

Miles spun the sword, pointing the silver handle at the Soldier.

With a sword in each hand, the Soldier held the blades to the flickering fire. 'I have seen nothing like these before.'

'Nor I,' Miles said.

'Light and dark,' Raquel said.

The Soldier handed the swords back. 'Have you found anything out?'

'There are a lot more women missing than we thought. It is noticeable in the entertainment district.'

'We don't go there often,' Raquel said. 'We need to visit our people there, Father.'

'Diners and bars are all looking to hire people as the women that used to work there have gone missing,' Miles said.

The Soldier let out a deep growl. 'The council has been holding back. I think it's time to make a change.'

'What do you mean, Father?' Raquel said.

The Soldier sat forward, extended a hand and took Raquel's in his own. 'Daughter, tomorrow I will relinquish my seat in the council.'

Raquel's eyes shot up. 'What on earth are you talking about?'

'It is time you take my seat as the leader of our house in the council.'

Raquel's mouth fell open.

'We need a sharper mind on the council now. That this problem has got this bad is a sign we need to change. I will still hold the General's authority, but you will make the political decisions needed.'

Raquel flopped back into her chair. 'I don't know if I am ready.'

The Soldier rolled his eyes at Miles. 'She was ready years ago. So dramatic isn't she?'

Raquel shot forward and punched her father on the leg.

The Soldier slapped his thigh and roared with laughter.

Raquel turned to Miles. 'Will you join us at the council meeting tomorrow?'

Miles shook his head. 'No. I need to be on the streets. The more I gather information, the more intelligence I can give you.'

'That's settled then,' the Soldier said. 'Now it's time for food.'

The doors opened and Rafa rolled in a trolley of food. He spread a white cloth on each side table and placed an equal amount of food on each.

'What do you think mama would say about me taking the council seat, Papa?' Raquel said.

A lump jumped into Miles's throat.

Rafa cleared his throat and raised an eyebrow at Miles. 'Would you care for extra bread, sir?'

Miles gave Rafa a thin-lipped smile. 'No thank you, Rafa.'

'She would be so very proud,' the Soldier said, smiling broadly at his daughter.

'This is delicious,' Raquel said. 'Thank you, Rafa.'

'My lady,' Rafa said, with a small bow.

'I have one more piece of information,' Miles said.

The Soldier blew on his spoon of hot soup. 'What is it, lad?'

'Your son is in Battleacre.'

'What?' the Soldier roared, sending his bowl of soup into his lap and all over the floor.

CHAPTER 13
GO NOW!

Raquel grabbed the cloth from Rafa's forearm. 'Clean yourself up, Father,' she said. 'And calm down.'

'Why did you leave that to the end?' the Soldier said while dabbing his trousers.

'I wanted to deal with all the other items before I told you,' Miles said, wiping some soup off his boot straps. 'I guessed you would explode.'

The Soldier tossed the cloth back to Rafa. 'We need to go to the inn now.'

Miles held up his hands. 'That is not a good idea.'

'I will go where I please,' the Soldier said, leaning forward. 'That son of mine needs to be brought home.'

'You need to go to the council,' Miles said. 'I have people looking out for your son.'

'I will not have that arrogant boy drag our good name through the mud.'

'Father,' Raquel said. 'You have given the title of the Hammer to Miles. Let him do his job.'

The Soldier sat back and folded his arms. 'Did this bartender say whether these vampires have turned my son?'

The room fell silent as all three stared at Miles.

'Tell me, boy,' the Soldier said, slapping his thigh.

'I am afraid it looks like he has been,' Miles said. 'I am sorry.'

The Soldier's hands covered his face as he shook his head. Raquel choked back a sob. The Soldier, hearing his daughter, leant forward and pulled her into a bear hug.

'What now?' Raquel said into her father's shoulder.

'We will bring him home,' the Soldier said, releasing Raquel and wiping a tear from her cheek. 'We will bring him home and we will look after him.'

'How?' Raquel said. 'We have no cure for this. How will we keep him here and how will we keep him safe?'

The Soldier looked at Miles. 'You mentioned your father might have a cure for Janie?'

Miles bit his bottom lip. 'My father and brother are excellent alchemists. If they don't have a cure, I am afraid nobody will have a cure.'

'You said they would,' the Soldier said, banging a fist on the armrest of the chair.

'I want Janie cured just as much as you want your son cured,' Miles said.

The Soldier held up a hand. 'Sorry, lad. I want answers now.'

'When will the messenger reach Fairacre?' Miles said.

'If they have permission to travel south out of the City, then they should be there in a few days,' the Soldier said. 'We will keep my son on the estate until they get here.'

Miles stood. 'I must return to the entertainment district and continue my search.'

'Take Rafa with you,' the Soldier said.

Miles gave the Soldier and Raquel a confused look.

'Rafa knows this city better than anybody,' the Soldier said. 'He has played in its streets since he was a young boy.'

'Go and get changed, Rafa,' Raquel said. 'I need to have a chat with my father and Miles.'

Rafa collected the bowls and the soup-covered cloth then left the room.

'Get changed?' Miles said. 'What is going on?'

'As you are the Hammer of our household,' Raquel said, 'Rafa is the Shield.'

'I thought Rafa was your servant?' Miles said.

'Rafa is no servant,' Raquel said. 'He waits on us because he wants to.'

'I don't understand,' Miles said.

'Rafa will accompany you to the inn as protection,' the Soldier said. 'When my son learns of your standing in my household, he will resort to violence.'

'The council meeting starts shortly, Father,' Raquel said. 'We need to get going. We can chat about Rafa another time.'

After a knock, the study door opened. Rafa strode in and stood with his hands behind his back.

'Well, you certainly look different,' Miles said, rising and standing in front of Rafa.

Rafa gave Miles a grin. 'My family's clothes,' he said, adjusting the wide multicoloured sleeve. 'The patterns are from the land where my grandparents were born.'

'I want to visit these lands,' Raquel said with a sigh.

'Be careful of Rafa's spear and shield, lad,' the Soldier said. 'I can assure you it would take both of us to disarm him.'

'And the vambraces?' Miles said.

Rafa held up his hands. 'The coin is below the crossed vambraces. The symbol of the Shield. I protect through defence.'

Miles took a step back and looked down at his own vambraces. 'The coin is above my vambraces. And I protect through offence.'

The Soldier walked up to both of them and placed a hand on each of their shoulders. 'You are the protectors of my house. I trust you to find my son and bring him back to me.'

Miles and Rafa inclined their heads towards the Soldier.

'Let's go, Papa,' Raquel said. 'You know how impatient the council gets.'

Miles watched Raquel and the Soldier leave the room. 'Ready?'

'I am,' Rafa said, striding to the study door.

Miles and Rafa sat on a bench opposite the amphitheatre's southern entrance. The crowd entering and exiting the amphitheatre cast wide eyes in their direction.

'I don't think anybody within Battleacre has seen the Hammer and the Shield together,' Rafa said, his voice low and measured.

Miles adjusted his boot. 'Either that or they are staring at my foot.'

Rafa grunted. 'That may be true.'

They sat in silence through the mid-afternoon. Miles winked up at the street sweeper who, humming a tune, worked around them.

'So you are not a servant?' Miles said.

'I serve,' Rafa said with a chuckle. 'So in that way, you can class me as a servant.'

'You know what I mean,' Miles said.

'You mean, I am free and not bound?' Rafa said.

'Yes,' Miles said. 'On the way to Battleacre I saw many black people bound to an owner.'

Rafa growled under his breath. 'I have seen more of this lately. And tidings from my homeland in the west are not positive.'

'Why don't you go back?' Miles said.

Rafa remained silent.

'I can see you turning a shade of red there, Rafa,' Miles said. 'Something you want to tell me?'

Rafa gave Miles a wide smile. 'No.'

Miles chuckled.

They sat and watched the shadows grow longer as the sun crawled west. The crowds grew thicker as the people left their places of work and came to the games.

Out of the crowd, a young boy ran up to Miles and showed him a bronze token.

'Which district, young man?' Miles said.

'The entertainment district,' the boy said, his chin high in the air.

Miles stood and grinned down at the boy. 'A job well done.'

'Best in Battleacre,' the boy said, his chin raising higher.

Miles pulled out a copper coin and slipped it into the boy's hand. 'Spend it wisely. If you see anything suspicious around Battleacre's streets, come and find us.'

The boy gave a toothless grin, then disappeared into the crowds of people.

Miles and Rafa marched around the eastern part of the amphitheatre until they reached the entertainment district's entrance. Revellers, drinking and singing filled the main street. As they wove between the crowd, the singing hushed to whispers as people either lowered their gaze or pointed at both of them. Jarod stood waiting at The Alphorn's entrance. At the sight of Rafa, he took a step backwards and his eyes widened.

'You look spooked,' Miles said, holding up a hand.

'Seeing the Hammer and the Shield walking the entertainment district would spook most people,' Jarod said.

'Why did you send for us?' Rafa said, leaning in.

'A regular is sitting at a table,' Jarod said, swallowing hard. 'She doesn't seem herself.'

'How so?' Miles said.

'I don't know. She's just different. Something about her. She seems pale and cold.'

'I think we need to go in separately,' Miles said to Rafa. 'We don't want to chase this woman away.'

'I will go in first,' Rafa said. 'I am not waiting out here when there is danger in there. Lead the way, Jarod.'

Miles watched Jarod and Rafa disappear through the door. He turned and cast his eyes across the crowd in the street. The revellers, now used to him standing there, ignored him and continued their singing and drinking.

Miles frowned as a dark shadow darted between the revellers. Lowering his eyebrows, he scanned the gaps between the people. After a minute of searching, he turned, opened the door and strolled into The Alphorn. On the far side of the bar, Rafa sat speaking to Jarod. Miles walked over to the opposite side of the bar and found an empty stool. He placed his back against the bar and ran his eyes along the tables. In the far corner, a pale woman sat with a group of men. She turned her gaze onto Miles and flashed him a brilliant smile. Miles gave her a nod and smiled back.

'Your drink,' Jarod said, thumping an ale on the bar.

Miles spun round and gave Jarod a thumbs-up. 'Thanks.'

'I see you have found her,' Jarod said.

Miles took a long draw from his draught and banged the glass down on the bar. 'Yes, the one in the corner.'

Jarod picked up a glass and started polishing it.

'Leave us alone, Jarod,' a woman's voice said.

Miles heard the scraping of a stool. He took another drink of his draught.

'Go on, get lost,' the woman said.

'It's fine,' Miles said, waving Jarod away.

'Why haven't I seen you before?' the woman said.

Miles smiled but said nothing.

'Not much of a talker?'

'I have just got into town,' Miles said.

The woman smiled sweetly. 'So where have you come from?'

Miles turned his head. 'From the horse farms. I am here because someone or something has been taking our women. Do you know anything about that?'

The woman gave Miles a broad smile. 'And why would I know anything about that?'

Miles leant in until his mouth was an inch from her ear. 'Because your kind have been taking them.'

'Is that so?' the woman whispered.

Miles pulled away from her and took another drink from his draught.

The woman leant in and whispered. 'Janie is dead.'

'What did you say?' Miles shouted, slamming his draught onto the bar.

The bar went quiet.

'You heard me,' the woman said.

Miles grabbed the woman's arm. 'How do you know?'

The woman pulled her arm away, stood, and walked to the exit of the bar where she looked over her shoulder and said, 'You failed to bring the wolf. For that, your Janie is dead.'

Miles took in a gulp of air to calm the roaring in his ears. He stood and followed the woman out. He turned east and wove through the crowd towards the eastern wall. Miles ignored his foot's throbbing pain as he stalked after her. Then, the woman disappeared. Miles stopped at the place where the woman had vanished. A thin alley between two high walls wended its way northwards. Turning into the alley, he scowled at the rotting food and stale ale that hit the inside of his nose. The alley walls grew narrow until suddenly he stepped out into a small stone yard.

'Well, that was easy,' the woman said, stepping out of the shadows.

Miles cast his eyes over the three men standing next to the woman. Behind the three men, a figure stood hidden in the shadows. 'What do you want?' Miles said.

The woman smirked. 'You know you have walked into a trap?'

'You told me Janie is dead.'

Two fangs extended from the woman's mouth as she chuckled. 'My dear boy. I don't know if Janie is dead.'

Miles snarled. 'Where is she?'

'I have no idea,' the woman said, spreading her hands.

'Enough of these games,' a man said. 'Let's get this over and done with.'

'Yes, let's,' the woman said, springing forward.

Miles pulled out both short swords, ducked to his left and sliced one of the vampire's heads off. With a snap, the vampire's body dissolved into dust.

The woman vampire hissed and took a step back.

'Did you think it would be that easy?' Miles said, curling his lip at the woman vampire.

The two other vampires drew swords of their own.

'Genevie won't get the wolf if you kill me,' Miles said, pointing a sword at each of the vampires.

'We are not here to kill you,' the woman said, taking another step back.

A vampire darted in with his sword, slashing wildly. Miles

parried, spun and stabbed the vampire in the heart. Another vampire disappeared into dust.

The woman snarled. 'That cannot be.'

'So I don't have to take your heads?' Miles said under his breath. 'A stab in the heart works just as well.'

The woman backed away further. 'What are those swords made of?'

Miles looked down at the two swords. Both the light and the dark shimmered as if alive.

The man from the shadows stepped out into the light. 'Who are you?' he said, walking over and standing next to the woman. 'And where did you get those weapons?'

Miles glanced at the vambraces on the man's arms. 'You are the General's son. He wants you to come home.'

The man bared his fangs. 'I am no longer part of that family.'

'Yet you still wear the vambraces,' Miles said.

The vampire turned both hands palms-up and stared at the vambraces tied around his wrists. With a hiss, he flicked out a nail and broke the bindings. After the vambraces hit the ground, the vampire kicked them at Miles.

'Come with me,' Miles said. 'Your father is waiting for you.'

The vampire reached behind his back and pulled out a long, thin sword. 'Why would I go back to my father when he has forsaken me? He has already given you the title of Hammer.'

'He knew they had turned you,' Miles said. 'You didn't give him much of a choice.'

The Soldier's son darted in with his sword stabbing at Miles's face. Miles parried with the dark sword and swung with the light. The vampire rolled out of the way, came to his knees and threw a handful of dirt into Miles's face. Miles coughed and spluttered while swinging his swords.

'You shouldn't have followed me,' the woman whispered into his ear.

Miles gasped at the stabbing pain in his stomach. Both his swords dropped to the ground with a clatter. He looked down through sand-filled eyes and gripped the handle of the knife sticking out just above his navel. He fell to his knees. With his eyes clearing slightly, he looked up at the Soldier's son. Behind the son, a stream of vampires dropped from the rooftops that surrounded the yard.

'Where is the wolf?' the Soldier's son said. 'Tell me now and I will take your life quickly.'

Miles opened his mouth, but all he could do was taste his own coppery blood.

The Soldier's son jumped back and hissed. Through his hazy vision, Miles saw the blur of a spear and shield. Vampires all around him dissolved into dust.

The yard fell silent.

With both hands, Miles grabbed the knife's handle and pulled it out of his stomach.

'Keep pressure on it,' Rafa said.

'Oh no,' Jarod said, placing a hand on Miles's shoulder. 'Quickly, stay off the main road and follow me through the alleys. There is a back door to my bar.'

Miles felt hands lift him off the ground. His vision swirled as the pain shot from his stomach up through his chest.

'Why isn't he dead?' Jarod said. 'Nobody should survive this wound.'

A door slammed open and Miles felt the cold steel of a tabletop underneath him. The sound of cloth being torn into strips filled his ears. He felt pressure on the wound as Rafa packed it with the strips of cloth.

Miles opened his eyes and grabbed Rafa by the wrist. 'You

need to find the Soldier and Raquel.'

'They are together at the council,' Rafa said. 'They will be fine.'

Miles let go of Rafa's wrist. He closed his eyes and concentrated on his breathing. Suddenly, shouts filled the bar.

'We are in here,' Rafa said.

'What the hell is going on?' the Soldier thundered. 'What happened?'

Miles opened his eyes and reached for him.

'I am here, son,' the Soldier said, grabbing Miles's hand. 'Tell me who did this.'

'Raquel.'

'Raquel did this?' the Soldier said. 'What are you talking about, son?'

'Where is she? Where is Raquel?'

'She is at home. I left her there after the council meeting,' the Soldier said, his voice trailing off.

'Go,' Miles said. 'Go now.'

The door slammed closed as Rafa ran out of the back room.

'Get me up,' Miles said.

'That is not a good idea,' Jarod said, still wide-eyed. 'You shouldn't be alive with that wound.'

Miles grabbed the Soldier. 'Help me up, now.'

The Soldier pulled Miles into a sitting position. 'Is it healing?'

'Yes,' Miles said. 'Slowly, but it's healing.'

Jarod looked between the two of them with his mouth open. 'How is he still alive?'

'Long story,' the Soldier said. 'Tell me what happened, son,' he said, looking back at Miles.

Miles placed both feet on the ground. 'I will tell you later. You need to go and help Rafa. If your son has gone to your estate, Rafa will not be able to handle him on his own.'

‘My son?’ the Soldier said.

‘He did this,’ Miles said, pointing to the wound in his stomach. ‘Go home and make sure they are safe. I will make my way back in a moment.’

‘Look after him,’ the Soldier said, laying a hand on Jarod’s shoulder. ‘If anything else happens, use the messengers and send for me.’

Jarod nodded.

Miles waited for the door to close. ‘Can you get me out of the entertainment district with no one seeing?’

Jarod thought for a moment. ‘I can get you to the entrance of the blacksmiths district.’

‘Take me,’ Miles said, placing both feet on the ground. ‘I should be able to keep up.’

‘I don’t know how you are doing this,’ Jarod said, walking to the back door. ‘I picked up your swords. They are over here.’

Miles hobbled over to the door and picked up his two swords. He took his hand away from the wound in his stomach. The hole left by the blade had reduced in size, but it was still leaking blood. Jarod took the blood-soaked cloths from Miles’s hand and replaced them with clean strips.

‘Lead the way,’ Miles said.

Jarod opened the door a sliver. ‘It’s got dark.’

‘Perfect for these blasted vampires,’ Miles said. ‘Let’s keep to the shadows.’

Jarod swung open the door and ducked into the alley. With his head low, Miles hobbled to keep up with Jarod as the high eastern wall of Battleacre loomed.

‘We go through here,’ Jarod said, pointing to a crack in the wall. ‘It will take us to the outside.’

‘Outside Battleacre? What then?’ Miles said.

'We follow it south,' Jarod said. 'There is another crack in the wall where we enter the blacksmiths district.'

Miles followed Jarod through the dark gap. With his hand on the wall, he trailed him until they broke through the other side. In front of them, a steep bank disappeared into the moat.

'I can get into a lot of trouble showing you this,' Jarod said, while moving south along the wall.

'I understand how a city works,' Miles said. 'There is always trade that doesn't go through the gates.'

Jarod grinned over his shoulder. 'We wouldn't make a living with the cost of legal goods.'

Fifteen minutes later, Jarod disappeared through another gap. Miles ducked his head, then froze. Across the moat, in the dark inky blackness, a long, mournful howl reached his ears. Miles held his healing wound and realised Waya must have suffered the same fate.

'I am sorry, girl,' he whispered. 'Well done for staying away.'

'Are you coming?' Jarod said, his head popping back through the gap.

Miles ducked and followed Jarod through the blackness. The bright lights of the blacksmiths district made Miles blink rapidly. 'You can leave me here,' Miles said. 'I know which way to go from here.'

Jarod shook his head. 'I am going to see you through to the estate. I have a favour to ask of you.'

'Oh?' Miles said.

'I need someone protected, but let's talk of this another time,' Jarod said, jabbing his chin at a curious blacksmith. 'Let's get you back to the General.'

Miles removed his hand from the wound. The skin left an angry welt, but it had closed.

'What magic is this?' Jarod said, looking down at where the

wound once was. 'That knife was deep inside you.'

'I will tell you one day, Jarod,' Miles said. 'For now, let's get to safety.'

With his back straighter and his limp lessened, Miles led Jarod through the blacksmiths district. They came out of the district close to the amphitheatre's eastern entrance. The shouts and screams from the baying crowd thundered around the outside of the arena. They walked south-west until they reached the southern entrance, then turned west towards the officers district. Miles started to breathe heavily as they followed the winding streets up into the hills.

They cleared the hill and reached the edge of the park, where Miles stopped and placed his hand on Jarod's shoulder. 'Need a minute to catch my breath.'

'I have never been up here,' Jarod said, his eyes running along the big estates surrounding the park. 'It is a lot different from the small houses where people live in the north of the city.'

'Let's go,' Miles said, letting go of Jarod's shoulder and moving into the park.

A whisper echoed through the park trees. 'Miles.'

With the breath catching in his throat, he froze.

'What is it?' Jarod said.

'Miles, over here,' came the whisper.

'Janie?' Miles said, squinting into the trees.

Janie stepped out from behind a thick tree trunk.

The twin swords on Miles's back sang out of their sheaths. Jarod's long sword appeared in his hand.

'I will not hurt you,' Janie said, her hands held out in front of her.

'I am not worried about you hurting me,' Miles said. 'Genevie controlling you is what I am worried about.'

'You need to leave Battleacre,' Janie said, taking a step

forward.

'Why?' Miles said. 'Why would I leave you here?'

'The royals,' Janie said. 'Genevie has asked them to come to Battleacre.'

'Royals? Who is this woman, Miles?' Jarod said, pointing his sword at Janie.

Miles ignored Jarod and took a step forward. 'How are you? Are you OK?'

Janie's nervous eyes darted around as she searched for movement in the darkness. She looked back at Miles and said, 'I am fine.'

'Are they hurting you?'

'She is a vampire,' Jarod hissed, taking a step forward. 'Why are we talking to her and not killing her?'

'Stand down, Jarod,' Miles said.

Jarod gave Miles a confused look.

A tree behind Janie rustled. In a flash, Janie disappeared into the blackness.

'What was that all about?' Jarod said.

Miles sheathed both swords. 'She is someone I know and am trying to save.'

Jarod replaced his sword. 'Not heard of any way you can save a vampire.'

Miles turned on his heel and walked towards the back of the park. Jarod hurried alongside. They wound up the street until they reached the gates of the Soldier's estate. Miles pulled open the gate and walked up the path to the steps.

'Son, let her go.' The Soldier's voice came from inside the house.

Miles hobbled up the steps and through the front door. He turned to Jarod. 'You need to go.'

Jarod inclined his head and disappeared back down the

winding street.

'Son, please, let Raquel go.'

Miles hobbled through the kitchen until he reached the back door.

'Why, Father?' the Soldier's son said. 'Are you scared you will lose your precious daughter?'

'Please, son. She has done nothing to harm you.'

'She was always your favourite, wasn't she?' the Soldier's son said. 'Always advising her, always looking out for her. But me, you spent no time with.'

The Soldier took a step forward. 'I tried, son. I have tried to understand the path you have taken.'

The man moved his mouth closer to Raquel's throat. 'You tried?' he hissed.

Miles stepped into the garden and drew his two short swords.

'And here is the new Hammer. How quickly you were to replace me, Father,' the Soldier's son said.

'Let go of her,' Miles said, pointing a sword at the man. 'You know what these swords can do.'

'I am sorry, Father, but it's time you feel the pain I feel every day,' the son said, opening his fang-filled mouth.

'No,' the Soldier shouted, jumping forward.

Miles threw the dark sword as hard as he could. The blade tumbled past Raquel and the Soldier's son. Rafa, who had peeled out of the shadows, caught the sword, and stabbed the vampire through the heart.

The man's mouth shut with a snap. His eyes turned wide. He opened his mouth, but before he could say anything, he dissolved into a cloud of dust.

Raquel dropped to her knees.

The dark sword Rafa had caught dropped into the grass. Sinking to his knees, he wrapped Raquel in a hug. 'I am sorry.'

CHAPTER 14
A ROYAL VAMPIRE

'Get out,' the Soldier screamed, his eyes wild.

'Papa,' Raquel said, jumping to her feet. 'Don't hurt him.'

'I said, get out,' the Soldier shouted, advancing on Rafa. 'I don't want you near me and I don't want you near my daughter.'

Rafa let go of Raquel, inclined his head and walked through the darkness of the garden to the kitchen door. He picked up his spear and shield and disappeared into the house.

'Where do you think you are going?' the Soldier said, grabbing Raquel's arm.

'Let me go, Papa,' Raquel said, pulling her arm away.

'I will not have you leave this house while those monsters are out there.'

'I will go where I please,' Raquel said, folding her arms.

'You will not,' the Soldier said, jabbing his finger into his daughter's face. 'Not while they are out there.'

Raquel took a step back and held up her hands. 'OK, Papa.'

The Soldier walked over to Miles and held him by the shoulders. 'As the Hammer of this house, I demand you rid this entire city of those murderous things. Do you hear me?'

Miles looked over at Raquel then back at the Soldier. 'I need the Shield's help to achieve this.'

The Soldier took a step back. 'He is no longer the Shield. That man murdered my boy!'

'Rafa did the right thing,' Miles said. 'You know he did.'

The Soldier bit back a snarl.

'Your daughter and your son would both be dead if he had not done what he did,' Miles said.

'I could have spoken to my son,' the Soldier said, fighting back the tears.

'He would have killed Raquel regardless,' Miles said.

'How do you know?' the Soldier said, his lip curling.

Miles shook his head. 'He said as much in The Alphorn. His hatred for this family was too deep.'

The Soldier lowered his head into his hands.

Raquel walked over and wrapped her arms around her father. 'Don't believe what he said, Papa.'

The Soldier choked back a sob.

'Rafa saved my life, Papa,' Raquel said. 'Let him help Miles.'

'What if that was Janie with a knife to my daughter's throat?' the Soldier said, looking at Miles over Raquel's shoulder. 'Would you have done the same thing? Would you have killed her?'

Miles placed his hands behind his back and looked up into the night sky.

'Not that easy, is it lad?' the Soldier said.

With a shake of the head, Miles turned and walked to the kitchen door.

'Go and find the Shield,' the Soldier said. 'Tell him he is no longer to serve in my house. He is to rid this town of these monsters. When it's achieved, I will forgive him.'

Miles bowed his head and walked through the kitchen door.

. . .

The cloudy night sky allowed the day's heat to escape. Miles pulled the cloak around himself as he walked through the gates of the Soldier's estate. The winding road down to the park sparkled with the ice crystals of the white and black snow. At the edge of the park, Miles crouched and squinted to get a better view through the mist hanging over the still trees. With no movement, he walked into the park and stopped at the children's play area. 'Rafa,' he said. 'I know you are here somewhere.'

'Good evening, Miles. We meet again.'

The two short swords appeared in Miles's hands. 'Who is that?' he said.

'I am surprised to see you walking,' the voice said. 'The Lady didn't do a very good job, did she now?'

'Knife slinger,' Miles said. The whirling sound of a blade whispered through the mist. Miles dropped to a knee just as a dagger flew over his head. 'Show yourself, you coward,' Miles said.

'As you wish,' the knife slinger said, appearing out of the mist. 'I am not going to take much pleasure in killing a cripple.'

Miles eyed the long, thin sword sitting in the knife slinger's right hand and the wicked curved dagger that spun in his left.

'No fire child to protect you in this lonely park here in Battleacre,' the knife slinger said. 'And I see you have downgraded from a greatsword to short swords. How pathetic.'

Miles ignored the jibing talk and kept his eye on the knife slinger's sword and the dagger. With a sudden burst of speed, the knife slinger darted in. Miles parried his long sword but missed the dagger. With a sharp gasp of air, Miles fell to one knee as the weapon sliced across his chest. The knife slinger sidestepped, spun and stood out of reach.

'You are slow,' the knife slinger said. 'The once-great weapon master of Fairacre is nothing more than a boy with two toothpicks.'

Miles again ignored his jibes. He kept his eyes firmly on the two weapons. The knife slinger darted in, but this time, Miles was ready for him. Parrying the sword and knife, Miles drove his forehead into the knife slinger's jaw. As the knife slinger stumbled backwards, Miles slashed his sword, nicking his thigh. 'You were always one for underestimating your opponent,' Miles said. 'I recall the young fire child driving you to your knees, once.'

The knife slinger's brow furrowed. 'Enough of these games,' he said. 'The Queen has requested you bring the wolf to her. And if you refuse to do so, I need to bring you. Dead or alive.'

'I am not going anywhere,' Miles said, pointing the light sword at the knife slinger. 'And if you kill me, you kill the wolf.'

The knife slinger smiled. 'We thought that to be true, but new information has come to light. The elemental animal will just choose a new partner if I kill you.'

Miles's heart skipped a beat. 'You know that is not true.'

'The elemental animal will be vulnerable while you are on death's door. We have knife slingers tracking her now.'

'You will never catch her,' Miles said. 'She has her pack for protection.'

'We will dispatch her entire pack if we have to,' the knife slinger said.

As Miles opened his mouth to respond, the knife slinger darted in with a flurry of sword attacks. Favouring his left foot, Miles bounced out of the way of each sword swing. After a minute of defending himself, Miles felt his breathing labour. A slow step to his right and the knife slinger jabbed a fist into his nose. Miles fell to his knees.

'I pity you,' the knife slinger said. 'It pains me to see such a formidable fighter reduced to this.'

Miles, panting hard, slashed his swords at the knife slinger. The mist swirled as he hit nothing.

'Fair tidings, my old friend,' the knife slinger said, lifting his sword over his head.

A yell from the mist spun the knife slinger around. A spear jabbed at his head. The knife slinger parried the spear, then took the full force of Rafa's shield into his face.

Miles battled to his feet and stood shoulder to shoulder with Rafa.

'A peasant with a spear and shield,' the knife slinger spat. 'What sacrilege is this?'

'He is the Shield of the General's house,' Miles said. 'And I am the Hammer. Together, we are the protectors of Battleacre.'

The knife slinger chuckled. 'What is this? Some children's tale told by court jesters?'

Rafa darted in with a jabbing spear that just missed the knife slinger's face. With a snarl, the knife slinger attacked with another flurry of swordplay. Miles and Rafa, working together, fought the knife slinger back. A few moves later, Miles found an opening and drove the tip of his sword into the knife slinger's shoulder.

The knife slinger darted into the mist. 'I will return, boy.'

'I plan on it,' Miles shouted. 'Bring some of your friends.'

Rafa chuckled. 'Goading him is not a good idea.'

Miles spat blood into the snow. 'Wherever I go, they seem to find me. I wish to get rid of them once and for all.'

'Let me see your nose,' Rafa said.

Miles ran a sleeve across his face. 'It is OK. We need to get back to the estate.'

'I feel I have caused irreparable damage in the General's house,' Rafa said, his eyes scanning the mist.

Miles replaced both his swords. 'The Soldier would have lost both of his children if you did nothing. He has asked that we rid Battleacre of these vampires.'

'We?' Rafa said, swinging his shield onto his back.

'Yes, we,' Miles said. 'He will forgive us if we finish this task.'

'Why us?' Rafa said. 'It was not you who killed his son.'

'It was my sword, Rafa,' Miles said. 'I knew what I was doing when I threw it at you.'

Rafa thought for a moment. 'What of Raquel? What did she say?'

'You care for Raquel, don't you?' Miles said with a sideways glance.

Rafa bit his bottom lip.

'Does the Soldier know?' Miles said.

'I don't think so. I don't know. If he does, he has said nothing,' Rafa said.

Miles sighed. 'Love is a merciless thing.'

Rafa turned his head and grinned. 'Are you talking from experience?'

Miles grimaced. 'I have no idea what I am thinking, feeling or talking about when it comes to this topic.'

'I will take that as a yes,' Rafa said, chuckling.

'Raquel,' Miles said, smiling back. 'We were talking about her, remember?'

A shadow of sadness crept through Rafa's dark brown eyes, yet a hint of a smile played on his lips.

'Let us go back to the estate and get some rest,' Miles said. 'The Soldier is going to expect results starting from tomorrow.'

Shoulder to shoulder, the Hammer and Shield, Miles and Rafa, walked back up the winding street.

. . .

With a start, Miles sat up straight in bed. He shook his head to clear the image of Janie held captive by Genevie and Gerald. Beyond the snow-streaked window of his room, the light of the sun crawled along the grey clouds. Miles left his bed, grabbed a cloth and wiped the sweat from his brow. He peered out of the window at the different flags fluttering from the top of the amphitheatre.

A knock sounded on his door. 'A minute, please,' Miles said, scrambling for his clothes. After getting dressed, he wrapped himself in a blanket to cover his disabled foot before opening the door a sliver.

'Hi,' Raquel said. 'Did I wake you?'

Miles shook his head. 'No, I was awake.'

'May I come in?' Raquel said.

'Oh, sorry,' Miles said, opening the door and standing aside.

Raquel walked over to a chair and sat. She looked up at Miles with a cloud of concern across her face.

'Are you OK?' Miles said, sitting down next to her.

'What did you say to Rafa last night?'

Miles frowned. 'What do you mean?'

'He is being distant,' Raquel said. 'I am worried he won't be careful and he will do something silly.'

'Will your father take him back after we complete this mission?'

Raquel's eyes dropped to her hands. 'I am not sure. I think he will because he is always true to his word.'

'I don't think Rafa will jeopardise the chance of being with you either,' Miles said.

Raquel's head shot up. She stared wide-eyed with her mouth open.

'The only people who think you and Rafa are a secret are you and Rafa,' Miles said, rolling his eyes.

Raquel looked down at her hands. 'Do you think my father knows?'

'I am sure he does,' Miles said. 'I think he knows exactly what is going on with his daughter.'

For the first time since Raquel walked into the room, she gave a smile. 'Will you look after him for me?'

'I do not need looking after, my lady,' Rafa said from the doorway.

Raquel's face turned a bright red.

'Are you ready, sir?' Rafa said, the corners of his mouth turning up.

Miles reached into his pocket and pulled out a token. 'These are the tokens you gave me. The messengers of Battleacre know me well enough now. If you need me or Rafa, give them the token and they will search for us.'

Raquel placed the token in one of her pockets. At the bedroom door, she pecked Rafa on the cheek, then disappeared down the hallway.

Miles's shoulders shook with laughter at Rafa's red face.

Rafa cleared his throat. 'Shall we get moving?'

Miles followed Rafa out of the estate and onto the icy, winding street.

'Where do we start?' Rafa said.

'We check my contacts,' Miles said. 'I have people looking out for anything suspicious. Let's get to the southern entrance of the amphitheatre.'

As they walked through the misty morning park, Miles flinched at the shifting shadows created by the trees. He pulled Billy's cloak tighter around himself and jammed his hands into his pockets. As they exited the park, Miles peered back and sighed.

'Are you OK?' Rafa said as they continued down the winding street.

Miles scratched his chin. 'I am worried about Janie. This park is the only place I have seen her.'

Rafa placed his hands behind his back. 'We will need to plan what to do with her.'

Miles gave Rafa a sideways glance. 'What do you mean?'

'She is a vampire,' Rafa said. 'After what happened with his son, I don't think the General is going to show much mercy.'

Miles shook his head. 'I didn't think of that. I need to warn her.'

'She will find out once we begin the General's work,' Rafa said, tapping his spear. 'News will travel fast.'

At the south entrance, they sat on the benches facing the amphitheatre. The sun broke over the eastern wall and lifted the mist covering Battleacre. Miles turned his head at the swish of a broom on the ground. The street sweeper stopped at the benches and donned his cap.

'Any news, my good man?' Miles said, looking up at the sweeper.

The street sweeper leant his chin on the end of the broom handle. 'The Hammer and the Shield sitting in the same place. Ominous indeed.'

Rafa gave the street sweeper a grin. 'It is good to see you again, old friend.'

'This young tyke occasionally stole my broom for an afternoon's entertainment,' the street sweeper said.

Miles smirked at Rafa. 'There is much to learn about you, my friend.'

The street sweeper chuckled then, looking at Miles, he turned serious. 'The Alphorn is where you need to be. All is not what it seems at that place.'

'What do you mean?' Miles said.

The street sweeper straightened his back. With a raised

eyebrow, he pointed at Miles and Rafa's feet. They raised their feet, then the sweeper swept under them and said, 'The owner of The Alphorn Inn has a daughter. It is her you seek.'

'What's so important about Jarod's daughter?' Miles said, casting his mind back to the young girl with blonde hair, running away from her father.

'It is all I can say,' the sweeper said. 'Have a good day.'

Miles and Rafa watched the sweeper move towards the amphitheatre's southern entrance.

'Who is he?' Miles said.

'He has been doing that job since the day I was born,' Rafa said. 'He has also been that same age since I can remember.'

The sweeper, now halfway to the southern entrance, reached into his pocket, took out a handkerchief, and hacked loudly into it.

Miles sat up straight.

'You look like you have seen a ghost,' Rafa said.

'Something is not right here, Rafa,' Miles said. 'I need to speak to that sweeper again.'

Miles and Rafa scanned the large yard. The street sweeper was nowhere to be seen.

'Very odd,' Rafa said.

'My father has a cough like that,' Miles said. 'He got it from the monstrous machines in the City of Lynn.'

'The General has spoken about these machines,' Rafa said. 'The cause of this black snow. It's like a plaque on our land.'

'What have we here?' Miles said, flicking his head at a messenger sprinting towards them.

The messenger skidded to a halt. He placed his hands on his knees to catch his breath.

'Your message, lad?' Rafa said.

'The Alphorn Inn,' the messenger said. 'There has been a fight. Someone injured the owner.'

Miles whipped out a copper coin and pressed it into the messenger's hand.

'I can go ahead?' Rafa said, with a look at Miles's foot.

'No,' Miles said. 'You cannot take them on alone. I will try to keep up with you.'

They walked as quickly as Miles's right foot would allow them to. The crowds, now gathered around the amphitheatre's southern entrance for the day's games, fell into a hush as the Hammer and Shield walked past them. At the entrance to the entertainment district, Miles could see the gathered groups of people outside The Alphorn Inn.

'Make way,' Rafa shouted. 'Create a path.'

The crowds parted as Miles and Rafa made their way to the inn.

Miles pushed open the front door and tutted at the mess of upturned tables and chairs. 'Jarod,' he said. 'Where are you?'

The storeroom door slammed open and Jarod walked in holding a blood-soaked cloth to his head.

'Is there anyone in your inn we need to worry about?' Rafa said, placing his hand on his spear.

Jarod shook his head. 'They have gone.'

'I will disperse the crowd,' Rafa said, walking back to the front door.

'Let me see,' Miles said, removing the cloth from Jarod's head.

'Just a bump,' Jarod said. 'A woman threw me right over the bar.'

'Genevie,' Miles said. 'Tall, with green catlike eyes and straight black hair that runs over one shoulder?'

Jarod nodded. 'That's her.'

'So she is in Battleacre,' Miles said.

'Who is she?' Jarod said.

'A royal vampire,' Miles said. 'She wants me, and she is the one stealing the women from Battleacre.'

Rafa returned and began righting the tables and chairs.

'Where is your daughter, Jarod?' Miles said.

Jarod frowned. 'How do you know about her?'

'I have been told she is important and that we need to keep her safe,' Miles said.

'Who told you this?' Jarod said, clenching his fists. 'You need to leave her alone.'

Miles rested his hand on Jarod's shoulder. 'I am the Hammer and Rafa is the Shield. The General of Battleacre trusts us. I need to take your daughter to the estate to keep her safe. You need to trust us too, Jarod. Was she the loved one you were talking about?'

'Yes,' Jarod said, dropping the cloth and placing his head in his hands. 'I don't know what to do. The woman asked me about her.'

Miles glanced at Rafa. 'The royal vampire? Genevie? She asked about your daughter?'

Jarod looked up. 'Yes. The vampire knew she wasn't really my daughter. Two seasons ago, I found her on the streets. She was cold and hungry. I took her in and looked after her.'

'Jarod, where is she?' Miles said. 'I have to get her before Genevie finds her.'

'I have her hidden,' Jarod said.

'Where?' Miles said. 'She is in danger, Jarod. Where is she?'

'She is staying with her grandmother in the weavers district,' Jarod said, scribbling an address and instructions on a piece of paper.

Miles took it. 'Will she know it's safe to come with me?'

'Show the note to my grandmother. I have left instructions and a code word that will tell her the note has come from me.'

Miles looked over at Rafa. 'Stay here please, Rafa, and get this inn back open. Let's make everything look as normal as possible.'

Rafa walked over and grabbed Jarod by the elbow. ‘Get me a serving apron. You have a new employee today.’

Jarod picked up the cloth and placed it back on his head. He walked into the storeroom to get an apron.

‘You going to be OK out there?’ Rafa said.

‘I will pick this girl up and drop her at the Soldier’s estate,’ Miles said. ‘Take this token. Give it to a messenger if you need me.’

Rafa pocketed the token. ‘Be safe, my friend.’

Miles walked north, then turned west as he followed the ring road around the amphitheatre. The weavers district in the north-east of Battleacre lay in a small valley below them. The streets, narrower than the housing streets of the officers district, rose and fell down into the valley. Miles checked the note and turned into a small street leading to the city’s north wall. A grey house with an unkempt lawn sat at the end of the street. Miles opened the squeaky gate and walked up to the front door.

‘Who goes there?’ an old lady said from behind the front door.

‘Jarod sent me. I am here for his daughter.’

The woman pulled open the door and checked up and down the road. ‘Who are you?’

‘I am a friend of Jarod’s. I have this note for you.’

The grandmother snatched the note from Miles. After reading the note, she placed it into her pocket and waved Miles into the house. ‘Luxea, there is a man here sent by your papa.’

At the end of the hallway, a small round face peered out of a doorway. She gave Miles a wide-eyed stare, then disappeared into her room.

‘Luxea,’ the grandmother said, raising her voice.

Miles walked down the hall and popped his head around the

door frame. The little girl with the long blonde hair sat on the end of her bed holding a small worn doll. She stared up at Miles with big round white misty eyes.

'You need to come with me, Luxea,' Miles said, swinging open the door.

'Where is my papa?'

Miles walked over to the bed and knelt. 'Your papa is at work in the inn and he sent me here to look after you. He wants you to be safe.'

The little girl pulled the doll tight to her chest. 'I don't know you. You are a stranger.'

'Yes, I am, and it is right you should go nowhere with strangers,' Miles said. 'But your papa gave your grandma a note that says you need to come with me.'

Her grandmother walked over to Luxea and sat on her bed. 'You need to go with this nice man. He is going to take you somewhere safe. Your papa has said it is OK.'

'Can Pippa come?'

'Pippa?' Miles said.

Luxea held out her little doll. 'Pippa!'

'Of course Pippa can come with us,' Miles said. 'She deserves to be safe as well.'

Luxea hopped off the bed, walked over to a small chest, and pulled out two sets of clothes which she stuffed into a bag. She walked over to her grandmother, gave her a hug, then stood in front of Miles.

'Is that all you have?' Miles said.

Luxea nodded. 'My papa says I can get new clothes on my birthday.'

Miles smiled. 'And when is your birthday?'

'When there is no snow,' Luxea said, with a smile missing two front teeth.

'Midsummer,' the grandmother said. 'We don't know the exact day of Luxea's birthday.'

'Well then,' Miles said. 'Are you ready to go? It is a long walk to the other side of the city.'

Luxea nodded. 'What will happen to Grandma?'

'Grandma will be just fine,' the woman said. 'I can take care of myself, dear.'

Luxea threw her tiny bag over her shoulders, tied Pippa to one strap, and marched out of her room.

Miles pulled out two gold coins and a silver coin from his purse. 'Take these,' he said, pressing them into the grandmother's hands. 'Luxea will be with us at the General's estate. You can visit whenever you want to.'

The grandmother pocketed the coins. She narrowed her eyes and wagged her finger in Miles's face. 'If anything happens to my grandchild …'

Miles smiled. 'I will look after her. I promise.'

'Come on, Mister,' Luxea said from the front door. 'Pippa says it's time to go.'

Miles took Luxea by the hand and walked out of the front door. They walked to the end of the garden and out of the creaking front gate. Patches of black snow dotted the streets and pavements. Luxea kicked her worn shoes at the snow as they walked up the valley.

'How do you know my papa?' Luxea said, skipping along.

'We met at your papa's inn,' Miles said. 'He is helping me with some things in the city. How often do you see your papa?'

Luxea scrunched up her face. 'Not a lot. He says he has to work all day and all night so me and grandma can have cake on Sundays.'

'Cake on Sundays?' Miles said.

'My grandma makes the best cake,' Luxea said. 'My papa brings home the stuff to make the cake.'

Miles grinned. 'It seems like Sundays are the best days.'

They continued through the winding streets until they reached the end of the weavers district. Turning south, the western wall of Battleacre rose high on their left. In the distance, the amphitheatre's flags peeked over the hills. The roar of the crowd touched their ears. They entered a wide cobblestone street that opened into the richer housing district of Battleacre. On each side of the cobblestone street stood a row of tall trees. Further south, the estates of the officers district sat on the hills. The crowds roared louder.

Suddenly, Luxea pulled her hand away from Miles and jumped into an elaborate show of swordplay. 'Papa says there is a lot of fighting in the arena. I would like to fight in the arena one day.'

Miles smirked at the young girl. 'Do you think you would win?'

Luxea jumped into the air and came down with an almighty sword strike. She threw her hands up and marched in a circle around Miles. 'I am the great Luxea. Beware the great Luxea.'

Miles's shoulders shook with laughter.

'Well, hello there.'

Miles froze.

Luxea skipped to Miles and hid behind his legs.

'Genevie.'

'Yes, my boy,' Genevie said, leaning against a tree trunk.

Miles reached out a hand behind him and pulled Luxea closer.

'Don't hide, little one,' Genevie said. 'I need you to come with me.'

'You leave her alone,' Miles said, pulling out the dark short sword.

'Sorry, my boy,' Genevie said. 'Orders from the City. It seems the little girl is even more valuable than you and your wolf.'

'She is staying with me, Genevie,' Miles said, pointing the sword at the royal vampire.

Genevie reached behind the tree and pulled out Jarod. 'So this is your daughter, Jarod.'

'Papa,' Luxea said, struggling to break free from Miles's grip.

'Stay there, Luxea,' Jarod said.

Luxea stopped struggling and peered around Miles's legs.

'What have you done to him?' Miles said.

Genevie ran the back of her hand across Jarod's cheek. A thin veil of smoke danced out of her fingertips and entered his ears.

The breath caught in Miles's throat.

'Why the wide eyes, boy?' Genevie said.

Miles eventually blinked. 'I can see your essence.'

'You are lying,' Genevie said with a snort.

'What is wrong with Papa?' Luxea said, peeking around Miles's legs.

Miles shoved Luxea gently backwards as he moved away from Genevie.

'Come here, little Luxea,' Genevie said. 'Your papa wants to give you a hug.'

'I want my papa,' Luxea said.

'Run, Luxea,' Jarod shouted.

Genevie pulled out a dagger and drove it into Jarod's chest. Jarod's eyes bulged before he dissolved into a cloud of dust.

The back of Miles's cloak fluttered. Miles spun and glared at the space where Luxea had once stood. 'Luxea,' he shouted.

'What have you done with her?' Genevie said.

Miles faced Genevie. 'Where is she?'

Genevie shrugged. 'Don't look at me. I have stood here the whole time. Don't tell me you have lost her?'

Miles scanned the length of the street. 'Luxea,' he shouted again.

'It looks like you have to make a choice, boy.'

Miles faced Genevie. 'What choice?'

'Who you're going to save? Your beloved Janie? The little girl? Or your dying friend in The Alphorn Inn?'

'Rafa?' Miles said. 'What have you done to him, Genevie?'

'Hurry, boy,' Genevie said before disappearing behind the tree.

'Luxea?' Miles shouted. 'Luxea, where are you?'

CHAPTER 15
NO DEAL

Miles kicked in The Alphorn's front door. Splinters from the door frame flew across the floor. 'Rafa?' he shouted. 'Rafa, where are you?'

A groan echoed from behind the bar. Miles slammed open the hatch, knelt and helped Rafa sit up. 'Where are you hurt?'

Rafa placed his hand on an egg-shaped lump on his head.

'Come on. Let's get you out of here,' Miles said, pulling Rafa's arm over his shoulder and then lifting him to his feet.

'She didn't bite me. I am sure of it, sir,' Rafa said, rubbing his neck with his other hand.

'I know she didn't. You wouldn't be lying on the floor with a wound if she had. It would have healed.'

They struggled from the bar to the front door. Miles brought his fingers to his mouth and whistled. A messenger ran up. 'Yes, sir,' the young girl said.

'I need two messengers,' Miles said. 'Can you call another?'

The girl jumped up and down while waving both hands in the air. A boy darted through the crowd and stood next to the girl.

'We need a doctor at the General's estate. Which one of you can fetch one?'

'Yes, sir,' the boy said.

Miles flicked a coin into the air, which the boy caught. 'Be quick. Tell the doctor they have injured the Shield.'

'I am fine,' Rafa said, still swaying on his feet.

'Go now,' Miles said, pointing his chin south.

The boy pocketed the copper and disappeared into the crowds of people.

'I need you to fetch the General for me,' Miles said to the young girl.

The girl's eyes widened. 'The General, sir?'

'Get Raquel,' Rafa said, smiling down at the girl.

The girl hopped from foot to foot. 'I can get Miss Raquel.'

Miles pressed the copper into the young girl's hand. 'Find Raquel and tell her the vampires have injured the Shield. Tell her we are on our way to the General's estate.'

The young girl pocketed the copper coin and ran, weaving through the crowds on the main street.

'Let's get you moving,' Miles said, pulling his arm tighter over Rafa's shoulder.

'What time is it?' Rafa said. 'And how did I get here?'

'You took a nasty knock to the head,' Miles said. 'I am taking you home.'

Rafa chuckled. 'The General is going to wonder why his food is not ready.'

Miles glanced at his friend. 'Hold on, Rafa, we will get you home. I shouldn't have left you there alone.'

With a grimace, Rafa said. 'Did you get the kid?'

'At least you remember that,' Miles said. 'I got her, but someone took her from me.'

'Jarod will not be pleased. He disappeared into the alley before that good-looking vampire got there. I wonder where Jarod got to?'

Miles ignored the comment. At the amphitheatre's east entrance, he turned south.

'Rafa,' Raquel shouted, as she ran up from the southern entrance. 'Miles, what is wrong with him?'

'They hit him on the head. I have sent a messenger to get a doctor. He has a terrible concussion.'

'Oh, Rafa,' Raquel said, pulling his other arm over her shoulder. 'Hold on, we will get you home.'

'Out of my way,' the Soldier's voice thundered through the streets. The crowds parted as the Soldier marched up towards them. In one sweeping movement, he swept Rafa up in his arms and doubled the pace towards his estate.

'Miles sent for a doctor, Papa,' Raquel said, double-stepping to keep up with her father.

They jogged past the amphitheatre's southern entrance and into the officers district. The Soldier filled his cheeks and panted as he walked up the hill. With the ground flattening at the children's playground, he picked up pace. At the end of the park, he powered up through the winding streets to the gate of his estate. A doctor, holding a medic's bag, stood at the front door.

'Place him on a flat surface please, sir,' the doctor said.

The Soldier walked into the kitchen and laid Rafa onto the table. He stepped back to give the doctor space to work.

'Why is he not awake?' Raquel said, wringing her hands.

The doctor tutted to himself as he ran his palms over Rafa's head.

'What happened?' the Soldier said, looking at Miles.

'The little girl,' Miles said, dropping into a kitchen chair and placing his head in his hands. 'Someone took her from me. Is Rafa going to be OK? I shouldn't have left him.'

The Soldier pulled over a chair and sat. 'Speak, son. What happened?'

Miles rubbed his eyes with the heels of his hands. 'Is he going to be OK?'

'Raquel,' Rafa shouted, sitting up.

Raquel barged the doctor out of the way. 'I am here, love.'

Rafa chuckled, fell back onto the table, and closed his eyes.

The Soldier rolled his eyes. 'He will be just fine. Tell me what happened, son.'

'Genevie,' Miles said. 'She hurt Rafa. Someone took Luxea.'

The Soldier's face turned red. 'Genevie is in my city? She is walking around in my city?'

Raquel moved out of the doctor's way and sat on another chair. 'Where is the girl now, Miles? Is her name Luxea?'

'She was behind me, and then, just like that, she disappeared.'

Raquel's forehead crinkled in confusion. 'You are not making sense.'

'And Jarod?' the Soldier said. 'Where is this girl's father?'

Miles looked up at the Soldier. 'Genevie changed him, and then she killed him in front of his own daughter. I don't know if Luxea saw.'

Raquel made a sound of disgust. 'What a horrible thing to do in front of a child. We need to go and look for her.'

'It is too dangerous, Raquel,' Miles said. 'Genevie has called the rest of the royals. They are coming here to destroy Battleacre. You cannot go out there.'

'Hang on,' Raquel said, raising both of her hands. 'Genevie is in town and she hurt Rafa. She also killed Luxea's father in front of her. Luxea is missing. And the royal vampires are going to attack Battleacre?'

'Yes,' Miles said.

'How do you know all of this?' the Soldier said.

Miles lowered his head back into his hands. 'Janie warned me.'

Raquel rolled her eyes.

'You cannot trust her, son,' the Soldier said, waving a finger in Miles's face. 'She is being controlled. You know that.'

'I think I have a way to stop her being controlled,' Miles said. 'We did it in the south. Is there any news on the messenger reaching Fairacre?'

The Soldier sat back. 'We won't know anything until your friends from the south arrive or the messenger returns to tell us they couldn't get there.'

'I know this is hard to believe, but there is a way I can help Janie.'

'But until then, son, you cannot trust her.'

'Can we not send someone from here to the south, Papa?' Raquel said.

'No,' Miles said, shaking his head vigorously. 'I don't want these vampires following us there.'

'They would know through Janie,' Raquel said.

'Maybe,' Miles said. 'But there is no reason for them to go there at the moment. Luxea and Waya are top of the agenda for them.'

Rafa sat up. 'Where am I?'

'You are home, love,' Raquel said, walking over and pulling him into a hug.

The doctor cleared his throat.

'Sorry,' Raquel said, releasing Rafa and sitting back in her chair.

'What happened in the council?' Miles said.

'My papa dealt with things in his usual subtle way,' Raquel said.

Miles snorted at the Soldier.

'Two vampires, son,' he said. 'Two vampires sitting right under our noses. Sitting on the very chairs my father's friends once sat on.'

'They were sitting under our noses,' Raquel said, shaking her head. 'Now they cover the council chambers with their dusty remains.'

'I will take back my seat in the council alongside my daughter,' the Soldier said. 'Until we eradicate these vermin from Battleacre.'

'I have done what I can, sir,' the doctor said, clipping his bag closed. 'He has a serious concussion. Someone must watch over him tonight. If he is no better in the morning, please call for me.'

Raquel stood and held one of Rafa's hands. 'I will stay with him this evening.'

The Soldier handed the doctor a gold coin and saw him out of the estate.

'I am going to look for Luxea,' Miles said. 'I cannot leave her out there.'

'Do you think she is even alive, son?' the Soldier said, returning to the kitchen.

'I need to find out. I will not let them turn her like they turned Janie.'

'Then I shall come with you,' the Soldier said. 'We will work quicker together.'

A soft tap sounded on the front door. The Soldier stood and lay a finger on his lips.

'Are you expecting anyone?' Raquel whispered.

The Soldier shook his head, then walked out of the kitchen to the front door. 'Who is there?'

'Open the door, mister,' a young girl said.

'Luxea,' Miles said, shuffling out of the kitchen.

'What are you doing here?' the Soldier said, reaching for his greatsword.

'Janie?' Miles said, barging the Soldier out of the way.

The Soldier grabbed Miles by the collar and pulled him to one side.

'Don't you hurt him, mister,' Luxea said, marching up to the Soldier and placing her hands on her hips.

'Papa, please,' Raquel said, grabbing his forearm. 'Not in front of the child.'

Miles knelt. 'Luxea. Are you OK?'

Luxea clutched Pippa tightly to her chest.

'Did they hurt you? Let me see,' Miles said, lifting her hair and checking her neck.

'Nobody hurt me,' Luxea said.

Miles stood and glared at the red rings in Janie's eyes. 'You took her?'

Janie nodded.

'She is one of them,' the Soldier said. 'Be careful, son.'

'Leave her alone, mister,' Luxea said, kicking the Soldier in the shins.

Miles rose and turned on the Soldier. 'She saved Luxea.'

The Soldier growled and walked back into the kitchen.

Miles knelt and pulled Luxea into a hug. 'I am sorry I didn't protect you.'

Luxea wrapped her arms around Miles's neck and squeezed. 'That is OK. This nice lady took me to the swings in the park.'

'Are you sure you are OK?'

'Where is my dada?'

Miles thought for a second, then told it as it was. 'I am sorry, Luxea. Your father isn't coming back.'

Luxea's bottom lip quivered. 'Did the nasty lady get him?'

Miles untangled Luxea's arms. 'I am sorry. There wasn't anything I could do.'

'What about my grandma?'

'Your grandma will be safe. They don't know where you came from, do they, Janie?' Miles said, looking up at Janie.

Janie shook her head. 'They don't know.'

'Can I go back to my grandma?' Luxea said.

Miles looked up at Raquel.

Raquel knelt. 'I don't think you can go back to your grandma,' she said. 'If you go back to your grandma, the nasty lady will get both you and your grandma.'

Luxea pulled Pippa closer to her chest and dropped her head.

'How would you like to stay here with me?' Raquel said, lifting Luxea's head by the chin. 'You can have your own room and nice food.'

'Cake on Sunday,' Miles said. 'And a new outfit for your birthday.'

'I don't think we need to wait for your birthday for a new outfit,' Raquel said, taking Luxea's hand. 'We can get a new one tomorrow.'

Luxea gave Raquel a half smile, then looked back at Miles. 'Will you stay here?'

'I will have to speak to him first,' the Soldier shouted from the kitchen.

Raquel huffed and picked Luxea up. 'Let's go and get you settled in your new room. We have a few rooms, so you get to pick one.'

Miles watched Raquel take Luxea up the stairs, then he faced Janie. 'I told you not to come here.'

'You knew she was in the city,' the Soldier shouted from the kitchen.

'I must go,' Janie said, backing away.

'Go to the swings in the park,' Miles said, grabbing her hand. 'Wait for me there.'

Janie squeezed Miles's hand, then disappeared out of the estate.

Miles walked into the kitchen and sat on the other side of the breakfast table.

'Janie is going to tell Genevie about Luxea,' the Soldier said.

'Something isn't right,' Miles said. 'She saved Luxea and brought her here. Why didn't she just hand her over to Genevie?'

The Soldier sat back and interlaced his fingers behind his head. 'You are right. That makes little sense.'

'I need to speak to her.'

'I will come with you,' the Soldier said, sitting forward.

'No,' Miles said. 'I need you to stay here and protect your house. An injured Rafa cannot protect your house or our guest.'

The Soldier sat back. 'Speak to Janie. See what she says. You are the Hammer of my house, son. We all need you here.'

Miles stood and checked his two short swords. 'I will be back shortly.'

The Soldier followed Miles out of the kitchen and into the foyer.

'Where do you think you are going, mister?' Luxea said from the top of the staircase.

Miles turned and grinned up at the little girl.

Luxea hopped down the stairs and marched over to Miles. 'Are you going to fetch Janie? I like Janie.'

Miles knelt. 'I am going to speak to Janie to find out what is going on.'

'Where did Janie go?' Luxea said.

'We have a special place at the playground.'

Luxea wrapped her arms around Miles's neck. 'I miss my dada and grandma.'

'We know,' Miles said, lifting his eyes up at Raquel. 'I am sorry about your dada.'

Luxea sniffed into Miles's shoulder.

'Raquel is waiting for you. I will see you when I get back.'

'Will you say hello to Janie?' Luxea said.

Miles untangled Luxea's arms from his neck. 'I will tell her you have your own room and that you will go shopping soon.'

Luxea gave Miles another half smile, then climbed the stairs up to Raquel.

'Be safe out there, son,' the Soldier said. 'Luxea has taken a shine to you and it would be heartbreaking for her to lose you.'

Miles checked his swords again and walked out of the estate. At the bottom of the winding street, he stopped at the edge of the park to scan the area. The children's playground lay eerily quiet. He walked over to the swings and turned in a circle, searching for movement. In a flash, Janie appeared in front of him.

'You scared me,' Miles said, putting his hand on his chest.

'Hold out your hand,' Janie said, looking nervously about.

Miles frowned.

'Quickly, before she gets here,' Janie said.

Miles opened his hand and blinked as Janie placed two devices on his palm. 'Valen's devices. His ear fans,' he whispered. 'So that's how you stopped her from influencing you.'

'I brought them with me purely by accident,' Janie said. 'They were in a pocket in one of my jackets.'

'Why are you giving them to me now?' Miles said.

'She will know she cannot influence me if I keep them in,' Janie said. 'I don't want her to know about these.'

'It's the same as the Lady,' Miles said. 'She transfers her essence into you and suggests things, controls you.'

Janie bit her bottom lip. 'It feels awful having someone control you.'

'What do we do now?' Miles said.

'The royals will be here tomorrow,' Janie said. 'They want the wolf.'

'And Luxea?' Miles said.

'They want to destroy Luxea,' Janie said.

Miles recoiled. 'She is a child. Why do they want to destroy her?'

'I don't know,' Janie said. 'Genevie asked me to do it.'

Miles looked down at the two devices in his hand. 'We need to get Luxea out of here.'

Janie froze. The red rings around her eyes flared. 'She is close.'

Miles pocketed the devices.

The rings around Janie's eyes dulled. She shook her head.

'What is she doing to you?'

'She is in my head,' Janie said, her voice catching in her throat.

Miles took a step backwards. 'Can she see what you see?'

Janie shook her head. 'No. She can only tell me what to do.'

'Where are you, Genevie?' Miles shouted. 'Show yourself.'

A twig at the border of the park snapped. Genevie stepped out from behind a tree and strode across to them. She placed a hand on the back of Janie's neck. Miles ignored the tentacles of grey smoke seeping out of Genevie's finger and into Janie's ears.

'I have a proposal for you,' Miles said.

Genevie smirked. Her long royal fangs extended over her bottom lip and down onto her chin. 'What proposal?'

'I will come with you if you release Janie,' Miles said. 'You can have the wolf.'

Genevie's head jerked back in surprise. 'Why the change of heart? And what of the young girl?'

'If you harm her, or this city, I will make sure you never see me or the wolf again.'

Genevie's mouth curved into a wide smile. 'My father and brothers will be here tomorrow. We will raze this city to the ground.'

Miles took a step forward and brought his face inches from Genevie. 'I will disappear with the wolf before your father and brothers get here. You will never find me. If you want me and Waya, let Janie go and leave the girl and the city.'

Genevie's brow knitted and her eyes rolled. A moment later, she shook her head, which cleared her eyes.

'Well?' Miles said.

'My father agrees we will leave them alone,' Genevie said. 'But Janie comes with us.'

'No deal,' Miles said.

Genevie snarled. 'You are testing me and my family, boy.'

Miles moved in closer yet. 'How well is the City of Lynn going to treat you when you go back empty-handed?'

Genevie closed her eyes. After a few moments, she opened them. 'We will leave the girl and the city alone. Janie comes with us as insurance. As soon as we have the wolf, we will let her go.'

'How do you guarantee her safety?' Miles said.

'That is the deal,' Genevie said. 'Take it, or we will unleash hell onto all the people here. And I will personally make the little girl suffer.'

Miles glanced at Janie. The rings around her eyes shone as Genevie controlled her with her essence. 'Janie?' he said.

'Do as she says, Miles,' Janie said, her voice hoarse. 'Or do you want me to die?'

With a curled lip, Miles looked back at Genevie and said, 'I accept.'

'Tomorrow, be at the northern gate at sunset,' Genevie said.

Miles took one last glimpse at Janie, then hobbled out of the park. At the highest point of the winding road, he took a moment to stare across Battleacre. The top of the amphitheatre stood high with its fluttering flags. With a sigh, Miles felt the dream of fighting there slowly fade from reality. The estate's gate squealed open and Miles made his way inside.

The front door of the villa closed behind Miles. He grinned at the laughs from Luxea and Raquel on the first floor. The door to the study lay slightly ajar. With a quick knock, Miles slipped in and sat opposite the Soldier.

The Soldier leant forward and studied Miles's face. 'You are going, aren't you? You are going with them.'

'I don't have a choice,' Miles said. 'If I don't go, the royals will kill Janie, kill Luxea, and then burn the city to the ground.'

The Soldier sat back and interlaced his fingers behind his head.

'But if I go, I have no guarantee they won't attack the city anyway,' Miles said.

'We can defend the city, son,' the Soldier said. 'You realise this place is full of warriors?'

Miles placed his elbows on his knees and lowered his head into his hands.

'What else is on your mind?' the Soldier said.

Miles looked up. 'I think we need to get Luxea out of here.'

'You mean out of Battleacre?' the Soldier said.

'Yes. We need to get her out of here with nobody seeing.'

'What about the horse farms?' the Soldier said. 'Heather and Jon are still wanting protection.'

'That could work,' Miles said.

'You are back,' Luxea said, skipping into the study. 'Can we go to the playground now?'

The Soldier's face softened as he looked down at Luxea.

'It will be dark soon,' Miles said. 'I don't think it's a wise idea to go into the park at night.'

Luxea sat cross-legged on the floor and placed Pippa in between her legs. 'OK, but only if you promise we can go tomorrow.'

Miles ignored the Soldier's raised eyebrows.

'Are you not going to promise?' Luxea said, gazing up at Miles.

Miles slipped off the chair and sat cross-legged in front of Luxea. 'We have a problem, which means I am going away for a while.'

Luxea twirled one of Pippa's ears in between her fingers. 'Is it the bad lady?'

'There you are,' Raquel said from the study door. 'I thought you were going to the kitchen?'

'I was asking Miles when we can go to the playground but he cannot promise because of the bad lady.'

Raquel walked over to the chairs and sat behind Miles.

Miles rubbed a finger on the top of Pippa's head. 'Can I ask you a question, Luxea?'

'Yes. If I can't answer, maybe Pippa can.'

Miles smirked and gave Pippa's head another rub.

'Well?' Luxea said. 'I am ready.'

'Is Jarod your real dad?' Miles said.

'Miles,' Raquel said, poking him with her shoe. 'What type of question is that?'

Luxea clutched Pippa tightly to her chest. 'It is OK,' she said, looking over at Raquel. 'Jarod isn't my real dada but I call him my dada.'

'Do you know who your real daddy is?' Miles said.

Luxea shook her head. 'My dada said he found me when I was small.'

'You are still small,' the Soldier said.

Luxea glared at him. 'I am not.'

The Soldier held up a hand and waggled his eyebrows.

'Why?' Luxea said, suddenly. 'Why are you asking if he is my dada?'

'Because you are special,' Miles said. 'Do you know if you have a brother?'

Luxea looked up at the ceiling, then back at Miles with a shake of her head. 'I don't think I have a brother.'

The Soldier suddenly sat forward.

Miles quickly shook his head.

The Soldier sat back and interlaced his fingers.

'I have my grandma, though,' Luxea said.

'And you have us,' Raquel said, clapping her hands together.

Luxea gave Raquel a wide smile.

Miles bit his bottom lip. 'I am in a tricky spot, Luxea. If I don't go with the bad lady, she and her friends will hurt everyone here in the city. But I don't want to leave you.'

'Will the bad lady hurt my grandma?'

'Yes. She will hurt your grandma if I don't go with her. Can you see my problem?'

The whites around Luxea's irises shimmered like swirling milk. A small frown creased her forehead. 'I don't want you to go with the bad lady, but I don't want my grandma to be hurt.'

'We have a plan though,' the Soldier said, sitting forward.

Luxea turned herself so she could look up at the Soldier.

'How would you like to go on a secret adventure?' the Soldier said.

Luxea's eyes widened, showing even more of the swirling,

swimming whites. She looked at Miles, then back at the Soldier. 'I like adventures.'

'We have friends on the horse farms in the south,' the Soldier said. 'We need to send protection to them. Protection from the bad lady. We are going to sneak you there so nobody knows where you are.'

Luxea jumped up and drew her imaginary sword. 'I can protect your friends too,' she said, slashing and hacking her sword.

The Soldier smacked the top of his thigh and roared with laughter.

'Aren't you the little warrior?' Raquel said, with a chuckle. 'I think it is time for your bed though before you chop someone's head off.'

'Aww,' Luxea said, peering up at the ceiling. 'Do I have to?'

'Yes you do, young lady,' Raquel said, sweeping Luxea off her feet.

'Once you have Luxea settled, can you come back and bring Rafa if he is able to join you?' the Soldier said.

Raquel nodded over her shoulder as she left the study. Miles dropped back into the chair opposite the Soldier. He looked down at the vambraces on his forearms. The vambraces of the Hammer. With a sigh, he unbuckled them and slipped them off. The Soldier sat on the end of his chair and squeezed one of Miles's hands. He gave Miles a nod and picked up the two vambraces. With a wiggle, he slipped the vambraces over his muscular forearms.

'They look good on you,' Miles said.

'I will keep them warm for you,' the Soldier said.

'Your city is going to need you,' Miles said. 'I don't trust Genevie. As soon as I go with them, they will launch an attack.'

'I wouldn't expect anything less,' the Soldier said.

The study door swung open. Raquel walked in, holding Rafa's elbow to guide him. Miles got off his chair and steered Rafa into it.

'How are you feeling?' the Soldier said.

Rafa rubbed the big lump on his head and grimaced. 'Sore, but I shall live.'

The Soldier sat back and laced his fingers around the back of his head. 'We have a plan.'

CHAPTER 16
A ROYAL FAMILY

'I have no choice, Raquel,' Miles said. 'If I don't do this, the royals will burn Battleacre.'

'We are a city of soldiers,' Raquel said, her hands planted on her hips. 'The city can defend itself.'

'We have Luxea and Janie to think of,' Miles said. 'Also, the women they have stolen. There is too much for us all to lose.'

'Father, speak to him,' Raquel said.

'Sit down please, love,' the Soldier said. 'I agree with Miles.'

Raquel dropped onto the chair and folded her arms. 'Next you will tell Rafa to go with him.'

The Soldier sat back.

'There is no way,' Raquel said, before the Soldier could interlace his fingers. 'Why does he have to go?'

'He is not going with me,' Miles said.

'I would go if the Hammer needs me,' Rafa said.

Raquel rubbed her forehead and sighed.

Rafa sat on the arm of the chair and placed an arm around her.

The Soldier nervously cleared his throat. 'I need Rafa to take Luxea to the horse farms.'

'Then I shall go with him,' Raquel said, looking up at Rafa.

'I need you here,' the Soldier said. 'Battleacre needs us now more than anything. You are a leader in the council.'

Raquel closed her eyes and shook her head.

'I am not happy leaving Raquel here with those vampires in the city,' Rafa said. 'Is there no other way?'

The Soldier's face hardened. 'I understand you both care for each other. But Luxea needs you, Rafa, and your city needs you, Raquel. There will be time to explore your new-found love at a later stage.'

Raquel's face turned a mild pink. 'It's not new-found,' she muttered.

'What of you, sir?' Rafa said, looking at Miles. 'Will you not be protecting little Luxea?'

'He is handing himself over to the royals,' Raquel said.

Rafa rubbed the bump on his head. 'Did I hear right? Or am I still concussed? I fear you will welcome your own death if you hand yourself over.'

'Not handing myself over will guarantee the death of everyone in this city,' Miles said. 'If I hand myself over, I will at least lead the royals away.'

'That may be so,' Rafa said. 'But as soon as they have your wolf, they will return.'

Miles sat back and closed his eyes. 'I know, Rafa. This is an exercise in buying time. I need Luxea hidden until my father, Dr Viktor, arrives. He will know what to do.'

The four of them sat in silence. The crackling fire popped and spat, sending sparks into the air. Miles cast his eye over to the table where the picture of the Lady sat.

Rafa cleared his throat, bringing everyone back to the present. 'How are we going to get Luxea to the horse farms?'

'My son had the job of sending protection to the people of the horse farms,' the Soldier said, with a glimmer of pain creasing across his face. 'I will send protection at sunset tomorrow. Rafa and Luxea will go with them.'

'I will keep the royals entertained while this is happening,' Miles said.

'They will know,' Raquel said. 'The royals will know something is happening, and they will send vampires.'

'I have thought of that and I think I have a solution,' Miles said. 'But it involves Janie.'

'What are you on about?' the Soldier said, slapping his thigh. 'You know I don't trust her, son.'

Miles held up a hand. 'I know, but I do, and I think she is the only one who can really protect Luxea right now.'

'You said Janie had to go with you,' the Soldier said. 'It was an order from Genevie.'

'If Genevie wants me to go with her, she is going to have to let Janie stay,' Miles said, pulling himself to his feet. 'It is late. I am going to find Janie tomorrow and speak to her. Can I assume you will organise the protection for the horse farms?'

'It is already underway,' the Soldier said.

Miles bowed his head and left the study to a chorus of whispers. With his hand on the banister, Miles hobbled up the stairs to his room. He walked over to the small desk in the corner. The desk drawer opened with a scrape and Miles pulled out paper, ink and a writing quill. For the next hour, he penned two letters that, once complete, he placed into envelopes. On one envelope, he wrote the name Dr Viktor and on the other, Chloe. He smiled to himself, thinking of Billy shaking his head at the lack of a letter. With both letters propped on the desk up against the wall, Miles removed his cloak and sat at the end of the bed. He kicked off his left boot, then sat staring at the three straps on the right boot. After a few moments of composure, he bent over and undid the straps. The pain streaked through his leg as his right foot turned inwards. Once his breathing settled, he pulled himself onto the bed and lay with his hands behind his head. He closed his eyes, knowing it would be a while until he felt comfort like this again.

The early morning mist swirled around the playground. Miles, sitting on the swing, pulled the cloak closer around his neck. He knew calling Janie would bring other vampires to the park, so he sat in silence. Thirty minutes later, Miles stood to stomp his cold feet on the ground. After turning around a few times, he jumped as Janie appeared in front of him.

'What are you doing here?' Janie said, trying not to smile.

Miles shook his head as he felt all the cold disappear from his body. 'I will never get used to you moving that quickly.'

'It feels normal to me,' Janie said. 'Why are you here? Are we not meeting the royals at sunset?'

'You are not to come with me,' Miles said, reaching for Janie's hand.

Janie took a step back and ignored his outstretched hand. 'What do you mean? Why don't you want to be with me?'

Miles took a step forward and took Janie's hand. 'It's not like that. I need you to do something else for me.'

'What do you mean, something else? I thought we were going to be together?'

'Put these in first,' Miles said, reaching into his pocket and pulling out the devices.

Janie took the devices and placed one in each ear.

'Now she cannot track you or influence you,' Miles said, leading Janie to the swings.

'She cannot track me, but there are eyes everywhere,' Janie said, looking nervously about. 'She knows I am here.'

Miles pulled Billy's cloak off and wrapped it around Janie. Once secure, he guided her to sit on a swing. 'Like I said before, I don't want you coming with me. I need you to do something way more important. I need you to look after Luxea.'

'I am the worst person to look after her,' Janie said. 'As soon as a vampire sees me, they can tell the royals where I am.'

'Then let's not let another vampire see you,' Miles said. 'I need you to take Luxea south-east, to the horse farms. They will hide you there.'

Janie reached over and laced her fingers through Miles's. 'I don't want to leave you. If I am not there, I cannot help you.'

Miles pulled Janie's hand up and rubbed her knuckles against his own cheek. 'Don't you see?' he said. 'If you are there, they can use you against me. They can influence you to do things to me and to yourself, which will bring us both pain. And I have this powerful feeling Luxea is very important.'

Janie turned her face and dropped a kiss on Miles's fingers. 'This feels like a goodbye.'

Miles took in a deep breath and looked up at the grey clouds. With a long sigh, he stood and pulled Janie off the swing into a hug. 'I don't know what it means. But believe me, I will fight to get back to you. That I promise.'

Janie held Miles tight. She sniffed as red tears trickled down her face and onto his shoulder.

'It's time we go,' Miles said. 'I need you to get to the estate with nobody seeing you.'

'Are you coming to the estate too?' Janie said.

Miles cupped Janie's cheeks with his hands. 'Of course I will.'

Janie dropped a kiss on Miles's cheek and, with a swirl of mist, she disappeared.

Miles walked out of the park and back up the winding street to the estate. He opened the gate and shuffled up the steps to the front door. To his right, hiding in a bush, Janie crouched with a smile on her face. Miles pulled open the door and, in a flash, Janie stood in the foyer. He closed the door behind them.

'Janie,' Luxea shouted, bouncing down the stairs. 'I didn't know you were coming to visit?'

Janie smiled, then closed her mouth quickly as she remembered her fangs. 'How are you?' she said, kneeling and holding out her arms.

'Did you and Miles go to the park without me?' Luxea said, jumping into Janie's arms.

'We met in the park, but we didn't get to play,' Janie said. 'Plus, there is no time for the park. We need to get ready for our adventure.'

Luxea wrestled herself away from Janie. 'And Pippa. I forgot Pippa in my room,' she said, running back up the stairs. 'Me and Pippa will be back.'

'I will look after her for a bit,' Raquel said, her face set in stone. 'My father and Rafa are in the study.'

'Is she OK?' Janie said as they walked to the study door.

Miles opened the door and stepped aside. 'She is going to miss Rafa.'

'Ahh,' Janie said, walking into the study.

The Soldier, his eyes never leaving Janie, rose from his chair and stood with his hands behind his back.

'Come, sit here please,' Rafa said, pointing to the chair opposite the Soldier.

Janie looked at Miles, who gave her a nod. She walked over and sat on the end of the seat with her hands in her lap.

The Soldier lowered himself into his chair. 'Miles has said we can trust you.'

'As long as I have these devices in my ears, they cannot compel me to do something I don't want to,' Janie said.

'What are these devices?' the Soldier said.

'It may seem like a kind of magic to you, so hear me out while I explain,' Miles said as he sat down in the chair next to the fire. 'Do you remember what it is like being in love?'

The Soldier glanced at the picture sitting on the table.

Janie looked too. Her eyes widened. 'The Lady,' she whispered.

'I beg your pardon?' the Soldier said.

'Just a person we knew back in Fairacre,' Miles said, sliding off his chair and kneeling in front of Janie. 'Old memories from a different time.'

The Soldier frowned and narrowed his eyes at Janie.

Miles reached up and touched her chin. 'It's OK. A conversation for another time.'

Janie tore her gaze away from the picture and looked down at Miles. She closed her eyes and gave him a nod.

Miles swung himself round and sat on the floor in front of Janie's chair. He looked up at the Soldier. 'It all has to do with one's essence.'

'Essence?' the Soldier said.

'When we are in love, we share essence with the person we are in love with. It is why we feel something is missing when we lose someone. It is why we feel more whole when we love someone. We share our essence,' Miles said.

The Soldier sat back and interlaced his fingers. 'Go on.'

'Some people can manipulate their essence. The royal vampires use their essence to control all the other vampires. It is how Genevie has been controlling Janie.'

'And my son,' the Soldier said. 'Was he controlled?'

'A royal ordered your son,' Janie said. 'Every vampire heard it.'

The Soldier closed his eyes and took in a deep breath. After a few moments of silence, he opened his eyes and said, ‘So how is Janie not being controlled?’

Janie moved her thick, red hair away from her ear and showed the Soldier the small device. ‘It is a device made by a master craftsman in Fairacre. It has a small fan that activates when it senses essence. No essence can get into me when I am wearing these.’

‘The little fans have a small piece of essence from the master craftsman,’ Miles said. ‘A little piece of him exists in the devices. It is what keeps the devices alive.’

‘What if someone removes the devices from Janie’s ears?’ Rafa said. ‘What do I need to do?’

Janie looked up at Rafa with a confused look. ‘Why would you be able to do anything?’

‘Rafa is going with you. He will be your Shield,’ the Soldier said. ‘His mission will be to protect you and Luxea at all costs.’

‘And to protect Luxea from you if I have to,’ Rafa said, looking straight at Janie.

‘If the devices fall out, I will go before you know,’ Janie said. ‘It takes a bit of time for a royal to find me. Especially if I am far away.’

‘Before you run, you need to tell me,’ Rafa said. ‘You will lead them back to the horse farms and I will need to get us away from there.’

Janie lowered her head. ‘I will tell you immediately.’

The Soldier sat forward and steepled his fingers in front of his face. ‘We need to get Luxea and Rafa out of here without the vampires knowing. Is that something you can take care of?’

‘We need a diversion,’ Janie said, looking up. ‘If a caravan of soldiers leave the southern gate, there will be vampires with them. So we cannot be in that caravan.’

‘I suggest we move the caravan while we’re transferring Miles to the royals,' the Soldier said. 'This will cause the greatest of distractions.'

Janie lay a hand on Miles's shoulder. Miles reached up and interlaced his fingers with hers.

'I can move them both, but it will be one at a time,' Janie said.

'Luxea first,' Rafa said. 'Make sure she is safe then come and get me.'

The study door banged open and in marched Luxea. 'Janie, come and see my bedroom.'

'I think we are done for now,' the Soldier said. 'Can you send my daughter in please, Janie?'

Janie stood and straightened her clothes. 'I will look after Luxea with my life. I can promise you that.'

'I can look after myself,' Luxea said, slashing the air with her swords. 'I am the great Luxea.'

With a slap of his knee, the Soldier roared with laughter. 'The great Luxea is among us.'

Luxea jumped into the air and slashed her swords in a figure of eight.

The Soldier stood and faced Janie. 'Looking after Luxea is all I can ask of you. Do not let what happened to my son happen to her.'

'Sorry about your son,' Janie said. 'Know he wasn't in his right mind. The royal who ordered him to take your daughter's life is Malik. He is the leader of the entire vampire kingdom.'

A muscle twitched in the Soldier's jaw. 'Thank you.'

Janie left the room with Luxea's hand in her own. Before the door could shut, Raquel marched in.

'I feel an ear bashing coming,' the Soldier said.

Raquel waited for Miles to move out of the way before she sat on the couch. She folded her arms and stared at her father.

'Love,' Rafa said, laying a hand on her shoulder.

'Oh, keep quiet,' Raquel said, swatting his hand away. 'I don't want to hear it.'

The Soldier sat and raised both hands. 'I am sorry, daughter, but you know what is at stake. We have to do it this way.'

Raquel bit her bottom lip. 'Everything I care for is being taken away from me.'

'I am not leaving you, love,' Rafa said.

'Well, you are, aren't you?' Raquel said.

The Soldier folded his arms. 'You two can deal with this later. We need to decide what we are going to do in Battleacre.'

'As soon as Miles goes with the royals, they will attack,' Rafa said.

'And we will be ready for them,' the Soldier said, unfolding his arms and tightening his vambraces. 'We have set traps and have leaked inaccurate information for the vampires to follow. Once they fall into the traps, our soldiers will be ready to take up the fight.'

'There will be a lot of vampire assassinations,' Raquel said. 'We have our eyes on many of them all over the city.'

'It's settled,' the Soldier said. 'At sunset, Luxea and Rafa leave with Janie, Raquel orders the citywide assassinations, and I hand over Miles to the royals. Once Miles leaves, I will join Raquel to protect the city.'

They sat in silence as each worked through the role they had to play that evening. Miles half smiled at the glances between Rafa and Raquel and the uncomfortable sighs of the Soldier.

A few minutes later, Miles stood. 'I am going to spend time with Janie and Luxea before sunset.'

Raquel jumped up and threw her arms around Miles's neck. 'You be safe when you are with those beasts.'

Miles squeezed Raquel and whispered into her ear. 'Make these monsters pay for what they have done.'

'We will,' Raquel said, stepping away from Miles and wiping a tear from her eye.

Rafa extended a hand, which Miles took. 'I will look after Luxea and Janie, my brother. That I will promise you.'

'Thank you, friend,' Miles said.

'Lead them as far away as you can, son,' the Soldier said. 'Buy us the time we need.'

The study door clicked closed. With his hand on the banister, Miles pulled himself up to the first floor and followed Luxea's voice. At the door of her room, he knocked gently.

The room fell into silence. 'Come in,' Luxea said, after conferring with Janie for a moment.

Miles opened the door and walked in. 'What are you two up to?'

'Miles,' Luxea said, jumping up and skipping to him. 'I have been doing drawings with Raquel.'

'I can see,' Miles said, brushing the charcoal from her small hands. 'Can I sit and watch?'

'Yes,' Luxea said, skipping back to Janie.

With a hand on the armrest, Miles lowered himself into a chair. 'Are you doing more drawings?'

Luxea, concentrating hard, stuck out her tongue and moved the charcoal about on the thick paper. 'It is a picture of the playground.'

Miles sat back and smiled at the little girl he would do anything to protect. A smile crept across his lips as he watched Janie, the girl he loved more than anything. A few moments later, his eyes closed as the chatter between the two of them sent him into a deep, dreamless sleep.

'It's time,' Janie said into Miles's ear.

Miles sat up and rubbed his eyes with the heel of his hand. 'What time is it?'

'An hour before sunset,' Janie said. 'Everyone is downstairs waiting for you.'

With a grunt, Miles pulled himself to his feet and wrapped Janie in a hug. 'I will be back. I promise you that.'

Janie squeezed Miles. 'Do you promise?'

'I do,' Miles said. 'I have something for you. Follow me.'

They walked out of Luxea's room, down the hall and into Miles's room. He walked over to the chair and picked up the sheath holding the two short swords. With the buckles loosened, he pulled the leather straps around Janie's shoulders so the swords criss-crossed her back. Janie pulled the straps tighter.

'Those are best suited for you,' Miles said, walking over to the cupboard.

'Are you sure?' Janie said.

'I am still a greatsword person,' he said, pulling out the weapon the Soldier had gifted him. 'I am going to ask them to safeguard this while I am gone.'

'I was never any good with swords,' Janie said.

'Remember your training and you will be great,' Miles said.

'I had a brilliant teacher,' Janie said, smiling up at him.

'Are we ready up there?' the Soldier shouted from the entrance hall.

'Get a move on, mister,' Luxea shouted. 'We haven't got all day, you know.'

Miles grinned at Janie. 'You are going to have your hands full with that little one.'

Janie giggled. 'I think it might be me that needs looking after.'

They climbed down the stairs hand in hand. At the bottom, Miles knelt and gave Luxea a hug. 'You listen to Janie and Rafa now, you hear?'

'I will,' Luxea said. 'And I will see you soon so we can play in the playground.'

Miles leant over and kissed Luxea's forehead.

'It's time. After you, my ladies,' Rafa said, sweeping his hand towards the front door.

Miles pulled Billy's cloak off and wrapped it around Janie. 'Too big, I know, but it will give you some cover.'

Janie pulled the drawstring closed, then leant in and kissed Miles.

'Ew,' Luxea said. 'Disgusting. Can we go now?'

Miles watched Rafa, Luxea and Janie walk out of the house and down to the gate.

'Ready, son?' the Soldier said, placing a hand on Miles's shoulder.

'I need you to keep this for me,' Miles said, reaching behind his back and pulling out his greatsword. 'The royals will just take it away from me.'

The Soldier took the sword and slipped it next to his own. 'I will keep her safe.'

With a last look around the house, Miles followed the Soldier out of the estate. After travelling through the city, Miles stood on the top of the northern wall. Three vampire royals on heavily armoured horses made their way to the northern wall of Battleacre. Members of the city trickled out of the gate and walked up the road, giving the royals a wide berth.

'Are you sure this is what you want to do?' the Soldier said, glancing over at Miles.

'I don't see another way,' Miles said.

The three royals stopped at the moat's edge and stared up at Miles. Genevie, growing bored, picked at her nails.

Miles faced the Soldier and extended a hand.

The Soldier looked down, ignored the hand and pulled Miles into an embrace. 'Take care, son.'

Miles took a last look across at the amphitheatre. He walked down the steps and through the northern gate. At the end of the moat, he turned and hobbled up to the three royals. The centre royal, much older than the other two, signalled to a vampire who walked over to Miles and bound his hands behind his back. The vampire pulled a collar from his robe and snapped it around Miles's neck. He secured a long piece of rope to the collar, then threw the end to Genevie.

'My name is Malik,' the centre royal said. 'And you have caused me a lot of trouble.'

Miles set his face in stone and glared up at the royal vampire.

Malik ran his hand through his long, braided beard. The hood of his cloak covered thinning grey hair and cast a shadow over his long nose.

'And I am Kaleb,' the other royal said, raising his hand. 'Son of Malik.'

Miles turned his eyes onto Kaleb and took in the strong angular jaw, wide eyes and strong nose. The rings around Malik and Kaleb's irises shone a bright red.

'And you know me,' Genevie said, tugging at the rope. 'Daughter of Malik. Time to go, wolf boy.'

Miles raised a hand. 'I wish to make sure we understand the terms of our agreement. Genevie has explained them to you both?'

'She has,' Malik said. 'But know this. If we do not receive the wolf, I will make sure the people you care about suffer for a very long time.'

Miles turned and took one last look at Battleacre. He looked back at Malik and gave the royal a nod. 'I understand.'

The royals swung their horses around and started a slow walk away from Battleacre. Miles looked to the ground to maintain his footing over the black-snow-covered cobblestones. Vampires walked in front, alongside and behind the royals. Their eyes constantly surveyed the surrounding area, looking for anything out of place.

'Once we have this wolf and hand her to the Queen, are we done?' Kaleb said.

Miles cocked his head to take in as much of the conversation as possible.

'The Queen is not the one who is after the wolf,' Malik said, raising his head and sniffing the air.

Genevie glanced at Malik. 'If not the Queen, then who?'

'The elder man with the four spheres requires the wolf,' he said. 'The Queen's request is for the women, which we have delivered.'

Genevie rolled her shoulders and rubbed the back of her neck. 'I wish to go home, Father. This land of cold, black snow has seeped into my bones.'

Malik looked over and smiled, showing his long thick fangs. 'As do I, my daughter. Your mother will be worried. We need to get home soon.'

'Mother will be displeased with the time we have been away,' Kaleb said. 'I will stay well away until you have calmed her down, Father.'

Malik chuckled. 'You will do as your mother wishes, my son.'

Miles stumbled and fell to his knees. Genevie looked behind her and tugged on the rope. Scrambling to his feet, Miles ignored the growing pain in his lower back and his right foot.

'I thought you said he is a capable warrior,' Malik said, flicking his head at Miles. 'Stumbling after such a short time does not match your assessment.'

Genevie shook her head. 'Underestimation will get you killed, Father. He may be a cripple but his swordplay is excellent.'

Kaleb grunted. 'Once we have his wolf, I would like to test his skill.'

The royals fell silent. To the north, a light mist formed over the rolling hills. The white of the mist kissing the black of the snow removed all colour from the world. The setting sun's glare through the clouds made Miles squint to stop his eyes hurting. One hill after the other came and went. Miles stumbled more often as he felt the skin split inside his shoes.

'He is faltering,' Genevie said, pulling on the rope again.

Malik sighed. 'There is a camp over the next horizon. Kaleb, go forward and clear it out.'

Kaleb clicked his tongue and his horse shot forward.

Miles tripped and fell onto his knees. He attempted to get up, but he fell forward onto his side. A vampire darted over and pulled him roughly to his feet.

'Come on, wolf boy,' Genevie said, glancing over her shoulder. 'Or you could just call your wolf and get this over and done with.'

Miles looked up. 'She will come if she wants to come. I have no control over her.'

Malik looked at Genevie. 'He cannot control this wolf?'

Genevie shook her head. 'He cannot but she is never far away.'

'When we get to the camp, send out a search team,' Malik said. 'I will not wait for her to come to us.'

They crested the next hill and made their way down the cobblestone path. At the bottom of the hill, a high fence appeared out of the mist. Kaleb, looking bored, sat on his horse on the other side of the fence.

'Is it clear, son?' Malik said.

'A few stragglers,' he said. 'We have sent them forward to the City of Lynn.'

Genevie hopped off her horse and handed the reins to a vampire. She walked back to Miles and unclipped the rope. Grabbing him by the shoulder, she led him to a fire pit where a vampire sat striking a rock to make a flame. She shoved Miles to the ground and then she sat on a log.

'I think we are going to need to get you a horse,' Malik said, sitting opposite them.

Genevie pouted. 'No fun in that, Father.'

'We are days away from the City if we are on horseback,' Malik said. 'At this pace, we are weeks away.'

Miles sat up and placed his back against the log Genevie sat against. He dropped his chin onto his chest and closed his eyes. The throbbing pain underneath the marks on the small of his back pulsed as a gentle reminder Waya was nowhere near them. He smiled, knowing the wolf had done what he had asked. The royals would never get the wolf this way.

'Eat,' Genevie said, nudging Miles with her elbow.

Miles looked at the bowl of vegetable slop, then back up at Genevie. 'How?'

Genevie reached behind Miles's back and undid his bonds.

The cold slop tasted of rotting vegetables. Miles ignored his gag reflex and sucked down as much of the food as possible. His stomach groaned and rumbled.

'We move at midnight,' Malik said. 'Find this boy a horse, Kaleb.'

After the food, Miles lowered his chin back onto his chest. He closed his eyes, knowing the best thing he could do was rest.

Miles jerked awake at the rough hands pulling him to his feet.

Genevie led Miles to a grey mare. 'Get on,' she said. 'You are lucky my father is merciful.'

'Only because we need the wolf,' Malik said. 'Once we have her, my mercy will fade.'

CHAPTER 17
GO, WAYA, GO

The black snow lay thick on the never-ending rolling hills. The long train of horses descended into yet another valley. Miles rocked backwards and forwards on his horse. Dry blood caked his mouth and nostrils from the daily beatings he received from the vampires. Over the next hill, he caught sight of the City of Lynn's tall steeples, which reached into the blackened, misty sky.

Genevie sniffed the air then looked over at Malik nervously.

'What is it, daughter?' Malik said.

'There is a slight warmth in the wind,' Genevie said. 'Spring will be here in a few weeks. The mists will lift and our kin will get caught in the direct sunlight. We need to end this, Father.'

'I know, my daughter,' Malik said. 'But we cannot return to the City of Lynn without the wolf. The old man has made it clear they would destroy mother if we came back empty-handed.'

Miles looked at Genevie through a blackened, enclosed eye. A small, painful smile spread across his face at the glimmer of fear rippling across Genevie's beautiful features.

'Do you think mother is OK?' Genevie said with another glance at Malik.

'You would feel it if she wasn't,' Malik said, also sniffing the air. 'For now, she is safe.'

'We cannot wait much longer for this wolf, Father,' Kaleb said, reining his horse in alongside Malik's. 'We will need to do something to draw her out.'

Malik turned his eyes towards the City of Lynn's steeples. 'I will think about it.'

'Can we not just kill the boy?' Kaleb said.

Malik glanced at Miles. 'If we kill him, the wolf will choose someone. If we don't know who that is, we will never find her.'

'I suggest we send Genevie back home then,' Kaleb said. 'If we cannot get this wolf, mother will need help and Genevie will be able to get closest to her.'

'I will not find it easy to leave you here alone, brother,' Genevie said, following her father's eyes towards the City of Lynn.

'I will have father with me,' Kaleb said. 'You are best suited to get close to mother to protect her.'

Malik lifted his hand to bring the slow-moving procession to a halt. He guided his horse off the cobblestone path and into the rolling field. He stopped at a lone, leafless tree. 'Genevie, it is time we try another tactic,' he said, jabbing his chin at Miles. 'Get him off his horse, please.'

Genevie slipped elegantly off her horse and pulled Miles from his. She watched him land in a heap on the ground.

Malik scanned the surrounding group and settled on a young vampire. With a raise of his eyebrow, he signalled the fresh-faced vampire over.

'Yes, master,' the young vampire said, bowing deep until his nose touched the ground.

'I wish you to turn the boy,' Malik said. 'But do not kill him.'

'An honour, master,' the young vampire said. He swaggered

over to Miles. With a clawed hand, he lifted Miles to his feet. He grabbed Miles's hair and pulled his head back to expose his neck. The vampire's small fangs extended. With a last look at Malik, he sank his teeth into the exposed flesh. Miles felt his blood being replaced with searing hot vampire poison. His eyes rolled into the back of his head as his heart missed a beat.

'Enough,' Malik said, raising an index finger at the young vampire.

Miles crumpled to the ground.

The young vampire ran his sleeve across his mouth. He smiled and raised his eyes towards the dark, grey clouds and let out a long, satisfying breath. Suddenly, the long breath caught in the vampire's throat. He levelled his head and stared wild-eyed at Malik, then back at Miles. His clawed hand grabbed his throat as he choked and gagged.

Miles struggled to his hands and knees and growled. His back arched as he coughed and spluttered. With a hack, he spat out a ball of thick black blood.

The vampire fell to his knees, ripping at his throat with his clawed fingers. He opened his mouth to scream but, before a sound came out, he dissolved into a pile of ash.

Miles threw up a second time before falling face-first into the ground. His body trembled as he lay holding his knees with his hands.

'I thought as much,' Malik said. 'Wolf blood coursing through those veins of his.'

'This is getting tiresome,' Genevie said, picking at her fingernails. 'Can we not just give him to the old man in the City?'

'I agree with you,' Malik said. 'I grow tired of this game. String him up please, Genevie.'

Genevie snapped her fingers at a nearby vampire. The vampire flashed to the lone dead tree and threw two ropes over the lowest bough. Two more vampires hauled Miles to his feet and dragged him to where the first vampire stood. Ropes snaked around Miles's wrists. The vampire yanked the ropes, pulling them taut. With a snap, Miles's arms spread high above his head.

Malik walked up to Miles and grabbed him by the jaw. 'This is your last chance, boy. Call your wolf.'

Miles coughed, spraying droplets of blood over Malik's face. The red circles around Malik's eyes flared at the taste of blood on his lips.

'Call her,' Malik growled.

'I can't,' Miles said, his voice hoarse. 'I don't know how.'

'Did I not warn you, boy?' Malik said. Miles gasped at the knife's cold steel driving into his side. He coughed and spluttered. Blood trickled out of his mouth and down his shirt. Malik let go of his head and watched Miles's chin bounce off his chest.

'Spread out,' Kaleb said, waving his hand at the surrounding vampires. 'If this wolf appears, we need to be ready.'

Miles groaned as the blood trickled out of the open wound just below his ribcage.

'Seems like this wolf doesn't care about you,' Genevie said, walking up to Miles and grabbing him by the chin. 'She is going to let you die.'

'You will never get her,' Miles said. 'She is too smart for you.'

'Look,' Kaleb said, pointing to the wound on Miles's side.

Genevie pulled up Miles's shirt. 'It is closing. Vampire blood?'

Kaleb shook his head. 'The boy threw the vampire poison up. Something else is healing him.'

'No,' Miles said under his breath. 'I told you to stay away.'

'Wolves,' Malik said, sniffing the air. 'I can smell them.'

'Is she with them?' Kaleb said.

'I am sure it is why the wound is healing,' Malik said. 'Make sure everyone is ready.'

A vampire's scream shattered the night's calm air.

Malik lifted his head and shouted. 'Find her.'

Vampires scattered in flashes into the mists.

'I cannot see anything in this blasted mist,' Kaleb said.

'Stay together, Kaleb,' Malik said. 'Do not get isolated.'

Miles spat out some more blood. The marks on his back crawled to his spine and knitted the nerve endings together at the lower part of his back. His right thigh muscles twitched at the pins and needles shooting from his lower back down to his feet. The wound on his side closed completely. The pressure of the three straps on his right boot eased as his right foot turned outwards. Strength filled his back, legs and feet.

'Truly remarkable,' Malik said, his long fangs inches from Miles's face. 'Even I do not heal that quickly. Tell me, boy, what are you? Why does the old man want you so badly?'

Miles's lips stretched into a smirk, exposing his blood-soaked teeth. 'I do not know what I am. And I don't know of this old man.'

'Is it this wolf?' Malik said. 'Is she healing you? Tell me, boy.'

Miles snarled at the royal vampire.

'I can see why the old man wants this wolf,' Malik said, looking back at Genevie and Kaleb. 'The power to heal this boy at this speed is unmatched.'

A snarl snapped Malik's head back to the right. A flash of fur took a vampire into the mists. His screams ended with a pop.

'Genevie, Kaleb, come closer to the boy,' Malik said. 'The wolf bites cannot kill us, but they can take us with sheer numbers. If they attack, stab the boy in the heart.'

Another vampire disappeared with a scream.

Malik, Kaleb and Genevie stood calmly, watching the mists.

In front of Miles, a wet snout and a set of yellow eyes

appeared. The black furred alpha wolf stalked into view. He lowered his head and snarled at the three royal vampires.

'Is that her?' Genevie said, slapping the back of Miles's head. 'Is that your wolf?'

The alpha wolf let loose a long, chesty growl. Kaleb drew a serrated sword and moved to circle the wolf. Another growl sounded out of the mists. Kaleb's eyes darted in the growl's direction. The alpha wolf crept forward with his belly just inches from the ground.

'Don't use that sword, son,' Malik hissed. 'We need the wolf alive.'

'She will heal, Father,' Kaleb said as he continued to creep around the wolf's side.

Behind Miles, a flash of brown-and-white fur streaked out of the mist and hit Genevie in the back. Waya chomped down on the back of Genevie's neck and, snarling, she shook her head from side to side.

'Let go of my daughter,' Malik said, drawing his sword and slashing at the wolf.

'Waya!' Miles screamed, spraying more blood on Malik.

Waya released Genevie and sprang out of the way of the falling sword. The sword's point pierced through Genevie's shoulder.

Malik's eyes grew wide as he pulled the sword out of his daughter's body. Waya snarled, then sprang into the mists.

'Genevie?' Malik said, offering his daughter a hand. 'Are you OK?'

Genevie grabbed her father's hand and pulled herself up. The wound from the sword knitted together. The wolf's bite oozed black-infected blood. 'You could have had my head, Father,' Genevie said, wiping the black blood from the wolf bite.

A yelp spun Malik and Genevie. The alpha wolf lay silent. Kaleb's serrated sword stuck through the alpha wolf's side.

'What have you done?' Malik shouted. 'I told you not to hurt the wolf.'

'He is not the boy's wolf, father,' Kaleb said, removing his sword. 'Waya, the brown-and-white wolf that just bit Genevie, is the one we need. Remember the one you nearly just killed?'

'Father,' Genevie said, poking Malik in the chest. 'I said you could have killed me.'

'It's just a flesh wound, my dear. Stop being so dramatic.'

Genevie folded her arms and pouted.

'There she is,' Kaleb said, pointing his sword past Miles.

'Run, Waya,' Miles said, his voice gravelly with the dried-up blood.

Malik crouched and stared at the snarling Waya. 'She has the same eyes as you, my boy.'

'Any ideas how to catch her?' Genevie said, flicking Miles in the face with one of her perfect nails.

With one quick movement, Malik rose and drove his dagger deep into Miles's side.

Miles cried out. Waya howled. With a limp, she scuttled backwards.

'They share the wound,' Malik said. 'Such a curious sight.'

'If you kill the boy, you kill the wolf,' Kaleb said. 'Be careful, Father.'

Malik twisted the knife in Miles's side. Miles and Waya both screamed out in pain.

'Father, be careful,' Genevie said.

'Hold the knife, daughter,' Malik said.

Genevie walked behind Miles and grabbed the dagger's hilt. 'Looks like you are going to live today, boy,' she said into Miles's ear.

Malik pulled a leather strap from his pocket. 'Twist the knife, Genevie.'

As the dagger turned, Miles's scream caught in his throat and his eyes rolled into the back of his head.

Waya's back legs collapsed underneath her. Yelping in pain, she rolled onto her side. Malik flashed over to Waya and swiftly wrapped the leather strap around her snout.

'Looks like we have her, boy,' Genevie said, gently kissing Miles on the cheek. 'We get to go home to Mummy now.'

Malik pulled out two more leather straps and bound Waya's paws. After checking they would hold the enormous wolf, he stood and faced Miles. 'Remove the knife, Genevie.'

Genevie pulled out the knife. She lifted Miles's shirt and watched the wound knit together. 'Faster than you can heal, Father,' she said, placing the knife into her belt. 'That is quite a skill.'

Miles's eyes fluttered open. 'Leave Waya alone.'

'Too late for that, my boy,' Genevie said, patting Miles on the cheek.

A long mournful howl rolled off the hills in the mists.

'They cry for their fallen leader,' Malik said. 'Call the rest of our kin together, Kaleb. We will begin the move to the City of Lynn immediately.'

Kaleb took a step towards Malik, then stopped and tilted his head. 'I hear horses.'

'As do I,' Genevie said, crouching and gazing into the mist.

'From the south,' Malik said, drawing his sword. 'Are they ours?'

In a thunderous roar, horses carrying men charged out of the mists. With his greatsword held above his head, the Soldier let loose an almighty war cry. Rafa screamed his battle cry in response as he jabbed his spear at a vampire. Battleacre soldiers with a multitude of different weapons all roared with bloodlust as they charged into the vampire group. Genevie spun away from

Miles and drew her long sword. Kaleb crouched and bared his long fangs at the attackers. The Soldier flourished his greatsword in an arc, sending vampire heads soaring into the air. Rafa bounded off his horse and ran towards Miles and Genevie with his spear aimed at Genevie's face. Malik's serrated sword sang through the air, and in one blinding flash after another, he dispatched the soldiers of their horses. The Soldier jumped off his horse, engaging Kaleb in a clash of steel that echoed through the valley. Rafa, reaching Miles, jabbed at Genevie's face but found nothing but misty air.

Genevie laughed from within the mists. 'Do you honestly think a few soldiers from Battleacre can take us on?'

'Show yourself,' Rafa shouted as he flicked his spear and sliced the bonds holding Miles. Miles dropped to his hands and knees and crawled to where Waya lay on her side with her bound snout and paws. With his strength returning to him, he freed Waya's paws and untied the leather strap around her snout. Waya struggled to her feet and shook herself. Miles pushed himself off the ground and onto his feet. The wounds on both their sides closed.

Malik turned and faced Miles and Waya. The red rings around his irises shone. 'Where do you think you are going, boy?' he said.

A blood-curdling scream spun everyone to look at the Soldier who stood behind Kaleb. The royal king's son stared back at his father with wide, fearful eyes. With a last gasp, he fell to his knees and dissolved into a cloud of dust.

Genevie screamed and clawed her face. 'Kaleb, brother, no!'

The Soldier turned his eyes onto Malik. 'Do you feel my pain? Do you feel the loss? You murderous animal.'

Malik glared at the pile of dust that lay at the Soldier's feet. With a deep guttural snarl, he flashed towards the Soldier with his serrated sword raised above his head.

'Run, son,' the Soldier shouted. 'Get out of here and take your wolf.'

'I cannot leave you,' Miles said.

'Rafa,' the Soldier screamed as he parried Malik's serrated sword. 'Get out of here.'

'Come on, friend,' Rafa said, moving away from the stunned Genevie. 'We need to obey the General.'

Miles took one last look at the Soldier then darted off into the mists. Waya, with her massive paws spraying black snow into the air, ran at his right side. Rafa ran alongside his left, his spear at the ready for any surprises.

A hiss sounded out of the mist. 'Come here, boy.'

'Genevie,' Miles said. 'She is following us.'

'Keep running,' Rafa said, peeling away into the mist.

'Rafa,' Miles shouted, looking over his shoulder. 'Where are you?'

'Run,' Rafa said from inside the mist.

Behind Miles and Waya, the shouts of fighting died out. An hour passed with them running side by side. The mists lifted, revealing more black-snow-covered boughs. Miles stopped running and walked up to a long line of dead trees. The dead forest's entrance loomed ahead. Waya turned back and looked into the mists. She raised her head and let loose a long howl. With a tilt of her head, she waited for a reply. Multiple howls within the mists answered her back.

Miles knelt and ran his hand over Waya's back. 'I am sorry about your alpha wolf.'

'Do you think she will be the alpha wolf now?' Rafa said.

'I think so,' Miles said, looking at Rafa.

Waya nudged Miles with her snout then, with a snort, she hung her head.

'We must be north of the inn,' Miles said, rubbing Waya's ears.

'I remember seeing the start of the dead forest from the eastern road.'

Waya gazed into the dark forest's depths. Miles followed her gaze and shivered.

'So many dead trees,' Miles said. 'Do we go around, or through?'

Waya growled.

A whisper of men came from behind them.

'It looks like we need to go through,' Miles said, taking a step into the forest. 'I don't know if those are men from Battleacre or if they are vampires.'

The gnarled tall trees created a canopy of thick intertwined branches above them. The ground squelched underneath boots and paws. Waya walked with her head low and her eyes shifting from side to side. Her nose twitched at the tar-like substance left by the black snow.

'We need to keep moving south,' Miles said.

Waya rumbled deep in her chest and slightly changed direction.

The mist lightened, making it easier for Miles to see further into the forest. Suddenly, Waya growled and lowered her belly to just inches off the slippery ground.

Miles knelt. 'What is it?'

Waya sniffed the air to the east.

Miles followed her gaze and froze. Through the trees, scores of undead shuffled aimlessly about. The smell of rotting flesh wafted through the light mist. 'Let's keep moving,' he said, running a hand over Waya's head.

As quietly as they could in the greasy, thick tar, Miles and Waya moved south.

Waya stopped, looked back and whined.

The sound of hundreds of feet dragging through the grease

echoed through the forest. An undead army shuffled towards Miles and Waya.

'Not good,' Miles said.

The undead, groaning and moaning, picked up their pace.

'Not good at all,' Miles said. 'Go, Waya, go.'

Waya darted off into the trees, with Miles running hard behind her. His legs and feet moved fluidly without pain as he dodged between the rotting, dead trees. He easily caught himself from slipping on the greasy blackness of the forest floor. A ghost of a smile played on his lips as he remembered the days of zero pain. Running past a large tree, Miles gasped as a hand wrapped around his neck. Fangs raked across the side of his face as a vampire wrapped his arms around his throat.

'Tell your wolf to back off, boy,' the vampire said, his fangs grazing Miles's neck.

Miles held up a hand. 'Stay there, Waya.'

Waya snorted and snarled at the vampire.

In the distance, the moans and groans of the undead grew louder.

The vampire swung Miles in the direction they had come. 'We are going back to our master, Malik.'

Miles held up a hand to keep Waya from attacking. The undead, sensing the vampire, slowed their shuffling and sniffed the air. Then, with a sudden pop, the vampire turned to dust.

Miles turned and sighed. 'Rafa,' he said.

'Run,' Rafa said, looking over his shoulder.

Miles darted off, keeping his eye on Waya's tail.

'Are you hurt?' Rafa said, jumping over a log.

Miles shook his head. 'I am fine. Genevie?'

'She suddenly disappeared,' Rafa said. 'I don't know why.'

'What about the Soldier?'

'I don't know,' Rafa said, skidding past a deep black hole. 'He is where we left him.'

'Fighting Malik,' Miles said. 'The king vampire.'

'And what about the vampire the Soldier killed?' Rafa said. 'That seemed to upset the king vampire more than the others.'

'It was his son,' Miles said, his breath catching in his throat.

'That would explain the rage in the king vampire's eyes,' Rafa said, through sharp intakes of air.

'And the woman vampire, Genevie, is his daughter,' Miles said. 'It sounds like she went back to their homeland if she disappeared from you.'

Rafa sprang past Miles, drew his sword, and slashed at an advancing undead.

'We need to go faster,' Miles said. 'They are everywhere.'

'Where do they come from?' Rafa said, as the undead's body hit the ground.

'There's a small boy who raises them out of the ground,' Miles said. 'I think Luxea is his twin sister. I am sure of it.'

Rafa's eyebrows shot up. 'Really?'

Waya changed direction. Miles and Rafa, dodging and ducking, sprinted after her.

'I have never seen you move so fast,' Rafa said, panting behind Miles.

'Having a wolf elemental has its perks,' Miles said over his shoulder.

Rafa chuckled, then cursed as a branch ripped at his clothes.

An hour later, the trees in the forest thinned. Up ahead, Waya suddenly disappeared.

'Waya,' Miles shouted.

'Watch out,' Rafa said, at the edge of a steep bank.

'The eastern road,' Miles said, skidding to a stop and looking up and down the cobblestone road.

'Is this the road you followed from the east to get to Battleacre?' Rafa said, sliding down the bank and standing on the cobblestone road.

'We didn't come along this road. We went south to the horse farms, then followed the road from there back up north to Battleacre,' Miles said, following Rafa down the bank. 'I followed this road from the eastern wall to the inn.'

Rafa turned west. 'How far do you think we are from Battleacre?'

'We aren't going to Battleacre, Rafa.'

Rafa stopped and looked at Miles with confusion. 'What do you mean?'

'The vampires are after me and Waya,' Miles said. 'I will not lead them to Battleacre.'

'They are probably going there anyway,' Rafa said. 'I need to get back to Raquel.'

Miles walked up to Rafa. 'Why are you with the Soldier, Rafa? Where is Luxea? I left her in your charge.'

With surprise in his eyes, Rafa took a step back. 'It was Luxea who demanded we find you.'

'She is a child, Rafa. Why on earth would you listen to her?'

Rafa sighed. 'You were right about her. There is something about that young girl. She is very persuasive. She was completely inconsolable when you left and demanded we find you. It got to where she threatened to tell everyone our plans if I didn't join the Soldier to come and look for you.'

Miles shook his head. 'You are not there to protect her anymore.'

'She is with Janie,' Rafa said. 'Janie is more than capable of looking after her. You know that.'

Miles shook his head, then rubbed his eyes with the heels of his hands. He turned around and started walking east along the road. A little way down the road, Waya lifted her head and let out a long howl. Howls in the north responded. Waya turned her head and gazed at Miles.

'Go,' Miles said. 'But don't go too far.'

Waya bounded back up the bank and ran towards the distant forest. As she got further away, Miles felt the nerve endings in his back unravel. He closed his eyes and controlled his breathing. He gritted his teeth as he waited for the first wave of pain. His right foot slowly turned inwards.

'Are you OK?' Rafa said, grabbing Miles by the shoulder.

'Yes,' Miles said. 'Pain gets worse the further she goes away.'

'What can I do?' Rafa said, holding Miles's elbow.

Miles waved his hand. 'I will be fine. We need to move.'

'Where to?'

'We need to go to the inn,' Miles said. 'The Soldier will know to come to the inn.'

Rafa took one last look to the west, where the love of his life sat in Battleacre, then followed Miles east.

The two of them walked side by side on the eastern road. A gust of warm air came and went as the promise of spring teased the eastern lands. The black clouds from the City of Lynn had turned away from the south and had now begun their move northwards.

'We are so exposed out here,' Rafa said. 'It will be light soon.'

A wolf howl sounded from the north.

'Is that your wolf?' Rafa said.

'They are shadowing us,' Miles said. 'We need to pick up the pace as I don't know how far the inn is.'

'I don't think we have to go much further,' Rafa said, pointing up the eastern road. 'Is that the inn?'

Miles stopped in his tracks. A thin trickle of black smoke rose high into the air. The inn's walls lay blackened and charred. Rafa jogged forward, leaving Miles behind. He disappeared around the side of the inn. A few moments later, he appeared on the other side and jogged back to Miles.

'Someone has burnt the entire inn,' Rafa said. 'It looks like they did it to escape the undead.'

Miles walked through the hole where the front door used to be. He navigated past broken bottles that lay scattered around the floor. Tables and chairs stood either shattered or smouldering. Rotting corpses of the undead lay scattered around the bar floor.

'This battle happened recently,' Rafa said. 'Early morning, I think.'

Miles walked behind the bar and peered into the storeroom.

'Someone came through here,' Miles said. 'It looks like they escaped through the back door.'

'Let me go around,' Rafa said, walking out of the front door.

Miles stepped into the storeroom and knelt to look more closely at the black greasy footprints. He gagged at the rotting corpses of the undead piled up next to the walls.

'I have the trail,' Rafa said, appearing at the back door.

Miles stepped through the storeroom and joined Rafa outside. 'Where does the trail go?'

'Towards the stables,' Rafa said, pointing at the wooden building behind the inn. 'At least they didn't burn that down.'

Miles walked over to the stables and opened the door. He peered in, checking for any movement. 'Can you see anything?' Rafa said.

Miles shook his head. 'Not a thing.'

Rafa closed the doors, then knelt at a set of footprints. 'They came through here.'

Miles walked over to the stable where the mare and foal used to stay. He opened the stable door and stepped in.

'Who are you?' A girl's voice echoed through the stable.

Miles jumped and banged his head on a stable beam. While rubbing his head, he walked out.

'I asked you who you are?' the girl said.

'Who may you be?' Rafa said.

Miles gawked at the tall girl with locs flowing over her shoulders. 'Chloe?'

CHAPTER 18
ADORABLE

'This is Chloe?' Rafa said. 'The one who leads the south?'

Chloe pointed at the stable doors. 'What are those things outside?'

Miles walked over to Chloe and gave her a hug.

'What are those things, Miles?' Chloe said into Miles's shoulder.

'The undead,' Miles said. 'Dead people walking about. And yes, Rafa, this is Chloe.'

Chloe pulled away from the hug and glared at the stable door. 'The undead?'

'Wait till you hear about the vampires,' Rafa said. 'They are worse than the undead.'

'And who are you?' Chloe said, her eyes narrowing at Rafa.

Rafa bowed dramatically. 'I am the Shield of the General's house. It is a pleasure to meet the leader of the south, my lady.'

Miles snorted.

'Have some respect, boy,' Rafa said. 'We require a proper greeting for a leader.'

'OK,' Miles said, with tears of laughter in his eyes. 'How are you, my lady?'

Chloe wagged a finger at Miles. 'Don't you start with me.'

Miles tried to keep his shoulders from shaking with laughter.

'It is a pleasure to meet you too, Rafa,' Chloe said. 'I would like to know more, but it seems we are being chased by walking dead people.'

Rafa gave another bow. 'Yes, my lady.'

Miles snorted again.

The stable doors shuddered with the relentless pounding of the undeads' fists beating against it. Their moans and groans filtered through the gaps in the walls and windows.

'Oh great, they are breaking through,' Chloe said, drawing her two short swords. 'How many more of these things are there?'

Miles picked up a plank and lay it across the two hooks to secure the doors. 'That will hold them for a while. Who else is with you? I assume you didn't come alone?'

'Billy, Alexa and Dr Viktor.'

'Dr Viktor?' Miles said. 'How did he get all the way here?'

'I should ask you the same thing,' Chloe said, glancing at Miles's feet. 'Valen built you a wheelchair, yet here you stand.'

The stable door rattled as an undead's body crunched against it with a massive thump.

'It's a long story,' Miles said. 'Where did the rest of you go?'

'The person you sent to Fairacre spoke of horse farms south of here,' Chloe said. 'Billy and the rest left yesterday in search of them. I hid here hoping for someone to show up.'

'You should not have waited,' Rafa said with a frown. 'You don't want to be caught out here alone at night.'

'On the way here, we camped outside,' Chloe said. 'We had no trouble until we reached this inn. When we got here, a steady stream of them appeared.'

'And your friends left you alone with them?' Rafa said, the muscles in his jaw twitching.

'I sent them south,' Chloe said. 'We needed to spread out to find you all.'

'You didn't see any vampires?' Rafa said.

'I think we distracted everyone with the fight north of Battleacre,' Miles said.

'Yes, that makes sense,' Rafa said. 'If your friends left yesterday, they should be near the horse farms.'

'We need to move,' Miles said. 'They will overrun us any second now.'

Just as Miles finished his sentence, the stable doors shuddered. With another massive thump, the doors splintered, sending bits of wood across the stable. Miles walked up to the doors and checked the thick plank. The doors rattled again as more undead threw their bodies against them.

'Any ideas?' Chloe said.

'We hide in the shadows of one stable,' Rafa said. 'When we open the door, most of them will walk past us. At the right time, we sneak out behind them.'

'Then we run for the south, right?' Chloe said, jabbing her thumb southwards.

'Hobble to the south,' Miles said, with a grim look on his face. 'Running is not something I do easily.'

Rafa walked over to Miles and laid a hand on his shoulder. 'I will stay behind you and make sure none catch you.'

'We do it the other way around,' Chloe said. 'Miles will need your strength to help him along. I will keep these things busy.'

Rafa opened his mouth but closed it as Miles lifted a hand.

'Chloe is more than capable, Rafa,' Miles said. 'Trust me when I say she can handle these things.'

Rafa's eyebrows shot up. 'Is that so?'

'Yes, that is so,' Chloe said, rolling her eyes. 'Can we get moving, please?'

Rafa waited for Miles and Chloe to move into a stable. He slid the plank off the hooks, then vaulted over the stable wall and crouched next to Chloe and Miles. The doors crashed open and a stream of undead flooded into the stable corridor. As the last undead shuffled past the stable, Miles snuck around the wall and hobbled through the main entrance towards the southern fence. At the fence, he glanced over his shoulder to see Chloe's two short swords flashing through the pursuing undead. He jumped over the fence and hobbled south across the field to the first of the rolling hills. Walking down the hill, sweat formed on his brow as he concentrated on keeping his feet moving. Miles crossed the valley floor, then slowed as he climbed the steep hillside.

'Hold on to me,' Rafa said, grabbing Miles's arm and throwing it over his shoulder. 'We need to keep going until we lose them.'

'Where is Waya when I need her?' Miles said, his voice ragged with the effort.

'Probably busy with vampires,' Rafa said. 'And I remember you sending her away, didn't you?'

Behind them, another undead body thumped into the ground.

'She is unbelievable,' Rafa said, glancing over his shoulder. 'Our women in my land are not known for any fighting skills.'

Miles smiled broadly. 'I have trained her well then.'

Rafa chuckled. 'I am not surprised you had a hand in her training.'

'She was formidable before I trained her,' Miles said. 'A force of nature.'

'I understand why people would follow her,' Rafa said.

At the crest of the next hill, Miles stumbled. He hissed as the pain streaked through his legs.

Rafa slowed and pulled Miles's arm tighter over his shoulder. 'We have to keep moving. Don't stop now.'

'I don't know how long I can go at this speed,' Miles said, stumbling down the next hillside.

'Aim for the valley,' Rafa said. 'We are increasing the gap between us and them.'

Miles's brow furrowed as he set his eyes on the valley floor. With all of his strength, he concentrated on moving one foot in front of the other. The three straps across his right foot creaked with each step. Beads of sweat rolled down his brow and down the bridge of his nose. His breath moved from laboured to sharp gasps.

'Nearly there,' Rafa said. 'Keep going.'

'Where is Chloe?' Miles said, his voice grating.

'She is still on the other side of the hill,' Rafa said.

'When we reach the valley, go and make sure she is OK,' Miles said. 'She is tough, but she could get overwhelmed.'

A minute later, the land flattened out. Rafa released Miles and ran back the way they came. Miles knelt and looked up at the hill they had just come down. Minutes passed with no movement.

'Come on, you two,' Miles said. 'Be OK. Please be OK.'

Then over the hill, Chloe and Rafa appeared, sprinting side by side. Miles dropped onto his back and smirked at the two tall figures dancing down the hill.

'We have left them behind,' Chloe said, her breathing controlled. 'There were not many when we crested that hill.'

'She has not even broken a sweat,' Rafa said, beaming.

Chloe shrugged. 'There are lots but they are not that quick.'

'I have never seen them outside the dead forest,' Miles said. 'Can you two stop admiring each other for half a second and help me?'

'Disgusting things,' Chloe said, grabbing Miles by the hand and pulling him up. 'How far are these farms?'

'At least another day away,' Miles said, circling his right foot to increase the blood flow. 'We will get there tomorrow if we leave first light.'

'Are you sure you don't want to carry?' Chloe said.

Miles rubbed the thigh on his right leg. 'Don't think I can. Sorry.'

Chloe's eyes widened. 'Sorry, I somehow keep forgetting.'

'That is OK,' Miles said. 'We need to move to those trees over there and make camp.'

A whistle sounded from the top of the next hill. Miles placed his hand over his brow and searched the hillside. A man with wavy blonde hair and a lopsided grin strode towards them. Miles couldn't help the wide smile spreading across his face.

'Brother,' Billy shouted. 'Do my eyes fail me? Am I seeing untruths? Does my brother stand there on his own two legs? What is this madness?'

'Oh, the drama,' Chloe said, rolling her eyes.

Miles waited for Billy to reach them, then grabbed him in a fierce embrace. 'Just about walking, brother,' he said. 'Not easily though, but walking nonetheless.'

Billy broke the embrace and looked Miles over. 'You have regained some of the muscle you had lost.'

'Every day, I seem to fight bad things or I'm running away from bad things,' Miles said. 'My muscles are aching more than ever. This is Rafa, my friend from the town of Battleacre.'

'A pleasure to meet you, sir,' Rafa said with a small bow.

'It is a pleasure to meet you too,' Billy said, also bowing. 'And you know Chloe?'

Rafa glanced at Chloe. 'Yes, only recently. A fierce one she is.'

Billy chuckled. 'Oh, I have stories, kind sir.'

'Enough,' Chloe said with a hint of a smile. 'Where is Dr Viktor?'

'He is at the horse farms,' Billy said. 'For a man of his age, he can move rather rapidly. As soon as I dropped them, I came back for Chloe.'

Miles suddenly gasped. He dropped to a knee and touched the small of his back.

'What is it?' Billy said, kneeling and grabbing Miles by the shoulder.

'Is it your wolf?' Rafa said.

A long, deep-throated growl sounded up on the hill.

'Wolves,' Chloe said, drawing her two swords.

'It is your wolf,' Rafa said.

Miles stood and rested his hands on his knees. He looked at the ground and breathed deeply. Once the nerves had finished knitting, he raised his head to the sky and took in a long breath.

'Miles, there are wolves on the hill,' Chloe said, moving into her defence stance.

Miles placed a hand on Chloe's wrist. 'It's OK. Everyone, I would like you to meet Waya.'

'Waya?' Billy said.

Miles waved Waya over. The enormous wolf padded over with a low, rumbling growl. Miles knelt and held either side of Waya's face. Waya whined with pleasure as he rubbed her cheeks.

'What is going on?' Chloe said.

'So this is why he can walk,' Billy said. 'Waya is an element, just like Chax.'

Chloe's mouth fell wide open. 'You have got to be kidding me?'

'Nope,' Miles said over his shoulder. 'Trust you to figure it out instantly, brother.'

Billy tapped his chin with his finger. 'I will not lie. I am truly gifted.'

Chloe filled her cheeks and blew the air out with a long sigh. 'This is what I have to deal with,' she said, looking at Rafa.

Rafa smirked.

'Who fancies a run?' Miles said. 'Let's see if you can all keep up with me and Waya.'

'Ha,' Rafa said, slamming his fist against his chest. 'A noteworthy challenge.'

Chloe secured her swords. Rafa checked his spear. Billy adjusted his staff. With a wink over his shoulder, Miles took off up the hill at great speed. Waya sprang forward and ran alongside him, her brown-and-white coat rippling with every stride. As they crested the hill, the entire wolf pack joined Miles and Waya. Down into the next valley, the wolves and the four friends sprinted. Miles threw his fist into the air and howled as hard as he could. The ground beneath his feet shifted and moved as the earth answered his every step. He slowed until his three friends caught up. Waya sprinted forward to lead her new pack. Hour after hour, Miles and his friends followed the wolves over rolling hill after rolling hill.

Behind Miles, Billy shouted with joy as he sprang over a rock. 'It is good to see you run, brother.'

Miles grinned over his shoulder. 'It gives new meaning to the word freedom.'

'Something I take for granted,' Billy said, dodging a pile of rocks. 'It must feel so sweet and free for you.'

Miles howled into the sky as he danced through a pile of boulders.

Chloe's locs bounced over her shoulders as her long strides easily kept up with the boys.' Rafa glanced at her and smirked at the smile stretching across her face. They crested another rolling hill and bounded down into the next valley. At the bottom, Miles watched most of the wolf pack break away. The four friends and Waya climbed the next hill and stopped at the top. The land out in front of them flattened. In the distance, streams of smoke escaped from the horse farms' chimneys.

Miles knelt and wrapped his arms around Waya's neck. 'It is time to make yourself scarce again.'

Waya grunted and let out a low growl.

'You know the deal,' Miles said. 'Now off you go.'

Waya lifted her head and howled. The wolves in the surrounding valleys howled back. With one last look at Miles, she bounded back down the hill.

Rafa walked up to Miles and held him by the shoulder. 'Are you ready?'

'You know me too well, friend,' Miles said, grabbing Rafa by the arm.

'What's wrong?' Chloe said.

The air escaped through Miles's teeth as the nerves in his back failed. His right foot tried to turn inwards but the three-strapped shoe stopped it. He doubled over and placed his hands on his knees.

'Come on,' Rafa said. 'Let's get you to the horse farms before the sun sets.'

Chloe came up alongside Miles. 'Why do you not stay healed like Juno?'

Miles shrugged. 'I don't know. I am hoping to speak to Dr Viktor about it.'

'What element is it?' Billy said. 'I cannot see any marks.'

'I think it's earth,' Miles said. 'The marks on the small of my back are brown.'

'Can I see?' Chloe said.

As Miles reached behind his back, he gasped with pain.

'I think that is enough for now,' Rafa said, raising an eyebrow at Billy and Chloe.

Billy pulled Miles's other arm over his shoulder. 'Let's get you home, brother.'

After another hour, they reached the high fences of the northern horse farm. They followed the fences until they got to the entrance to the horse fields. Chloe took the lead and walked through the field towards the inn that Miles and the Soldier had previously stayed in. The door opened and Dr Viktor walked out with his cane thumping on the wooden decking. Dr Viktor stopped in front of Miles and stared up at him with a face set in stone.

'Dr Viktor, sir,' Miles said.

'You ran away,' Dr Viktor said, his face contorted in anger. 'You ran away from me, your brother and your friends.'

Miles remained silent.

'Father,' Billy said.

'Silence,' Dr Viktor thundered, pointing his cane at Billy.

Billy took a step back and lowered his head.

After a few moments, Dr Viktor reached up and embraced Miles. 'It is good to see you, son.'

Miles hugged his adoptive father fiercely.

'You have some explaining to do,' Dr Viktor said. 'I may be old, but my eyes clearly see you standing and walking.'

'Hobbling rather than walking,' Miles said.

'Good to see you, Miles,' Alexa said from the inn doorway.

Miles released his hug from Dr Viktor and inclined his head towards Alexa. 'And you, Alexa. I trust this lot has not been too much trouble.'

Alexa inclined her head to the side. 'Nothing Chloe and I cannot handle.'

'May we go inside, please?' Miles said. 'I could do with some food and I am sore all over from our run.'

'And what a run it was,' Rafa said.

'And who are you?' Dr Viktor said, jabbing his cane at Rafa.

'I am the Shield of the General's house within the city of Battleacre,' Rafa said with a deep bow. 'It is an honour to meet your acquaintance.'

'A free man from the west,' Dr Viktor said. 'It is unusual to meet a western man with his freedom in these parts.'

Rafa smiled. 'I am one of the lucky ones.'

'Very lucky indeed,' Dr Viktor grunted, before walking back into the inn.

'Miles,' Heather said, walking over and embracing him. 'Jon, look who it is.'

With a wide smile and a polished glass in his hand, Jon gave Miles a nod.

'Jon, can we pull these tables together?' Heather said.

Jon walked over and pulled the small square tables together. 'I will bring food and drink.'

Miles sat and cast his eyes around the table. A smile played over his lips as his old and new friends spoke loudly among themselves. The smile disappeared as a twinge of pain shot down his thigh. He grabbed his leg and massaged it slowly. Looking up, he grinned at the intense stare of Dr Viktor.

'Here we go,' Jon said, placing tankards of ale on the table. 'As it is nearly dark out, I will serve dinner.'

'Thank you, Jon,' Miles said.

'Move, please,' Heather said as she laid out cutlery in front of the guests.

'Are Janie and Luxea here?' Miles said. 'Where have you hidden them?'

A look of worry spread across Heather's face.

'What is it, Heather?' Miles said, bringing the table to silence.

'They aren't here,' Heather said. 'Janie took Luxea away.'

'What do you mean, she took her away?' Miles said, his voice rising.

Jon walked over. 'Vampires came. Janie took Luxea away before they got her.'

Miles struggled to stand.

'Sit, boy,' Dr Viktor said, his voice low but firm.

Miles fell back into his chair.

'Did Janie give any information?' Dr Viktor said.

Jon shook his head. 'She had to move quickly.'

'We need to find them,' Miles said.

'We will wait here,' Dr Viktor said. 'You do not know where she is and she will come back when the time is right.'

Miles placed his head in his hands.

'We need to trust Janie,' Chloe said. 'She will do the right thing, Miles.'

Miles lifted his head and looked at Chloe. 'The plan was to bring Luxea to you in Fairacre. She is important, Chloe. I don't know why, but she is.'

Chloe reached over and grabbed Miles's hand. 'And so are you, Miles. You and Waya.'

'Waya?' Dr Viktor said.

'Earth element, Father,' Billy said. 'It is why Miles can walk.'

Dr Viktor leant forward. 'You are the vessel for the earth element?'

Jon interrupted by dropping plates of stew on the table. Heather placed big serving boards piled high with buttered bread.

'That is a lot of food,' Billy said with a chuckle.

Miles hungrily grabbed some bread and dipped it into the stew. The group ate in silence. When finished, Miles leant back and interlaced his fingers behind his head. He closed his eyes and felt the exhaustion take over.

'You need to sleep, son,' Dr Viktor said.

Miles's eyes snapped open. 'I need to look for Janie and Luxea.'

'He definitely needs to sleep,' Chloe said with a frown.

'You are going to sleep,' Billy said. 'Come on, up you get.'

Miles placed his head in his hands. 'If anything has happened to them, I will unleash hell.'

Billy chuckled. 'And I will be there with you, brother. But now it is time for you to turn in.'

With a hand on Billy's shoulder, Miles stood. 'It is good to have you here, sir,' he said, looking at Dr Viktor. 'I wish your advice and guidance on things.'

'We shall speak when you have rested,' Dr Viktor said. 'Go now.'

Miles followed Billy across the inn and up a narrow flight of stairs. Billy kicked the second door open and guided Miles to the bed. With a groan, Miles fell onto the bed and closed his eyes.

'Have we heard anything?' Miles said, walking up to the table the next morning.

Billy shook his head.

'So what do we do?' Miles said. 'Just sit around and do nothing?'

Billy shrugged. 'I think that is the plan.'

The clump of Dr Viktor's cane jerked both their heads around. Miles pulled out a chair and sat.

Chloe followed Dr Viktor in and sat opposite Miles. She smiled up at Heather, who put a mug of tea in front of her.

Dr Viktor lowered himself into a chair. 'So tell me what is going on, son?'

'The messenger you sent was adamant we came immediately,' Chloe said.

'You don't know about Janie,' Miles said, with a shake of his head. 'The messenger would not have known.'

Chloe placed her mug on the table and began bouncing her leg. 'What of Janie?'

Miles sat in silence with his head bowed.

'Well?' Chloe said, her leg bouncing angrily.

'They turned her,' Miles said. 'Genevie, a royal vampire, turned her into one of them.'

Chloe's leg stopped bouncing.

Miles looked at her. 'I am sorry.'

'She wouldn't have come here if you hadn't left,' Chloe said, her voice turning to ice.

'I know. Is there something we can do?' Miles said, looking at Dr Viktor.

'I do not know,' Dr Viktor said. 'I would have to check my books.'

'How could you let this happen, Miles?' Chloe said, her hand slapping the table. 'You, of all people. How could you let this happen to the girl that loves you?'

Miles lowered his head again.

'Answer me, Miles,' Chloe said, her voice stabbing him in the gut.

'I didn't know she would follow.' Miles's voice was barely a whisper.

'What happened?' Billy said. 'How did she get turned?'

Miles walked through the entire story. From arriving at the inn, to meeting the Soldier, Waya, the undead, Battleacre, and finally how he gave himself to the royal vampires to save Janie, Luxea and Battleacre. He finished the story by wiping a tear from his eye. 'I love Janie,' he said to Chloe. 'I truly do.'

Chloe walked around the table and pulled Miles into a hug. 'I am sorry,' she said. 'I didn't know you felt for her like she feels for you.'

Miles couldn't control it anymore. The tears flowed down his face as he sobbed into Chloe's shoulder. Billy walked over and wrapped them both in a big bear hug.

'We need to save her,' Miles said, his voice muffled. 'There must be a way.'

Billy and Chloe let go of Miles and pulled up chairs to sit on either side of him.

'I will have to go back to Fairacre,' Dr Viktor said. 'I will check my books to see if I can find anything.'

Miles lifted a finger. 'I forgot to tell you one thing. I can see essence.'

Chloe's eyes widened. 'Like Juno can see it?'

'I think so, yes,' Miles said.

'Makes sense if he is the vessel for the earth element,' Dr Viktor said. 'Whose essence can you see?'

'The essence of the royal vampires influences all vampires,' Miles said. 'They transfer their essence just like the Lady and Valen do.'

'So how is Janie free now?' Billy said.

Miles grinned at Chloe. 'Because she accidentally brought a set of Valen's devices. They are purring in her ears right now.'

A fondness melded over Chloe's face.

'Even from afar, Valen is with us,' Billy said.

'May I see these marks, son,' Dr Viktor said.

Miles stood and raised his shirt.

'Remarkable,' Dr Viktor said. 'Brown marks means earth. Have you learnt to control them?'

With his shirt lowered, Miles sat. 'I have no control. The earth has rumbled once or twice when I am angry. But I have no power like Juno has.'

'Remember what we had to do to bring Juno's power forth,' Dr Viktor said.

'I have tried it, Father,' Miles said. 'It isn't the same. I also don't stay healed. Not like when Juno nearly got stabbed to death then fully recovered. I only partially heal when Waya is close to me.'

Dr Viktor rubbed his chin. 'That is certainly not the same.'

'The City of Lynn has tried to capture Waya,' Miles said. 'They are also stealing the women like they did in Fairacre. And now they want little Luxea.'

'So much happening,' Chloe said with a shake of her head. 'Where do we start?'

'I must return to Fairacre,' Dr Viktor said. 'If I find a cure for this vampire issue, it will eliminate most of the problem.'

'We need to find Janie and Luxea,' Rafa said.

'We need to keep Miles and Waya safe,' Billy said.

'Yet, we cannot bring anyone back to Fairacre,' Chloe said. 'We do not want the vampires entering our lands.'

'Which means we stay here until Dr Viktor comes back with a solution,' Miles said.

They sat around the table again in silence. Jon and Heather arrived with more tea, breads and jam for breakfast. Miles moved a piece of bread around on his plate.

'I suggest we wait here for another day,' Rafa said. 'After that, I will return to Battleacre to find out what is going on.'

'The Soldier should be back,' Miles said. 'If Battleacre is safe, we can all return.'

'I will leave first thing in the morning,' Dr Viktor said.

'Alexa will accompany you,' Chloe said with a nod towards Alexa. 'Go through the southern gate. It is safer.'

'I cannot stand waiting around,' Miles said, sitting back and interlacing his fingers behind his head.

'Yet it is the smartest thing to do,' Dr Viktor said.

They continued eating breakfast until Heather came over and cleared the plates and mugs away.

'Chloe, Billy, I have something to show you,' Miles said, pushing his chair back. 'Follow me.'

They left the inn and walked along the path leading south. Miles pulled open the squeaking gate that led to the large horse farm owned by Norman. He tapped his knuckle on the door. A few moments later, locks scraped back, and the door opened a crack.

'Hello, Norman,' Miles said. 'How are you?'

Norman swung the door wide open. 'Good day, sir,' he said with a broad smile. 'It is good to see you.'

'It is good to see you too,' Miles said. 'I think you can guess why I am here.'

'Yes, yes,' Norman said, moving back into his house. 'Just a second, please.'

'Where are we going?' Chloe said.

'Wait and see,' Miles said.

Norman reappeared and closed the door behind him.

'How are they doing?' Miles said.

'Fine, just fine,' Norman said. 'The little one is not in hiding anymore. The horse farmers know he belongs to the General and yourself, so they have accepted him. Naughty little fellow he is.'

Miles grinned as he followed Norman into the barns.

'They are in the fourth one along,' Norman said.

'Where are you, little fellow?' Miles called out.

A whicker and a snort came from the fourth stable.

Miles reached the stable and peered in. The not-so-small foal took one look at Miles and raised his head and showed his teeth. He nickered and pawed the ground.

'Looks like he has missed you,' Norman said, opening the stable.

The foal stumbled out and rubbed his face against Miles. His eyes rolled and his ears twitched.

'He is adorable,' Chloe said, 'May I?'

'Of course,' Miles said.

Chloe walked up to the foal and ran her hand over his nose. The foal shook his head, then jammed his nose into Chloe's armpit. His enormous eyes stared at her.

'What is he doing?' Chloe said, her voice a whisper.

'He is hiding,' Miles said. 'He thinks nobody can see him if he hides his nose.'

Chloe chuckled and rubbed the horse's ears.

'Are they both yours?' Billy said, peering into the stable.

'They were Jon's. He was going to put them down,' Miles said. 'They frown upon disabled horses in the horse farms. Nobody wanted this little guy. So I said I would take them.'

'I want him,' Chloe said, rubbing her face against the foal's. 'What do I need to do to have him?'

'He is all yours,' Miles said with a chuckle. 'As long as you treat him like a normal horse. That's all he wants.'

Chloe smiled at Miles. 'I love him to death.'

The foal removed his nose from Chloe's armpit, then showed her his teeth.

'Cute,' Chloe said, rubbing the foal's cheeks.

Miles walked into the stable and wrapped his arms around the mare. After giving her a hug, he picked up a brush that hung on the wall and started brushing her down. A few minutes later, her coat shone.

'What was that?' Billy said.

Miles stopped his brushing.

A moan trickled through the barn. The stench of death hit their nostrils.

'Undead,' Miles said, replacing the brush back on the wall. 'Undead in the horse farms.'

CHAPTER 19
A WESTERN VISITOR

'Stay here with the horses, Norman,' Miles said. 'Don't go outside.'

Norman's eyes widened as a moan filtered through the stables.

'What are these things?' Billy said, his voice low.

'The walking dead,' Miles said. 'There is a young boy who raises them out of the ground somehow.'

'I think it is moving away,' Billy said, tilting his head to listen.

Miles walked up to the stable door and opened it a crack. He waved Billy and Chloe over. 'Look,' he said, opening the door a bit more. 'Can you see it?'

'Disgusting,' Billy said, wrinkling his nose.

The door creaked open further and Miles stepped out into the morning sunlight. The undead, hearing the door, turned and looked at Miles.

'Now what?' Billy said, moving alongside him.

With a low moan, the undead stretched out a hand and shuffled towards them.

'Now we get rid of it,' Miles said, reaching over his shoulder and grabbing the hilt of his greatsword.

The undead stopped, turned in a circle and sniffed the air. With another groan, he moved south, away from the three of them. Miles replaced his greatsword.

'Over there,' Chloe said, pointing to the corner of a barn. 'A young boy just peeked around.'

'We think that is Luxea's brother,' Miles said.

'Stay behind me,' Billy said. 'You two look too scary with your sharp swords.'

'I am not too scary,' Chloe said.

Billy flashed a lopsided grin. 'You are both scary. Follow me.'

Misty eyes peered around the corner, then quickly disappeared.

'At least he isn't running,' Miles said.

'Quiet,' Billy said, flapping his hand at Miles.

Miles held up both hands.

Billy slowed even further as they approached the corner of the barn. He stopped at the sound of small feet scampering away. 'It's OK, son,' Billy said. 'All we want to do is say hi.'

The small feet fell silent.

Billy moved his head around the corner of the barn. 'What's your name?'

Miles strained his neck to get a view over Billy's shoulder. Chloe grabbed his arm and pulled him back. 'Behave,' she said.

'Lazriel,' the little boy said.

'Hi Lazriel,' Billy said. 'I am Billy. Miles is my brother. And the girl is Chloe. We are going to come to you now, OK?'

Miles followed Billy around the corner and lifted a hand. 'Hi, Lazriel.'

Lazriel looked at Miles nervously.

'Hi, Lazriel,' Chloe said.

Lazriel gave Chloe a small smile.

'Do you remember me?' Miles said. 'You helped me when the

evil vampires came after me. Near the enormous wall. Remember?'

Lazriel nodded.

Billy crouched. 'Where are your mama and papa?'

Lazriel looked down at his fidgeting hands. He looked back up at Billy and shrugged.

'He is so thin,' Chloe said. 'And his nails are black.'

'Not sure how he is alive,' Billy said.

Chloe sat cross-legged. 'Lazriel, what have you been eating?'

Lazriel shifted his black misty eyes from Billy to Miles and back to Chloe. He reached into a worn trouser pocket and pulled out roots.

'The poor kid has been digging for food,' Billy said with a shake of his head.

A low moan sounded behind them.

Miles tensed and reached for his greatsword.

'Stop,' Billy hissed. 'You will scare him away. If he wanted to harm us, he would have already.'

Miles let go of his greatsword's hilt.

'Are you injured anywhere?' Billy said. 'Are you sore?'

Lazriel bit the bottom of his lip and shook his head.

'Lazriel, do you have a sister?' Miles said.

'Wow,' Billy said. 'Just jump straight in there, brother.'

Miles ignored Billy. 'Lazriel, do you have a sister? Do you know who Luxea is?'

Lazriel froze. He opened his mouth, then closed it again.

'He knows her,' Miles said. 'You don't have that type of reaction without knowing.'

'It's OK, Lazriel,' Billy said. 'Is Luxea your sister?'

Lazriel stood deathly still. His mouth fell open as he gawked at Billy.

'What is he doing?' Miles said.

'Luxea,' Lazriel said, the mist in his black eyes swirling. 'Sister.'

'Yes,' Miles said, a smile breaking across his face. 'I know Luxea. She is safe. Would you like to see her?'

Lazriel bit his lip, then nodded.

'She will be back soon,' Miles said. 'Do you want to come with us and have some food?'

A bang came from the stables. Lazriel jumped then ran around the corner of the barn.

'Stop!' Miles said, hobbling after him.

'Gone,' Chloe said, walking up next to Miles. 'That poor kid. He looks scared out of his mind.'

'I think we need to get Luxea in front of him,' Miles said. 'That might bring him around.'

'We've got to get back to the inn,' Billy said, his hand over his forehead to stop the sunlight. 'Something is happening.'

The three of them walked back to the inn at a pace Miles could handle.

Miles opened the door and frowned at a young boy who stood doubled over with his hands on his knees.

'I have asked this young gentleman to catch his breath,' Dr Viktor said. 'It seems he has come from the city with a message.'

Miles pulled out a chair and sat. The boy stood and took in another deep breath. Jon walked over and handed him a glass of water.

After draining the glass, the boy sat on the chair Jon held out for him.

'I remember you,' Miles said. 'You ran a few messages for me in Battleacre.'

The boy smiled widely. 'Yes, sir.'

'What message do you have?' Rafa said.

The boy cleared his throat. 'Vampires have overrun the city of

Battleacre. A vampire by the name of Gerald holds the lady Raquel captive.'

A loud clatter made everyone jump. Rafa's chair lay on its side next to the table. 'I must go back immediately,' he said.

'Please, Rafa,' Miles said. 'Let us ask questions and find out more information.'

Rafa righted his chair and sat. He placed his elbows on the table and gazed unblinkingly at the young messenger.

'Did Raquel send you?' Miles said.

The young boy cleared his throat again. 'One of her trusted friends sent me,' he said. 'I was to find the Hammer and the Shield and tell them Battleacre needs them.'

'Where is the Soldier?' Miles said. 'Has he not returned?'

'The Soldier, sir?' the young boy said with a confused look.

'He means the General,' Rafa said. 'Has he not returned from the north?'

'I do not know,' the boy said. 'I did not see him, but then I don't see many people from the officers district.'

'We must go,' Rafa said. 'I cannot wait around here.'

Miles held up a hand. 'I know, Rafa, but you and I must speak first.'

Rafa sat back in his chair and folded his arms.

'Any other news?' Miles said to the messenger.

The boy shook his head.

'Did you see a young girl with white misty eyes?' Miles said. 'Her name is Luxea.'

The boy's eyes widened. 'The lady Raquel spoke of a vampire named Janie, and a girl named Luxea. She thinks they are hiding somewhere in Battleacre.'

'Jon, can you get this young man a room?' Miles said, summoning Jon over with a wave. 'Spare no expense. I want him to have the finest room where he can rest. It must have been a lengthy journey.'

'Two day's run,' the boy said. 'I ran right through the night to find you, sir.'

Miles gave the boy a single nod. 'An honourable achievement. I will make sure the lady Raquel rewards you correctly. Off you go.'

The boy stood, bowed and followed Jon up the winding staircase.

Miles spun in his chair and, resting a finger on his lips, asked for them all to remain silent.

A few minutes later, Jon walked back down the stairs and gave Miles the thumbs-up.

'Something doesn't look right here,' Miles said, looking at Rafa. 'If Battleacre is overrun, then why have they not sent vampires here? And, this boy still thinks I am the Hammer when I am clearly not.'

'I do not care,' Rafa said. 'Raquel is in danger. The house is in danger. I am the Shield and I must return.'

'I agree you need to return,' Miles said. 'But I fear you will walk into a trap.'

'It is a chance I have to take,' Rafa said. 'I cannot bear to think that Raquel is being held by this vampire. This Gerald.'

'I will go with you,' Chloe said.

'What?' Miles and Billy said in unison.

'I am going with Rafa,' Chloe said. 'If Janie is there, I've got to get there and help her.'

'Battleacre is not overly friendly to people from the western land,' Miles said.

'What Miles is trying to say is that it will be unusual for you to be there and not be someone's slave,' Rafa said.

Chloe folded her arms and lifted her chin. Her left leg bounced angrily on the chair's armrest. She narrowed her eyes at Miles and Billy.

'You know she has decided, brother,' Billy said with a lopsided grin.

'I know,' Miles said with a sigh. 'Make sure you have a believable story about why you are there.'

'She is my sister visiting from the west,' Rafa said. 'A guest of the General's house.'

'That is a good story,' Billy said. 'When will you leave?'

'Now,' Rafa said, standing and adjusting his spear. 'I wish nothing more than a skin of water if possible.'

Chloe stood and checked her swords. 'A skin of water for me too, please.'

Heather walked over with two small skins. She handed one to each of them. Rafa gave a small bow, then marched out of the inn.

'Make sure Dr Viktor gets home safely,' Chloe said to Alexa. 'His research on these vampires is going to be most important.'

Alexa inclined her head. 'You have my word.'

'When will you two join us?' Chloe said, looking at Miles.

'I will leave tomorrow morning, first light,' Miles said.

'We will leave tomorrow morning,' Billy said. 'I am coming with you this time, brother.'

'If you wish,' Miles said, grinning at Billy. 'It will take us three days to get there by road. If you go as the crow flies, it will take two days for you and Rafa to get there.'

'Be safe, you two,' Chloe said, then walked out of the inn.

'We shall leave tomorrow morning,' Dr Viktor said. 'I wish to make the southern gate in one day.'

Jon walked over and placed some fruit on a small square table next to the inn's fireplace. Heather collected the mugs on the breakfast table and showed the group to the more comfortable chairs near the crackling fire. Throughout the rest of the afternoon, they sat on couches and spoke of the old days. Alexa jokingly needled Miles about his love for Janie. Miles held his head in his hands and blushed a bright pink. Billy, spurred on by Alexa, did a small play in front of them, depicting Miles and Janie's love. Dr Viktor clapped and chuckled at his son's antics.

'Stop, stop, please,' Miles said, holding up a hand.

Billy flopped into his chair and wagged his eyebrows at Miles. 'I have only just started, brother.'

Miles covered his face and groaned.

'You mentioned you wanted some advice, son?' Dr Viktor said, after the antics had died down.

'I do, sir,' Miles said. 'I wish to speak to you alone on a matter.'

Billy stood. 'Right. That is our signal to turn in. I wish you all a good night.'

'As do I,' Alexa said. 'It is good to see you, Miles. I will be ready first thing for our journey, Dr Viktor.'

Dr Viktor smiled up at Alexa.

'It is great to see you too, Alexa,' Miles said with an incline of his head.

'Do you two require another drink?' Jon said from the bar.

Dr Viktor held his hand up. 'I have had my fill, thank you.'

Miles shook his head at Jon, then leant back in his chair. He interlaced his fingers behind his head and closed his eyes.

'Out with it, boy,' Dr Viktor said.

'The Soldier, who is General of Battleacre, lost his wife a few seasons ago. When I was staying at his estate, I noticed a picture of his wife on a table in his study.'

Dr Viktor pulled out a handkerchief and coughed loudly into it.

'His wife is the Lady,' Miles said.

Dr Viktor's mouth fell open. He sat completely still and stared at Miles. After a moment, he said, 'Who else knows of this?'

'Only Janie has seen the picture,' Miles said. 'And I have told Rafa about it.'

'What did the General say about his wife?' Dr Viktor said. 'How did he lose her?'

'They didn't tell me much other than they buried her a few seasons ago,' Miles said.

Dr Viktor rubbed his stubbled chin. He took a deep breath and closed his eyes. Miles knew his father well enough to know now was not the time to interrupt him. His father sat deep in thought.

'We need to keep this among ourselves for now, son,' Dr Viktor said. 'We need to think about the General's daughter. You said her name was Raquel?'

'Yes, she is the one Rafa is in love with,' Miles said.

'It is indeed important we keep this quiet for now,' Dr Viktor said. 'It will have a profound effect on Billy and Chloe. We want to help Raquel.'

'I think so too,' Miles said. 'I fear this will distract them from the key priorities.'

'You are the key priority, son,' Dr Viktor said. 'You cannot hand over the wolf to the vampires. Do you understand me?'

Miles stared into the fireplace.

'Son?'

'Yes, I understand,' Miles said. 'I just find it difficult being the centre of attention.'

'Luxea and this young boy have a part to play in all of this,' Dr Viktor said. 'They should also be our key priority.'

'The boy's name is Lazriel,' Miles said. 'And Janie is my most important priority.'

Dr Viktor pulled himself forward. 'You are all important, son. You are the earth element's vessel, which means the earth element relies on you. Janie, who you love, is important because I fear you will do something noble for her and put yourself in danger. And these two children are important. You must do everything you can to make sure you are all safe.'

Miles looked at the ceiling and sighed.

'It is time for bed, son,' Dr Viktor said. 'Think about what I have said. I will leave at first light with Alexa for the south.'

'Yes, sir,' Miles said. 'I will turn in shortly, too. Now I need to think.'

Dr Viktor struggled to his feet. With a thin smile and a nod at Jon and Heather, he moved up the stairs.

Miles interlaced his fingers behind his head and stared at the flickering fire. He smiled at Heather, who walked over and threw a new log into the flames. Miles closed his eyes and thought of Waya running with her pack. He knew he must protect her at all costs.

Miles jerked awake. The fire smouldered in front of him. Sunlight streamed through the large windows.

'Morning,' Billy said from the table behind him. 'Didn't even get up to your bed?'

Miles groaned as he stood. 'I am stiff as a plank. Falling asleep in that chair was a bad idea.'

Billy filled his mouth with bread and gave Miles a lopsided grin. Miles walked over to the table and sat.

Heather dropped a plate of eggs and bread in front of him. 'We heard you are travelling to Battleacre,' she said. 'Jon is organising some horses for you.'

'That is kind of you,' Miles said.

'I wouldn't thank me just yet,' Heather said. 'Battleacre has depleted the horse farms, so we are not sure what we will find.'

'We will take weeks if we walk,' Billy said, pointing a slice of bread at Miles. 'No way that leg of yours will hold up.'

Miles instinctively rubbed his right thigh. 'When I spend longer with Waya, it feels better.'

'Don't know why you don't stay healed,' Billy said. 'It's all very different from Juno and Chax.'

The inn door banged open. Jon walked in and dumped a pile of wood next to the fireplace. Back at the breakfast table, he pulled out a chair and sank into it. 'I have two horses called Titch and Twitch. They are small and a little old. It will take you a few days to get to Battleacre.'

'Thanks for organising them,' Miles said, slipping Jon a gold coin. 'We will finish breakfast and leave.'

Jon gave Miles a nod, then moved back to the bar. Miles and Billy finished breakfast, waved their goodbyes, and stepped out into the sunlight. Two small horses with big, kind eyes stood tied to the side of the inn. Miles walked up and rubbed the horse's ears.

'This is going to be interesting,' Billy said, eyeing the horse.

'It's going to be painful for you at first,' Miles said. 'Watch how I get on.'

Billy watched Miles, then pulled himself onto the horse. Miles ran through the art of horse riding, then pointed them east along the road.

'Jon said it would take three days?' Billy said, gritting his teeth as he slammed into the horse's back.

'Two if we maintain pace and we travel into the night tomorrow,' Miles said. 'Today we aim for the first camp over the river.'

They moved along the path at an easy pace. The sun bathed them in warmth, which was something Miles had not felt in a long time. The brothers chatted about what had happened after Miles had left. Billy told of a thriving Fairacre with new trade with the City of Lynn. The women of Fairacre now owned their own shops or trade carts. Every person in the town now had the privilege of voting for leadership and change.

The sun set in the west as the first bridge came into view. They moved across and chose a spot in the circular camp. Miles placed the horses into the internal circle and joined Billy at the fire. After a meal of dried meats, they slept for two hours each, swapping for the night watch. At first light, they retrieved the horses and moved over the second bridge, then turned north. The first of the rolling hills appeared and the small horses blew hard with the steep inclines. Miles slowed them down to keep them from exhaustion.

'These hills are hypnotic,' Billy said, as they crested another hill.

'Ideal for wolves and horses,' Miles said. 'It's mid-afternoon and we should reach the last camp before Battleacre.'

'What do you suggest, brother?' Billy said. 'Camp or continue on?'

Miles rubbed his chin. 'The trip has been quiet. I think we should continue, but let's decide at the camp.'

A long howl filled the late afternoon. Miles turned his head and gazed up the hill they had just come down.

'Is that Waya's pack?' Billy said.

Miles shook his head. 'I cannot feel anything. She won't come to me unless it's necessary.'

They reached the bottom of the hill and began the steep climb up the next. Billy adjusted himself on his horse. Miles grinned, knowing how sore his brother must be. They reached the top of the hill and Miles pulled the horses to a stop.

'What's the matter?' Billy said.

Miles placed his hand over his brow. 'The camp is below but it seems quiet.'

'Too quiet?' Billy said.

'Battleacre is half a day's ride away,' Miles said. 'The camp should have a lot more people.'

'No point sticking around,' Billy said, spurring his horse forward. 'Let's check it out.'

Miles followed his brother down the hill. They stopped just short of the small bridge over the river. A few streams of smoke from the back of the camp curled up into the late-afternoon sky. The inner circle lay empty.

'There is a large wagon around the back,' Billy said, standing in his stirrups.

'A slave trader,' Miles said, spitting into the ground. 'I have seen him before.'

'Didn't we abolish trading people, though?' Billy said, a frown streaking down his forehead.

'I thought so too,' Miles said. 'But it seems things have changed.'

Billy spurred his horse forward. The sound of the horse's hooves on the cobblestone bridge rang out through the afternoon. They circled the camp and slowly walked past the wagon. A man dressed in jewels and emeralds sat in a chair. Western people ran around the campsite keeping the man in constant luxury.

'I wish to do something,' Billy said, with disgust etched on his face. 'I wish to do something to that pig of a man.'

'Once we sort out Battleacre, we will certainly come back and deal with it,' Miles said. 'But right now, brother, we have to deal with the threat of the vampires.'

Billy turned his head and snarled at the man.

The man smiled, then gave Billy a rude signal.

'Certainly going to deal with him,' Billy grumbled.

The steep incline slowed the two small horses. At the top, Miles pointed to the north.

'Is that Battleacre?' Billy said.

'What you can see there is the top of the great arena,' Miles said. 'It will amaze you when you see the size of it.'

Billy smiled at the look of dreamy wonder on Miles's face.

Suddenly, a small blade whistled past Miles. He turned to his left and his breath caught in his throat. At the side of the road, two knife slingers stood in front of their horses. Miles slid off his horse and drew his greatsword.

'Stay behind me, Billy,' Miles said, as he moved into his defence stance. 'I am going to take the one on the right.'

The knife slingers stood staring with their swords drawn.

'Billy?' Miles said, turning around. 'Billy, no!'

With his sword clattering to the ground, Miles stumbled around Billy's horse and fell to his knees. 'Billy!' he shouted, turning him over. The dagger protruded from his brother's chest. There was little blood. Billy's eyes stared lifelessly at Miles. No air made his chest rise and fall.

'No, Billy, no,' Miles said, grabbing the dagger's hilt. 'Forgive me,' he said, yanking the dagger from his chest. Miles placed his hands over the wound. He kept the pressure firm to stop any further bleeding. A shadow blocked out the sun as a knife slinger towered over the two brothers.

Miles turned his head and snarled up at the knife slinger.

He smirked, then placed the tip of his sword on Miles's neck. 'Where is your wolf?'

Miles ignored the sword and looked back at his brother.

'The royal vampires know they don't need you,' the knife slinger said. 'It will take longer to find your wolf, but they do not need you. This is your last chance. Tell me where your wolf is and I will spare you.'

Miles turned his head. 'You murderer. You will never have Waya. Never.'

The knife slinger lifted his sword. Just as he began to bring it down, a rotting corpse slammed into the back of the knife slinger, sending him sprawling to the ground. The moans and groans of undead sounded through the hills. With a flick of his legs, the knife slinger sprang to his feet and slashed at the closest undead. The other knife slinger whistled, calling for his friend. With his sword hacking a path to the side of the road, the knife slinger jumped onto his horse and the two of them rode down into the valley.

Tears streaked down Miles's cheeks. He stayed kneeling with both hands over the hole in Billy's chest. A smaller shadow broke the sun's rays.

Lazriel knelt next to Miles. He placed his hand on Billy's shoulder. The black mist swirled in his eyes as he chanted unintelligible words to himself. Miles felt Billy's body warm. A moment later, Lazriel let go of Billy's shoulder.

'Is he alive?' Miles said, looking at Lazriel.

Lazriel shook his head. 'Luxea.'

Miles frowned with confusion. 'What do you mean, Luxea?'

Lazriel pointed at Billy. 'Luxea.'

'I need to take Billy to Luxea?' Miles said.

Lazriel nodded vigorously. 'Luxea.'

Miles walked over to the two horses and brought them next to Billy. With strength he did not know he had, he bent over and deadlifted Billy up onto his horse. He tied the stirrups to Billy so he wouldn't fall off.

'Is Luxea in Battleacre?' Miles said to Lazriel.

Lazriel shrugged. 'Luxea,' he said, pointing at Billy.

Miles pulled himself onto his horse and kicked them into a trot. On all four sides, the undead escorted him and his dead brother to the city of Battleacre.

CHAPTER 20

I NEED HIM

The small hooves of the sweating horses clopped on the wooden drawbridge. Large black clouds lay over the city of Battleacre. The wind was absent. Mist threatened to lower past the arena rooftop and blanket the entire city.

'Open the gate,' Miles said.

'Who goes there?' a guard said.

'The Hammer,' Miles said. 'I need to get to the General's estate.'

The chains clacked. The thick wooden gates creaked open. A soldier ran onto the drawbridge and grabbed the reins of Billy's horse.

Miles slipped off his horse. 'I will take this one. Can you stable my horse, please?'

The guard saluted. 'Certainly, sir. Shall I send a message to the General's estate?'

'That won't be necessary,' Miles said. 'I don't want to wake his household.'

The guard gave Miles the reins of Billy's small horse. He

grabbed the reins of Miles's horse and guided him through the gates and up to the stables.

Miles pulled the small horse through the gate and onto the wide cobblestone road. Up ahead, with the games finished for the evening, the arena loomed in darkness. After a few minutes, Miles turned into the steep, winding lane leading into the officers district. The small horse rattled his lips as he blew hard with the effort of the climb. The winding road flattened into the children's playground. After crossing the park, they wound up the street to the front gate of the Soldier's estate. The enormous house sat in darkness. Thick mist almost touched the top of Miles's head. The gate squeaked open and Miles led the small horse up to the steps. He tied off the horse and shuffled up to the front door. With a shove, the door opened halfway. Miles hobbled down the steps and pulled Billy from the horse. With his leg and foot screaming with pain, he climbed up with Billy on his shoulders. He kicked the door open and carefully guided Billy into the foyer. With another kick, the Soldier's study door flew open. Miles carried Billy to the cold, dark fireplace and lay him in front of it. After he threw kindling and wood onto the grate, he struck flint until sparks brought the fire to life. The soft glow of the flickering light danced across the walls. Miles held the back of his hand to Billy's forehead. A small sliver peeled off Billy's skin.

'Undead. He is turning into the undead,' Miles said. 'Hold on Billy. I am going to find Luxea.'

Miles walked out of the study and shouted into the house. 'Hello? Anybody here?' After no reply, he used the banister to pull himself up the stairs. With every door he opened, darkness greeted him from inside each room. He reached Luxea's bedroom and opened the door. Miles walked in and stood in the middle of the room. He turned in a slow circle, looking for clues. On the bed, nestled between the pillows, sat Pippa, Luxea's doll. The bed creaked as Miles sat on it. Pippa flopped about as he turned the doll in his hands.

'Grandma's house,' Miles said, standing up and stuffing Pippa into his jacket. 'It's the only place I know of where she might go.'

Miles climbed down the stairs and hobbled back into the study. He threw another log into the grate and stoked the fire with a poker. With a last look at his brother, he left the study and walked out of the front door.

'Going to throw caution to the wind,' Miles said as he untied the small horse. 'Sorry, my boy, but we are on the move again.'

Titch nodded his head and rattled his lips. Miles guided Titch out of the estate and down the winding road to the playground. Instead of crossing the playground, he trotted north alongside it until he met the road to the north. Titch trotted along with his head nodding and his eyes rolling. A few minutes later, they passed the spot where Genevie had murdered Jarod. Up ahead, the hills and valleys of the poorer district loomed. Miles stopped at the district's entrance to get his bearings. Titch, getting bored, chose to go to the right. They went up and down the roads until Miles found the small street leading to Luxea's grandmother's house. At the bottom of the street, he hopped off Titch and tied him to the fence. Miles ground his teeth as the gate squeaked open. He walked up to the small dark house.

'Anyone home?' Miles said, knocking on the door.

Miles waited, but no answer came. He placed his ear against the door and heard a quiet whisper.

'I can hear you,' he said. 'It's Miles. I am looking for Luxea.'

The sound of small feet ran up to the door. With a creak, the door opened.

'Luxea,' Miles said, kneeling and holding out his arms. 'Are you OK?'

Luxea ran into Miles's arms and squeezed him tightly.

'Where is your grandma?' Miles said. 'Can I come in?'

'She went to the nice place in the sky,' Luxea said, pointing up. 'I sent her there.'

Miles walked into the house and covered his nose. The mild stench of death floated out from a closed door next to the kitchen. He opened the door to Luxea's grandmother's bedroom and walked over to the bed. The old woman lay peacefully with her hands crossed over her chest.

'It was her time,' Luxea said, standing next to Miles. 'She is happy now.'

Miles led Luxea out of the room and into the kitchen. He lifted her up onto a kitchen chair, then sat opposite her.

'I have Pippa,' Miles said, pulling the doll out from under his jacket.

'Pippa,' Luxea said, clapping her hands together. 'We had to run from the other house and I left her behind.'

Miles gave Luxea a moment to say hello to Pippa. 'Luxea,' he said. 'Who did you run here with?'

'Janie, of course,' Pippa said with a small frown. 'Raquel had to go to work and then she didn't come back. Janie said we should come here and hide.'

'And where is Janie now?' Miles said.

Luxea shrugged. 'I don't know. She hasn't been here for two days.'

Miles leant forward and gave Luxea a hug. 'You are so brave looking after yourself on your own.'

'My grandma taught me how to make food,' Luxea said, making chopping moves with her small hands. 'Eggy bread.'

Miles chuckled. 'Eggy bread?'

'I will make it for you one day,' Luxea said.

'What do you mean you sent your grandma to the sky?' Miles said.

Luxea looked at Miles with her white misty eyes. 'I help people go to the sky.'

Miles frowned. 'I am not sure I understand?'

With a hop, Luxea jumped off the chair and ran to her room. A few moments later, she walked out with a bunch of paper in her hands. She placed the paper on the kitchen table, then climbed back onto the chair.

'Good drawings,' Miles said, shuffling the papers.

Luxea pulled over a picture. 'When people are dead, I see smoke come out of them. I can talk to the smoke.'

Miles's eyebrows shot up into his hairline. 'You can speak to people's essence?'

'What is essence?' Luxea said, her eyes wide.

'The smoke that comes out of people, we call it essence. It is like their soul,' Miles said. 'There are not many people who can see it.'

Luxea pulled over another picture. 'If the smoke, the essence, needs help, I can speak to it. See?'

'Why would the essence need help?' Miles said.

'If the person needs to finish something, or if some of their essence is missing,' Luxea said.

Miles cast his mind back to Valen and the worry Chloe had if he passed away without all of his essence. Doomed to be stuck between this world and the next.

'My grandma's essence was worried about me because I was on my own,' Luxea said. 'But I told her it was OK.'

'You can bring the essence back if they don't want to go into the sky?' Miles said.

Luxea turned her head to the side. 'Well, I fix the body so the essence can come back.'

'Billy,' Miles said, standing up suddenly, which sent his chair toppling over.

'Who is Billy?' Luxea said.

Miles knelt in front of her. 'He is my brother. A knife slinger stabbed him. He is in the Soldier's house. Do you think you can help him?'

'Janie said I shouldn't leave the house,' Luxea said, looking at her hands. 'It is safer here.'

'We can go there and I will bring you right back,' Miles said. 'I have a horse outside. I will hide you in my cloak.'

Luxea wrung her hands together. 'I don't know. The bad man with the red eyes will hurt me.'

'I promise I will look after you,' Miles said. 'And we can bring Pippa along.'

Luxea thought for a while. 'OK, Pippa said she would like to go on a horse ride.'

Miles hobbled into Luxea's room and opened her small wardrobe. It stood bare, apart from an old, worn jacket. The coat hanger clattered as Miles ripped the jacket off it. He walked back into the kitchen and held it up for Luxea.

'We are going right now?' Luxea said, her eyes widening. 'It is dark outside.'

'That is even better,' Miles said. 'Few people will see us.'

Luxea struggled into her worn jacket, then tucked Pippa into it.

'Ready?' Miles said.

With a nod, Luxea marched out of the house. She stopped at the front gate. 'He is cute,' she said loudly.

'We need to keep quiet, Luxea,' Miles said, placing a finger on his lip. 'Nobody must know you are with me.'

Luxea pulled a face. 'Sorry,' she said, her whisper louder than her normal voice.

Miles grimaced then, with one movement, he picked up Luxea and placed her on the front of Titch. Miles jumped on behind and pulled her into his cloak. With a click of his tongue, he moved Titch down the street and out of the district.

Miles grinned as Luxea giggled all the way down the western road. When they reached the playground, Miles slowed to a walk.

'Swings,' Luxea whispered. 'You promised me one day.'

'I did,' Miles said. 'And one day we shall.'

They turned up the winding road and stopped at the Soldier's estate. Miles hopped off Titch and pulled open the gate. He guided the horse up to the front door, where Miles lifted Luxea out of the saddle and led her up the steps.

The front door moved.

Miles pulled Luxea behind him and reached for his greatsword. 'Who goes there?'

The door swung open.

'Janie,' Luxea said, escaping Miles's grasp and running at Janie.

She knelt and hugged Luxea. 'I told you to stay at Grandma's house.'

'Grandma went to the sky,' Luxea said.

'What do you mean?' Janie said, frowning up at Miles.

'Her grandma passed away,' Miles said. 'She was sitting there on her own.'

Janie pulled Luxea out of their hug. 'I am sorry about your grandma.'

'That is OK,' Luxea said. 'She was happy when she went to the sky.'

'I am sorry I went for so long,' Janie said. 'I didn't know you were on your own.'

'That is OK,' Luxea said. 'I made eggy bread.'

Janie frowned up at Miles.

'Janie,' Miles said, waving his hand to change the subject. 'Billy is in the study.'

She stood. 'He is here?'

'I need Luxea to help him,' Miles said.

'Why would Luxea help Billy?' Janie said.

Miles bit his lip, then dropped his eyes.

'Miles,' Janie said. 'What is wrong with Billy?'

'A knife slinger killed him,' Miles said, voice cracking. 'He is in the study.'

'Oh, Miles,' Janie said, walking over and hugging him. 'I am so sorry.'

Miles squeezed Janie tight. 'I think Luxea can help him. Follow me.'

Miles opened the door to the study and walked over to the fireplace. The last of the logs spat embers into the fireguard. Billy lay with his arms crossed over his chest. His skin had turned even whiter.

'Oh, Billy,' Janie said, kneeling next to him. 'I cannot hear his heart, Miles.'

'Is this your brother?' Luxea said, walking over and then kneeling next to Janie. 'He doesn't look like your brother.'

Miles knelt on the other side of Billy. 'We are not brothers from the same mother. But we have lived together since we were smaller than you.'

Luxea frowned at Miles. 'Someone has trapped his smoke. Why is his smoke trapped?'

'Lazriel did something to him,' Miles said. 'He touched him and said something, then told me to find you.'

'Lazriel,' Luxea said under her breath. 'I have heard that name before.'

'Can you help Billy?' Miles said.

Luxea laid a hand on Billy's forehead. The mist in her eyes swirled as she spoke the same unintelligible language as Lazriel. Miles's breath caught in his throat as a thin line of white smoke escaped Billy's nose. Billy's essence danced in front of Luxea's face as she continued to speak in the language nobody could understand.

After a few moments, Luxea turned to Miles. 'Billy is ready to go to the sky,' she said, her voice lowered with the strain. 'He does not have anything to finish.'

'No,' Miles whispered. 'I need him. Does he have to go? What about Tilly?'

Luxea tilted her head. 'You want me to not let him go into the sky?'

'Miles,' Janie said. 'This isn't a good idea.'

Miles placed his head in his hands. 'I need him, Janie. I cannot let him go.'

Her voice getting heavier, Luxea continued speaking in the language Miles couldn't understand.

'I need him, Luxea,' Miles said, tears pouring down his face. 'Please bring him back.'

Billy's essence spun once, then dived back into his body through his nose. Instantly, Billy's skin changed from a white to a bright pink. Luxea placed her hand over the hole in his chest and continued to speak the language. The wound closed up, leaving nothing but a small red mark.

'Miles,' Billy shouted, sitting up suddenly.

Janie let out a small yelp in surprise.

'Brother,' Miles said, grabbing Billy and pulling him into a hug. 'I am so sorry. I had to. I just had to.'

Billy hugged Miles back, then gently pushed him away. He gave Miles a lopsided grin. 'Were you not supposed to protect me from those daggers?'

Miles laughed with relief. 'Is that really you?'

'Who else would it be?'

Miles glanced at Luxea. 'Are you OK?'

Breathing heavily, she opened her eyes and gave Miles a thin smile. 'I am not supposed to break the rules.'

Miles glanced at Janie, who shrugged.

'What rules?' Miles said. 'I don't understand.'

Luxea placed her thumb in her mouth and laid her head in Janie's lap. 'Very tired.'

Miles picked Luxea up. 'Janie, can you check this house for somewhere to hide?'

In a flash, Janie disappeared. A second later, she reappeared. 'There is a large basement area with a room.'

'Lead the way,' Miles said.

Billy and Miles followed Janie to a door under the stairs. They climbed down the stairs and walked through a dark corridor that led into a large bedroom. A double bed and two single beds filled the space.

'Servants' quarters,' Billy said.

'I think we rest up here for the night,' Miles said, placing Luxea on one bed.

Billy walked over to the single bed and sat on the end. He lowered his head into his hands and sighed.

'Are you sure you are OK?' Miles said, walking over and sitting next to Billy.

'I think so,' Billy said with his lopsided grin. 'I feel like I have been away for a long time.'

Miles glanced at Janie.

'Go to bed,' Billy said, nudging Miles with his shoulder. 'You look shattered.'

Miles squeezed Billy's shoulder, then walked over to the double bed. He kicked off his left shoe, then struggled with the three straps on his right. Eventually, the shoe fell away, and his right foot turned inwards. He swung both legs onto the bed and lay down. With his hands behind his head, he stared at the ceiling. The bed creaked as Janie climbed on. She placed her head on his shoulder and wrapped an arm around him.

'I think I might have done something stupid,' Miles whispered.

'Billy?' Janie said.

Miles nodded.

'I think we need to trust Luxea,' Janie said. 'She wouldn't have done something if she thought it would be bad.'

'I hope so,' Miles said. 'I just feel I might have robbed Billy of something.'

Janie snuggled into Miles's neck. 'There is nothing you can do about it now. Get some rest.'

Miles closed his eyes and took in a deep breath. Exhausted from the last two days, he fell into a deep sleep.

'Morning,' Billy said. He jogged on the spot in front of the double bed. 'It's good to be alive. Time for breakfast.'

Miles sat up. 'Are you OK?'

Billy frowned. 'And why wouldn't I be OK? I slept like a baby.'

'Where is Luxea?' Janie said, sitting up.

The three of them stared at the small bed. With a pop of air, Janie flashed out of the room. Miles scooted to the side of the bed and gingerly placed his right foot on the floor.

'Does it still hurt?' Billy said.

'I am so used to it now,' Miles said, pulling the three straps tighter. 'It's a part of my life now.'

There was a sudden rush of air and Janie popped back into the room. 'She is in the kitchen making breakfast.'

'She is a bit young to cook, isn't she?' Billy said. He walked to the door. 'Won't she hurt herself?'

'She is more than capable,' Miles said, hobbling past Billy.

They walked through the kitchen doors and stood stock-still.

Luxea stood with both her hands on her hips. 'I thought I'd need to wake you all.'

'How could we stay asleep with this lovely smell through the house?' Billy said, walking up to a chair. 'What are you making?'

'Eggy bread,' Luxea said, flipping over a piece of egg-soaked bread. 'It is my favourite.'

'We need to eat breakfast, then get you back to your grandma's house,' Miles said.

A look of sadness rippled over Luxea's face. 'I will bury her in her favourite garden.'

'I will help you with that,' Janie said, accepting a plate from Luxea. 'And we can plant some flowers on top of her.'

Luxea came back with two more portions of eggy bread and placed them in front of Miles and Billy. She returned with her own plate and hauled herself up onto the chair.

'What is the plan for today, then?' Billy said, while chewing on a piece of bread. 'Wow, this is fantastic. I think it is also my favourite from now on.'

Luxea took another big bite and beamed at Billy.

'The plan is to get Luxea to safety, and for us to search for Chloe and Rafa,' Miles said.

'Who is Chloe?' Luxea said.

'Chloe is the leader of the south,' Billy said. 'She is strong and smart and fierce like you.'

Luxea jumped off her chair and practised her sword moves. 'I am Luxea, the great! Fight me, bad people. I will protect my friends. I am the greatest.'

Billy threw back his head and howled with laughter. 'You and Chloe will definitely get on well.'

After they had finished their toast, Luxea ran upstairs and got Pippa.

When she returned, Miles knelt and gave her a hug. 'Janie will be with you all the time. I have given her tokens to use if you want to send messages to us. We are going to help our friends and Raquel.'

Luxea threw her arms around Miles's neck. 'Remember, you promised we would play in the playground.'

'We will,' Miles said, squeezing her. 'Go with Janie, and when we have finished what we need to do, I will fetch you.'

Billy knelt next to Miles and took his turn to hug Luxea. 'I don't know how you did it, but thanks for bringing me back.'

Luxea gave him a thin-lipped smile. 'Don't tell anyone,' she said, placing her fingers on her lips. 'I will get into lots of trouble.'

'My lips are sealed,' Billy said, dragging his finger across his lips and throwing away a key. 'And thanks for the eggy bread.'

'Let's get going,' Janie said.

Miles stood and embraced Janie. 'I will see you soon. Be careful.'

Janie smiled up at Miles. 'Be safe.'

Billy put his finger in his mouth and made loud gagging noises. 'You two are gross.'

Luxea hopped from foot to foot while giggling.

Janie grabbed the hood of her cloak and pulled it over her head for protection from the sun. She picked up Luxea. 'Hold on tight,' she said.

'Here we go,' Luxea said. 'Bye.'

And with a pop, they disappeared.

'Who needs a horse when you have someone like Janie, right, brother?' Billy said, punching Miles on the shoulder.

Miles sat back down and waited for Billy to sit. 'Are you sure you are OK?'

'I am fine,' Billy said. 'Why the worry?'

'Luxea keeps saying she broke the rules,' Miles said. 'What

rules? And how would a young girl know rules around life and death? It seems very mature.'

'I don't know,' Billy said, spreading his hands. 'All I know is I am here now, so let's embrace it and get on with it.'

'You are right,' Miles said with a sigh. 'Let's find our friends.'

They left the estate and made their way on horseback to the south entrance of Battleacre. The stablehand took Titch and led the small horse into a stable. Twitch bobbed her head and snorted as her friend entered the stable. With the horses settled, Miles and Billy walked up the southern road towards the amphitheatre. As they entered the southern square, the horns blared, signalling the start of the day's fighting.

'Unbelievable,' Billy said, craning his neck to see the top of the arena. 'This place is massive.'

'Wait till you see the inside,' Miles said, moving to the southern gate.

'You sure it's a good idea for you to go in there?' Billy said.

'The Soldier, his family, the mayor, his family, and the entire council have special areas they sit in,' Miles said. 'We need to get a good look to see what is going on.'

'Where do you think Chloe and Rafa are?' Billy said, following Miles through the gate and to the first staircase.

'Rafa would come to the games,' Miles said. 'But he would have gone straight up to the special areas.'

He sucked air through his teeth as they made their way up the long spiral staircase. Three tiers before the top, he stepped off the staircase and walked into the arena. He turned to watch Billy's expression grow from surprise to wonder. 'Big, isn't it?' Miles said.

Billy shook his head. 'I could never have imagined something this big.'

Miles faced the arena and breathed in the last of the winter air.

The surrounding crowds jostled each other to get to their prescribed seats. Miles covered his eyes with his right hand and peered over the arena at the special area. His breath caught in his throat.

'What is it?' Billy said, covering his own eyes and gazing in the same direction.

'Gerald,' Miles said. 'They have erected an awning for him so he can watch protected from the sunlight.'

'Is that woman sitting next to him tied up?' Billy said, frowning.

'Raquel,' Miles said. 'She has a collar around her throat.'

'Raquel is the General's daughter?' Billy said.

'Yes, and she is also a council member,' Miles said. 'I need to get her away from that animal.'

The trumpets sounded to start the first game. The four massive steel gates around the arena clacked open. Out marched four soldiers, ready to begin the contest. Gerald waved a dismissive hand, giving the mayor the authority to continue. The mayor rose from his jewelled seat and walked up to the long alphorn. The horn reverberated around the arena. With the panels slamming open, the combatants grabbed their weapons and began the fight.

'Something isn't right here,' Miles said, squinting down at the arena floor.

'What do you mean?' Billy said.

'Those weapons look real,' Miles said.

'Are you sure?' Billy said, also squinting.

Just as the last word came out of Billy's mouth, a sword pierced the chest of a combatant. The crowd screamed and cheered. The soldier fell forward onto his face and the light sand around him turned a dark red.

Miles stood and walked back to the spiral staircase.

'Where are we going?' Billy said.

'This ends now,' Miles said. 'Gerald is at his most vulnerable out here in the sun. We need to stop this madness. He has everyone under his control. He's doing this for his own sick pleasure.'

They walked down the staircase and out of the southern entrance. At the end of the square, they walked north until they came to the western entrance square. Miles slowed and grabbed Billy by the wrist. 'Guards,' he said, flicking his chin to the two figures standing on either side of the entrance.

'Vampires?' Billy said.

'Or knife slingers,' Miles said.

Billy shivered. 'Not a group of people I ever want to see again.'

'We need a distraction,' Miles said, turning around and walking to a set of benches on the edge of the square.

'I could cause a scene,' Billy said.

Miles shook his head. 'I need you with me. I don't think it's as easy as climbing the stairs to Gerald. We might have to fight our way up.'

The crowd roared again. Horns blared to signal the start of the battle between the final two combatants. Miles sat down on the bench and eyed the two guards at the gate. Billy sat, crossed his legs, and tilted his head back to take in the sun's rays.

'I have an idea,' Miles said, raising a hand in the air.

A messenger appeared. 'Yes, sir.'

Miles pulled out a gold coin and held it up in the air.

The messenger gasped.

'Do you see those two guards at the western entrance? I need you to distract them for me.'

The messenger peered at the western gate. 'That is not a good idea, sir.'

'Why not?' Billy said. 'It's a distraction and I am sure you can get away.'

'Vampires, sir,' the messenger said. 'There is no way for me to get away from them. They are too quick.'

Miles held up the coin. 'I am sure you can be creative. This coin can set you up for many years.'

The messenger took the coin and turned it around in his fingers. He pocketed the coin, then gave Miles a nod. 'Be ready, sir.'

'Let's get close,' Miles said. 'I think we will only have a moment.'

They walked across the square and stood a short distance from the vampires. Billy threw his arm over Miles's shoulder and laughed loudly. Miles let his brother play the game of just two people milling about. A few moments later, food and water tumbled out of the arena's second tier and landed on top of the two guards. Miles grabbed his brother and made a beeline for the entrance as the guards turned and shouted up at the tiers. Once inside, Miles hobbled up the spiral staircase.

'Clever kids, these messengers,' Billy said, through heavy breathing.

Miles remained silent as he climbed the stairs. His right foot ached more and more with each step. At the third tier from the top, Miles climbed off the spiral staircase and leant on the wall. Up ahead, he could see Gerald lounging in his chair with his fangs extended. Raquel sat stone-faced, her eyes bulging. The collar had rubbed harshly, forming a red ring around her neck. Visible vampire-teeth marks left angry red welts near the veins on her neck and shoulders. Miles drew his greatsword and placed it against the wall. He stood stock-still and waited for a distraction. A few minutes later, the mayor stood and approached the alphorn. With a deep breath, he placed his lips on the horn and blew. As the deep rumbling sound ran around the arena, Miles jumped forward with his greatsword raised. With every muscle tensed, he brought the greatsword down as hard as he could. The blade entered Gerald's shoulder and cut down to his heart. The vampire crumbled into dust.

Raquel turned her head and screamed. 'Watch out.'

Something hard hit Miles on the side of the head. His legs buckled underneath him, sending him to the ground. Miles blinked to clear the fog.

A tall figure bent over him. Long thick fangs descended from his mouth. 'Well, hello there, son,' the Soldier said, his eyes turning a deep red. 'Nice to have you back.'

CHAPTER 21

FIGHT, FIGHT, FIGHT

'Leave him alone, Father,' Raquel screamed.

Miles blinked hard to stay conscious. The Soldier's teeth-filled smile appeared inches from his face. Hands grabbed him roughly by the shoulders and dragged him to the stairs. He looked to his right and saw Billy moving towards him. Miles shook his head, then pointed his chin at Raquel. Billy backed away and moved towards her.

'Take him to the arena jails,' the Soldier said. 'Once we finish today's games, I will come down and deal with him.'

Thick rope bound Miles's wrists and ankles. Six men lifted him onto their shoulders and walked down the spiral staircase. Miles struggled at first, but then stopped as the punches to his head came thick and fast. The Soldier's voice boomed out into the arena, asking for the games to continue. At the bottom of the stairs, the six men turned south and walked along the arena wall. A large wrought-iron gate clacked open. Miles watched the bricked ceiling go by as they descended deeper under the arena. The light disappeared until a single torch flickered against the wall.

'Open up,' a vampire said.

Bolts banged and a thick metal door creaked open. The vampires hauled him through the narrow door and down a stone staircase. Rows of cells sat in near complete darkness. The door of the third lay open. With a heave, the vampires threw Miles up against the back wall. With fangs extended, they growled as they lifted Miles's wrists above his head and shackled them to the wall.

'Not getting out of these, boy,' a vampire said.

Another knelt and punched Miles square in the face. 'Gerald was my father,' he hissed. 'He turned me a century ago. I hope the vampire king makes you suffer.'

Miles turned his head and spat blood onto the ground.

'Leave him alone,' another vampire said. 'The king will end you if you kill this dog.'

The vampire hissed inches away from Miles's face. Miles turned his head to get his nose away from the smell of rotting flesh.

'Let's go,' the vampire said.

With a squeal, the iron gate slammed shut. The key's clink sealed Miles into the cage. He waited for the metal door at the top of the stairs to slam shut, then pulled against the circles of steel around his wrists. The chains clinked on the walls above him.

'It's no use,' a gravelly voice said.

Miles turned his head to the left. 'Who are you?'

'Is that you, Miles?' a girl's voice said.

'Chloe? Rafa?'

'Oh, that is just great,' Chloe said. 'Here we have been waiting for you to rescue us.'

Miles spat more blood onto the ground. 'Sorry. What happened to you two?'

'Your big General buddy caught us and locked us up in here is what happened,' Chloe said. 'He didn't take too kindly to the Shield asking questions.'

'What is going on, Rafa?' Miles said.

Silence echoed through the jail.

'Rafa is sulking,' Chloe said.

'I am not sulking,' Rafa said. 'I just cannot believe what is happening.'

'The Soldier is a vampire,' Miles said.

'Not just a vampire,' Rafa said. 'The vampire king.'

'How can that be?' Miles said.

'I don't know,' Rafa said. 'We left him fighting the old vampire king. Maybe the king bit him and the General killed him. I have no idea.'

'I don't care who bit who,' Chloe said, her chains clinking as she struggled. 'We have to get out of here.'

The metal door above them slammed open. Footsteps clacked down the stairs, then disappeared into a room at the bottom. A few minutes later, a vampire walked up to Miles's cell with a plate. He unlocked the gate and walked in. With the plate placed next to Miles, the vampire undid one wrist, then went back out of the cell. Miles pulled a face at the rotting meat and mouldy bread on his plate. With his eyes closed, he ate it all.

'Disgusting,' Chloe said.

'Eat it all,' Miles said. 'Keep up your strength, Chloe.'

The sounds of Chloe gagging bounced off the jail walls.

For what seemed like days, Miles fell in and out of consciousness. Rats ran across his jail cell, squeaking as they looked for food. Miles kicked out when one would test out his shoe.

The door at the top of the stairs slammed open. Footsteps echoed through the jail. The Soldier stopped in front of Miles's cell and stared through the bars.

'Good morning,' the Soldier said, cheerfully. 'I hope you are enjoying your stay in the top-rated arena inn.'

The surrounding vampires snickered.

'What has happened to you?' Miles said.

The Soldier chuckled. 'I think you can figure it out.'

'You killed the vampire king?'

'Open this gate and get me a stool,' the Soldier said to a vampire, then he pulled open the unlocked gate and walked over to Miles. He slammed the small stool into the ground.

'Let me go,' Miles said, pulling against his chains.

After sitting on the stool, the Soldier leant in. 'You know what I want.'

Miles snarled.

'The wolf,' the Soldier said. 'And that little brat of a kid. Where are they?'

Miles stared at the Soldier but said nothing.

The Soldier grabbed Miles by the hair and pulled his head up. 'Where are they?'

'You know I cannot control the wolf,' Miles said. 'Yet you still ask me.'

'You are lying,' the Soldier said. 'I have seen you call her.'

Miles shook his head to attempt to release his hair from the Soldier's grip.

'And the young girl,' the Soldier said. 'Where is she? I know she is with this love of yours. Janie is it?'

Miles licked his lips and grimaced at the taste of fresh blood.

The Soldier leant in further. 'If you tell me where your wolf is or where Luxea is, I will spare your friends.'

'They are your friends too,' Miles said. 'Rafa is the Shield of your house. Why would you harm them?'

The Soldier sat back and looked up at the ceiling. With a sigh, he interlaced his fingers behind his head.

'Tell me,' Miles said. 'What is making you do all of this? Who is making you do all of this?'

'They will kill mother,' the Soldier said.

Miles shook his head in confusion. 'What do you mean they will kill your mother?'

'Mother and Genevie are the only pure women bloodline of our race,' the Soldier said. 'Genevie cannot have children for centuries. Our mother is the only one who can give our race pure-blood children.'

'And who has her?' Miles said.

'The old man has threatened her,' the Soldier said. 'He will kill her if we don't give them the wolf and the girl.'

'Pretty stupid of the king to send Genevie home then, wasn't it?' Miles said. 'Placing both women in the same place.'

'Enough of this talk,' the Soldier said, shaking his head to snap out of the conversation. 'None of these things matter. Where is the wolf and where is the girl?'

Miles kept quiet.

'We are searching every corner of Battleacre,' the Soldier said. 'When we find this child, I will make sure Janie suffers a slow and painful death.'

Miles's eyes flew open. He jerked his head at the Soldier trying to headbutt him. He kicked with both feet but missed.

The Soldier flashed to the door. 'I will leave you to think about what I have requested.'

Miles's cell door slammed shut. A minute later, he heard the door at the top of the stairs close.

After a few minutes, Rafa said. 'Now we know. The General is the new vampire king.'

'What do I do?' Miles said, his voice catching in his throat. 'I cannot see a way out of this. I am going to have to give Waya up, aren't I?'

Chloe and Rafa remained silent.

Miles let his chin drop into his chest. He closed his eyes tight as the salty taste of his tears trickled into his mouth.

. . .

'Time to wake up,' the Soldier said, running a metal bar along the cell bars.

Miles jumped awake. He grimaced with pain as the loud clanging rang through his ears.

'It's time to go top side,' the Soldier said. 'Get him out of there and get him up to the arena.'

Miles struggled as the vampires tied his legs together. They released his metal bonds, tied his wrists, and hoisted him onto their shoulders. The same journey as before felt twice as long because each step sent stabbing pains all over his body.

'Put him on that chair,' the Soldier said. 'That chair is where my pathetic son used to sit.'

The vampires dumped Miles onto the chair. A metal collar snapped around his neck. A chain led from the collar down to the ground. The vampires undid the ropes around Miles's wrists.

'Where is your daughter?' Miles said.

'Raquel?' the Soldier said. 'She went missing yesterday. I will find her and turn her.'

Miles let a ghost of a smile play across his lips.

The Soldier leant in. 'I am going to show you what will happen to your friends if you defy me.'

'Leave them alone,' Miles said, the smile disappearing. 'They have done nothing to you.'

'I think you have already met Walter,' the Soldier said, pointing behind Miles.

Miles spun and looked behind him. Jewels sparkled on the rotund man's fingers. Two western black people sat on either side of him. One fanned him to keep him cool. The other offered an assortment of food.

'Your friends are from the west, aren't they, son?' the Soldier said, leaning back in his chair and interlacing his fingers.

With a snarl, Miles struggled with the chain and collar.

'It seems we are running out of soldiers to take part in the arena,' the Soldier said. 'So why not entertain ourselves with some men from the west? Walter here has opened up a steady stream of slaves from the City of Lynn.'

'You disgust me,' Miles said, spitting at the Soldier's feet. 'You despise slavery.'

The Soldier threw his head back and howled with laughter. Once he had finished, he walked over to the alphorn and let go a long blast. The four gates of the arena opened. Vampires shoved four western men out of each of the arena's three gates. A knife slinger strode out of the fourth. The twelve western men looked around in confusion. When the knife slinger reached his quadrant, the Soldier blasted the alphorn again. The knife slinger walked up to the first panel and pulled out a pole with a blade on the end. Within a minute, it was over. All twelve western men lay lifeless on the ground.

'That is going to happen to your friends if you don't hand over the wolf and Luxea,' the Soldier said, with a wide smile.

'Where is your honour?' Miles said. 'You were the most honourable man I know. Now look at you.'

The Soldier placed his chin on a fist. He sat there in silence with his red eyes looking at Miles. A moment later, he slapped him with the back of his hand. 'I said, where is the wolf and where is Luxea? Do you want your friends in the arena with the knife slingers?'

'I will give you nothing,' Miles said, sitting back in his chair.

A long snarl came from the Soldier. His thick fangs extended, his eyes turned a deep red, and his nails became sharp claws. He raised his clawed hand to strike Miles. He stopped mid-strike. The red in his eyes disappeared as he lowered his hand. 'If you will not give me the wolf or Luxea, I might as well have some fun with you.'

Miles curled a lip. 'I don't call this fun.'

The Soldier stood and walked onto the platform so he could address the crowd. 'Ladies and gentlemen. This man, once the Hammer of my old pathetic house, wants to be a part of the Queen's Guard. How do you become a member of the Queen's Guard?'

'Win, win, win,' chanted the crowd.

'Yes, you have to win,' the Soldier said, raising his thumb in agreement. 'You need to be the last man standing.'

'Win, win, win,' the crowd chanted.

'This man has a disability,' the Soldier shouted, pointing back at Miles. 'Do we give him special dispensation?'

'Boo,' the crowd chanted. 'Boo.'

The Soldier looked back at Miles and smiled. 'No dispensation, for the Queen's enemy won't be showing him any dispensation.'

'I have never wanted a head start or a leg-up,' Miles said. 'I would always do this through my own merit.'

The Soldier turned back to the crowd. 'Under this arena, there are two formidable fighters, captured by me. One fighter is from the southern land and one from the western land. They are the friends of this man.'

'Fight, fight, fight,' chanted the crowd.

'If this man reaches the end of the day, he will need to fight these formidable fighters,' the Soldier thundered.

The crowd roared. 'Win, win, win.'

'And I decree that this will be a fight to the death.'

The crowd deafened Miles with a roar that reverberated around the arena.

'If this man wins, I will allow him to choose between the small girl and the wolf,' the Soldier said. 'If he fails, I will put to death all he knows here in the east, and everything he knows in the south.'

'You wouldn't dare,' Miles shouted, struggling against his collar.

The Soldier walked back and sat next to Miles. 'These are your choices. You fight and win, and you get to save the girl or the wolf and your beloved southern town. You fight and lose, and I will destroy everything you love, your friends, and everything in the south. You don't fight – well, you know the answer to that statement.'

Miles kicked out at the Soldier. 'I will kill you!' he shouted. 'Do you hear me? I will kill you!'

The Soldier threw his head back and roared with laughter. He waved his hand at the surrounding vampires, then sat back and interlaced his fingers behind his head.

The vampires tied Miles's wrists and ankles. The collar fell to the ground with a clang. Miles struggled hard against his bonds. The vampires lifted Miles onto their shoulders and walked down the spiral staircase. At the bottom of the staircase, they moved south against the wall to stay out of the sunlight. They went through the cast iron gate, down the corridor, and through the metal door. With a thump, Miles hit the cell floor. They yanked his arms above his head and tied the steel shackles to his wrists. The vampires slammed the cell shut, then walked up the stairs and through the metal door.

Miles dropped his chin onto his chest.

'Miles,' Chloe said. 'Are you OK?'

'No,' Miles said, his breath catching in his throat.

'What is it?' Rafa said. 'What have they done?'

Miles took in a deep breath. 'The Soldier is making me fight.'

'What do you mean?' Chloe said.

'If I fight and win, I get to save either Luxea or Waya and Fairacre. If I lose, the Soldier will destroy everyone here and everyone in Fairacre.'

Chains clanged against the jail's brick walls. 'Get me out of here,' Chloe said. 'I will kill that disgusting creature. I will not let them hurt the people of Fairacre.'

After a few moments of silence, Rafa said, 'There is a catch, isn't there?'

'Yes,' Miles said, his voice barely higher than a whisper.

'What is the catch?' Chloe said.

Rafa let out a knowing laugh. 'The General is going to make Miles fight us.'

Chloe sighed. 'I wasn't expecting that.'

CHAPTER 22
BATTLEACRE

'Come on,' the vampire said, banging the cell door open. 'It's a new day, and it's your turn to fight.'

'I will not fight,' Miles said, dragging his feet as the two vampires lifted him out of his cell.

'The king says you will fight, so you will fight,' the vampire said.

Instead of turning towards the big iron gate near the west entrance, the vampires turned in the opposite direction. They travelled down a long corridor until they hit a T-junction. The vampires turned right into a large room lined with wooden benches. Above each bench, a set of iron rings held thick chains. The vampires dumped Miles on a bench and tied his hands above his head. Miles turned his head to his right as the crowd's roar filtered through the room. The two vampires walked up to the gate to watch the current match. Fifteen minutes later and it was over.

'It's time,' a vampire said, walking over to Miles and untying him. 'Don't keep the king waiting.'

The second vampire spun a wheel, which opened up the gate. Miles approached the gate and placed his hand on his brow. Thick clouds lay over Battleacre, but the sun still burnt Miles's eyes as they adjusted to the first light he had seen in a while.

'Ladies and gentlemen,' the Soldier's voice boomed across the arena. 'It is the day you have all been waiting for.'

The crowd roared, clapped their hands, and stamped their feet.

'The Hammer of my house,' the Soldier thundered, 'will fight against two westerners and a soldier. If the Hammer loses, we hunt every one of his cherished people down both here and in the south. If he wins, we move to the next round.'

'Win, win, win,' the crowd chanted.

'Looks like you are up,' a vampire said, pushing Miles into the arena. 'Remember what is at stake.'

Miles stumbled forward, then fell to his knees. The crowd's roars quietened to whispers. Miles lifted his head and curled a lip at the people pointing at him. The first laugh brought the second, then the third, until the whole arena was pointing and laughing.

'Look at him,' the Soldier said. 'The great Hammer of my previous house crawling like a dog.'

Miles closed his eyes and took a deep breath. A tear fell from his face and hit the pale soil of the arena floor.

'You better get up and get to your quadrant,' a vampire said. 'If the king blows the alphorn, you won't be able to get your first weapon.'

Miles looked at the special area. The Soldier stood with arms folded and a smile on his face. His fangs reached down to the end of his chin, and his claw-like fingernails lay across his biceps. With a grunt, Miles pushed himself to his feet. He stumbled again but maintained his footing. Cautiously, he hobbled to his quadrant. A small part of the crowd clapped. As soon as Miles entered his quadrant, the alphorn rang through the arena.

Miles slammed his fist against the first panel in the arena wall. The panel sprang open. Miles reached in and pulled out a weapon called a Jo, the short pole preferred by Juno. He tested its weight, then turned to assess his opponents. Two western black men and a Battleacre soldier stood in each of their quadrants. The soldier stood with his arms folded and a sword leaning against his leg. He eyed Miles, then snorted a laugh. The two western men ran to the centre, engaging in a ferocious fight. Miles moved to the centre of his quadrant and settled into his defensive stance. One of the western men slashed at his kin, missed, then gasped wide-eyed as his opponent's dagger sank into his chest. The soldier marched up behind the second western man and slashed twice, sending him to his death.

He faced Miles and laughed out loud. 'Are you really the General's Hammer? What a joke.'

Miles ignored the taunting and kept his eyes trained on the soldier's weapon.

'Fight, fight, fight,' the crowd chanted.

He ran at Miles, then slashed his sword in a figure of eight. Miles parried, sank to a knee, and jabbed the stick into the soldier's wrist. He yelped, dropped his sword, turned and ran for his quadrant. As they were the only two fighters left, the fifth panel automatically opened. The soldier pulled out his preferred weapon, a chain with a spiked ball at the end. He ran at Miles.

'Win, win, win,' the crowd chanted.

He leapt into the air and swung the ball at Miles's head. Miles wrapped the chain of the soldier's weapon around his Jo, then whipped the spiked ball in a circle. With a crunch, the ball slammed into his chest. With wide eyes and a gasp of air, the soldier fell face down into the dirt.

The crowd roared. 'Winner, winner, winner.'

Miles turned and lifted his chin at the Soldier. He curled a lip, then spat into the ground next to him. 'I am going to kill you,' he whispered. 'I will have your head soon.'

The Soldier's smile disappeared as, with acute hearing, he heard Miles's words float on the wind. Miles walked back through the metal gate and sat on the bench. The two vampires showed more caution as they tied him to the chains.

Two more fights rang out through the lunch period. Miles placed his chin on his chest and closed his eyes. The dying men's screams and the crowd's cheers echoed through the room incessantly.

'Your turn,' a vampire said, unlocking the chains.

Miles stood before the vampires laid a hand on him.

'Easy there,' one vampire said. 'You know where to go.'

Miles shuffled into the arena and up to his quadrant. A western slave and two soldiers occupied the other quadrants. The Soldier placed his lips on the alphorn and blew a reverberating blast across the arena. Miles turned and slammed his fist against the panel. The panel sprang open. Miles pulled out a short sword and a shield. The crowd roared as the two soldiers tackled each other. The western man stood back, holding a pole with a blade on the end.

'They don't know that's his weapon of choice,' Miles said, looking up at the Soldier.

The Soldier unlaced his fingers and leant forward.

Miles cursed. 'I am going to kill you.'

The Soldier slapped his thigh and roared with laughter.

A sickening scream sounded as a soldier fell face-first into the dirt. The second eyed Miles and the western man. Choosing the western man, he advanced with his hooked sword. The western man placed his long-bladed pole, a Naginata, at the ready. With a feint to the right, the soldier pressed hard on his right leg and jumped to the left. He slashed his hooked sword at the western man but hit nothing. With a flick of his wrist, the western man hooked the sword and ripped it out of his hands. The soldier turned to run for his quadrant but collapsed after two steps. With a snarl, the western man pulled his blade from his back.

Around the arena, the crowd clapped and cheered.

The western man looked at Miles with narrowed eyes.

Miles held up his shield with his left arm. He swished his sword through the air to check its balance.

'I will kill you, dog,' the western man said. 'I will kill you for what you have done to my people.'

'Sir, I have done nothing,' Miles said. 'I don't want to fight you.'

The western man darted in with a flurry of jabs. The blade cut gashes through the wooden shield. Miles hobbled to his right and continued to hold up his shield for defence.

The western man roared, then jumped high. As he came down, he stabbed the Naginata at Miles's face. Miles turned a full circle to evade the blade and slammed the shield into the western man's face. With a sickening crunch, the man hit the dirt. He lay there dazed, with his eyes blinking. Miles stood over him with his sword at his throat.

'Kill, kill, kill,' the crowd chanted, their thumbs pointing down.

Miles saw the fear in the western man's eyes. He lowered his sword.

'What are you doing, boy?' the Soldier said. 'You know the deal. You lose, I will take everything from you.'

'I will not kill this man,' Miles said. 'This is barbaric. You are barbaric.'

'Kill him,' the Soldier thundered. 'Kill him now or I will make everyone you love pay with their lives.'

'No,' Miles said, stepping back.

The Soldier flicked a hand.

'Let go of me, you smelly, greasy, small-brained peacock,'

Chloe said. 'Let me out of these chains and I will send you to the hell you came from.'

'Ladies and gentlemen,' the Soldier said. 'Please say hello to the leader of the south.'

The crowd, laughing and smiling, waved at Chloe.

'How is a black woman slave the leader of the south?' Miles heard a man in the crowd say.

The Soldier grabbed Chloe by the locs and exposed her throat. 'Kill him now or I will start with this friend of yours.'

'I have seen more brains in a field mouse, you son of a booger butt,' Chloe yelled.

'Let her go,' Miles said.

'Kill him,' the Soldier said, pulling out a dagger. 'I won't even turn your friend; I will let her die slowly.'

'You pin-brained muscle head,' Chloe said, struggling hard. 'Fight me like a man, not like a coward.'

The Soldier brought a blade up to Chloe's throat.

Miles closed his eyes and gritted his teeth. With one movement, he stepped forward and dealt a swift death stab to the western man's heart.

'Win, win, win,' the crowd cheered.

Miles discarded his shield. He stared at the dead man.

'Let go of me,' Chloe said.

'Take her back,' the Soldier said.

Miles's face turned to stone. The light in his eyes faded. He shuffled back to the room and sat on a bench. He placed the back of his head against the wall and stared straight ahead. The light and sound of the occasion faded into a muffled background noise. His breathing remained steady.

'A warrior's look,' a vampire said with a chuckle.

'All humanity is leaving him,' the second vampire said. 'Is this your first kill?'

Miles closed his eyes. After half an hour, the gates snapped open. Miles hobbled out into the bleak grey day and made his way to his quadrant. The alphorn sounded. Panels slammed open. Bodies hit the pale dirt. Miles glared up at the Soldier with a chiselled, unmoving and unfeeling face. He then made his way back to the room and sat back on his bench. The gate clacked closed. The sun headed for the horizon in the west. Torches flickered to life all around the arena. The gate clacked open. Miles walked to his quadrant.

'The quarter-finals,' the Soldier said. 'Are you ready for the spectacle?'

Miles swayed on his feet, his eyes never leaving the Soldier.

Feet thumped in unison as the crowd chanted and cheered. 'Fight, fight, fight.'

Miles pulled his eyes away from the Soldier and checked each quadrant. No more western men, just hardened Battleacre soldiers. The alphorn sounded. Miles approached the panel and slammed his fist against it. The panel flew open. Miles grabbed the Bo, a long fighting stick, and turned to face the enemy. The soldiers, having seen Miles's previous battles, grouped together and walked towards him.

In a blur, Miles spun the Bo in a circle around himself to test its balance. He settled into a defensive stance with the Bo's tip facing the soldiers. The soldiers held an axe, a short sword and a pike. As they came into striking distance, Miles's Bo spun and twirled, crunching against thigh, shin, face and chest. Each soldier sprang backwards with a yelp of pain. Not one soldier could get close to their opponent. Twice, Miles disarmed a soldier, sending them back to the panels for another weapon. No sweat appeared on Miles's brow. His breathing came easily. Drenched from head to foot, the three soldiers breathed heavily.

Then, with a sudden burst of speed, Miles crunched his Bo

against the heads of two soldiers. Both soldiers dropped dead. The third soldier stared at Miles with fear in his eyes.

'Kill, kill, kill,' the crowd chanted.

The soldier ran back to his quadrant and retrieved his preferred weapon. Miles didn't bother retrieving his.

As the soldier approached, Miles bounced to the right, twirled his Bo, and sent the last soldier to his death.

The crowd roared.

Miles turned his empty eyes towards the special area. He glared at the Soldier. 'I am going to kill you,' he whispered.

No smile played on the Soldier's lips. His dark red eyes stared back.

The gate in the arena wall clacked open. Miles spat on the ground, then hobbled back to the room, where he sat on the bench. With the back of his head against the wall, he stared forward, unblinking.

'Miles,' came a faint whisper. 'Miles, can you hear me?'

The muscles in his jaw twitched.

'Miles, it's me. Can you hear me?'

The sound of the crowd rushed into the room. Miles blinked once and shook his head.

'Look here, Miles.'

Miles turned his head and stared through the bars.

'It's me, Janie.'

'Janie?' Miles said, his voice coarse. 'What are you doing here?'

'I need you to hold on, Miles,' Janie said. 'We plan to get you out of here soon. We have a plan.'

'Go away, Janie,' Miles said. 'There is nothing you can do.'

'Who are you speaking to?' a vampire said, walking up to Miles and jabbing a finger in his face.

Miles kept his eyes staring forward.

'Leave him alone,' the other vampire said. 'He is going to be dead soon.'

Miles closed his eyes and lowered his chin into his chest. The darkness of sleep took him.

The back of a hand slapped Miles's face. 'Wake up, dog, they have finished the last quarter-final. Semi-finals are next.'

Dark grey clouds still hung over the arena. The sun had finished its journey over the horizon, leaving an end-of-winter chill in the air.

Miles snarled at the vampire.

'Take it easy,' the vampire said, stepping back.

Miles shuffled his way through the gate and over to his quadrant. The crowd murmured and pointed. Two quadrants had enormous, seasoned soldiers, but the third quadrant stood empty.

'Ladies and gentlemen,' the Soldier said. 'Are you ready for the semi-finals?'

'Who is the last person?' a crowd member shouted through the hollering and cheering.

The Soldier called for calm with his hands. 'As this is a special occasion, we have a special guest appearing.'

'Who, who, who?' the crowd chanted.

'Are you ready?' the Soldier thundered.

The crowd stamped their feet in unison. 'Ready, ready, ready,' they chanted.

With a squeal, the fourth gate opened. A tall, thin man with close-set eyes strode into the arena. His long, flowing cloak flapped around him. With a hint of a nod at the Soldier, he walked over and stood in his quadrant.

'The Queen's elite assassin, ladies and gentlemen,' the Soldier said. 'This is what this boy wanted to be when he came to Battleacre. Do you think this cripple is worthy?'

The crowd this time cheered, but without conviction. Some murmured among themselves. Others stood with their mouths shut and their arms crossed.

The Soldier sneered at the crowd. He walked up to the alphorn and signalled the start of the battle.

Miles approached the arena wall and hit his fist against the panel. He pulled out a heavy two-blade axe. After testing its weight, he turned just in time to see a soldier launching through the air with a large hammer. Miles fell onto his back and rolled to the side. The hammer hit the dirt, spraying light-coloured sand in every direction. With his axe abandoned, Miles used both hands to back-pedal on his rear. The Battleacre soldier lifted his hammer above his head. Before he could bring it down, the soldier's eyes widened and his mouth fell open. He collapsed to his knees. Behind him, the knife slinger stood with a blood-soaked dagger in his hand.

A grin broke across his face as he wagged a finger at Miles. 'You are all mine.'

Miles scooted back further.

The knife slinger turned and strode towards the other soldier.

Miles cried out in pain. With both hands, he reached down to his right foot. The three-strapped boot lay in the dirt with two of the straps broken. His foot turned inwards, sending sharp jolts of pain up through his leg. In the distance, the knife slinger toyed with the soldier for the crowd's entertainment. Miles undid the laces of his left boot and gingerly slid his foot out. Using the arena wall for balance, Miles pulled himself upright.

The crowd roared as the knife slinger sent the soldier to his knees.

Miles's toes dug into the fine, pale sand. A distant thump jolted the bottom of his feet. The sand vibrated around his toes. Slowly, a small amount of pain drained away into the earth. Another thump, stronger than the first, jolted through his legs. Miles pushed himself away from the arena wall. He stood without help. The pale sand shimmered around his feet, holding him in place. Mother Earth's heart thumped again. Miles felt the power pass from the ground up through his legs.

The soldier fell face-first into the dirt.

With an almighty roar, the crowd jumped to their feet. 'Fight, fight, fight,' they chanted.

The fifth panel in each quadrant slid open.

Miles held his breath. He flexed his right knee, which lifted his right foot off the ground. The marks on his back shifted over his muscles. Miles maintained his balance. His right inwards-facing foot turned outwards just enough for him to walk with a small limp.

The knife slinger reached his own quadrant and pulled out his long, thin sword and short dagger from the fifth preferred panel.

Miles moved to his quadrant with easier steps, the marks on his back shifting to trigger the muscles he needed to move. He maintained his balance. For the first time since the Lady had cut the nerves across his back, Miles walked unaided without Waya nearby. At the arena wall, Miles reached into the fifth panel and pulled out his greatsword.

Miles turned and looked up at the Soldier in the special area. 'This is the sword you gave me. And this is the sword that is going to kill you.'

The Soldier sat back in his chair and interlaced his fingers behind his head. His face sat in stone with his deep red eyes trying to bore a hole into Miles.

The knife slinger walked to the middle of the arena and bowed.

With another roar, the crowd chanted, 'Honour, honour, honour.'

Miles walked to the centre and bowed.

The two walked in a circle with their weapons ready. In a sudden burst of speed from both, their weapons clashed. Backwards and forwards they went, from defensive to offensive stances. Miles moved with the thumping heartbeat of Mother Earth.

The experienced crowd, never seeing such skill, fell silent in awe.

Two blades twirled in a blur.

After a minute of intense fighting, Miles and the knife slinger broke apart and circled each other. Sweat dripped down Miles's nose.

The crowd found its voice and roared.

The knife slinger smiled. Not a bead of sweat appeared on his face. 'You have fought bravely,' he said, with a slight inclination of his head.

Miles kept his eyes trained on the knife slinger's hands.

'Your honourable death will please this crowd,' the knife slinger said. A flick of the wrist and the knife slinger's sword stabbed straight at Miles's chest. Miles turned sideways, then fell to the ground. He kicked his feet hard against the ground to push himself backwards. The knife slinger raised his sword.

Miles heard a roar in his ears. The ground beneath him vibrated. Black and blue spots shot across his eyes. Miles flung his hands at his opponent. Small shards of sand sprang from the ground and ripped through the knife slinger. With wide eyes, he fell to his knees. All over his body, small beads of blood appeared from the holes the shards of sand had made. With a last gasp of air, the knife slinger fell forward onto his face.

The crowd fell silent.

Miles blinked hard to clear the black and blue dots. He commanded the pale sand to help him to his feet. The earth pulsed and lifted Miles up. He looked up at the Soldier. 'Mother Earth is going to swallow you whole. I am going to kill you.'

'Winner, winner, winner,' the crowd chanted.

The Soldier got to his feet and walked over to the announcement platform.

'Fight, fight, fight,' the crowd chanted.

The Soldier raised his hands. The crowd fell silent. 'You wish me to fight this cripple? This dog?'

'Fight, fight, fight,' the crowd chanted.

A smile broke across the Soldier's face. 'If this dog wins the final, I will fight him.'

With a deafening roar, the crowd stamped their feet.

Miles's unblinking eyes never left the Soldier's face.

'You have thirty minutes before the final, boy,' the Soldier said. 'Thirty minutes before you die.'

The gate behind Miles banged open. Mother Earth rippled underneath Miles's feet as he walked back to the room. The bench creaked with his weight. Miles stared forward. No vampires sat in the room. The gate to the arena stayed open.

'Miles,' Janie said. 'We are coming. Please hold on.'

Miles sat still.

'Can you hear me, Miles?' Janie said. 'Please look at me.'

Not a flicker of movement escaped Miles's body.

Thirty minutes later, trumpets sounded through the arena. The crowd roared.

Miles strode into the arena and over to his quadrant. The other three quadrants lay empty.

The Soldier walked up to the announcement platform. 'Ladies and gentlemen, are you ready for the final battle?'

'Fight, fight, fight,' the crowd chanted.

'I have something special for you tonight,' the Soldier said. 'First, the undefeated cripple. The sand devil standing in front of you. If he loses tonight, I will kill everything dear to him.'

The crowd murmured and pointed. Some shook their head at the Soldier.

'Next,' the Soldier said, pointing to the gate that clacked open, 'the Shield. Defender of the realm. A member of my old pathetic household.'

The crowd's murmurs grew louder.

Two vampires walked into the arena and threw a beaten Rafa to the ground. In an instant, Rafa was on his feet, scanning the arena. Seeing nobody else, he settled his gaze on Miles.

Miles kept his dark, lifeless eyes on the Soldier.

'In the next quadrant,' the Soldier thundered, 'the leader of the south, an imposter, a western dog.'

Two vampires threw Chloe into the arena. Just like Rafa, she sprang to her feet and surveyed her surroundings. Her eyes found Miles and she shouted. 'Miles, look at me.'

Miles ignored her. His eyes sat firmly on the Soldier.

'Snap out of it, you greatsword-loving tortoise,' Chloe said. 'Or I will teach you how to make fairy cakes. Look at me!'

Not a hair on Miles's body moved.

'The Hammer, the Shield and the southern leader,' the Soldier thundered. 'What more could you ask for?'

'Fight, fight, fight,' the crowd roared.

'And in the final quadrant,' the Soldier roared. 'Mine and the City of Lynn's finest warriors.'

Out of the last gate, two vampires and a knife slinger walked over to the quadrant.

Miles frowned at the knife slinger's disfigured face.

'Why is this fair?' Chloe shouted up at the Soldier. 'Hey, wannabe dentist, why is this fair?'

The Soldier smiled down at Chloe.

Chloe gave the Soldier a rude gesture.

Miles turned his head to Chloe. 'Remember your training and stay alive. If you are to be ended, I will do it rather than one of these dogs.'

'Oh my, that is so very sweet of you, Miles,' Chloe said, rolling her eyes. 'Do I get to choose how you kill me?'

Miles snarled. 'Remember your training, Chloe.'

Chloe lifted a hand. 'OK, OK, I get you warrior boy.'

The Soldier walked over to the alphorn. He looked directly at Miles. 'Remember what is at stake, boy. You lose, I will eradicate everything you love, including the south.'

'Do you even know which way south is, cupcake?' Chloe shouted up at the Soldier. 'Come down here and I will show you,' she said, pointing a finger at the ground. 'Six feet south, I tell you. That's the only south you are going to know.'

The crowd cheered and pointed at the Soldier. 'South, south, south.'

The Soldier snarled, placed his lips on the alphorn, and blew. The sound reverberated around the arena.

Each combatant walked over to the arena wall and punched open the panels.

Miles pulled out a Naginata. Rafa pulled out two short swords. Chloe pulled out a greatsword.

With a look at Miles and Rafa, Chloe burst out laughing. She looked up at the Soldier. 'You are as dumb as you look, princess.'

The Soldier looked at Chloe with confusion.

'Time for us to swap,' Chloe said, flinging the greatsword at Miles. Rafa spun and let loose both short swords that pegged into the ground at Chloe's feet. Miles flung the Naginata at Rafa, who caught it with one hand.

The two vampires stood with no weapons. Their nails and fangs extended. The knife slinger held a shield and a short sword.

'The knife slinger has instructed them to leave each other alone,' Rafa said, circling towards Chloe. 'We are going to have to stick together.'

Miles ignored Rafa and moved to the middle of the arena.

'Get back here, Miles,' Chloe said. 'We have a better chance if we stick together.'

'We are all dead anyway,' Miles muttered.

'What did he say?' Chloe said.

A vampire flashed forward and raked his claws along Miles's chest. Miles cried out in pain and sank to a knee. The second vampire flashed forward and raked his claws along his neck. His shirt turned red as blood oozed from the gashes.

'Get back here, Miles,' Chloe said.

Miles lifted a hand. 'Stay with Rafa. I am warning you, Chloe. Stay with Rafa.'

Chloe let forth a string of rude words.

The crowd laughed, then cheered.

The vampire flashed with blinding speed and raked his claws down Miles's back. Another scream escaped his lips.

'Pathetic,' the Soldier said. 'He cannot even see my kin. They are too fast for him.'

Miles dug his hand in the dirt. He closed his eyes just as another set of claws raked across his body. The earth beneath him rumbled. The marks on his back split, forming more marks. Miles felt them crawl over his back and shoulders. The wounds from the vampire's claws slowly closed.

'Stop fooling about,' the Soldier shouted. 'End him now.'

A vampire flashed towards Miles but stopped dead as he snatched out a hand and caught him by the throat. Miles felt the strength of the earth run through him. He threw the vampire to the ground and stabbed him with his greatsword. The vampire collapsed into a pile of dust.

The second vampire stood staring at Miles, then suddenly turned to dust.

'Poof,' Chloe said, waving her short sword in a circle. 'Stupid vampire thought he could have rest.'

Miles turned his eyes to the knife slinger.

'Do you remember me, boy?' the knife slinger said.

'Isn't that the knife slinger Juno set on fire in the orchards?' Chloe said.

The knife slinger curled a lip at Chloe. 'It is. My name is Dimitri. Remember it, for it shall be the last name you say.'

Miles flicked his greatsword at the knife slinger's face. The knife slinger darted out of the way then, ignoring Miles, he went for Chloe and Rafa. Miles chased the knife slinger but slowed as he neared the trio. Chloe and Rafa, working as a team, slashed and hacked at the knife slinger. With each attack, the knife slinger stepped backwards towards the arena wall. Rafa jabbed his bladed pole at the knife slinger's shield. With a crack, the shield split in two. Chloe flicked her sword and sent the knife slinger's sword flying.

'Kill, kill, kill,' the crowd chanted.

Rafa lifted his Naginata and slashed his death blow. The knife slinger dodged, then ran through a gate and out of the arena.

'Not so tough after all,' Chloe shouted. 'We will find you!'

'Boo,' the crowd sang. 'Boo.'

Miles dropped his greatsword and looked up at the Soldier. He spread his arms. 'Fight me, you coward.'

The Soldier walked to the edge of the platform and showed his hands, asking for quiet. 'The battle isn't complete. There must be only one combatant standing.'

'Follow the knife slinger,' Miles hissed at Chloe and Rafa.

Chloe and Rafa sprang for the gate. The gate slammed shut. 'Well, there goes our escape,' Rafa said.

'Running now, are we?' the Soldier said. 'I always knew you western slaves were cowards.'

'Whatever you say, pretty boy,' Chloe said, sticking a finger in her mouth to make herself gag. 'Who is the one hiding up there in the stands? Come down here and fight.'

'Fight, fight, fight,' the crowd sang.

'You know the rules, boy,' the Soldier said. 'Last person standing. If you do not complete this fight, I will send an army to the south and destroy everything.'

'Do you not want the wolf?' Miles said. 'I will give you the wolf.'

The Soldier threw his head back and howled with laughter. 'I am hunting for your wolf already, boy. And we will find the little girl and your lover soon. I do not care about bargaining right now.'

Chloe looked at Miles. 'Well, this looks like it's the end then.'

'I am not touching either of you,' Miles said. 'I cannot.'

Rafa lifted his Naginata. 'I shall take Chloe's life. Use your anger to take mine.'

'That is actually brilliant,' Chloe said, her eyebrows raised. 'That way, you can blame Rafa.'

Miles's mouth hung open. 'Don't be stupid. None of you need to die.'

Chloe walked over to Miles and pulled him into a hug. She placed her mouth onto his ear. 'This is bigger than us. Fairacre is bigger than us. He will kill thousands of people, Miles.'

'He will still go there,' Miles said. 'If I lose and he kills me, he will still go to Fairacre.'

'Not if you kill him in the next round,' Chloe whispered. 'Make sure you take his head. Make sure he cannot come back.'

Miles choked back a sob.

'Tell Valen I love him,' Chloe said.

'I will,' Miles said.

Chloe pushed away from Miles and walked over to Rafa. 'Make it quick, will you?'

Rafa gave her a nod.

'Hey, you son-of-a-slug, my friend is going to take your head,' Chloe shouted at the Soldier.

The crowd hooted and cheered.

Chloe dropped to her knees.

Rafa raised the Naginata high above his head. 'I am truly sorry. I would have liked to have got to know you in another life.'

An ear-splitting scream came from the crowd. Miles spun his head to the south. More screams sounded.

'What is going on?' Rafa said, lowering his weapon.

A man jumped from the spectator area into the arena. His bones crunched as he hit the arena floor. More screams could be heard from the west and the east of the arena. And then, in one massive tidal wave, countless undead streamed into the amphitheatre's spectator stands The crowd jumped from their chairs and headed for the exits. More undead streamed into the upper tiers. Miles looked over at the special area. The Soldier hacked and slashed with his greatsword, his claws and his teeth. Body after body of undead crunched at his feet. But for every one he sent to the ground, two more appeared.

'Let's get out of here,' Rafa said.

'Over here,' a voice said.

'Janie,' Chloe shouted. 'Let's go, boys.'

Miles and Rafa followed Chloe to the gate Janie had opened. Once through, Janie let the gate slam shut.

'What is going on?' Chloe said.

'Raquel and Billy,' Janie said. 'They took Luxea to look for Lazriel, and they found him.'

'Did you hear that, Miles?' Chloe said. 'We don't have to die today.'

Miles's cold eyes looked away from his friends. He took in a breath and strode towards the western gate.

'Where are you going?' Janie said. 'Miles, stay in here. It is dangerous out there.'

'Stay here,' Miles said, shoving Janie away. 'Stay inside here until this is over.'

Janie's mouth fell open.

The gate just about stayed on its hinges as Miles ripped it open, the full force of Mother Earth thumping through him. All around him, undead shuffled about. Miles turned north and ran freely, using the earth to help him.

'Where did he go?' Miles said, grabbing a messenger.

'Who?' the messenger said.

'The vampire king,' Miles said. 'The General. Where did he go?'

'North,' the boy said, pointing up the northern road.

Miles ran along the street towards the northern gate. The marks moved over his back and shoulders knitting nerve endings. Undead ran about moaning and growling. People huddled together, screaming in fear. The undead shuffled past the people without touching them. A vampire hissed at Miles, but before Miles could raise a hand, a bunch of undead pounced on the vampire and pulled him to the ground. Miles carried on running until he reached the gate, where he climbed the steps. At the top of Battleacre's northern wall, Miles narrowed his eyes to search for the Soldier. In the distance, sitting astride a horse, the Soldier looked back.

'Stop, Miles,' Janie said.

Miles spun round.

'I need you to stop, Miles,' Janie said, holding her hands up.

'It's me, Janie. Everyone is safe. You don't need to chase after him right now.'

Miles's eyes cleared. 'Janie?' he said, staggering.

'Yes,' Janie said, dashing forward and grabbing Miles as he fell to his hands and knees.

'I think I am going to be sick,' Miles said. 'Why are the undead not hurting you?'

'Can someone help me here?' Janie shouted.

Miles turned and lay on his back. The dark clouds above Battleacre opened with a torrent of rain. Janie's face appeared above Miles, her wet hair plastering against her head. The marks on Miles's back and shoulders moved to the base of his spine. His right foot turned inwards. Miles's eyes rolled into the back of his head as the stabbing pain returned.

'Hold on, Miles,' Janie said.

CHAPTER 23
GRR

Miles opened his eyes. He sucked air through his teeth.

'Miles,' Janie said, rushing over from the armchair she was sitting on. 'You are awake.'

'It hurts,' Miles said, his jaw clenched. 'It hurts so much.'

'Your leg and foot?' Janie said, grabbing Miles's hand. 'What can I do?'

Miles rolled onto his side and pulled his knees up to his chest. His breath came in small gasps.

'I don't know what to do,' Janie said, her voice cracking.

'Hello,' Luxea said, skipping into the room. 'I heard you talking. Oh, what is wrong, Miles?'

'Miles is in a lot of pain,' Janie said, biting her bottom lip. 'And I don't know what to do.'

'Oh no,' Luxea said, squeezing Pippa against her chest. 'Can I have a look?'

Janie frowned. 'What do you mean?'

'Here, hold Pippa, please, Janie,' Luxea said. 'Be careful, her arm is falling off.'

'What are you going to do?' Janie said, taking Pippa from Luxea's small, outstretched hands.

Luxea walked up to the bed and placed her hand on Miles's forehead.

'What are you doing?' Miles said through his teeth.

The whites in Luxea's eyes swirled. Thin tendrils of white smoke fluttered out of Luxea's fingertips and slowly crept into Miles's ears. She hummed to herself as the whites in her eyes swirled faster. After half a minute, the tendrils of smoke retreated into her fingers.

'What did you see?' Janie said, her eyes wide in wonder.

Luxea grabbed Pippa and pulled her to her chest. 'Miles must find Waya.'

'Why?' Janie said. 'What did you see, Luxea?'

'Miles does not want to change,' Luxea said, looking at Janie. 'He must find Waya if he wants the pain to stop.'

Miles pushed himself up with a grunt. 'You heard Luxea. I need to go to Waya.'

'What do you mean, Miles doesn't want to change?' Janie said. 'Miles, what is she saying?'

'I don't know,' Miles said.

'Wolf kills vampire,' Luxea said. 'If he changes, he cannot be with you.'

'But his blood already kills vampires,' Janie said. 'I have seen it with my own eyes.'

Luxea shrugged. 'It is what his smoke is telling me. He must find Waya if he wants the pain to stop.'

'Right,' Miles said. 'Waya, here I come.'

Luxea skipped to the door, where she stopped and looked back at Janie. 'Miles is also in pain because he loves you.'

'What?' Janie said, jerking her head around. 'How am I hurting him?'

Luxea disappeared down the hall.

'Ignore her,' Miles said. 'She is just a kid.'

'A kid who knows what she is talking about,' Janie said. 'Why does your love for me hurt you?'

Miles chuckled. 'Doesn't love always hurt?'

Janie playfully punched Miles on the shoulder. 'You know what I mean. Why does loving me hurt you physically?'

'I don't think she means that,' Miles said, pulling his legs over the side of the bed. 'I think she means my heart is hurting. We need to find Waya.'

'Are you positive that's a good idea?' Janie said, rubbing a cloth across Miles's brow.

'You don't understand how painful this is,' Miles said, taking short, sharp breaths. 'I feel like throwing up. My back, my right leg and foot feel like they are on fire.'

Janie organised Miles's clothes then helped him get dressed. Dr Viktor's cane stood propped against the door. Miles hobbled to it and gripped it with white-knuckled fingers.

'How far do we need to go?' Janie said.

'Just to the southern gate,' Miles said, his cane thumping on the wooden floors. 'I can call her from there.'

Janie held onto Miles's elbow as they walked down the stairs. Voices came from inside the Soldier's study.

Miles placed a finger on his lips. 'Let's sneak out,' he said. 'I will bite someone's head off right now if they ask me how I am doing.'

Janie quietly opened the front door. The night's cool air gently kissed both of their faces.

'How long was I out for?' Miles said, looking up into the night sky.

'A full night and day,' Janie said. 'Billy said you were fine. Just that you needed to rest.'

A moan sounded from outside the front gate.

'Undead?' Miles said, frowning.

'Lazriel is here, and it seems there are always a few about when he is around.'

Miles touched his forehead. 'I think I remember asking you something about the undead?'

'You asked why they were not attacking me,' Janie said. 'We have Luxea to thank for that. She asked Lazriel to make sure they don't attack me.'

'So he has that much control over them?' Miles said.

'Looks like it,' Janie said, opening the gate.

'Does that mean there are no vampires left in Battleacre?' Miles said, walking onto the winding road.

'There are no vampires left in Battleacre,' Janie said. 'Lazriel made sure of that.'

The undead stared at Miles with one bloodshot eye. 'That must have scared the people of Battleacre.'

'Really badly,' Janie said. 'Raquel has had to work hard to bring order. Everyone is staying indoors at the moment.'

'What has happened with Luxea and Lazriel?' Miles said.

Janie pulled Miles's arm over her shoulder. 'Long-lost brother and sister reunited. Lazriel is saying a few words rather than just pointing and grunting.'

'Anyone asked them about their abilities?' Miles said.

'We have tried but they just change the subject or disappear to play.'

Miles pulled Janie closer as they walked through the playground. Janie looked up at him and smiled, her small fangs poking out over her bottom lip. The swing creaked as a small gust of wind blew up against it. Another undead moan came from behind a tree. They continued out of the park and down the road until they met the two-lane road to the south. Battleacre sat eerily quiet. Even the amphitheatre lay empty and lonely.

Miles stumbled. He sucked in air through his teeth.

'Is it getting worse?' Janie said, holding him up.

A pale-faced Miles nodded at Janie.

'It's not far now,' Janie said. 'What do you have to do to call her?'

'I just have to think her name when we get there,' Miles said, dragging a hand over his brow. 'It won't take too long for her to get here.'

'Are you sure she is OK?' Janie said.

Miles stopped walking. He stood deathly still. 'Janie,' he said, 'get back to the house and get my greatsword.'

'What is wrong?'

'Go now and meet me at the southern gate. Hurry, please.'

The air popped, and instantly Janie disappeared.

With Janie gone, Miles put his weight on his cane and continued hobbling south. The closed drawbridge of the southern gate loomed up ahead. At the gate, Miles turned left and headed for the stables. Horses neighed and bobbed their heads as he walked through, checking each of the stalls. Titch and Twitch popped their heads out of their stall. Miles hurried over, opened the gate, and led them out of the stable.

Another pop of air and Janie appeared. 'Is Waya in trouble?'

'I don't know,' Miles said, taking his greatsword from Janie. 'Usually, if she gets injured, I would feel a stab of pain. The pain I am feeling now is constant.'

Janie adjusted the light and dark sword on her back, then flashed away. Miles groaned with pain as he climbed onto Twitch. The southern gate clicked open as Janie turned the gate wheel. Twitch trotted out of Battleacre. Janie and Titch trotted up alongside Miles.

'She is south,' Miles said. 'We need to move quickly.'

The two small horses trotted forward. Thick sludge from the melted black snow flew up into the air as the horses trotted through it. Twitch and Titch blew hard as they tried to keep their balance in the slippery black gunk.

They went up and down the rolling hills until Miles slowed. 'She is close,' he said as they climbed the next slope.

Janie hopped off Titch and flashed up the hill. A second later, she was back with Miles. 'They have her.'

'Who does?' Miles said.

'Vampires have her,' Janie said. 'They caught her in a net and they are hurting her.'

Mile spurred Twitch forward. As he crested the hill, the muscles in his jaw clenched as the marks on his back shifted. His breath caught in his throat. All around the group of vampires lay dead wolves. Waya lay on her side under a thick net. The vampires circled her with spears and poked her with the bladed end whenever she moved.

'I am going to kill them all,' Miles said, his eyes turning dark and cold.

Waya howled as a vampire used a blade to cut open her right side.

Miles gasped at the shock of pain tearing through him. He gripped Twitch with his legs and drew his greatsword.

The vampires turned and faced the two charging horses.

With a roar, Miles sprung off Twitch and landed on top of the vampires. Two pops sounded as his greatsword took two heads. Before Miles could get another swing in, the vampires pounced with claws and teeth slashing and ripping. Miles snarled with rage as he punched with one hand and stabbed with the other.

Suddenly, a vicious growl stopped the vampires. They turned and took a step back. Waya's haunches bristled. Saliva dripped off her thick white teeth as she growled menacingly. Janie stood next to her with the light and dark short swords drawn.

'You abomination,' one vampire said, pointing at Janie. 'You would side with your food?'

Before another vampire could open their mouth, Waya and Janie sprang forward. Vampires screamed, then crumbled into grains of sand as Janie's sword took heads and Waya's teeth broke skin.

Miles jumped to his feet, picked up his greatsword, and joined in the fight. The brown marks on his lower back spread to his upper back and over his shoulders. Mother Earth rumbled beneath his feet, guiding him, and supporting him. His greatsword turned into a blur as he engaged with the vampires.

A few seconds later, the last vampire's head flew into the air.

Miles slipped his greatsword into its sheath and knelt in front of Waya. He ran his hands along the side of her face. 'I am sorry they hurt you. And I am sorry about your pack.'

Waya dropped her head and whined.

'How did these vampires kill these wolves?' Janie said.

'Nets,' Miles said, rubbing Waya's ears. 'They sprang a trap for them.'

'How many other wolves are they doing this to?' Janie said. 'How many packs?'

Miles stood and stretched his arms into the sky. The marks on his back held his nerves together. His right foot faced forward. 'I don't know. But we need to stop this as quickly as possible.'

'Waya needs to come with us,' Janie said. 'She is being actively hunted now and she will have a lot more protection with us.'

Waya whined again.

'Agreement then,' Miles said, rubbing the top of Waya's head. 'Let's get back to Battleacre.'

'I will run ahead and warn the others,' Janie said. 'I think Waya may frighten them if they are not expecting her.'

Miles pulled Janie into a hug. He kissed her on her forehead. 'I will never leave your side again. You know that, don't you?'

Janie grinned up at Miles. 'I know, and I will never leave you. We need to finish this, though. The king will hunt you, Waya, me and Luxea until he has either captured or killed us.'

'We will need to ask the city of Battleacre for help,' Miles said. 'Go quickly, and I will see you there.'

With a pop, Janie disappeared.

Miles tied Titch's reins to Twitch's saddle. 'Let's go, you two,' he said, jumping onto Twitch and digging his heels into him.

The two horses and Waya galloped up and down the rolling hills. Waya's tongue hung out of the side of her mouth as she bounded easily alongside. The horses' eyes rolled as they kept their eye on the predator alongside them. The amphitheatre loomed over the next hill. Miles broke over the crest of the hill and galloped towards the city. Chloe, Janie and Rafa waited at the entrance.

Miles pulled Twitch to a halt, then hopped off.

'I will take them,' Rafa said.

'So this is the wolf,' Chloe said. 'She is absolutely massive.'

'Her name is Waya,' Miles said.

Waya whined and growled.

'It's OK, girl,' Miles said. 'They are friends.'

Waya trotted up to Chloe and whined.

Chloe tentatively placed a hand on her head. 'Hello, pleased to meet you.'

'Is she going to be OK with the undead in there?' Miles said.

'I have spoken to Lazriel,' Chloe said, removing her hand. 'From what little he says, I think he has laid most of the undead to rest because he has chased all the vampires out of Battleacre. So Waya should be OK.'

Rafa returned and walked over to Miles. He pulled Miles into a hug. 'It is good to see you up and about.'

Miles hugged Rafa hard. 'I am sorry about the arena. I am sorry I put you in that situation.'

'That is OK, my friend,' Rafa said. 'I think it was Chloe calling the shots, anyway.'

'Come on, you two,' Chloe said, smiling at the two men. 'Everyone is waiting for us and we need to discuss what to do next.'

Miles walked up to Chloe and pulled her into a hug. 'Thank you.'

'For what?' Chloe said, frowning.

Miles pulled away and shrugged. 'Thank you for being strong enough for the both of us. You pretty much instantly decided what was going to happen.'

'If Rafa had taken my head, and you had defeated the Soldier, you would have been the one that would have had to face Valen,' Chloe said, placing a hand on her hip.

Miles's eyes widened. 'I didn't think of that. I think I would have taken my chances with a horde of vampires, rather.'

Chloe doubled over with laughter.

'Valen?' Rafa said.

'Someone you don't want to mess with, my friend,' Miles said. 'He is a gentle giant who wields a club like a toothpick.'

'That's enough chitter-chatter, you two,' Chloe said. 'Let's get back to the estate.'

Miles walked into the Soldier's study.

Chloe stood in the corner holding the picture of the Soldier's family. 'Have you seen this?' she said with a raised voice. 'The Soldier's wife is the Lady. Juno would go ballistic.'

'Who is Juno?' Luxea and Lazriel said at the same time.

Luxea held her hand to her mouth and giggled.

'I will tell you all about Juno in a second,' Chloe said, smirking at Luxea and Lazriel.

'I have never seen this place so full,' Miles said, walking over to Billy and hugging him. 'Yes, Chloe, I know about the Soldier's wife. She passed seasons ago. Something for us to talk about at another time.'

'What are you talking about?' Raquel said, walking over and hugging Miles. 'Why are you saying my mother is the Lady?'

Chloe's eyes widened with realisation. 'I am sorry. It is a talk for another time. Don't worry about it for now.'

Raquel frowned. 'OK, but we will talk about it.'

Chloe walked over to Raquel and took her hand. 'I hear you have been leading this city on your own. I have great admiration, as it is the hardest thing I have done. Once we rid this world of this threat, you and I will sit and talk.'

'I would like that very much,' Raquel said, inclining her head.

Miles sighed with relief.

At the fireplace, Chloe sat cross-legged and pulled Billy down next to her. 'Juno is a superhero who saved our land with fire magic,' she said, blasting fireballs at Luxea and Lazriel. 'She has a big cat that goes roar!'

'Ohh,' Luxea and Lazriel said, clapping their hands. 'Can we meet her? Where is she?'

Miles smirked as Chloe, leaving out the Lady, told small pieces of the story that happened in the south.

'It has been a long time since the sound of children has echoed between these walls,' Raquel said, looking up at Rafa. Rafa pulled Raquel into a hug.

A contented look spread across Miles's face as he scanned the room. Raquel and Rafa held each other without fear of being caught. Chloe turned her hands into lion's claws and made the loud sounds of a growling cat. Luxea and Lazriel sat wide-eyed, listening to Chloe's story. Billy leant against the fireplace, his eyes staring into the leaping, crackling flames. Down by his side, Janie stood with her arm around Miles's waist. And behind him, in the room's corner, Waya lay with her eyes closed and her head on her paws.

Rafa walked out of the room and returned with trays of food and drink. Lazriel ate the most, devouring everything Luxea handed to him. The colour in his cheeks grew with each mouthful.

With everyone finished, Raquel clinked on her glass, asking for quiet. 'I think we all know what we need to talk about.'

'Playing in the playground,' Luxea said, clapping her hands.

Everyone chuckled.

'That is very important, yes,' Raquel said. 'But we have something just as important. We need to deal with my father.'

Rafa dropped a small kiss on Raquel's temple, then squeezed her tight.

Raquel tried a half smile, then continued talking. 'He has a whole vampire army at his disposal. He will come back to Battleacre as soon as he has them with him.'

'And he will know Waya is here with us,' Miles said.

Waya's ears pricked up. She lifted her head, tilted it to one side, and growled.

'Vampires, yuck,' Lazriel said, as he pulled out a piece of bread from his trouser pocket.

'He doesn't mean you, Janie,' Luxea said, her eyes wide.

'I know,' Janie said with a smile.

'The only way we can take on my father is if we ask the soldiers of Battleacre,' Raquel said.

'We can also ask Waya to bring wolves,' Miles said.

'Ra ra ra,' Lazriel said, holding his hand out in front of him.

'Lazriel will bring the yuckies from the ground,' Luxea said, crinkling her nose up.

'The undead, Waya's wolves and Battleacre's soldiers,' Rafa said. 'Do you think it is enough?'

The study fell silent.

'Don't forget the knife slingers,' Billy said. 'They are the only ones who can fight in the daylight.'

'We can fight in the daylight,' Janie said. 'We just don't let the sun touch our skin. And don't forget the sunlight doesn't affect the vampire king.'

Billy gave Janie a thumbs-up. 'Good information.'

'So how do we get Battleacre's soldiers to fight with us?' Raquel said.

The study fell silent again. The fire crackled, spitting hot embers onto the carpet. Lazriel went to pick them up, but Luxea slapped his hand.

'The games,' Miles said, eventually. 'We host another day of the games. At the end we explain what and why we need all of them.'

'That might work,' Rafa said.

'What of the council?' Miles said, looking at Raquel. 'Do we need to speak to them?'

Raquel snorted. 'They have holed themselves up in their mansions. The undead terrify them and there are no vampires around to protect them.'

'So we do this off our own back?' Miles said. 'How do we get word out about the games?'

'That is easy enough,' Raquel said. 'We send out Battleacre's finest. Our messengers.'

Miles grinned. 'They have served me well in the past.'

'So we have decided,' Raquel said. 'I will get the games ready for the day after tomorrow. We need to leave here before the week's end, otherwise my father will hold this city to siege.'

'Do we have that amount of time?' Billy said. 'Will he not be here sooner?'

'I fear we have no other option,' Raquel said. 'I think he will also need to get help from the knife slingers.'

'In the interim, we need to guard Battleacre,' Billy said. 'Maybe Lazriel can help with that?'

'Ra, ra, ra,' Lazriel said, holding his hands up in front of him to depict the undead.

'Leave that with me,' Miles said, nodding at Billy. 'Tomorrow we will go to the playground and I will ask him there.'

Luxea jumped up. 'Yes! Did you hear that, Pippa? Tomorrow we go to the playground. Can Lazriel come?'

'Of course he can,' Miles said. 'And Janie.'

'And Janie,' Luxea said, hopping from foot to foot.

'Playground,' Lazriel shouted, then clapped his hands.

'I think it's time for bed,' Chloe said, standing up. 'Come on, you two.'

'Do we have to?' Luxea said, her shoulders slumping. 'We can sleep in here.'

'If you want to go to the playground tomorrow, then yes, it is time for bed,' Chloe said.

'Oh, OK. Come on Lazriel,' Luxea said, pulling her brother up. 'Bedtime.'

After the two children had left, everyone said their goodnights and made their way to their separate rooms.

Miles locked the bedroom door behind him. He walked over to Janie, picked her up, and laid her on the bed.

Janie pulled Miles into a deep kiss. 'Nobody to disturb us for the first time.'

Miles bit his bottom lip. 'I am new to this.'

'So am I,' Janie said, leaning over and blowing the candle out.

'Just don't forget,' Miles said. 'No biting.'

Janie chuckled.

'Playground, playground, playground,' sang Luxea as she marched around the kitchen holding Pippa in the air. 'Can we go now, please?'

'Where is Lazriel?' Janie said, placing food into a bag.

Lazriel walked in and sat on a chair. He pulled out a piece of bread from his pocket.

'Old habits die hard,' Miles said, smiling at Janie. 'I don't know where he finds the food.'

'Yum, yum,' Lazriel said, taking a bite of bread.

'Going to work on his talking,' Janie said. 'It looks like their parents abandoned them at a very young age.'

Miles tutted. 'Poor kid. Chloe seems to get through to him, though. Maybe she can help with his talking?'

'I will speak to Chloe,' Janie said, picking up the bag and throwing it over her shoulder. 'Time to go.'

'Yay,' Luxea said, skipping to the kitchen door.

'Luxea, don't forget your brother,' Miles said.

Luxea stood at the kitchen door and lifted an eyebrow at Lazriel. The chair squeaked as he jumped off and ran over to his sister.

'We must go down together,' Janie said. 'Don't go running off on your own. It's still not completely safe out there.'

They walked out of the entrance, down the steps, and onto the winding road. Luxea held her brother's hand; Miles held Janie's hand. The dark clouds still swam above, shrouding Battleacre in a gloomy morning. Janie pulled the cloak over her head in case the sun appeared.

'What are you going on first?' Luxea asked Lazriel.

Lazriel smiled at his sister but said nothing.

'How about you, Luxea?' Janie said. 'What do you want to go on first?'

'Swings,' Luxea said, doing a whooshing motion with her hand. 'And I am going to go this high.'

'Are you sure you are brave enough to go that high?' Miles said.

'Huh,' Luxea said, a little unsure of herself. 'Will you catch me if I go that high?'

Miles chuckled. 'Of course I will.'

'Then I am going this high,' Luxea said, jumping up in the air.

Janie looked up at Miles with sorrow in her eyes. 'You would have been a wonderful dad, you know that.'

Miles grinned. 'Don't give up just yet. There is still hope. Dr Viktor will find a cure, I am sure of it.'

A thin-lipped half smile spread across Janie's face. 'I hope so. Just as long as you don't leave me again.'

'I promise,' Miles said, kissing Janie on the end of her nose.

'We are here,' Luxea cried, as she squeezed Pippa to her chest. 'Can we go to the swings?'

'Of course,' Miles said. 'I will race you. Ready, steady, go!'

Luxea and Lazriel squealed with laughter as Miles chased them. For the next few hours, Janie and Miles played with Luxea and Lazriel on the playground swings, seesaws, roundabouts and climbing frames.

At lunch, Janie found a nice grassy area. 'Time to eat,' she said, waving everyone over. 'What do you want, Lazriel?'

'Yum, yum,' Lazriel said, pulling out another piece of bread from his pocket.

'Unbelievable,' Miles said, sitting next to Janie. 'That kid is resourceful.'

'Luxea?' Janie said. 'What do you want?'

'Anything,' Luxea said, sitting down next to Miles. 'As long as Pippa can have some.'

Janie passed sandwiches to Luxea and Lazriel. They sat in a circle, eating and talking.

'So, Luxea,' Miles said. 'Can you tell me what you two actually do? Your brother pulls people out of the ground and you speak to people's essence? Their smoke?'

The whites in Luxea's eyes swirled. She beamed at Miles. 'I fix the smoke in the bodies my brother pulls out of the ground.'

Janie raised an eyebrow. 'So these undead your brother has been raising need fixing?'

Luxea shook her head. 'No. When I am not here, he just raises them because he can.'

'Ra, ra, ra,' Lazriel said.

Janie chuckled.

'OK,' Miles said, biting into his sandwich. 'So he can just raise old bodies out of the ground.'

'If he wants to,' Luxea said. 'He can raise anything that is dead.'

'And you fix people's essence?' Janie said.

Luxea nodded. 'Sometimes people's smoke gets broken. I fix their smoke so they can go up into the nice place in the sky.'

'I need to speak to Dr Viktor about you two,' Miles said.

'We need to ask your brother to do a couple of things for us,' Janie said. 'One should be easy, but the other thing may be dangerous.'

'Oh no,' Luxea said, her eyes widening. 'Is he going to get hurt?'

'No,' Miles said. 'My friends will make sure of that. I promise.'

Luxea bit her nail. 'OK. Can Pippa help too?'

'Of course,' Janie said, reaching over and patting Pippa. 'She can keep an eye on Lazriel.'

'First thing,' Miles said. 'We need Lazriel to protect the outside of Battleacre. The big nasty man might come at night and we can't see him. Can he do that?'

Luxea lifted her hands. Her eyes swirled as white smoke escaped.

'What is she doing?' Janie whispered. 'Can you see anything?'

'She is using her essence to speak to her brother,' Miles said. 'Let's wait and see.'

A minute later, Lazriel's eyes turned dark. Black mist swirled as he opened his mouth and spoke unintelligible words.

'OK, he has ra, ra, ra dead things all around the city,' Luxea said.

'Great,' Janie said, clapping her hands.

'Second thing. We are going to chase the evil man in a few days,' Miles said. 'That means we are going to leave Battleacre and go north. We need lots of undead to fight the vampires.'

'Oh, OK,' Luxea said. 'He is already helping with that.'

Miles raised an eyebrow at Janie.

'What do you mean?' Janie said.

'He chased the bad things away from here,' Luxea said. 'He will chase them again.'

Miles slapped his forehead. 'Of course he did.'

Both Luxea and Lazriel slapped their foreheads. 'Ouch,' Luxea said.

Janie chuckled. 'Don't hurt yourself.'

'One more thing, Luxea,' Miles said.

Luxea let out a dramatic sigh. 'You said two things.'

'Sorry,' Miles said with a grin. 'There will be lots of wolves like Waya with us. Can you ask Lazriel not to harm them?'

'Grr,' Lazriel said, making his hands into claws. 'Wolf.'

Luxea clapped her hands together. 'He is learning.'

'Yes, he is,' Janie said, reaching over and ruffling Lazriel's hair. 'He is definitely learning.'

Luxea sent her smoke to Lazriel to communicate the request. 'Lazriel likes Waya,' she said.

'Good,' Miles said, clapping his hands.

For the rest of the day, Miles and Janie played with the two children in the playground. As the sun tipped over the horizon, Miles picked up Lazriel and Janie picked up Luxea for the trip back to the Soldier's estate.

'Sleeping like babes,' Janie said, as Luxea snored in her armpit.

'A bit of food and I am also going to get some sleep,' Miles said. 'Any news from Raquel?'

'The games are on for tomorrow,' Janie said. 'It is going to be an interesting day.'

CHAPTER 24
LITTLE TERRORS

The clash of soldiers reverberated around the arena. The crowd stamped their feet to the rhythm of their chants. Winter had broken and the warm spring air swirled into the amphitheatre. With its rays pointing from west to east the sun journeyed to the western horizon. The last soldier in the second semi-final knelt and held up his hands in surrender.

The combatants left the arena and sweepers moved in with their rakes to flatten the fine pale sand.

Miles sat on the same bench that the vampires had once chained him to. He stared forward with a face of stony concentration.

Raquel's voice boomed across the amphitheatre. 'Ladies and gentlemen, welcome to the final of today's games.'

'Fight, fight, fight,' the crowd chanted as they stamped their feet.

The first iron gate clacked open and an enormous soldier walked through. He stood in his quadrant and bowed to the special area. The crowd cheered and sang. The second gate clacked open and in walked a thin man with a cap on his head. He marched to his quadrant while waving to the crowd. He turned and inclined his head at the special area. His knees slightly trembled.

'And in the third quadrant,' Raquel said, 'please welcome the Shield of my house. Rafa from the western lands.'

The crowd stamped and cheered as Rafa walked into the arena. He stood in his quadrant and bowed. With a small glint in his eye, he grinned at Raquel.

Raquel cleared her throat. 'And in the final quadrant, the Hammer of my house, the weapons master from the south, Miles.'

The arena shuddered with the deafening roar. Chloe and Billy clapped harder when their friend appeared at the iron gate. Miles marched up to his quadrant and bowed at the special area. He grinned at Janie, who sat covered by Billy's hooded cloak.

Raquel walked up to the alphorn and took in a deep breath. After a moment of hesitation to build up the tension, she leant forward and sent a resounding note around the arena. On each quadrant, the first panel sprang open. The combatants retrieved their practice weapons and tested them for balance. After a moment's hesitation, they sprang forward and met with an almighty crash in the middle of the arena. Backwards and forwards they fought, only breaking off to retrieve their next weapons from the panels. Finally, the first combatant, the large, muscled man, fell to a knee and surrendered. The crowd lifted their hands and gave the finalist a round of applause. The three remaining combatants fought until Miles, his last weapon flying from his grip, knelt and held up his hand in surrender.

Rafa and the smaller man ran to their quadrants and pulled their preferred weapon from the panels. A ferocious battle raged until Rafa's Naginata flew into the air and pegged into the pale soil.

The crowd roared. 'Winner, winner, winner.'

The thin man thrust up his short swords in victory.

'I would never have thought you were such a formidable fighter, Almond,' Miles said, walking up and embracing him. 'I will fight alongside you any day of the week.'

Almond bowed. 'Yes, sir, I was a soldier a long time ago, sir.'

Miles grabbed Almond's wrist and held his hand up in the air. 'Your champion,' Miles shouted. 'Almond, the master blacksmith.'

'Win, win, win,' the crowd chanted. 'Almond, Almond, Almond.'

Almond bowed dramatically, sending the crowd into another stamping, raging roar of approval.

Raquel lifted her hands in the air. The crowd's roar died to whispers. 'It is good to be back,' she said, her voice carrying to every corner of the amphitheatre.

The crowd clapped and cheered while nodding their heads.

'We have eradicated the vampires from our city,' Raquel said.

In unison, the crowd stopped clapping and hissed.

'From this day forth, we are free,' Raquel said, raising her voice. 'Free from the vampires that have ripped this city apart.'

The hissing stopped and a roar of approval followed.

'But it is not over,' Raquel said. 'The vampire king has fled north and he will, alas, be replenishing his vampire army.'

The crowd fell silent as they recognised Raquel was talking about her father.

'She reminds me of Chloe,' Miles said to Rafa. 'So full of strength.'

A ghost of a smile appeared on Rafa's lips.

'Let's get up there, Rafa,' Miles said, making a beeline for the western gate. 'We are going to be needed in a second.'

Raquel continued. 'We have a choice. Either we stay here and defend Battleacre, or we mobilise and we hunt the vampire king and his army.'

'Hunt, hunt, hunt,' the crowd chanted.

The mayor rose from his chair and cleared his throat. 'Is this wise? Are we not sending our men to their deaths? Will it not be easier to defend Battleacre?'

'Defend, defend, defend,' the crowd chanted.

Raquel gave the mayor a look of disgust. With a finger pointed at him, she turned and addressed the crowd. 'For too long, those monsters, those vampires, have dressed our leaders in finery. Our leaders live in comfort as the vampires steal our women from us. They live in comfort as they send our sons away from us. I say we chase this vampire king and rid our land of him and his kind once and for all.'

'Hunt, hunt, hunt,' the crowd chanted.

'They will slaughter us,' the mayor shouted. 'We are no match for them. This is madness.'

Chloe walked onto the announcement platform and stood next to Raquel. The crowd fell quiet.

'My name is Chloe. I am the council leader of Fairacre, the farming and trading town in the south.'

The crowd murmured and pointed.

'We had our women stolen from us by the City of Lynn. To this day, we do not know why.'

An increase in volume came from the crowd.

'They stole our women, but we fought back. This terror will not stop unless we eliminate the threat. If we stay here and hide, your women will continue to be stolen.'

The crowd snarled. A man close to the special area shouted. 'They have my wife, my daughter and my son. I wish for them to be returned home.'

'And mine. And mine,' came the chorus of agreement from the rest of the crowd.

Chloe placed a hand on Raquel's shoulder. 'Lead them, sister. They will follow if you lay out your plan.'

Raquel squared her shoulders and took a step forward. 'I have organised an army. An unorthodox army, but an army.'

Miles and Rafa walked into the special area and stood next to Raquel.

'It is an army of unlikely allies and unlikely beasts,' Raquel said, turning her head and smiling at Miles and Rafa. 'We are asking the soldiers of Battleacre to join us. Join our small army and help us hunt this vampire king and the monsters that follow him.'

'Hunt, hunt, hunt,' the crowd chanted.

The large soldier in the arena stepped forward. He waited for the crowd to fall silent. 'Who are these unlikely allies, my lady? If I must go into battle, I wish to know who my friends are and who my foes are.'

Miles approached him. 'What is your name, soldier?'

'My name is Claude, sir,' the soldier said, bowing slightly.

Miles knelt and waited for Waya to trot next to him. He curled his arm under Waya's head and rubbed her opposite cheek. Waya growled with pleasure. 'This is Waya. She is the alpha of the wolves that grace the western land. She will fight alongside us.'

Claude frowned in confusion. 'How is this possible? How do you command this wolf?'

Miles shook his head. 'I do not command her. I have asked her. She and her wolf pack will join on her own accord.'

'Will she not harm our men?' Claude said.

'She will not,' Miles said. 'The wolves' hatred for the vampires is as strong as our own. We do not have to worry about her or anyone in her pack attacking our soldiers.'

Waya trotted forward, raised her head, and let loose a long calling howl. The crowd fell silent. A moment later, a howl from the west answered. Then another from the east, and another from the south. Within half a minute, the wolves' language consumed the whole of Battleacre.

A murmur spread across the crowd.

Claude waited for Waya and her kin to stop howling. 'Is this enough?' he said. 'There will be a mountain of vampires to contend with. I don't think we can win with soldiers and wolves.'

'We did not say this would be easy,' Raquel said, clasping her hands behind her back and lifting her chin. 'To protect our freedom will take sacrifice. To save the ones we love will take bravery and strength. And above all else, it will take our superior soldiers to fight shoulder to shoulder. But we cannot sit here and do nothing. We will be lambs to the slaughter.'

'What of the undead?' Claude said. 'They seem to have the same hatred for these vampires.'

'The undead will remain here to protect Battleacre,' Raquel said. 'We cannot bring the persons who control them with us.'

'Excuse me, miss,' Almond said, stepping forward to stand next to Claude. 'But why does it just have to be the Battleacre soldiers? What of Battleacre's citizens? Do we not get the chance to defend our beloved city?'

'He is right,' a man in the crowd shouted. 'Why is it only soldiers? We were all soldiers once upon a time. Why can it not also be us, the citizens of this city?'

A rumble of agreement rippled through the crowd.

'Hear me,' Miles said, holding both hands up in the air. 'This is not a battle we will come out of without loss. Look around you. If you join this battle, your friends you are standing next to may not be here at the next games. This is a decision not to be taken lightly.'

The crowd fell silent.

'We understand the risk,' Almond said. 'We know the life of a soldier, sir.'

'Then we will not stop you,' Raquel said. 'If you wish to join us, then come prepared. We will leave tomorrow.'

'I will rally the soldiers,' Claude said. 'Battleacre's soldiers will be ready for the march at first light.'

'Claude, you will report to me throughout this endeavour,' Miles said. 'I will report to Raquel. Does that serve you well?'

'Most certainly, weapons master,' Claude said, with a bow.

'And I will take charge of the citizens,' Almond said. 'We will be ready at the northern gate at first sun. We will fight for our city.'

The crowd slammed their fists against their chests and sent out a long cheer.

'Tonight, we celebrate,' Raquel said. 'Tonight, the entertainment district will serve food and drink for every citizen of Battleacre. But, be responsible, for tomorrow's march will not be easy.'

The crowd, sensing the end, filtered out of the amphitheatre.

Raquel walked back from the announcement area. 'I fear I am walking my citizens to their deaths.'

Chloe embraced Raquel. 'They do so of their own free will. They know what's at stake and they are willing to defend their city.'

A tear escaped Raquel's eye and rolled down her cheek. 'I cannot believe my father is at the heart of this.'

'It is not your fault,' Miles said, squeezing her hand. 'He was like a second father to me. But he is no longer the man we once loved.'

Raquel filled her cheeks and let out a long breath. 'Be ready. We gather at the northern gate at first light.'

'Let us get these two little ones back to the estate,' Chloe said. 'I think I will slightly upset them when I tell them what is happening.'

Miles bent over and picked up Luxea. 'Time to go home and have some food, little one.'

'Can we stop at the swings?' Luxea said.

'For one go,' Miles said, walking down the spiral staircase.

Luxea punched the air. 'Swings, swings, yes.'

At the western exit, the arena crowd cheered and clapped as Miles walked out onto the square.

'Seems like you have commanded respect here in Battleacre,' Chloe said, smiling.

'I will take it,' Miles said. 'Not quite the Queen's Guard, but then, my priorities have changed, haven't they?'

'Yes, they have. Love does that, you know?' Chloe said with a coy smile. 'If only you had listened to me in Fairacre.'

Miles rolled his eyes. 'Yes, I should have listened to you, oh great mighty wise leader.'

'Watch it, warrior boy,' Chloe said, smirking.

'Swings,' Luxea and Lazriel both shouted.

Miles and Chloe let the two children run off to the swings. Half an hour later, after lots of laughs and giggles, they made their way back to the estate. In the study, they all tucked into snacks Raquel served.

'Listen, you two,' Chloe said, looking at Luxea and Lazriel. 'In a day's time, we are all going to be leaving for a short while. But, we need you two to stay here.'

Both Luxea's and Lazriel's bottom lips pouted. 'Where are you going and why can't we come?'

'We are going to the north to deal with the horrible man,' Miles said. 'The horrible man and woman who have been hurting everyone here.'

'The ones that hurt my dada?' Luxea said, her eyes welling up.

'Yes,' Miles said, leaning in and wiping a tear away. 'We need to stop them before they hurt more people.'

'There is a job for you two, though,' Chloe said. 'We need you to protect Battleacre.'

Luxea's face brightened. 'For when you get back?'

'Yes,' Chloe said, clapping her hands. 'We will be back in a few days and we don't want any nasties in Battleacre.'

'And you know what?' Billy said, sitting cross-legged next to the two of them. 'I am staying here with you and we can play in the playground every day.'

'Every day?' Luxea said, her eyes growing wide.

'Every day?' Lazriel shouted.

'Yes, every day,' Billy said.

'Are you sure, brother?' Miles said.

Billy's forehead crinkled over. 'I don't think I can take another battle like the last. I would much prefer to stay here and look after these two lovely terrors.'

'We may need you to heal people,' Chloe said with a raised eyebrow.

'I will give you salves and wound dressings,' Billy said. 'You know how to administer them. Tilly and I have shown you many times.'

Chloe smiled and touched Billy's cheek. 'You look after these two now, you hear? I have grown quite fond of these little terrors too.'

Billy gave Chloe a lopsided grin. 'With the undead protecting us, we won't have a problem.'

'It's settled then,' Raquel said, sitting cross-legged in front of Rafa. 'So for the rest of the evening, can we speak about something else? I don't want to talk about my father or my mother anymore.'

Miles chuckled. 'I vote yes on that.'

. . .

Miles and Janie stood on Battleacre's northern wall. The sun was yet to rise, but an orange glow peeked out of the eastern horizon. In front of the northern gate, hundreds of soldiers and Battleacre artisans gathered ready for the northern trek. Claude barked orders at the Battleacre soldiers. Almond marched between the artisans, giving encouragement and instructions.

'Luxea and Lazriel were not happy before we left,' Janie said.

'There is no way we are taking children into battle,' Miles said. 'As much as I am going to miss the two of them.'

'I know,' Janie said. 'Although the undead would really help.'

Miles rubbed his chin. 'If we get pushed back to Battleacre, I am sure we are going to need them.'

'Are you two coming?' Raquel called from just inside the gate.

Miles and Janie double-stepped down the wall and walked over to Twitch and Titch.

'Good to see you moving so freely,' Chloe said, glancing at Miles's legs.

Miles jumped onto his horse and flashed Chloe a grin. Using the reins, he guided Twitch to follow Raquel out of the northern gate.

Raquel spurred her horse forward. Miles and Janie followed on Twitch and Titch. And behind them Chloe and Rafa followed with their Naginatas protruding over their shoulders.

A howl sounded from the plains in front of them. Hundreds of howls answered. Miles felt the marks on his back roam over to the places he needed them most.

Miles turned and looked past Chloe and Rafa. Behind them, a long train of soldiers marched side by side along the cobblestone road. Behind the soldiers marched blacksmiths, entertainers, traders and people of every other profession.

'We will be pretty safe during the day,' Janie said, pulling the cloak around herself as the sun appeared. 'Night-time we will be in trouble.'

'We are going to have to rely on the wolves to protect us at night,' Miles said.

Janie adjusted the two swords on her back then touched her ear to check the device that kept her safe from the wandering essence of the Soldier and Genevie.

'Protected by such a small thing,' Miles said, reaching over and squeezing her gloved hand.

'I want them gone,' Janie said. 'I want the royals gone so I can give these devices back to Valen.'

'Even if we don't rid the land of all the royal vampires, you might not need the devices if Dr Viktor finds a cure,' Miles said.

Janie gave Miles a thin-lipped smile. 'I cannot think of anything better than going home to Fairacre. I am tiring of this desolate black sludge-covered land.'

'Something that may befall the lands of the south if the City of Lynn continues with their machines,' Miles said.

Janie curled a lip as they passed another pool of toxic black sludge.

A few hours later, as the sun passed mid-morning, the first of the rolling hills appeared. Down the slopes, they travelled until they reached the valley floors. Once over the flat, grass-covered floors, they started their ascent to the top of the next hill. The train slowed considerably as the men panted with the steep climb. Up and down, they marched through the hypnotic landscape. Wolves to their left and right bounded up and down the rolling hills with ease. They ate lunch in their saddles. The soldiers ate as they marched.

Hours later, dusk arrived.

Raquel held up her hand at a camp at the bottom of a valley.

'We stop here for the night. If we continue, they will catch us out in the open.'

Rafa led the horses into the camp's middle circle. The rest of the group sat around a crackling, spitting fire. Raquel served up a feast of cold meats and bread.

On the outside of the centre group, the artisans of Battleacre formed their own circled defensive lines. The soldiers followed with their own defensive circles on the artisans' outside.

'I am going to take first watch,' Miles said.

'Wake me in two hours, my friend,' Rafa said.

Just as Miles laid his head on the grass, a howl from the hillside sounded through the camp.

Miles sprang to his feet and pulled his greatsword. 'That's a fighting howl. Everyone up.'

The rest of the group stood and pulled their weapons. A second later, shouts came from the encampment's edge.

'I will be back,' Janie said. With a pop, she disappeared.

'How does she move that fast but the other vampires don't?' Chloe said.

'Royal blood,' Miles said. 'Genevie turned her, which means she has a stronger bloodline.'

Another pop and Janie appeared. 'It is a vampire scouting party. They are testing our defences.'

'Have we lost anyone?' Raquel said.

Janie shook her head. 'The wolves and soldiers took care of them. It seems like Waya hates them as much as we do.'

'We double the guards,' Raquel said to Claude and Almond. 'Make sure the citizens know about these scouting parties.'

'Yes, my lady,' Claude and Almond both said, before walking away and barking orders.

'I wish they wouldn't call me my lady,' Raquel said, sighing.

'You will get used to it, my lady,' Miles said, with a twinkle in his eye.

Raquel huffed and rolled her eyes, but she couldn't help the corners of her mouth turning up.

'I think this is going to be a long night,' Chloe said, sitting down on a log. 'Not much we can do from here but wait it out.'

'Try to get some sleep,' Miles said.

Throughout the night, the entire group fell in and out of sleep as wave after wave of scouting parties tested each area of the Battleacre army's defences. Eventually, the sun broke the horizon and the scouting parties stopped. Miles stood and stretched. Chloe and Rafa stifled yawns. Raquel, with sleepless bags under her eyes, covered her brow to look north.

'They are doing this on purpose,' Janie said. 'They are going to tire us out.'

'We have little choice but to continue,' Raquel said. 'Let us get moving.'

Another day passed as the army made slow progress over the rolling hills. At nightfall, they camped at the bottom of another valley. Throughout the night, the warring noises of the vampires, wolves and soldiers rattled through the air. Most of the army sat blurry eyed with their weapons ready as they fell in and out of sleep.

The sun broke over the horizon, signalling for everyone to get ready for the march. Soldiers' feet dragged as they made their way up the hills. On the way down the hills, people stumbled more frequently. Two more nights came and went.

'My Lady, we are going to need to rest during the day,' Claude said. 'The vampires will pick us off easily at night if we don't sleep.'

'I agree,' Raquel said, turning and looking back with concern.

'Let us continue to the next valley and we can make camp for the rest of the day.'

The orders filtered through the army, giving them renewed vigour. They marched up the long hill with a bit more urgency. At the top of the hill, Raquel pulled to one side and raised her hand to her brow.

'Those spires are from the City of Lynn,' Miles said, approaching Raquel and placing his hand over his brow. 'The city and the spires look so tiny from here.'

Rafa and Chloe came to a stop next to them. 'The valley below is larger than the ones we have crossed,' Chloe said. 'It will be ideal to rest in.'

Raquel spurred her horse forward. Miles waited for Janie to pull up next to him and then continued after Raquel. Down the winding hill the army went. An hour later, as the sun hit midday, they reached the lush grass of the valley floor. Spots of black tar pooled here and there. The army created their circular defensive positions. Within half an hour, most of the men lay in the grass with something on their faces to block the daylight. An eerie silence descended on the valley as soldiers fell into an exhausted sleep. As the hours passed, the sun travelled towards the western horizon.

'Miles,' Janie whispered.

Miles sat up with raised eyebrows.

Janie pointed her chin north.

Miles placed his hand over his brow and looked ahead. His breath caught in his throat. On the hilltop stood a lone horse. Atop the horse sat the Soldier who stared down at the Battleacre army.

Miles slowly got to his feet. One by one, the rest followed.

'Father,' Raquel whispered, as she got up.

Rafa walked over and laid a hand on Raquel's shoulder. 'We are here with you, my love.'

Suddenly, another horse appeared on the hilltop.

'Genevie,' Miles said. 'I wasn't expecting to see her.'

'I assume that is the royal daughter?' Chloe said.

'My sister, in a disgusting kind of way,' Raquel said. 'Defences, everyone.'

Claude barked orders that rippled through the army. The soldiers drew their weapons and solidified their defensive ring around the entire encampment. Behind the ring, the citizens stood in their own circles with their chosen weapons drawn and ready. In the middle stood Raquel with her hands behind her back. The bottom of the sun touched the western horizon. An orange glow blazed across the valley floor.

'And so it starts,' Miles whispered, adjusting the grip on his greatsword.

'And today, it ends,' Raquel said. 'We will rid our land of these monsters.'

As the last of the sun disappeared over the horizon, a horde of vampires poured past the Soldier and down into the valley. Trumpets sounded through the Battleacre army. A few seconds later, shouts, screams and pops filled the air.

'I will not stand in the middle and wait for them to get to us,' Miles said.

'Yes, you are staying here, Miles,' Chloe said, walking up to him. 'I know you want to get into the thick of it, but remember, it's the Soldier we are after. We need you here. Claude is leading the Battleacre army.'

Miles cast his eyes to the top of the hill. The Soldier sat with his elbows resting on the pommel of his saddle. Genevie sat, picking at her long fingernails.

The sun disappeared. A full moon cast an eerie light on the battlefield. The shouts and screams of combat continued to fill the night air. A haze of dead vampire dust wafted into the centre of the army. Every few minutes, the citizens stretchered a wounded soldier through the defences and set them on the ground just in front of the centre circle. Chloe and Rafa walked among them, applying healing salve.

An hour passed of intense fighting. The horde of vampires continued to stream over the hill. Slowly, the outer circle of soldiers depleted.

'It is nearly our time, boys,' Almond shouted. 'For freedom of Battleacre.'

The citizens lifted their weapons and cheered.

'Here he comes,' Miles said.

Everyone in the inner circle stopped what they were doing and stared up the hill. The Soldier moved lazily down the hill with his elbows still resting on the saddle.

'Time to bring in the cavalry,' Miles said. 'Go get them, girl.'

A long howl sounded from the hill behind the Battleacre army. Waya and her packs of wolves streamed down the hill towards the soldiers. The citizens separated as the wolves thundered through their defensive lines. Waya halted as she entered the inner circle.

Miles knelt and placed his forehead against Waya's. 'It is time we end this.'

Waya snorted. She shook her head then looked north at the advancing vampire king.

CHAPTER 25
A LUNA WOLF

As Miles stood, he drew his greatsword in one movement. Up ahead, the Soldier, now off his horse, swatted Battleacre soldiers off him, sending them flying into the air. The wolves steered clear and attacked the vampires surrounding him. Slowly, the Battleacre army shifted the battle in their favour and pushed the vampires back. Only the Soldier continued forward.

'I am coming for you, boy,' the Soldier said, slashing his greatsword at another soldier.

Waya stalked towards the vampire king. Her thick coat bristled and rippled as the muscles in her shoulders tensed with every step. Miles walked next to her with his greatsword pointed at the Soldier. The muscles in his body rippled in unison with Waya's.

'Give me that wolf,' the Soldier said, his fangs extending down his chin. 'Do you see how your kin suffers? All you need to do is give the wolf to me.'

'You will never have her,' Miles said, his eyes narrowing and his pace increasing.

'Then your friends will pay for your decision,' the Soldier said, a smile spreading across his face. 'I will make them all pay. Even your little vampire girlfriend.'

Miles closed his eyes and concentrated on the marks. The power of Mother Earth thumped a deep rhythmic beat that pulsed through the bottom of his feet and up to the swirling marks on his back. He opened his eyes and ran at the Soldier. With a crack, the Soldier sent another soldier flying. The pupils in Miles's eyes suddenly expanded. The world around him slowed to a crawl. Vampires and wolves moved at a snail's pace. For the first time, Miles could see the royal vampire moving at speed. The Soldier's sword clashed with Miles's in a shower of sparks. Blow by blow, the swords blurred as each of them attacked, then defended.

'This is not possible,' the Soldier said. 'You are not a royal. Your speed is not human.'

Miles jabbed the pommel of his greatsword at the Soldier's chin. With a crunch, the pommel found its mark. The Soldier staggered backwards. He brought up his hand and wiped his sleeve across his mouth. With a roar, the Soldier re-engaged. His sword, teeth and claws raked and slashed.

Miles expertly used his sword, fists and elbows to parry the attack. After each attack, he launched his own. 'You may have royal speed, but I have Mother Earth on my side.'

'I am going to kill you,' the Soldier said. 'It was not a wise choice bringing your wolf here. If I kill you, she will choose another vessel. Perhaps her next vessel will be one of my kin.'

'She will never choose an abomination,' Miles said through his teeth. 'She is smarter than that.'

'Your wolf is more like me than you care to accept, boy,' the Soldier said, just before taking another blow to the chin. 'She is a predator. A killer.'

'She is nothing like you,' Miles said. 'She does not kill for fun.'

The Soldier snarled, spun and raked his claws down Miles's back. Waya dived in, her jaws snapping at the Soldier's heels. She yelped as the Soldier's fist connected with her snout. The claw marks down Miles's back knitted together. He placed both hands on the handle of his greatsword and attacked with a flurry of wide slashes and stabs. The end of his sword found its mark and cut through the Soldier's chest. The Soldier staggered back and fell to a knee. Waya pounced again and wrapped her jaws around the Soldier's arm.

'Your time is up,' Miles said, raising his sword above his head.

'Look,' the Soldier said, pointing with his free arm.

The air in Miles's lungs escaped with a gasp. Just a few steps away, a vampire held Janie by the throat.

'Tell your wolf to let me go,' the Soldier said.

'Waya, let go,' Miles said.

Unable to speak, Janie shook her head at Miles. Waya growled then let go of the Soldier's arm.

'Step back,' the Soldier said. 'And lower your sword.'

Miles looked back at Janie. She shook her head again.

'I am warning you,' the Soldier said. 'You step back or she will turn to dust.'

'Let her go,' Miles said.

The Soldier got to his feet. He smiled at Miles, then turned to the vampire. 'End her.'

'No,' Miles shouted.

Waya sprang forward at the vampire holding Janie. Fear spread across the vampire's face. Janie fell to the floor with a thump. The vampire screamed just as Waya tackled him to the ground.

Before Miles could move, the Soldier flashed forward and picked Janie up.

'You should have taken the shot,' the Soldier said, while

shaking Janie by the throat. 'Your love for this traitor has now killed you both.'

'No,' Miles said, fear spreading across his face. 'Please don't hurt her.'

Waya stopped her attack on the vampire and backed towards Miles.

The Soldier raised his head and roared. In his clawed hands, Janie struggled as the Soldier held her high in the air. The vampires, hearing the king's signal, stopped their attack and ran to the edge of the valley. The soldiers lowered their weapons and moved back into their defensive circles. Waya howled, calling the wolves to retreat behind the soldiers.

'Let her go,' Miles said, the muscles in his jaw clenching.

Again, the Soldier shook Janie until her eyes bulged in her head.

'Do not hurt her,' Miles shouted, lowering his greatsword. 'Please. Leave her alone.'

The Soldier snarled at Janie. 'Do you think I care about this worthless annoyance? My kin, who has turned on me?'

Miles pointed at the Soldier. 'If you hurt her, I will hunt your entire family down. Genevie, the mother, everyone. I will hunt them until the day I die.'

'You know what I want,' the Soldier said. 'Give me your wolf and I will give you your girlfriend.'

'Miles,' Chloe said, walking towards him. 'You cannot do this.'

Miles held out a hand. 'Stay where you are, Chloe.'

'The wolf for the girl,' the Soldier said. 'If you do not give me the wolf, I will finish your girlfriend and friends right here, right now. I have had enough of these games.'

'Miles,' Chloe said.

Miles ignored her.

'Don't do it, Miles,' Janie choked. 'You cannot trust him. Fight him.'

Miles raised his greatsword. 'Let her go, you coward.'

'I know what you want, son,' the Soldier said. 'You want to be a member of the Queen's Guard. A knife slinger. The best fighters these lands have ever seen. It's all you have ever wanted. You abandoned this girl to become one. Hand me the wolf and come with me. I will make it happen for you.'

'He is lying,' Janie said. 'Don't do what he asks.'

'The wolf for the girl,' the Soldier said. 'I will let your little girlfriend live if you give me the wolf and come with me to the City of Lynn.'

'You cannot trust him,' Janie said, a blood tear running down her cheek. 'He is lying and he will kill everyone when he has the wolf. You need to fight, Miles.'

'Enough of this,' the Soldier said, his grip tightening on Janie's throat. 'My kin are being held hostage by the old man in the City of Lynn. Choose, boy! Give me the wolf and you can have your girl.'

Waya lowered her head and, with a rumble in her chest, she walked towards the Soldier.

'What is Waya doing, Miles?' Chloe said. 'If they get the wolf, we will lose everything. You know this is what Dr Viktor told us.'

'I choose Janie,' Miles said, his chin held high in defiance. 'Give her back to me.'

'Finally the little crippled boy chooses the girl,' the Soldier said.

Waya dropped to her belly and crawled in submission towards the Soldier. A few paces from him, Waya looked up at the vampire king and whined.

Miles walked towards him. 'Let Janie go.'

The Soldier threw his head back and laughed.

'Miles, no,' Janie said, struggling against the Soldier's grip. 'You cannot let him take Waya.'

Suddenly, everything slowed as Waya sprang from her belly and wrapped her massive jaws around Janie's leg.

Janie's eyes widened as she screamed in agony.

'No,' Miles yelled. 'Waya, what are you doing?'

The Soldier let go of Janie. 'Stupid wolf,' he said, a sneer spreading across his face. 'It looks like she has killed your girlfriend for me. I will take your wolf, your girlfriend will die and, again, I leave you with nothing, boy.'

With Waya dragging Janie away from the Soldier, Miles sprang forward and stabbed his sword at the vampire king. With a side step, the Soldier parried Miles's sword and sent his own deep into Miles's stomach.

'Miles, no,' Chloe shouted.

The Soldier pulled his sword from Miles's stomach and kicked him in the chest. After a few backwards steps, Miles fell, clutching the large hole in his body.

Waya continued to drag Janie until Janie lay next to Miles. She opened her jaws and let go of Janie's leg. Janie's breathing came in quick gasps as black poison from the bite spread from her leg up into her torso.

'Janie,' Miles said, reaching a hand over to her. 'Waya, what have you done?'

Janie pushed Miles's hand away and turned onto her hands and knees. Her breathing came in short, hard gasps. She opened her mouth and gagged. With a look at Miles, she said, 'What is happening? I cannot breathe.'

Miles's eyes slammed shut. He gripped the side of his body and let out an ear-piercing scream. His right foot turned inwards, ripping his shoe from his foot. He opened his eyes and stared at Janie. The nerves in his back separated, sending spasms of pain down his right thigh. His eyes rolled in his head as black spots danced around his vision.

'Miles,' Janie said as, with a crack, her two vampire incisors fell from her mouth onto the blood-soaked ground.

'Janie, Miles,' Chloe said, running up and kneeling next to them.

Miles looked down at the gaping wound in his belly. 'It's not healing, Chloe. Why is the wound not healing?'

Chloe placed both of her hands over the hole in Miles's stomach. She cast an eye on Janie's leg to check the wolf's poison. Her brow furrowed. 'The marks,' Chloe said. 'The earth marks are all over Janie's leg.'

Janie opened her mouth, gagged again, then vomited a pile of black poison. 'Help me,' she said, reaching out a hand for Chloe. Before Chloe could take her hand, she placed it back on the ground and vomited again.

Miles reached across and touched Janie's cheek. 'Waya has chosen you.'

'What do you mean?' Janie said, through another gasp. 'I don't understand.'

'I love you, Janie,' Miles said. 'I chose you.'

Janie grabbed Miles's hand. 'I love you, too. Please, Miles, what is happening?'

'Look after Janie, please, Chloe,' Miles said again, his voice soft and distant. 'And make sure you look after little Luxea. Promise me.'

'I promise,' Chloe said, tears streaming down her face. 'But hang in there. I have salve from Billy.'

Miles grabbed Chloe's hand. 'It's too late. Tell Billy I love him too. I love all of you.'

'Help him, Chloe,' Janie said.

The last of Miles's breath escaped from his lips.

. . .

'Miles!' Chloe screamed, placing an ear to his chest. 'No, no, no. Please don't leave us.'

Janie's chest heaved as a distant roar started forming in her ears. Spots of brown and green flashed before her eyes. The ground rumbled and shook. Janie shoved herself to her knees and held out her trembling hands. Her back arched as she flung her head rearward and screamed up into the sky.

'No,' the Soldier said, sneering at Janie. 'She chooses a weak thing like you.'

The ground shook harder. The brown and green marks slipped into two and travelled over her entire body. Her auburn hair turned brown with streaks of green.

The ground underneath Waya's paws rumbled. She snarled at the Soldier as the ends of her coat turned into sharp thorns. Green roots sprouted out of her shoulders and wrapped around her body, forming a thick plant armour. She lifted her head to the sky and howled. The ends of her teeth turned to diamonds and sparkled as the moonlight kissed them. At the end of her paws, thin, hard-stoned claws extended and bit into the ground. Her thick fur tail hardened as the roots wrapped around it. Small razor-sharp spikes sprang out at the tip of her tail.

Janie roared at the Soldier. The marks on her arms swirled as they answered her internal rage. Stones scattered around, lifted off the ground and shot through the air, punching holes through the Soldier's chest. The Soldier stumbled backwards with a snarl. The holes in his chest quickly closed. With a bellow of his own, he ran at Janie, his greatsword high above his head.

The light and dark swords whipped off Janie's back and slashed through the air. The Soldier dodged out of the way and brought the pommel of his sword onto Janie's skull. She crashed to the ground, with blood pouring out of the side of her head.

Waya howled.

Instantly, the wound on the side of her head healed. Janie sprang to her feet and attacked with both swords.

Waya sprang at the Soldier and sank her diamond teeth deep into his leg. The Soldier sucked in air as the teeth crunched through bone. With a swat of his hand, he sent Waya somersaulting to the ground.

The Soldier raised his head and shouted orders for the vampires to attack. The hill shimmered as waves of vampires ran down the hill and jumped into battle.

Janie re-engaged with her two swords, stabbing and slicing the Soldier. Waya jumped to her feet, shook her head, and attacked. She slashed with her stone claws and bit with her razor-sharp diamond teeth. Janie picked up stones and ripped them through the Soldier. Yet, each wound created by Janie and Waya continued to heal just as quickly.

The vampires, gaining the advantage, beat the soldiers back until they streamed into Battleacre's citizens. With screams of terror and pain, the citizens fell to their deaths or turned into vampires.

'You will be the only one left standing,' the Soldier said, with a snarl. 'I will kill or turn everyone here.'

Janie slashed her swords at his face. The Soldier parried with his greatsword and slashed with his claws.

'You can stop this. Hand me your wolf. You have lost the man you love. Why lose your friends too?' the Soldier said.

'Never,' Janie said. 'I will send you to the hell that you came from.'

'Then I will make you watch your friends fall,' the Soldier said, flashing past two citizens and killing them instantly.

Janie stabbed at the Soldier with her swords. She flung pebbles and stones from the ground into the Soldier's body. Waya chomped, snapped and ripped.

'Enough,' the Soldier roared, punching Janie hard in the face.

Janie flew to the ground with a crunch. The Soldier flashed to Waya and dragged a claw down her side. Waya and Janie screamed in pain. The wounds on their sides healed quickly. With another snarl, the Soldier tore into Waya again, leaving deep gashes. Waya and Janie, lying on their sides, screamed again.

The Soldier pulled out ropes and tied them around Waya's paws. He walked over to Janie and pulled her up by her hair. 'Do you see what you have done? I told you none of this needed to happen. Now I will order the death of all of your friends.'

Janie's eyes widened as she looked into the centre of the Battleacre army. Chloe, Rafa and Raquel knelt with their hands on their heads. In front of them, with a sword trained on their throats, stood Genevie.

'It is over, wolf child,' the Soldier said. 'My daughter will kill your friends. You and your wolf are coming with me to the City of Lynn. The old man wants you.'

Janie struggled against the Soldier's clawed hand. 'Leave me alone, you animal.'

'Go ahead, daughter,' the Soldier said, raising his sword.

Genevie lifted her sword.

From atop the southern hill, an almighty roar sounded down into the valley.

Silence fell over the battlefield.

A ball of fire flew from the hilltop and slammed into the vampires, setting them ablaze.

'Oh, you are in so much trouble now,' Chloe shouted. 'So much trouble!'

Down the hill streaked Juno and Chax. Juno, with her Jo in her hand, stood on Chax's back. She waved her hands and sent another fireball flying past Genevie's head. Genevie jumped back, lowered her sword and hissed.

Chloe sprang to her feet and slashed at Genevie. In a flash, Genevie disappeared and reappeared next to the vampire king's side.

'What is this?' the Soldier said, glaring at the ball of fire that now entered the valley.

Juno jumped off Chax's back and skidded to a halt next to Chloe. She flicked a fireball at the Soldier who let Janie go to dodge out of the way. Janie walked over to Waya and severed the ropes that bound her paws.

'Who are you?' the Soldier said, pointing his greatsword at Juno.

Chax roared at the Soldier sending a fiery blast of air into his face.

'She is fire,' Janie said, lifting her chin and snarling at the Soldier. 'I know how much you love fire, don't you, vampire king?'

The Soldier's eyes darted from Juno to Chax. He placed an arm in front of Genevie and took a step backwards.

'Fire, Father,' Genevie said, with fear etched in her face.

The Soldier and Genevie continued to walk backwards.

'Where is Miles?' Juno said.

'That snivelling cripple is dead,' the Soldier said. 'The wolf killed him.'

Juno's red-specked eyes looked at Janie. 'What is he talking about?'

'This monster stabbed him. Waya transferred her bond to me before Miles could heal. He died from the vampire king's stab wound.'

Fire flared over Juno's hands. 'You did this,' she said, pointing a finger at the Soldier.

'All he had to do was give us the wolf so we could save our kin,' Genevie said.

With flames lapping around her coat, Chax stalked towards the Soldier.

'Keep that animal away from me,' the Soldier said, placing his greatsword across himself and Genevie.

A snarling Chax pounced on the vampire king. The Soldier flashed away and appeared in front of Juno. He slashed his greatsword at her throat. Juno ducked then blasted a fireball into the Soldier's chest, which sent him to the ground. Waya bit into the Soldier's arm. The greatsword sprang out of his grasp. Juno lit up her hands and flung the fire forward, engulfing the Soldier in flames. The Soldier flashed away, then reappeared with the flames extinguished.

'Together,' Juno said, giving Janie a nod.

Janie picked up rocks from the ground and flung them at the Soldier. Just before the rocks hit the vampire king, Juno sent blasts of fire into them. The rocks turned into molten lava and slammed into the Soldier's chest.

The Soldier grabbed his chest and dropped to his knees. He screamed as the lava burnt from the inside. Together, Chax and Waya sprang onto the Soldier. Waya sent vines into the Soldier's body, pinning him to the ground. Chax sent waves of flames over his body, covering him from head to toe. After a moment of struggle, the Soldier exploded into a crackling, spitting cloud of hot dust.

Genevie fell to her knees and howled with anguish.

Janie walked over to Genevie and aimed her swords at her throat.

'Wait, Janie,' Raquel said, waving a hand. 'Don't hurt her.'

Janie lowered her swords. 'What are you doing?' she said. 'We need to rid these lands of these monsters.'

Genevie sat on her heels and placed her head in her hands. 'No, no, no,' she said under her breath.

Janie watched the vampires move away from the battlefield. The wolves backed into the defensive circles of the citizens.

'They are going to kill my mother,' Genevie mumbled, red tears streaming over her hands.

'What do you mean?' Janie said, placing her sword under Genevie's head and lifting her chin.

Genevie swatted the sword away and wiped her eyes. 'The old man in the city. He will exterminate us now. We have failed in our task.'

'Do you think I care?' Janie shouted. 'You have killed too many people to count. You helped kill my Miles. Your kind are murderers.'

Silence descended on the battlefield as the wrath of the earth elemental shuddered the valley.

Janie walked back to where Miles lay. She dropped to her knees and placed her head on his chest. She wrapped her arms around him and closed her eyes.

'We did not have a choice,' Genevie said. 'They ordered us to bring the wolf, the little girl and as many women as possible. If we had not done this, they would have killed my mother. My mother is the only one of us who can keep our species alive.'

'You turn humans into vampires all the time,' Raquel said, walking up to Genevie. 'How is your kin in danger of extinction?'

'The sun kills the vampires we turn,' Genevie said, looking up at the moon. 'Our royal blood line is immortal. If she dies, our species will slowly die out.'

Juno walked over to Janie and placed a hand on her shoulder. 'Get up, sister.'

Janie stood and curled a lip at Genevie. The surrounding earth rumbled.

'Be calm,' Juno said, squeezing Janie's shoulder. 'You have untold power that you do not know how to control.'

Janie closed her eyes and controlled her breathing. She slowed her loud, thumping heart.

'Why does this old man need our women?' Juno said, walking over to Genevie.

'Lower your weapons,' Genevie said, pointing at Janie. 'I will tell you what I know if I and my kin have a safe passage from here.'

'Never,' Janie growled. 'You are not leaving here alive. You are a murderer.'

'We will let you go if you tell us what is going on,' Chloe said, walking up next to Raquel.

'We will not,' Janie shouted. 'She will not leave this place alive.'

Juno squeezed Janie's shoulder. 'Our leader has spoken, Janie. We do not get to break orders because of our gifts.'

Janie snarled at Genevie. 'Today, you are the luckiest being alive. I swear if I hear anything more about you in the future, I will hunt you down.'

Genevie inclined her head. 'I understand.'

'We agree with your conditions,' Chloe said. 'Now talk.'

Genevie lifted her hand and signalled to the horde of vampires waiting on the northern hill. The horde slinked back up over the hill until there were none left. 'It is just me now,' Genevie said, holding up her hands.

Raquel pointed to a set of logs in the centre of the defensive circle. Chloe, Raquel and Genevie sat. Rafa, Janie and Juno stood behind.

'Why are the women being stolen?' Chloe said.

'The City requires the essence of women to keep the enemy

from storming the City,' Genevie said.

'Why do they need their essence?' Chloe said.

Genevie spread her hands. 'How it is being used, I do not know. All I know is women are holding the enemy from getting close to the City walls.'

'She is telling us nothing,' Janie said with a snarl. 'She does not get to live if she holds back information.'

'I have not seen what is happening in the north,' Genevie said.

'We prevented women from being stolen in the south,' Juno said. 'Where else are they getting women from?'

'Everywhere,' Genevie said. 'Slaves from the west and women from the underground kingdom.'

A low growl escaped Chloe's mouth.

'Why do they want the young girl?' Rafa said.

'The old man's eyes lit up when he heard of her,' Genevie said. 'You need to protect her with everything you have. The old man is giving directives to the Queen's Guard to capture her alive.'

'You didn't have a problem hunting her,' Janie spat. 'If it wasn't for us, you would have taken her to him.'

'I would do anything to save my family,' Genevie said. 'Surely you understand this.'

Janie looked away.

'You haven't told us much,' Chloe said.

Genevie shook her head. 'It is all I know.'

'What of this old man who has been threatening you?' Chloe said. 'What can you tell us about him?'

A distant look flashed across Genevie's face. She shook her head, then looked at Chloe. 'A powerful being who is an advisor to the Queen. He knows of our land and will burn it to the ground if we do not comply with his demands.'

'And you choose to destroy our land rather than fight him,' Janie said.

Juno pulled Janie into a hug. 'Calm yourself, sister. I know you are hurting.'

'He is a warlock,' Genevie said. 'Nobody fights a warlock and survives. You do as you are told.'

'What does he look like?' Chloe said.

Suddenly, a shout came from the edge of the defensive circles. Raquel stood and looked south.

'Let him pass,' Claude said, moving soldiers out of the way. 'There is a messenger for you, my lady.'

The messenger ran into the area and placed both hands on his knees. He took a second to catch his breath.

'What is it, young man?' Raquel said.

The messenger straightened his back. 'They have captured the two youngsters and taken them south,' the messenger said. 'We tried to fight, but the undead overran us.'

'Are you talking about Luxea and Lazriel?' Chloe said, jumping to her feet. 'Billy is looking after them.'

'We think they have captured him too,' the messenger said. 'We could not find him anywhere.'

'Who captured them?' Chloe said.

'We do not know who,' the messenger said. 'There is talk of a man with jewels all over his hands and a man with long thin blades.'

Chloe's hands balled into fists. 'Walter. The slave trader. And knife slingers. The undead are attacking you because they are making Lazriel do it. I am going to feed this Walter to Chax and Waya.'

Chax and Waya both nodded in unison.

'And they travelled south?' Chloe said.

'Yes, my lady,' the messenger said. 'A day and a half ago.'

'The young girl is missing?' Genevie said.

'It is no business of yours,' Janie said.

Genevie held up a hand. 'You need to find her and protect her. If they take her to the City, I dread to think what this warlock would do to her.'

'We need to go,' Chloe said. 'We need to go now.'

Rafa stood and pulled Raquel into an embrace. 'I need to help Chloe.'

'What about her?' Janie said, pointing at Genevie. 'We cannot leave her here with Raquel.'

'She is free to go,' Raquel said.

Genevie took one last look at everyone then flashed away. She appeared at the top of the northern hill.

'Please retrieve our horses, Claude,' Chloe said.

'Janie and I are coming with you,' Juno said.

'I am not leaving Miles,' Janie said, peering over his covered body.

Raquel approached Janie and pulled her into a hug. 'Help your friends. We will take care of Miles. He will be in Battleacre for when you return.'

Janie pulled away from Raquel. 'You will look after him?'

'We will carry him as a deserved champion,' Raquel said. 'He will receive the highest honour back at Battleacre.'

A thin smile appeared on Janie's face. 'He would like that.'

Juno walked over to Chax and sprang onto her back. Waya trotted over to Janie and nuzzled her hand.

'Don't be afraid,' Juno said. 'Your elemental and you are one. She knows what you need. Get onto her back and let her do the work.'

The vines the covered Waya's body unwrapped then disappeared into her shoulders. Janie gripped the fur around Waya's neck and sprang up onto her back where she pressed firmly with her knees to hold on.

Claude appeared, holding Twitch and Titch. Their eyes rolled and their feet stamped at the sight of the wolf and the lioness.

'Thank you,' Chloe and Rafa said, taking the reins from Claude.

'Are those little horses going to keep up?' Juno said, with a raised eyebrow.

'They may be small, but they have heart,' Chloe said. 'They will take us halfway, then we let them go and Rafa and I will run. Do you remember how we used to run back in Fairacre, Juno?'

Juno stared into the distance with a blank look on her face. 'I think I remember, sister.'

Chloe frowned at the distant look on her friend's face.

Rafa kissed Raquel, then jumped onto Titch. 'Lead the way,' he said, looking at Chloe.

Chloe dug her heels into Twitch's side. The little horse sprang forward and darted through the Battleacre army. Behind her, Titch, Chax and Waya ran with their wards on their backs.

The crowd cheered and clapped as they passed.

As they stepped onto the southern hill, the animals slowed at the steep incline. The moon high above gave them enough light to see where they were going. At the top of the hill, the rolling hills waited for them. Over the next few hours, up and down they went. The horses blew hard, but their legs never faltered. Chax and Waya used their elements to keep up.

'You are doing well,' Juno said to Janie.

Janie held onto Waya's fur for dear life.

After another hour, Rafa slowed his horse. 'It is time,' he said. 'I can feel Titch tiring.'

Chloe stopped Twitch and sprang off his back. 'Time to go home, little one,' she said, slapping Twitch on the rump. The horse bobbed his head and took off south. Titch followed her friend.

'Do you think they will go to Battleacre or the horse farms?' Rafa said.

'I am hoping for Battleacre. Not sure what the horse farms are looking like if that slave trader went south,' Chloe said.

'Let's get moving you two,' Juno said.

Chloe snorted. 'Let's see if your pets can keep up.'

Rafa's smile stretched from ear to ear. 'It has been a while since I have run for any length of time.'

'Then let's put them to the test, brother,' Chloe said, stretching her long legs into a run.

Rafa stretched his own legs and kept up easily. Behind them, the two elemental animals grunted and snarled at each other as they kept pace with the running westerners.

A couple of hours later, a glow of orange spread from the eastern horizon. To the west, the tops of the amphitheatre broke over the horizon. Another hour and Chloe slowed as they approached the desolate black forest.

'Do we go around or through?' Rafa said.

'I don't think we have anything to fear if we go through,' Chloe said. 'The vampires have gone north and the undead are in the south.'

The four of them entered the forest and walked through the tightly packed trees. Chax and Waya sniffed the air, looking out for trouble. Chloe shared out dried meats and skins of water.

Juno walked next to Janie and placed an arm around her. 'Are you OK?'

'I cannot believe Miles is gone,' Janie said, tears streaming down her face. 'I want to kill everything that hurt him.'

Juno squeezed Janie tight. 'I will miss him too.'

Janie's eyes widened. 'I forget he was your friend too.'

A glimmer of pain spread across Juno's face. 'He was like a brother to me.'

The two of them continued walking arm in arm.

'He would want me to get little Luxea back,' Janie said. 'And to look after Billy.'

'Then that is what we will do,' Juno said. 'But be careful. There is a lot to learn with this new power of yours.'

Janie looked down at the green and brown marks spreading across her hands. She looked at Juno with wide eyes. 'Have I got these marks everywhere?'

Juno chuckled. 'They are everywhere. Welcome to being stared at for the rest of your life.'

'I don't care if people laugh,' Janie said. 'Miles wouldn't have laughed.'

'No, Miles would have immediately started training you,' Juno said, with a grin. 'He was very particular with discipline.'

Ahead of them, Chloe snorted. 'That boy never listened. Even when he fell in love, he did stupid things. Stupid boy!'

A chuckle escaped Juno's lips. 'He just never listened to you, Chloe.'

'Ha!' Chloe shouted over her shoulder. 'He came around eventually though, didn't he? Falling in love with our little seamstress over here.'

'Earth element seamstress, you mean,' Juno said.

Rafa shook his head. 'Oh how I long for an evening with just the boys.'

'I will tell Raquel you said that,' Chloe said.

They all laughed a little. Even a small smile played across Janie's face. The chuckles died down as they continued through the dead, dense black forest.

'Who is going to tell Billy?' Janie said, her voice cracking. 'How can I tell him knowing it was me he died for?'

Juno squeezed her again.

'We shall cross that bridge when we get there,' Chloe said, over her shoulder. 'For now, we need to get Luxea, Lazriel and Billy back.'

An hour later, the trees thinned. Suddenly, Chloe stopped and held out her hand. The ground fell steeply away and ended on the east–west road.

‘Which way?’ Chloe said.

‘We go east,’ Rafa said. ‘Past the inn, then south to the horse farms.’

They slid down the embankment and met in the middle of the cobblestone path. Janie and Juno climbed back onto Chax and Waya and spurred them east. Chloe and Rafa stretched their legs. An hour later, the burnt-out inn came into view. They continued past the inn and ran until the path turned south. The sun worked its way up to the middle of the sky. After another hour, the rolling hills began. Their breathing became laboured as they went up and down the hills.

‘Stop,’ Chloe hissed.

They all stopped at the crest of the hill. Juno and Janie jumped off Chax and Waya.

‘Can you see them?’ Chloe said, pointing.

On the crest of the next hill, the undead walked aimlessly about.

CHAPTER 26
MILO

'Is Walter making Lazriel do this?' Chloe said.

'Or the knife slinger,' Juno said, her voice crackling with fire. 'I should have ended him when I had the chance.'

'If he has hurt the little ones, I will end him myself,' Janie said. 'Lazriel only throws up the undead when something has scared him or he needs to defend himself.'

They stood and watched the undead walk around in circles. Every minute, they raised their noses into the air and sniffed.

'Something is going on,' Rafa said. 'They are leaving. Let's get to the other side.'

The four of them ran down the hill and into the valley. Chax and Waya, still both eyeing each other suspiciously, followed behind at a distance.

Before they began the climb to the top, Chloe stopped them so they could listen. 'It is quiet,' she said.

They ran up the path of sand and stones. Chloe held out her hand just before they reached the crest of a hill. She crouched and walked up ahead until she could see over the hilltop. A moment later, she moved back with a grave look on her face.

'What is it?' Juno said.

'The knife slinger is standing in the doorway of Heather and Jon's inn,' Chloe said.

The fire in Juno's eyes flared. 'So help me if he has hurt anyone.'

'What of the undead?' Rafa said. 'Did you see any?'

'None,' Chloe said. 'They have disappeared into the ground.'

Rafa's brow furrowed. 'That makes little sense. What was that knife slinger doing, Chloe?'

'He is just standing there,' Chloe said. 'It looks like he knows we are here.'

'Well, there is only one way to find out what is going on,' Juno said, starting up the hill.

Janie, Chloe and Rafa followed until all four of them stood on the hill's crest. The land in front of them flattened into green pastures and horse farms. Farm houses dotted the land with fenced-off areas ready for horses. Today, though, they all stood empty.

'What is the knife slinger doing?' Janie said. 'It looks like he is signalling.'

Juno walked forward, her hand resting on her Jo. The surrounding air crackled as the marks on her body pulsed with heat. A few minutes later, they slowed as they reached the gate to the farm that housed the inn. The knife slinger folded his arms and hid his hands in the ends of his sleeves.

'It's a trap,' Chloe hissed. 'I am sure of it. Be careful, Juno.'

Just as Juno stepped through the gate, the inn door slammed open and Luxea ran out. 'Janie,' she shouted, running towards them with Pippa in her hands. Halfway across the field, she stopped and stared with wide eyes.

Janie trotted forward. 'Are you OK, Luxea?'

Luxea's mouth hung open. 'Why did you paint your face?'

Janie touched her face instinctively. 'Do you like it?'

A big smile spread across Luxea's face. The smile instantly disappeared as Juno walked up and stood next to Janie.

'Whoa,' Luxea said. 'You are like sisters. Can I paint my face also? I will be Luxea the magnificent.'

'Oh, here we go,' Janie said.

'The magnificent Luxea,' Luxea said, drawing her imaginary sword and swiping it in front of her. 'Luxea, the protector of all things.'

Janie turned to Juno and grinned.

'I am the hero of the land,' Luxea shouted as she jumped into the air and stabbed her sword.

Juno placed a hand on Janie's shoulder. 'Have you seen the sword on your back, sister?'

With a frown, Janie reached over her shoulder and began to draw her sword.

'Keep it where it is,' Juno whispered. 'It will draw too much attention.'

Janie peered over her shoulder at the sword. She raised one eyebrow as the white metal swirled, just like Luxea's eyes. With a snap, she shoved the sword back in its hilt.

'So can I paint my face like you?' Luxea said. 'What about Pippa?'

'I am sure one day we can organise that,' Janie said. 'Come here, will you?'

Luxea replaced her imaginary sword, then wrapped her arms around Janie's legs.

Juno took a few steps closer to Dimitri. 'I see your face has healed, old friend.'

The knife slinger thrust his chin out. 'You jest. You scarred my face. The only thing that hurts today is my pride.'

Chax let out a low rumble. Dimitri eyed the big cat.

'Chax won't hurt you unless I tell her to,' Juno said, seeing Dimitri's nervous eyes. 'Care to tell me what is going on here?'

'The slave trader captured the young boy,' Dimitri said. 'He threatened to harm the boy, so your friend Billy had to comply with his demands. I waited until they reached the horse farms and then freed them from him.'

'Where are Billy, Heather and Jon?' Chloe said.

'I am right here,' Billy said, walking out of the inn.

'Look at Janie, Billy,' Luxea said. 'She has face paint.'

Billy stopped dead in his tracks and glared at Janie. Silence descended across the horse farms. Billy placed his head in his hands and sank to his knees. Chloe walked forward but stopped as Billy held out a hand.

'I am sorry, Billy,' Janie said, walking over.

Billy pushed himself off the ground and straightened his back. He looked at Janie with tired, sad eyes. His lopsided grin stayed absent. Lines grew across his face, making him look much older. He cleared his throat. 'Is my brother dead?'

'I am sorry, Billy,' Janie said. 'He didn't make it.'

A tear ran down Billy's cheek. 'Did he do the right thing?'

Janie tilted her head to one side. 'What do you mean?'

'What I mean is, did he die honourably?' Billy said. 'Did he do the right thing?'

'He did not hand me over to the vampire king,' Janie said. 'He should have, but Waya made the choice for him.'

Billy closed his eyes. 'So he died the right way. He acknowledged his love for you.'

A sound caught in the back of Janie's throat. She grasped her mouth to stop the cry that wanted to escape.

'He told us he loved you, Billy,' Chloe said. 'He asked us to look after the little ones.'

Billy opened his eyes and looked fondly at Luxea. 'Then that is what we shall do.'

Chloe took another step towards Billy, but she stopped as he held up his hand again.

'I do not want comfort now, Chloe,' Billy said. 'We have work to do.'

'I understand,' Chloe said, taking a step back.

'I have your cloak,' Janie said. 'He wore it to the end. He wanted you to have it.'

Billy walked over, took the cloak and slipped it around himself.

'Dimitri here has been telling us his tale,' Juno said. 'Care to fill us in, Billy?'

'He tells the truth,' Billy said. 'The slaver captured Lazriel and Luxea and threatened to hurt them if I did not comply. Dimitri intervened and freed us.'

'Can we trust him?' Juno said.

Billy looked over at Dimitri. 'I suggest we go inside and listen to him. He has information regarding Battleacre.'

'We will meet you inside,' Janie said, kneeling and wrapping her arms around Waya's neck.

Juno knelt and hugged Chax. 'You two need to get going, but don't be too far away.'

Waya backed away, turned and sprinted back towards the rolling hills. Chax bounded south towards the forest in the distance.

Janie entered the inn and embraced Heather with a smile. Heather sat everyone around the big centre table and signalled for Jon to bring them drinks and food.

Billy sat at a table in the corner of the inn with the cloak's hood hiding his face.

'Billy is sad,' Luxea whispered. 'Is it because of Miles?'

Janie gave Luxea a thin-lipped smile. 'Yes. Miles was his brother.'

Luxea placed her elbows on the table and her chin on her hands. 'He will be sad for a long time.'

'We will all be sad,' Janie said, a tear escaping down her cheek. She reached up and brushed it off before Luxea could see.

'Where is the slave trader?' Chloe said, changing the subject.

'He is in the cellar,' Dimitri said. 'I unfortunately had to tie up the westerners as they kept following his orders even after we said they were free.'

'He is secure down there?' Chloe said.

'If he gets out of his bonds, he will still need to get through the cellar door,' Dimitri said.

'Billy says you have some information?' Chloe said.

Dimitri placed his hands inside the ends of his sleeves. 'Battleacre will be under attack shortly.'

Rafa sat up straight. 'What do you mean? We rid the land of the vampires.'

'The City of Lynn,' Dimitri said. 'They will attack with a full squad of my brothers and a City of Lynn war machine.'

'I need to get back to Raquel,' Rafa said, sliding his chair back.

Chloe placed a hand on Rafa's forearm. 'Sit, brother. We all need to get to Battleacre. Let us first find out what we are dealing with. Go ahead, Dimitri.'

'It is a war machine built by the old man,' Dimitri said. 'The warlock. We use them in the northern war and I fear he is sending it to the south to test Battleacre.'

'We need to leave,' Rafa said. 'Raquel is defenceless.'

'I agree,' Chloe said. 'But we need to find out what this machine is and we also need to rest. I suggest we go first thing in the morning?'

'I will go now,' Rafa said. 'At least to warn them.'

'Then I will go with you,' Juno said. 'I can provide protection for the journey and for Battleacre.'

'I will go too,' Luxea said, reaching for her sword.

Janie grabbed her arm. 'You are staying with me, young lady.'

'Aw,' Luxea said.

'Are you sure you don't need to rest, brother?' Chloe said.

Rafa inclined his head. 'I will rest when I am with Raquel.'

'What do we need to know about this machine?' Juno said.

'I do not know too much about it other than sword and shield is useless against it,' Dimitri said.

'What about fire?' Juno said, lighting a flame at the end of her finger.

'Whoa,' Luxea said.

Dimitri touched the side of his face. 'That you will need to find out. I cannot say because I do not know.'

'We must go,' Rafa said, walking over to the inn door. 'I will see you in a few days.'

Juno hugged Chloe and Janie. She knelt next to Luxea. 'Look after my friends for me, will you?'

'I will and so will Pippa,' Luxea said, holding up her doll. 'And Lazriel.'

'Good,' Juno said, embracing the little girl. Juno turned to Janie. 'If this man does anything suspicious, make sure the ground swallows him whole.'

'I will make sure he doesn't harm anybody,' Janie said.

Juno followed Rafa out of the inn.

After the inn door closed, Chloe stood. 'Take me to this slave trader, please, Dimitri.'

Janie followed Chloe and Dimitri to the stockroom and up to the cellar door. After sliding the bolt back, Dimitri opened the cellar. Walter sat on a chair in the centre, bound and gagged and, along each wall, black westerners suffered the same fate.

Chloe walked over and pulled off his gag. 'Got yourself into a spot of trouble now, haven't you, Walter?'

Walter spat blood onto the ground. 'You are the one in trouble. Once the governor of the west finds out you had me prisoner, he will unleash untold misery on you and your people.'

'Who is this governor?' Janie said. 'What does he govern?'

Walter sneered at Janie. 'I will say nothing to you and any of your friends.'

Chloe cursed in Walter's face, then slid his gag back over his mouth. She walked over to the nearest westerner and pulled down his gag.

'Untie me,' the man growled.

Chloe knelt. 'Hold your tongue, brother. How did you become property of this man?'

The man sneered at Chloe. 'He is my master. I am bound to look after him. How this happened is none of your business.'

'What does this man have to maintain this hold over you?' Chloe said. 'I am offering you your freedom, yet you defend him.'

A flicker of worry flashed across the man's face.

'So he is holding something over you,' Chloe said. 'What is it? Money? Family?'

After a few seconds, the man cleared his throat. 'He holds nothing over me.'

Chloe snorted. 'You are lying. Why would you deny your own freedom if he is not holding anything against you?'

The man kept his eyes trained on Chloe. After a few more moments, he dropped his chin in resignation. 'It is the governor. He holds all our families. They put our children to work in the mines and they send our women to the City of Lynn.'

Chloe rose and walked over to Walter. She ripped off his gag. 'From this point, my kin will serve you no longer. If your governor hurts any of their families, I will send you to the arena in Battleacre.'

Walter's eyes bulged. 'You cannot do this. I bought them. They are mine to command.'

Chloe stood aside and closed her eyes. 'I must leave this room before I do something I regret. Untie these people and bring them up to the inn please, Dimitri.'

Janie followed Chloe back out into the inn's main room, where she sat next to Luxea and Lazriel.

Billy continued to sit in the corner with his cloak draped over his head.

One by one, the westerners entered the inn and sat at the table Chloe pointed to. Dimitri, with his long thin blade drawn, kept all of them from attacking anyone in the inn. When the last westerner sat, Chloe stood and waited for them all to face her.

'From this day forward, you are free,' she said. 'You are free because Walter will no longer be there for you to serve. I will throw him into Battleacre's prisons, ready for trial.'

'Then I will stay with him in the cells,' a westerner said.

Chloe pulled over a chair and sat. She draped a leg over the armrest and sent her leg bouncing in anger. 'You will be free to choose what you do. But know this. You will be free to return to the west and retrieve your family. This is what your freedom will allow you to do.'

The westerners glared at Chloe. 'We have no chance of getting our families back.'

'That may be so, but if you try to harm me, Billy or any of these children, I will ask Janie or Dimitri to deal with you rather harshly.'

Janie lifted her hand and closed it into a fist. The inn shook lightly, causing the glasses in the bar to rattle.

'Ra, ra, ra,' Lazriel shouted.

Luxea peered at the ceiling. 'Boys!'

The westerners gawked at Janie.

Jon appeared from behind the bar with large trays of dried meat, hot bread and glasses of ale. He dropped a tray at each of the westerner's tables. A few moments later, the westerners dug into their food as the hunger overtook them.

Chloe stood and joined Janie at the table with Luxea and Lazriel. She glanced at the table where Billy sat.

'Billy is very sad,' Luxea said, her misty eyes swimming. 'His smoke is very sad.'

Janie placed her head in her hands and breathed in deeply. She wiped away the tears that ran through her fingers.

'Janie is also sad,' Luxea said, climbing off her chair and walking over to Janie.

Janie lifted Luxea onto her lap and wrapped her arms around her. 'Yes, I am very sad.'

Luxea squeezed Janie hard.

'We need to get to Battleacre quickly,' Dimitri said. 'We have the slaver's carriage with four horses around the back. I don't think the carriage is enough to carry us all to the city. We need more horses.'

'We will go and see Norman,' Chloe said, standing.

'I am going with Chloe,' Janie whispered to Luxea. 'Can you go and see if Billy is OK?'

Luxea jumped off Janie's lap. 'Me and Pippa will say hi.'

Janie followed Chloe out of the inn and up the hill towards Norman's horse farm. They turned into the gate and walked up to his front door. Janie rapped her knuckles against the wood.

'Who is there?' Norman shouted.

Janie rapped her knuckles a second time.

The curtain next to the door moved aside. A second later, Norman undid the locks and slid aside the bolts on the door. He pulled open the door and stared with his mouth agape at the two women in front of him.

'I keep forgetting I look like this,' Janie said.

Chloe chuckled.

'We are here to pick up the two horses,' Janie said.

Norman held up his hand, then disappeared back inside to put on his boots. Once back, he led them to the stables and up to the stall that held the mare and the foal.

Janie slid open the door and chuckled at the foal rolling his eyes at her.

'The foal has grown,' Chloe said. 'And his shoulders don't look that bad.'

'He is cute,' Janie said.

'I have it under good authority that my colleague has paid you?' Chloe said to Norman.

'Yes, my lady. However, it will be good to get these two off my farm. They deserve to roam freely, but the horse farms will not accept this foal.'

'You shouldn't underestimate something just because it is different,' Janie said.

Norman scratched the side of his head. 'After meeting Master Miles, I have learnt that even the different can achieve good things. Tales of his endeavours have reached the people of the horse farms.'

Chloe chuckled. 'If only you knew the half of it, sir. I would like to thank you for looking after them. We will take them from here.'

Norman walked into the stall and retrieved two saddles. Once he had the saddles strapped to the horses, he led them out of the barn and onto the path. Chloe took the mare's reins and Janie grabbed the foal's. On the way down to the inn, the foal nudged

Janie with his snout, then rolled his eyes as she looked over her shoulder at him.

'He is going to be a handful,' Chloe said.

'I am not sure what to do with him,' Janie said. 'I cannot take him with Waya being about. The wolves terrify them.'

'I was going to ask you and Billy if I could take them back to Fairacre,' Chloe said. 'I can use them there to help transport wares around the town. Light work to keep them exercised.'

Janie grinned at her leader. 'I think Miles would be pleased.'

They reached the inn where they tied up the horses onto one wheel of the slave trader's carriage. A pile of gold and silver cutlery lay on a wide piece of cloth on the ground.

Jon stuck his head out of the carriage. 'Dimitri has asked me to strip it down.'

'Keep everything, Jon,' Chloe said. 'At least you can put this stuff to good use.'

Luxea ran out of the front door. 'You are back.'

'Yes, and we brought Miles's horses from the stable,' Chloe said.

'Whoa, he has funny shoulders,' Luxea said. 'He is like Miles with the broken foot.'

Chloe knelt. 'Yes, I think that is why Miles loved him so much, because they were similar.'

'What is his name?' Luxea said.

'I don't think he has a name,' Chloe said. 'Can you think of one?'

'Um,' Luxea said, putting her finger on her chin. 'I think you should name him Milo.'

'Milo,' Chloe said. 'I like that name. It sounds like Miles.'

Luxea beamed at Milo. 'Hello, Milo.'

The foal pricked its ears at Luxea.

'Let's get back inside, shall we?' Chloe said, walking back to the inn.

In the corner, Billy still sat, but this time, Lazriel was opposite him.

'Billy is teaching Lazriel extra words,' Luxea said. 'Billy is a little less sad.'

Janie squeezed Luxea's hand. 'That is good news. I think it's time for some food and then it is off to bed. We have a long trip over the next two to three days.'

Janie and Chloe sat at the large table in the centre of the inn and dug into the food Jon had laid out.

As they finished, one of the westerners came over and asked to sit.

Chloe nodded at a seat. 'I see you have decided,' she said.

'We will accompany you to Battleacre and then follow you to the south,' a westerner said. 'We will get provisions, then continue to the west to find our families. Does this sound acceptable to you?'

'That is a good plan,' Chloe said. 'But I am afraid we will not have space in the carriage. You will need to run alongside me.'

For the first time, the westerners smiled at Chloe. 'It will fill us with joy to run free again.'

They finished the food, then made their way to the inn's bedrooms. Janie put Luxea down to bed, then went to the door of the room where Lazriel and Billy slept. Billy lay on his bed with his cloak wrapped around Lazriel. Both of them snored gently as they slept. Janie made her way to her room, undressed and climbed into bed. She pulled the covers over her head and allowed the pain of loss to sweep over her. After many minutes of tears, exhaustion took over and Janie fell fast asleep.

CHAPTER 27
THE FIRST WOMAN

At the top of the hill, Janie stopped and placed her hand on her forehead to block the glare of the setting sun. Raquel, Juno and Rafa stood just outside Battleacre's southern gate. The mare nickered as she caught the first smells of the Battleacre stables.

'I cannot wait to get cleaned up,' Chloe said, walking up next to Janie. 'I didn't expect it to take four days to get here.'

'Walter's horses are fat,' Janie said, looking over her shoulder at the sweating horses that pulled the slave trader's carriage. 'When waited on hand and foot by the westerners, it seems haste was never on his agenda.'

Chloe curled a lip at the miserable-looking slave trader who sat on the carriage bench with his hands tied.

'Raquel,' Luxea said, running past Janie. 'Raquel, Rafa, Raquel, Rafa.'

'Ra, ra, swings,' shouted Lazriel, as he followed his twin sister.

Raquel knelt and held out her arms. A second later, she fell on her backside as both the children bowled her over.

Rafa bent over and scooped Lazriel into his arms.

Juno walked up to Janie and embraced her.

'You look upset, sister,' Janie said, holding Juno at arm's length.

The red flecks in Juno's eyes flared. 'I found a picture of a certain someone in the study.'

'The Lady,' Janie said, interlocking her arm into Juno's as they made for the gate. 'I have seen it too.'

'I was at first angry, but I am calm now,' Juno said. 'Raquel has lost her entire family in such a short time.'

'Yes, and she has so much on her shoulders right now,' Janie said. 'Have you spoken to her about Dimitri?'

'He will have safe passage,' Juno said. 'Once I explained how he saved the twins, she agreed.'

Janie gave Dimitri a quick nod over her shoulder.

Dimitri bowed his head slightly.

A flurry of activity started as the travelling group walked through the gate. Stablehands took the horses and carriage into the stables. Guards marched Walter off to the Battleacre jails. The travellers gave their bags to the waiting porters. Messengers received messages and ran off into Battleacre's streets. Once the frantic activity at the gate passed, Janie followed Billy, Raquel and Rafa up into the officers district, through the playground, and into the estate.

'My staff are preparing food and drink,' Raquel said, while ushering everyone into the study.

Luxea yawned and placed her head on Raquel's shoulder.

'I think it's best we get these two to bed,' Rafa said, a grin spreading across his face. 'This young man is already asleep.'

'I will also turn in for the night,' Billy said.

'Do you wish to talk, Billy?' Chloe said with a frown.

Billy held out a hand. 'No, thank you.'

Janie waited for Raquel, Billy and Rafa to leave before she sat cross-legged in front of the glowing fireplace. She gasped as a small ball of fire flew past her and hit the logs.

Juno sat cross-legged next to Janie and grinned at her.

'Do we need to worry about Billy?' Janie said, ignoring Juno and peering at the study door.

'He will come around,' Juno said, taking Janie's hand and squeezing it.

Janie looked at Juno and smiled. 'Sorry, there is just so much going on.'

'You two look like artwork,' Chloe said, flopping down into a chair and throwing her leg over an armrest. 'We are going to have to warn the residents of Battleacre you are friendly or they might decide to throw you out.'

Janie traced a hand over her neck.

'You look good, sister,' Juno said, a smirk spreading across her face.

'You are just saying that because you are no longer the weird one,' Janie said, while shoving her friend gently by the shoulder.

Juno chuckled. 'I suppose it is nice to have someone a bit like me.'

'So have you seen it, Juno?' Chloe said. 'The monster in the north?'

Juno nodded at Chloe, then turned her eyes on Dimitri. 'I have, but it is just sitting there doing nothing. Care to fill us in, Dimitri?'

Dimitri stepped out from the corner of the room. 'What does this monster look like?'

'It looks like a man, but it is twice the size. It is made out of shiny metal and it spews black smoke from holes in its shoulders,' Juno said.

'Are the legs out of proportion?' Dimitri said. 'Are they longer than they should be?'

'That is correct,' Juno said.

'It is a scout machine,' Dimitri said. 'Less deadly than the war machines, but destructive enough. What is it doing?'

'Nothing,' Juno said. 'It is just standing there. Far enough away from our soldiers' bows and arrows, but close enough for us to see it properly.'

Dimitri folded his arms. 'It is scouting. It may seem dormant, but it is searching.'

'Searching for what?' Janie said.

With a glance at the door, Dimitri sighed. 'I fear it is looking for the young one. And secondary, it may look for the two of you. Have you shown yourself to it?'

'I have stood on the wall to look at it,' Juno said.

'Were your marks exposed?' Dimitri said.

Juno thought for a moment. 'It would have seen the markings on my face.'

'Then it knows an elemental is here,' Dimitri said. 'I suggest the two of you escape to the east and take the young ones with you.'

Raquel and Rafa walked into the room. Raquel sat in her father's chair opposite Chloe. She placed her finger and thumb on her forehead and rubbed.

'I hear you have been discussing your mother with Juno?' Chloe said.

Raquel glanced at Juno, then looked at Chloe. 'We have been talking, yes. I find what she has said very hard to believe.'

'After what I have seen over the last few seasons, I find nothing hard to believe,' Chloe said.

'That is a good point,' Raquel said.

'I hope you understand Raquel had nothing to do with any of what happened in the south,' Rafa said.

Chloe smiled up at Rafa. 'There is no need to worry, brother. We are not a people that cast blame unjustly.'

Raquel relaxed into her chair. 'It is good to hear you say that. I have lost my entire family, and I do not wish to sit here and lament their failings. Battleacre needs a leader now.'

Dimitri cleared his throat. 'On that note, did any of you heed my warning?'

Chloe closed her eyes and steepled her fingers. Her leg bounced on the chair's armrest.

'I am sorry,' Dimitri said. 'Do I need to repeat myself?'

'The boss needs to think, Dimitri,' Juno said, with a half smile.

Dimitri held out a hand and stood back.

After a minute, Chloe opened her eyes. 'Dimitri, what is more important to the City of Lynn? The elementals, the little ones or the women?'

Dimitri stepped forward. 'I cannot say, as I do not know.'

'Try to guess,' Chloe said, spreading her hands. 'We need to make some assumptions here.'

'Then the little ones are the most important,' Dimitri said. 'Those two need to be protected from the City of Lynn and the old man.'

'Do you know why they are in demand?' Raquel said.

Dimitri shook his head. 'I do not. All I know is the powerful people in the City speak of them often.'

'Then I suggest you take them south,' Raquel said.

'We cannot leave the city unprotected,' Chloe said. 'If the City of Lynn takes control of Battleacre, who knows what they will do with its people?'

'I will stay,' Janie said.

'You cannot stay, sister,' Juno said. 'You need urgent training with your new powers.'

'I cannot leave Raquel and Battleacre at the mercy of that machine and the City,' Janie said.

Juno steepled her fingers. 'Then I shall stay here with you.'

Chloe held up a hand. 'That is all very well, but we also need to think of the south.'

'I will stay but will come to Fairacre when called,' Juno said. 'It will take me just over two days to get home.'

'How will you send a message?' Raquel said.

'My Valen has a way,' Chloe said. 'We will send one of his little beasts.'

Juno shuddered at the thought of the spider and bumble bee.

'What of the children?' Dimitri said.

'We will hide them in the horse farms,' Chloe said before anyone could give another suggestion. 'I will take them there and make sure Heather and Jon hide them.'

Janie opened her mouth, but Juno gently jabbed her in the ribs with her elbow.

After a moment's silence, Raquel turned to Janie. 'If you are going to stay, may I request something of you?'

'Of course,' Janie said.

Raquel stood and walked over to the small cabinet at the end of the study. She knelt, opened the door and pulled out a wooden box. After closing the small door, she walked back to her father's chair and sat. 'As I am now the new leader of this house, I would ask that you accept these vambraces. Would you do me the honour of being the Hammer of my house?'

Janie took the vambraces from Raquel and stared at them.

'We will adjust them so they fit you,' Rafa said. 'You will be the first woman to hold this position.'

'It also means you will need to acquire new weapons,' Raquel said. 'Weapons of your choice.'

Janie cleared her throat. 'This is a great honour. I will accept, but only once Juno has trained me.'

'Wise choice,' Chloe said. 'Nobody knows what those powers of yours can do yet.'

'I will be back,' Janie said, rising and walking out of the study.

'Will you continue being the Shield?' Chloe said, smiling at Rafa.

Raquel turned a bright pink. She placed a hand over her mouth as she bit her lip.

'I cannot be the Shield of the house,' Rafa said, a wide grin spreading across his face.

'What are you two up to?' Juno said, smirking.

'Rafa has asked me to marry him,' Raquel said. 'He will head the house with me so he cannot take the position of the Shield.'

A wide smile spread across Chloe's face. 'Congratulations,' she said, leaning forward and hugging Raquel. 'How is Battleacre going to take you marrying a westerner?'

'I think it is time Battleacre progressed into the new world, don't you think?' Raquel said.

'No issues from me,' Chloe said, sitting back and draping her leg over the armrest.

Janie walked back into the room and sat cross-legged next to Juno. She ran her hands over the two sheathed short swords that lay across her lap. 'I think you should take these with you,' she said to Chloe.

Chloe took the swords Janie held out. 'Are you sure? They were Miles's.'

Janie took in a deep breath. 'They need to stay with the twins.'

The light sword came easily away from its sheath. Everyone turned their heads as Dimitri gasped.

'What is it?' Juno said, frowning at her old foe.

Dimitri stepped away from the corner of the room to inspect the sword. 'A master swordsman must have created this. And I have never seen such material. It looks like swirling mist.'

Chloe replaced the light sword and pulled out the dark sword.

Dimitri's eyes widened even further. 'Remarkable. Truly remarkable.'

The dark sword slid back into its sheath. 'And that is the last time you get to see those, knife slinger,' Chloe said.

A smile cracked across Dimitri's burnt, deformed face. With a nod, he took a step back and placed his hands into his wide sleeves.

After a few minutes of Raquel telling Janie of her marital news, followed by the subsequent smiles and congratulations, the study fell silent.

Janie took a breath. 'Where have you put Miles?'

Raquel leant forward. 'He is in the catacombs underneath Battleacre. I intend to bury him there next to the weapon masters of old. Of course, only with your blessing.'

Chloe's leg bounced. 'We need to tell Billy and Dr Viktor.'

'We have a ceremony prepared for tomorrow,' Rafa said. 'After that, we will place him in the visitor's catacombs for thirty days. If you wish him to be moved, you will need to tell us before that time is over.'

'I will get a message to Dr Viktor from the horse farms,' Chloe said.

'What is the ceremony tomorrow?' Janie said.

Rafa sat on the armrest of Raquel's chair. 'You will see tomorrow, Janie. All I will say is it will be grand enough for a king.'

'And Chloe will be very busy tomorrow,' Raquel said with a smirk.

Chloe frowned. 'What do you mean?'

'Ha,' Raquel said. 'Now that would be telling. I suggest we all get cleaned up and have a good night's sleep. Dimitri, there is a room prepared for you. I trust it will be safe to let you stay overnight in my household?'

Before Dimitri could answer, Juno lifted a hand and set it on fire. 'Oh, he will behave, won't you, Dimitri?'

Dimitri chuckled. 'I would behave even if we were still enemies. I am a guest in your house and I shall act as such.'

'Good, that is settled then,' Raquel said. 'I wish you all a good night and I will see you in the morning.'

The next morning, the group lined up at the villa's front door.

'Where are we going?' Luxea said, stepping out into the brilliant sunshine. 'Are we going to the swings?'

'We are going to the arena,' Janie said. 'Here, hold my hands.'

'Are you sure it's a good idea letting everyone see the kids?' Dimitri said.

'They need to say goodbye to Miles,' Janie said. 'And if we expose them to everyone at the games, the City will train its monsters on Battleacre rather than search for them.'

Dimitri folded his hands into his cloak and frowned, deep in thought.

'Swings!' Luxea shouted as they entered the park.

'Swings!' Lazriel shouted, pulling on Janie's hand.

'We will play on the swings on the way back,' Janie said. 'We need to get to the arena.'

'Oh, OK,' Luxea said, with a huff.

They followed the winding road out of the officers district. They turned north and walked alongside the arena until they reached the western entrance. The guards bowed deeply at the sight of Raquel.

'Up you get,' Rafa said, picking up Luxea. 'It will take us all day getting up these winding stairs with those little legs.'

Dimitri picked up Lazriel and stuck him on his shoulders.

'Ra, ra, ra,' Lazriel said, holding his hands out in front of himself.

Rafa shook his head. 'Attempts at teaching that young man have failed.'

Raquel wound her arm into Rafa's. 'I think he needs a safe place away from this crazy world before he will learn anything.'

At the top of the spiral staircase, they all moved into the area owned by Raquel's family. Behind them, the mayoral and council seats all sat empty.

'Sit here please, Chloe,' Raquel said, pointing to a seat next to her. 'You are going to be needed shortly.'

Chloe raised both of her eyebrows. 'What are you up to?'

Raquel smiled coyly. 'Oh nothing.'

Once they were all seated, Raquel walked up to the announcement area. The crowd cheered, shouted, clapped and stamped their feet. She lifted her hands, asking for silence. The crowd died down. 'Welcome back to the Battleacre games,' Raquel said, spreading her arms.

The crowd exploded into a deafening roar.

'Today we will begin with the usual round of games, which will lead to the finals this evening,' Raquel said. 'Just after lunch, as the sun crosses the top of the sky, there will be a special event.'

The crowd whispered among themselves. Raquel walked up to the large alphorn and blasted the signal to start the games. The special event forgotten, the crowd roared.

'Where is Billy?' Chloe said, leaning over to where Juno sat.

Juno's eyebrows raised into her forehead as she shrugged. 'I don't know. I know he needs his space, but I am not happy with him missing.'

Raquel came and sat on her seat and spread her arms as Luxea and Lazriel fought to sit on her lap.

'I am going to fight in the games one day,' Luxea said. 'Miles said I would be a great warrior one day. Luxea the great.'

'Is that so?' Raquel said.

'Yes,' Luxea said. 'Look, Pippa, they are going to fight.'

The games continued throughout the morning. At Raquel's request, the combatants now used practice weapons rather than live weapons. As the sun reached the top of the sky, Raquel signalled for the porters to bring food and drinks.

'Don't eat too much, Chloe,' Rafa said.

Chloe shook her head with her mouth open.

After they had finished their food, Raquel walked up to the announcement platform. The crowd cheered, then slowly calmed to a murmur.

Raquel cleared her throat and spoke softly, but firmly. 'The vampires turned my father into one of our mortal enemies. This you have seen with your own eyes.'

The murmurs disappeared into silence.

'We, however, faced our mortal enemy and were victorious,' Raquel said, her voice raising.

'Victory, victory, victory,' the crowd chanted.

'We lost many men that day,' Raquel said.

The crowd quietened.

'On that day, my family lost our champion,' Raquel said, turning and signalling for Janie to join her. 'The Hammer of our house, Miles, the weapons master of the south.'

'Champion, champion, champion,' the crowd chanted.

'Proceed,' Raquel said, raising her hand.

The northern, eastern and western gates of the arena clacked open. Three mighty warriors walked into the arena and stopped in the centre.

Raquel placed her arm over Janie's shoulder and whispered in her ear. 'It is customary for the fallen to be represented by someone they loved and respected. I would say that would be you, but you cannot with your new skills. It is too dangerous. Therefore I have chosen Chloe. Is this acceptable?'

Janie smiled. 'I would have chosen her over me, anyway.'

Raquel lifted a hand, asking for silence. 'We have decided the person who will represent the fallen is someone who Miles, the Hammer, respected with his life. He was her weapons master and master tactician. The leader of the south, Chloe.'

The crowd turned their collective eyes on Chloe.

Chloe lifted her eyes to the heavens. 'So that's what you were planning!'

'Get over here,' Janie said, waving her hand frantically.

Chloe stood and walked over to the announcement platform. She cleared her throat. 'Miles was my friend, my advisor and a complete idiot in love.'

The crowd chuckled. Janie turned a bright pink under her green and brown marks.

'This is a true honour,' Chloe said.

Janie pulled Chloe into a hug. 'Fight like he taught you.'

With a wink, Chloe took off down the spiral stairs. The crowd whispered and spoke among themselves. A few moments later, the southern gate clacked open and Chloe entered the arena. The four combatants faced each other and bowed. They then faced the announcement platform and bowed.

Raquel pointed Janie to the alphorn. 'If you please.'

Janie placed her lips on the horn and sent out a long blast. The crowd jumped to their feet and cheered.

'I think the crowd is going to get a bit of a fright,' Juno said after Janie had sat. 'Let's see if these soldiers can handle themselves.'

The four warriors engaged with an almighty clash. As each one became disarmed, they flew back to their quadrant and bashed open the next panel. After fifteen minutes of furious fighting, the first warrior fell to his knee and lifted his hand in submission. The fighting continued and Chloe spun the ball and chain, her third weapon, at one of the remaining warriors. The warrior ducked and lashed out with his mace, hitting Chloe's hand. The ball and chain fell to the ground. With a growl, Chloe ran up to the second panel and pulled out a greatsword.

'Oh dear,' Juno said, smiling broadly. 'I think they are in a bit of trouble now.'

Chloe attacked with moves that would have put a smile on Miles's face. A few moments later, a warrior held up his hand in submission. The remaining two fighters, Chloe and the soldier eyed each other before they each ran to their quadrants and punched open the fifth panel. Chloe pulled out her two short swords. The soldier pulled out a pair of double-edge axes.

'Fight, fight, fight,' the crowd chanted.

The two combatants darted in and out as they tested each other's defences. Seeing the soldier would overpower her easily, Chloe stayed nimble. As the crowd's cheering grew to a roar, the soldier finally caught Chloe by the legs. With a puff of dust, Chloe fell onto her back. Chuckling, the soldier dropped his axes and held out a hand. Chloe grabbed it and jumped to her feet.

'A formidable fighter you are,' the soldier said, his voice carrying across the arena. 'Your weapons master would be proud.'

Chloe bowed. 'Thank you.'

'Ladies and gentlemen, what a spectacular match,' Raquel said. 'Over the next thirty days, Miles, the Hammer of my house will accept gifts in the catacombs for his journey to the afterlife.'

The crowd clapped and cheered.

'Where is Billy?' Janie said to Juno.

'He is here,' Juno said, pointing high into the stands.

Janie followed Juno's finger to a man sitting in the last row of seats. The hood of his cloak covered his face. In his hand, a small thin dagger glinted in the sunlight.

'Are you going to speak to him?' Janie said. 'He looks very angry.'

Juno shook her head. 'There is no point. He will come to us when he is ready.'

'Yay,' Luxea cheered as Chloe sat back down. 'You were nearly as good as the great Luxea.'

Chloe chuckled. 'I tried my best.'

'I will train you one day,' Luxea said, swishing her imaginary sword about. 'For I am Luxea the great.'

Raquel ruffled her hair. 'Yes, you are Luxea the great.'

'Thank you, Chloe,' Janie said, with tears in her eyes. 'Miles would have tutted and called you all kinds of names because you lost, but he would have been proud.'

'He would have, wouldn't he?' Chloe said, wiping her forehead. 'I am glad you are happy.'

They all sat watching the games through the afternoon. As the sun set in the west, Chloe nudged Janie. 'Time to get the kids back to the estate.'

'Good plan,' Janie said.

'I think we will all join you,' Rafa said. 'It has been an emotional day.'

Rafa and Dimitri picked up the two tired children and walked down the spiral stairs. Janie, Juno, Chloe and Raquel followed arm in arm after the two men. Half an hour later, the four women walked into the villa and sat together in the study. Rafa and Dimitri took the children to their room.

'Janie, Juno, I am leaving tonight,' Chloe said. 'I am going to take the two kids and the horses and get back to Dr Viktor's house.'

'I thought you were up to something,' Juno said. 'Are you going alone?'

'I am,' Chloe said. 'I need to bring as little attention to myself as possible. We also want Dimitri to think I have gone to the horse farms.'

'Wise idea,' Juno said. 'I still don't trust him.'

'What about Billy, and what about the monster at the northern gate?' Janie said.

'I am sure the two of you can deal with both,' Chloe said. 'Tell Billy where I am going when you speak to him. Dr Viktor does not know about Miles. When he finds out, he may need his other son there for comfort.'

The study door opened and Dimitri entered. 'The little boy was asleep before I got him into his bed.'

'Thank you, Dimitri,' Chloe said. 'What is your next move? You said you had family in the City of Lynn.'

Dimitri took in a breath. 'I have been thinking about this. If it pleases the lady of Battleacre, I would like to pick them up and bring them here. And to show my gratitude, I am going to get rid of the machine at the northern gate.'

'How do you propose to do that?' Janie said. 'If you do that, will that not compromise your coming back here?'

'It will,' Dimitri said. 'But at least my wife and daughter will be safe.'

The study fell silent.

'I am sure we can think of something else,' Rafa said.

'The machine will stay there as they have seen the fire woman,' Dimitri said, nodding at Juno. 'I will tell them she has left. That should get the machine to leave. Be vigilant though, as it may come to search the horse farms for you.'

'I will make the preparations,' Chloe said. 'But let's continue discussing this tomorrow. It has been an emotional day and we may think of a better option if we sleep on it.'

Janie stood and began embracing everyone in the study. She wrapped her arms around Chloe and squeezed tightly. After letting Chloe go, she turned to Raquel. 'Thank you for doing what you did for Miles. Battleacre was always his dream and being buried here with his heroes fills me with joy.'

'You are welcome,' Raquel said. 'We loved him too.'

'I wish you all a good night,' Janie said, walking out of the study and up the stairs. She sneaked into the room where the two children slept. With her fingertips, she brushed the hair out of Luxea's face and kissed her forehead. 'Be safe, little one,' she said. A minute later, she crept over to Lazriel's bed and dropped a kiss on his forehead. 'Look after your twin sister.'

The bedroom door crept open. 'It's time,' Chloe said.

'Look after them, boss,' Janie said, giving Chloe another hug. 'I am not too far away if you need me.'

'I will look after these two as if they were my own,' Chloe said, squeezing Janie's hand. 'Listen to Juno now, you hear? She knows what she is talking about.'

Janie gave Chloe a nod, then walked out of the bedroom without looking back.

CHAPTER 28
CHLOE

'I am sorry,' Chloe said.

'Where is Billy?' Dr Viktor said, a little too harshly.

'The last we saw him was in Battleacre,' Chloe said, as she rested her elbows on the kitchen counter.

Dr Viktor rubbed a hand over his face. He closed his eyes and sighed. 'My boy,' he said. 'My poor boy.'

'He died doing the right thing,' Chloe said, trying to hide the quiver in her voice.

'He shouldn't have left,' Dr Viktor said. 'The vessel would have chosen him even if he had stayed. I could have helped him then.'

Chloe remained silent.

'Whoa,' Luxea said, running into the kitchen. 'There is a big place at the back with trees and flowers and grass and bees and whoa.'

'It's a greenhouse,' Chloe said, smiling. 'It's where Billy and Tilly usually work.'

'Who is Tilly?' Luxea said.

'She is a friend of ours who lives in Fairacre,' Chloe said. 'One day, when it is safe, I will take you there to meet everyone.'

'Am I staying here now?' Luxea said. 'Do I have my own room? Can Pippa stay? Does Lazriel get his own room? I don't want to share with Lazriel. He is a boy.'

Dr Viktor stared at Luxea with wide eyes and his mouth hanging open. 'How am I going to cope with these two?'

'I am going to send Alexa,' Chloe said. 'She will be their guardian while they stay here.'

Dr Viktor hacked into his handkerchief.

'And yes, Luxea, you will get your own room,' Chloe said.

'Yay,' Luxea said, throwing her little hands into the air.

'Yay, yay, yay,' Lazriel shouted, running into the kitchen. 'Nom, nom, nom?'

'I suppose that means the child is hungry?' Dr Viktor said.

Chloe pushed out her stool and walked over to the pantry. She grabbed an assortment of meats, breads and jams. Back at the breakfast table, she placed Luxea and Lazriel onto stools of their own.

'Nom, nom, nom,' Lazriel said, reaching for a jam jar.

'Wait,' Chloe said, grabbing his hand. 'I will make some bread.'

'Wait,' Lazriel said.

'I am going to need to work on this young one,' Dr Viktor said, reaching over a gnarled hand and ruffling Lazriel's hair.

'I trust you know what to do with these two?' Chloe said. 'Their gifts are pretty scary.'

'The boy is a necromancer. The girl is a luxmancer,' Dr Viktor said. 'One raises the bodies of the dead, the other can access people's essences, their souls. So yes, I know of them.'

'Will you be able to help them?' Chloe said.

'It is highly unusual for them to be found together,' Dr Viktor said. 'Unheard of them being from the same family. And practically impossible to be twins.'

'But can you help them?' Chloe said.

'I cannot help them with their powers,' Dr Viktor said. 'But I can help them with discipline.'

Chloe narrowed her eyes.

'Don't worry,' Dr Viktor said, raising his hand. 'My old ways will not take part in their discipline. I have learnt there are better ways to do things.'

'That is good to hear,' Chloe said, her voice low and her eyes trained on Dr Viktor. 'I shall, however, still keep an eye on you.'

Dr Viktor chuckled, then pulled out another handkerchief and hacked into it.

'I like your big book in the other room, Dr Trickster,' Luxea said.

Chloe snorted. 'It's Dr Viktor.'

'That is what I said,' Luxea said. 'Dr Trickster.'

'You shouldn't be in that room,' Dr Viktor said.

'Oh,' Luxea said, lowering her head. 'The door was open.'

'I am sure it is fine, right, Dr Trickster?' Chloe said with a twinkle in her eye.

Dr Viktor grumbled under his breath.

'The brown ball, all shiny and swirly, is pretty,' Luxea said. 'And so is the red one.'

Chloe frowned at Luxea. 'Brown ball, red ball?'

'Four balls on the table, two shining and two dark,' Luxea said, just before shoving a thick jam-covered slice of bread into her mouth.

Dr Viktor cleared his throat. 'Just toys I play with to light up my study when I am writing.'

Chloe picked up a cloth and wiped Lazriel's mouth with it.

'You are going to need to get used to not leaving stuff lying around, Dr Trickster.'

'Nom, nom, nom,' Lazriel said.

'I have placed the two short swords in my new vault that Valen has created,' Dr Viktor said. 'Those swords are truly remarkable.'

'Janie decided they needed to stay with the twins,' Chloe said. 'They match their eyes for some reason.'

'I will look into it,' Dr Viktor said.

Luxea yawned.

'Alright, young lady,' Chloe said. 'It is time to get you and your brother into your new rooms.'

'And Pippa,' Luxea said, holding up her doll.

'Of course,' Chloe said with a smile.

Once Chloe had settled the two children, she gathered her things and placed them on the mare that waited outside Dr Viktor's house.

'When will Alexa be here?' Dr Viktor said from the doorway.

'Before sunrise,' Chloe said.

Dr Viktor flung a key up into the air, which Chloe caught. 'Give her this key. Tell her to pick up a cane from the basket at the front door and to strike the ground three times once she has entered. That way I will know it is her.'

Chloe nodded. 'Look after them, will you?'

Dr Viktor gave Chloe a thin-lipped smile. 'I will and when you see Billy, tell him I need to see him immediately.'

'I will,' Chloe said, leading the mare to the path. 'Take care, Dr Trickster.'

'Get out of here,' Dr Viktor said, pretending to throw something at Chloe.

. . .

Chloe placed the mare and Milo into their new stables. Milo rolled his eyes at Chloe, then buried his snout into a bale of hay.

'I want you to put these two to work, please,' Chloe said to the stablehand. 'But keep it light. Especially on the foal.'

'Yes, my lady,' the stablehand said.

With the east entrance behind her, Chloe walked up the wide road leading to the centre of Fairacre. She turned left and wound down the small roads until she reached the shop with the little bell on the door.

'Who goes there?' Valen shouted as Chloe opened the door.

'Oh, just a friend of yours,' Chloe said as she walked into the arts and crafts shop.

After an almighty crash of a desk falling over, Valen came charging out of his office. 'My love,' he shouted, wrapping Chloe up in his massive arms. 'You are back.'

Chloe wrapped her arms around Valen's neck and squeezed tight. 'I am back.'

Valen unwrapped her from his embrace. 'Are you OK? You look sad.'

'Lots has happened, my love,' Chloe said quietly.

Valen scooped Chloe up and carried her to the couch in the back office. He went to the kitchen and made two mugs of sweet tea. A minute later, he walked into the office and sighed.

With a leg draped over the armrest, Chloe lay stretched out on the couch with her hands under her head.

'I don't see you for weeks and you fall asleep on me,' Valen muttered.

'I heard that,' Chloe said, opening an eye.

Valen ran a hand through his hair. 'I thought you had fallen asleep on me.'

'I am tired, but I am awake,' Chloe said, smiling.

The bell on the shop door tinkled. 'Valen, are you here?'

Chloe swung her leg off the armrest. 'We are in here, Alexa.'

'You need to come with me urgently, miss,' Alexa said. 'There is something happening north of the town.'

Chloe stood and frowned at Valen. 'What's going on now?'

Valen shrugged.

'Hurry, miss,' Alexa said.

Chloe walked out of Valen's office and gave Alexa a quick hug. 'Why the urgency, sister?'

'There is something out there, miss,' Alexa said, opening the shop door. 'I have never seen anything like it.'

'Let's get moving then,' Chloe said, jogging up to a crate and then climbing up onto the rooftops.

'I will see you there, love,' Valen said, jogging up the winding street.

Chloe stretched her legs as she made her way along the rooftops. At the northern wall, she placed her hand over her forehead.

'What is it, miss?' Alexa said.

'It's a scout from the City of Lynn,' Chloe said, curling a lip. 'Raise the alarm, Alexa. We are under attack.'

NEXT UP...

Petra and the Sewer Rats: A Juno and the Lady Novella (An Acre Story Book 1.2)

AUTHOR REQUEST

Hello,
Thank you for taking the time to read **Miles and the Soldier**. We have reached the second book of The Acre Series and there is a lot more to come.

If you have a moment, I would really appreciate a review on either Amazon or Goodreads. The reviews help us indie authors a great deal.

Please consider joining my mailing list where I will keep you up to date with book release dates, news and upcoming events. https://gjkemp.co.uk/mailing-list/

Again, thank you for spending your precious time reading my books.

Take care,
G.J.

ABOUT THE AUTHOR

A nomad at heart, GJ has lived in nine countries across Africa, Europe and the Middle East. His career has included working as a Divemaster in The Red Sea, a zookeeper in Israel, and a proof-reader in Sweden. Born with cerebral palsy, GJ has spent a lifetime trying to tie his shoelaces while standing up in the hope of not falling over. It is a constant challenge, but sometimes he occasionally succeeds.

Finding the love for writing later in life, GJ spends most of his free time going for walks and dreaming of story ideas. He hopes to one day have a small place on the oceanfront where he can walk his dogs on the beach.

For more information please visit gjkemp.co.uk

facebook.com/gavin.kemp.92505

twitter.com/kemp_gj

instagram.com/gjkempauthor

linkedin.com/in/g-j-kemp-4a76b03

bookbub.com/profile/g-j-kemp

Printed in Great Britain
by Amazon

32494131R00267